THE HOT
FLASH CLUB
Chills Out

NANCY THAYER

THE HOT FLASH CLUB
Chills Out

A Novel

BALLANTINE BOOKS • NEW YORK

tha

The Hot Flash Club Chills Out is a work of fiction. Names, characters, places, and incidents are the products of the author's imagination or are used fictitiously. Any resemblance to actual events, locales, or persons, living or dead, is entirely coincidental.

Published in the United States by Ballantine Books, an imprint of The Random House Publishing Group, a division of Random House, Inc., New York.

BALLANTINE and colophon are registered trademarks of Random House, Inc.

ISBN 0-345-48553-X

Printed in the United States of America on acid-free paper

www.ballantinebooks.com

2   4   6   8   9   7   5   3   1

First Edition

Book design by Susan Turner

This book is dedicated, with love,
to Musicall

ACKNOWLEDGMENTS

Thanks to the wonderful Ballantine crew:

Gina Centrello and Libby McGuire

Jacket designer Royce Becker

Art directors Gene Mydlowski and Robbin Schiff

Gilly Hailparn and Kim Hovey

Dan Mallory and Howard Mittelmark

And especially my editor, Linda Marrow.

THE HOT
FLASH CLUB
Chills Out

Faye released the tiebacks on her bedroom curtains. With a silky whisper, the heavy, luxurious panels fell together, blocking out the night, turning her bedroom into a private chamber. Crossing the room, she folded back the floral quilt, exposing the crisply ironed ivory linen sheets. She plumped the already puffy pillows, leaning them invitingly against the headboard.

She paused, listening. Aubrey was still in the bathroom. Always fastidious, she knew he would be especially particular with his grooming tonight.

Tonight they would make love for the first time.

She didn't want to be caught admiring herself, but her full-length cheval mirror invited her to appreciate her appearance. The curves of her voluptuous body were enhanced by the drape of her silk nightgown. The slenderest of straps supported a bodice of exquisite lace dipping to reveal her full breasts. The loose cut allowed the material to skim the rest of her body without emphasizing her other bulges. She'd kept her long white hair in the low chignon she often wore—she was planning, at some appropriate moment, perhaps when she was on top of Aubrey, to reach up with both arms and remove the barrette, so that her hair would tumble down around her shoulders, just as it did on the heroines in romance novels.

Bringing her face closer to the mirror, she inspected a freckle on her nose. In spite of her straw hat, the work she'd done in her garden had let the spring sun darken the small, pea-sized blemish. Because it was on the same level as her eyes, it gave her the unfortunate appearance of having three eyes, so she'd had it lasered off a few years ago, even though it wasn't precancerous. Now she'd have to do it again. Taken with all the other changes on her face and body, it made her look not just older, but peculiar.

Water ran in the bathroom. Faye squinted at the mirror. She wore the beautiful gold filigree necklace Aubrey had given her for Christmas this December. Should she remove it? She never wore jewelry to bed. But then, she hadn't gone to bed for *this* purpose for years. The necklace was very pretty, lying against her chest. It led the eye down to her bosom. She'd leave it on.

Walking around the room, she took up a pack of matches and lighted all the candles she'd set out earlier in the day. The candles made eager, almost erotic, little gasps as their wicks took the flame. The sound sent her into a hot flash. Oh Lord, she hoped she didn't have a hot flash while they were making love! She grabbed a perfume bottle and pressed its cool glass against her flaming cheek. Did she have time to get a glass of ice water? Probably. But if she had a drink of water, she'd have to get up to pee right in the middle of this long-awaited romantic interlude. No, she couldn't take the chance. She picked up another bottle and held it to her other cheek. Wow, she really was a little radiator. What a shame she couldn't somehow channel all this extra heat into some kind of battery. She could run her house for the winter.

Aubrey was *still* in the bathroom. She chided herself for impatience. After all, what was the hurry? She had all evening. All night. But her back hurt from standing all day painting, and her arms and shoulders ached from preparing the light dinner of fish, fruit, and salad. She folded back the covers and slid into bed. Ah, it felt so good to lie down! She chuckled to herself, thinking how sexual cravings changed during a lifetime. In her youth, desire often made it impossible for her to sleep. Now she was in her fifties, and she wasn't sure she could stay awake to make love.

Well, that was only to be expected, she supposed, now that she'd traded her birth control pills for K-Y Jelly. She opened the drawer of the bedside table and took out the new tube she'd bought yesterday. When should she put it on? Should she wait and let Aubrey put it on? Would he want to? He was a bit finicky when it came to the earthier parts of being human.

Which reminded her, she should bring some towels to the bed. Sex was such a messy business, and Aubrey was such a tidy man. The only child of a wealthy family, he'd been coddled and fussed over and raised to live up to certain standards of elegance. He was the only man she'd ever met who actually owned, and sometimes wore, a cravat. He loved squiring Faye to operas, ballets, concerts, and the many charity events to which he donated generously. Tall, handsome, possessing a thick head of gleaming silver hair, Aubrey was also deeply kind. Faye didn't know that she loved him, but she was terribly fond of him, and thought he was equally fond of her.

That didn't necessarily equate to sexual passion, but the night they first met, that exciting, surprising *spark* had been there. One spring evening, at an open house at The Haven, they'd begun chatting in front of the art exhibit. Over the course of the evening, they'd lingered, feeling more and more drawn to one another. In fact, by the end of the evening, they'd found themselves making out in the front seat of Aubrey's Jaguar like a couple of hormone-driven teenagers. Yes, Faye remembered, with a smile and a little shiver, they *definitely* had been sexually attracted to each other.

Unfortunately, Aubrey's daughter Carolyn had interrupted them, rapping on the window, nearly snarling at Faye. That had cooled their ardor, and since then, events had conspired to make it difficult, if not impossible, to regain that passion. They were busy people, occupied with family duties and private interests. They were older, and they were less energetic. Furthermore, Aubrey, who was in his early seventies, almost fifteen years older than Faye, had made a brief, bad, marriage to a young gold digger just before he met Faye. While the marriage had been annulled and his fortune safely protected, his self-esteem had been damaged. He knew only too well how sexual desire could get him into trouble.

Well, everyone at the hot-flash stage came with a burden of history. Faye knew she was one of the lucky ones. She had loved her husband Jack for all the thirty-five years of their marriage. His unexpected death when he was only sixty-four had plunged her into a well of grief. With her daughter and granddaughter around, she'd eventually struggled back into a life of something like happiness, and with the help of her Hot Flash Club friends, she'd begun to have fun again. They'd encouraged her, a year or so after Jack's death, to try dating. What a bizarre quartet of experiences *that* had occasioned! She snickered now, remembering the four different men and the disastrous dates. At least she'd ridden a motorcycle—she'd always be just a bit proud of that.

Jack had been the only man she'd ever slept with in her life, except for the brief affair she had the year she turned thirty. Back then, Jack had put in eighteen-hour days at a law firm, and Faye had kept house, mothered her baby, and organized the obligatory cocktail parties. Zeke, an old friend, just back from leading a hiking tour in New Zealand, had seemed like freedom, danger, fresh air. He didn't love her, he didn't even care for her—he was just furiously sexually attracted to her. When they made love, it was fierce and completely physical. Kindness, trust, love, and the responsibilities of family weren't in the same room—they weren't even in the same universe.

Remembering those few, brief, crazy meetings brought a smile to Faye's face, and then—oh, damn!—another hot flash! This one was accompanied by its familiar comrade, irrational crankiness. Why was Aubrey taking so long? She huffed in exasperation. In a way, it seemed rather cold, making love this way, after they'd performed their necessary ablutions, but Aubrey was easily embarrassed by the indignities of age.

The bathroom door opened. Finally! Faye's heart did a little salsa step and she sat up, smiling.

"Sorry to be so long," Aubrey apologized. "Candlelight. How nice."

He was completely naked as he came toward the bed, and Faye gave him full points for courage. She wasn't ready to walk naked in front of him. With her clothes on, she felt attractive, and she wondered briefly whether it would be possible for her to keep her nightgown on while they made love.

Aubrey slid into the bed next to her. He was in excellent shape for a man in his seventies, yet beneath his silver chest hair, little pouches of fat hung, and Faye was glad. They lay side by side, smiling at each other.

Aubrey put a warm hand on Faye's arm. "You look very elegant."

She blinked in dismay. "I look like an elephant?"

Aubrey laughed. "I said," he repeated carefully, enunciating each word, "you look very elegant."

"Oh," Faye laughed, too, relieved. *Great, I'm going deaf, too,* she thought.

Aubrey moved his hand, gently slipping the nightgown strap down her arm. The lace bodice folded delicately over, revealing her breast.

Aubrey said, "You're beautiful, Faye."

Leaning forward, he kissed her. His mouth tasted of both mint and cinnamon, and Faye was slightly amused at all his careful grooming, but as they moved together, touching with hands and mouth and lips and teeth different parts of each other's body, she was glad he smelled so very good, so clean, and slightly spicy. As he delicately explored her, bits of her body woke up, like plants lifting their faces to the sun after a long winter. Now she was glad he moved so slowly. Her flickering thoughts— the day's warm sun, the delicious evening meal, her lovely house, this shadowy room—melted away in concentric rings, like the reverse of a stone tossed into a lake. The world grew smaller, tighter, more concentrated, on the bed, on their bodies, on her skin—and then, beneath her skin, in the warm, nearly forgotten space between her thighs. Aubrey spotted the tube of moisturizing jelly. Without speaking, he opened it and gently and very slowly spread it on Faye, his fingertips painting spirals of sensation on tender, long-unnoticed skin. He lay on his back, pulling Faye on top of him, and for just a moment, she thought *Oh, no. All my double chins!* but he adjusted himself, moving her hips with his hands, and she gave herself over to pure feeling.

Oh, my, her body said. *I remember this. This is very nice.*

Goodness! her body said. *This is very, very . . .*

Scoot forward just an inch! her body demanded. *Tilt forward! No, more! More! NOW!*

"Aubrey," she gasped.

Tilting her pelvis forward, her body found a spot she'd forgotten existed. She moaned aloud as she adjusted herself. In response, Aubrey put his hands on her breasts, both arousing and supporting her as she lifted and lowered her hips. She'd forgotten to take out her barrette, but her hair fell loose of its own accord, a strand of it sticking in the sweat on her forehead. This was really a kind of labor, like climbing a mountain, a breathtaking endeavor, a struggle, and she was so close, so close, so close, she was almost—

"Aaah!" Aubrey cried out, dropping his arms to his chest.

With the sudden loss of his support, Faye fell forward, losing her momentum and nearly crashing into Aubrey. She caught herself on her hands just in time.

"Aaah!" Aubrey groaned. He grasped his right arm at shoulder level.

"Aubrey?" Sexual sensations vanished. Dear God, was he having a heart attack? "What's wrong?"

"Shoulder," he groaned. His face was contorted in pain.

Faye moved her confused, trembling body off Aubrey's. Kneeling next to him, she touched his arm. "How can I help?"

"Aspirin," he gasped. "Heating pad. Brandy."

Faye hesitated. "Um, is it safe to take aspirin with alco—"

"Please!" Aubrey's voice was thick with pain.

"But are you—"

"It's only bursitis," Aubrey panted. "But it hurts like the devil."

Faye scooted off the bed, nearly tripping as her foot caught in one of the straps of the silk nightgown that had been discarded at some point in their lovemaking. Grabbing it up, she wrapped it around her like a makeshift towel to cover her rear as she scuttled toward the bathroom. She grabbed her robe off a hook, pulled it on, filled a glass with water, sorted through her medicine cabinet, found the aspirin, and hurried back to Aubrey, who lay clasping his arm, his teeth gritted in pain.

"Shall I help you sit up?" she asked.

"Don't touch me," he barked, adding, "please."

As she watched, Aubrey rolled over to his left side, got his feet on the floor, and sat up, all the time keeping hold of his right arm. He took the glass she held out and swallowed the aspirin. Beads of sweat gleamed on his forehead in the candlelight.

"I'll go downstairs and pour you a brandy," Faye told him. "Then I'll get the heating pad."

"Thank you." Gingerly, Aubrey leaned against the headboard, his face etched with pain.

Faye brought him the snifter of brandy. She blew out all the candles and plugged the heating pad into the electric socket just behind the bed-side table. When Aubrey said he'd like to lie down, she arranged pillows to support his arm. He closed his eyes. His face relaxed. Faye slipped her nightgown on and sat down on the other side of the bed.

"Ouch!" Aubrey's eyes flew open.

Faye jumped up, alarmed. "What happened?"

"You made the mattress move. Any movement jiggles my shoulder and makes it hurt."

Faye winced. "Oh. Sorry. Well, um, would it help if I slept in the guest room?"

"Would you mind? When my shoulder goes out like this, even the slightest alteration is agony."

"Of course I don't mind. I'm so sorry, Aubrey." Very, very lightly, she kissed the top of his head. "I'll see you in the morning. Sleep well."

2

Alice loved the ever-changing view of boats, ships, storms, and sea displayed in the windows of her chic, stylish condo on Boston's harbor front.

She loved—she *adored*—her son Alan, his wife Jennifer, and especially their six-month-old baby girl Aly.

She did *not* love the drive back and forth between her condo and her son's home.

Alan, Jennifer, and baby Aly lived in the gatehouse of The Haven, the wellness spa Alice and the other Hot Flash friends had helped Shirley plan and create. Alan and Jennifer provided baked goods and catering for The Haven. In exchange, they had use of the cozy cottage for their home, and in its kitchen they'd begun their bakery and catering business. As their business grew, they often walked up the drive to use the professional equipment in The Haven's kitchen. When they continued to expand, they asked permission from Shirley and the board of directors of The Haven to transform the sunporch at the back of the gatehouse into a small shop front, complete with glass cases and a few old-fashioned, sweetshop-style wrought iron chairs and tables. A swinging door led from the shop to the efficiently designed commercial kitchen, complete with one of the industrial-size refrigerators and one of the enormous stainless-steel gas ovens from The Haven. From the kitchen, another swinging door led into the smaller kitchen of their private quarters, where Alice spent her days tending the baby and helping with the housework.

The Haven was located on a winding rural road thirty miles west of Boston, not such a very long distance. It only *seemed* endless, because of the constantly congested traffic along 128 and the other east-west roads.

In her secret grumbling soul, Alice admitted that she was growing just a little weary of all this driving.

She was growing just a little weary *period,* and she didn't know what to do about it.

She'd always been powerful, energetic, really kind of invincible, or at least she'd felt that way until the hot-flash years exploded through her system, vaporizing much of her energy. When she retired from the national insurance company where she'd been vice president in charge of administration, she'd received a handsome financial packet, so money would never be a source of stress, certainly not the way it was years ago, when she was a young single mother struggling to raise her two boys and fight her way up the corporate ladder. Over the past few years, in spite of her darling beau, Gideon, their bridge groups, her four Hot Flash Club friends, and her membership on the board of The Haven, Alice had felt just slightly bored. Edgy. Missing something.

Then, last summer, she'd had a small, very minor, really almost insignificant heart attack. After that, she'd been instructed by her physician to cut down on stress. She dropped the competitive bridge clubs for more relaxed groups, paid attention to her diet and attended the damned yawn-inducing, brain-sogging yoga classes Shirley was always raving about, and did the best she could to relax.

She'd felt even *more* bored. Boredom made her cranky, and that hadn't been good for her blood pressure, and for a while she felt almost itchy with ennui.

And then her granddaughter was born.

Alice had never known such love, such pure unadulterated joy. When she was with her grandchild, the music of life transformed from irritating rap to a soaring symphony. She'd never had much interest in babies before, but then little Aly wasn't any normal baby. Aly was the most beautiful, fascinating, precious infant ever born.

Her son and his wife had paid her the ultimate compliment, naming their daughter after her. When she offered to take care of the infant while Alan and Jennifer ran their catering and bakery business, they eagerly accepted, which made Alice love them so much she had to restrain herself from becoming a babbling fool. The baby was born prematurely, and Jennifer had suffered from toxemia, so for the first couple of months worry clouded Alice's joy. Gradually both mother and child flourished.

Things went back to normal. Alice's morning and evening drives became routine.

Since both grandmother and grandchild were named Alice, the three adults deliberated on how to nickname them to avoid confusion. Little Alice and Big Alice didn't work, because Alice—tall, broad-shouldered, big-boned, and well-padded—was just *slightly* sensitive about the word "big." Young Alice and Old Alice wasn't so great, either. Alice One and Alice Two? Nope. Numbers carried too many negative connotations. When Alan and Jennifer considered Granny, big, old Alice diplomatically refrained from telling them that while she loved being a grandmother, the word *Granny* made her feel even older and grayer than ever. Fortunately, they all three fell into the habit of calling the baby Aly, and the problem was solved.

Today, Alice took care of Aly while Alan and Jennifer ran the bakery. While Aly slept, Alice did the piles of laundry a baby makes, and scrubbed the kitchen and bathroom because her son and his wife hadn't the time or energy, and put a hen in the oven to roast for the dinner Alan and Jennifer would eat with the potatoes, vegetables, and salad she'd prepared. Alan and Jennifer were so grateful for all her help. They were working furiously, taking all the private orders and catering jobs they could get, because they wanted to save enough money for a down payment on a house. They loved living in the tidy stone gatehouse of The Haven, but it was small, and they hoped to have more children eventually, and naturally wanted their own home.

At five o'clock, they closed the bakery at the back of the house and came through the industrial kitchen into the cottage kitchen, where they hugged Alice and showered her with gratitude. They told her she was an *angel*. They said they couldn't imagine what they'd do without her.

Now the universe's crankiest *angel* was driving home. She adjusted the seat on her BMW, grateful for the technology that allowed her to relieve the stress on her back as she began the long slog east, toward home and the blissful quiet of her apartment. WGBH was playing a Vivaldi piece she'd heard a thousand times before. She turned from the country road onto Route 2, and then entered the eight thundering lanes of cars, trucks, and SUVs speeding along 128 in a hypnotic blur, like a pack of roaring metallic monsters. The bright spring sun bounced off the hoods and roofs, lasering into her eyes.

Now Vivaldi's perky little notes irritated her. She snapped the radio off. Usually classical music buoyed her, providing a psychological lift that helped her survive the drive in heavy traffic. Tonight it just wasn't working. She craved chocolate, so she reached over, opened the glove compartment, and brought out a bag of chocolate-covered almonds. She knew she shouldn't eat them, she knew she was gaining weight again, but almonds were good for one's health, and the caffeine and sugar and sheer pleasure of the candy was a necessity tonight. She was tired.

Behind her, an impatient driver honked his horn. Alice flicked her turn indicator and began to edge over into the slower middle lane just as an idiot on a motorcycle cut in front of her with suicidal recklessness. She missed hitting him by only inches. Her heart jumped into her throat.

She hit the button that rolled down the window. "Watch what you're doing, you moron!" she yelled, realizing, as the warm, gasoline-scented air flooded in, that of course the moron couldn't hear her.

Behind her, Mr. Impatience's horn blared. She jerked her wheel right, lurching into the next lane, nearly kissing the bumper of a lumbering cement truck.

Her heart quivered and kicked inside her chest. She hated this feeling. She tried to remember all the advice she'd received about calming down. She couldn't visualize a cool pool of water because she had to keep visualizing the freaking traffic, so she forced herself to inhale deeply and exhale slowly. Gideon was always reminding her to relax. *Get in the right lane and just poke along,* he advised. Well, she would, except at the end of the day, in spite of the aspirin she took, arthritis threatened to cripple her with cramps in her legs, hands, and back. At any moment she'd find herself curling up like a pretzel, not the safest posture while driving seventy miles an hour. At home, she'd take a hot soaking bath, or collapse on her heating pad, or have a nice glass of wine. She wanted to *get home*. She didn't want to dawdle.

She was so tired, so stressed—tears rolled down her cheeks. Was it possible that she'd gone from being a woman who had it all to a woman who had too much?

Finally she reached her exit and threaded her way through the narrow Boston streets to her condo. As she slid her car into its calm, waiting spot in the cool shade of the parking garage, her pulse slowed. She took a minute to redo her makeup—she didn't want Gideon to see her with tear marks. Gideon kept telling her to step back and let Alan and Jennifer manage their lives without her, but she saw, every day, firsthand and close-up, how overwhelmed the younger people were. Gideon's advice was well-meant, but it only increased the tension Alice felt. She didn't want to argue—which was only another sign of her exhaustion. Alice usually loved a good argument. In her younger days, her talent for confrontation had sent her flying right up the corporate ladder. In her younger days, she'd always won her arguments. In her younger days, the drumroll of her excited heart and the flush of blood through her body had been an exhilarating experience, making her keen, articulate, triumphant.

Now the same drumroll made her anxious. She couldn't let Gideon know how often, how easily, her heart went trippy.

It was so quiet in the garage. So soothing. Alice wanted to recline her seat and fall asleep right there. But of course that would only present her cranky old bones with brand new ways of aching. Besides, Gideon was waiting for her. Most evenings he fixed dinner, which she truly appreciated. He was a retired schoolteacher with lots of hobbies and interests. Thank heavens *one* of them was cooking.

Alice left her car and entered the elevator. As it ascended, the sleek chrome box soothed her. She felt as if she were in one of *Star Trek*'s transporters, conveying herself from chaos to calm.

Gideon looked up at her from his recliner when she entered the living room. "Damn, Alice. You look beat."

It was the wrong thing to say.

"I look *beat*?" Alice burst into tears. "What you mean is I look old, right? Just go ahead and spit it out, don't pussyfoot around!" Slinging her purse onto a chair, she stomped into the kitchen and snatched out the ice-cube tray. She wanted a drink. A nice cool vodka tonic. She twisted the tray to release the ice, but she must have used more force than necessary, because ice cubes exploded from the tray, flying around the room like manic ping pong balls. "Damn!" she cursed.

"Alice." Gideon was calm, in control. "Go sit down. Let me make you a drink."

"I'll do it myself! I'm not too *beat* to make my own damned drink!"

"Really."

Alice glared. "Don't you go all superior on me!"

Gideon stared at her. He looked sad. He said, "Alice." The warmth in his voice made her cry even harder. He took the ice tray from her, set it in the sink, and wrapped his huge arms around her, pulling her against him. He was so big, so strong, so calm. He was infinitely comforting.

"Why don't you go sit down and take your shoes off, and I'll fix your drink," he suggested.

She gave in. "All right." She sniffed. "Thanks."

Man, it felt good to sink down onto her sofa. She eased off her shoes, brought her legs up, and stretched out. Gideon brought her the drink, then sat at the other end of the sofa, taking her feet in his lap. He began to massage them gently.

"Heaven," Alice sighed.

"I've had a thought," Gideon said.

"Oh, yeah?"

"Yeah. I think Jennifer's mother ought to come up for a while. I'm sure she'd love to spend some time with her grandchild."

"Jennifer's mother is a babbling hysteric."

"Not really. She was pretty upset when Jennifer was having such a tough time when the baby came early. But that's only natural. She did manage to raise Jennifer, after all, and Jennifer's a gem."

"She was younger when she raised Jennifer."

"And you were younger when you raised Alan."

Alice closed her eyes. She really was too tired to argue.

"I worry about you, Alice." Gideon's voice was soft. With his thumbs, he pressed the balls of her feet, then the arches. "You're not taking care of yourself. When was the last time you went to yoga or rode your exercise bike? I'd bet all the money I have you're having heart episodes you're not telling me about."

"This really isn't fair." Alice forced herself to pull her feet away, drawing her legs under her as she readjusted herself on the sofa. She was relaxed now and had regained her sense of humor. "Seduction by foot massage—if men only knew, they'd never have to buy flowers."

"Have you been hearing a word I've said?" Gideon looked stern.

"I hear you." Alice stared at her glass, rattling the ice cubes. "Gideon, I appreciate your concern. But first, I'm just fine. And second, the kids really need help. They want to buy a house. They need someone to take care of Aly. Otherwise, they'll have to hire help in the bakery, and there goes part of their profits. Besides, I love taking care of little Aly. She's the light of my life."

"But why not let Jennifer's mom take over now and then?"

"I don't know if she'd do it."

"You don't know that she wouldn't. Has Jennifer asked her?"

Alice shrugged. She thought of Jennifer's mother, whom she'd met only a few times. The woman was like some kind of overwound mechanical toy, talking incessantly, throwing her arms out in manic gestures, unable to sit still for a minute.

"The baby won't stop loving you if you're not there every day," Gideon said softly. "She won't forget you if you're not there all the time."

"I know that!" Alice snapped. "I just don't think Jennifer's mother can run that house as well as I can."

"Because you're a control freak," Gideon said bluntly.

Alice opened her mouth to object, but she knew what he said was true. "I'll think about it, Gideon, all right?" She frowned. "But if I suggest it to Jennifer and Alan, will it hurt their feelings?"

"Of course not. Jennifer might be thrilled to have her mother around."

As Alice bit her lip, thinking, the phone rang. Gideon rose, picked it up, and brought the handset over to Alice.

"Hi, Mom." It was Alan. "Listen, there's a movie Jennifer and I really want to see. Is there any chance you'd want to do a little more babysitting for Aly this evening?"

Alice closed her eyes. She knew her son and his wife hadn't seen a movie for at least six months. Probably more, because Jennifer had been confined to bed rest for the last few months of her pregnancy. If Gideon drove her out, she wouldn't mind making the trip again. It was only forty minutes, more or less.

"I'd love to," she told him. "We'll leave right away."

3

As sunlight filled the room, Marilyn floated out of her dreams into a dream come true. She lay on her side in the warm bed, her fiancé Ian next to her, his arm wrapped over her, holding her close. Never before in her life had she felt so secure with a man. Never before had she been so much in love.

Marilyn had lived her life like a tugboat: sturdy, homely, helpful, significant only in her usefulness to others.

Now, at fifty-three, she found herself transformed into a pleasure barge like the one Cleopatra rode gliding down the Nile: sensual, laden with rose petals, scented with exotic perfumes.

"Awake?" Ian whispered.

Marilyn turned over to face him. "Awake." She nuzzled her face into his chest. It was a bit scrawny and bony . . . she thought of it as an *intellectual* chest.

"I wish we didn't have to get up," Ian murmured, caressing her back.

Marilyn sighed as the myriad complexities of real life claimed her thoughts, turning her romantic mood into a vanishing mist.

It was early May, and she had to give her final lecture at MIT in Analytic Techniques for Studying Geologic Samples at nine o'clock. Ian had to be at Boston University to teach his classes.

"We'll talk about the wedding tonight?" she suggested.

"Tonight." He kissed her forehead and threw back the covers.

Marilyn slid from bed, and the day began.

She rushed into the shower while Ian hurried downstairs to start the coffee. By the time she was zipping up her brown skirt, he arrived with a mug for her, just the way she liked it. She sipped it as she bumbled around the bedroom, searching for her comfortable gray pumps, strapping on her watch, wondering where she'd left her briefcase. She headed down to the kitchen for a quick bowl of All-Bran. As she gobbled her food, she moved around the kitchen, preparing a tray of coffee, juice, toast, and a banana. She set her bowl in the dishwasher. Ian hurried down, hair still wet from the shower, pecked her forehead, and left for the university. Marilyn picked up the tray and climbed the steps to the attic.

This past December, when her beloved Ian Foster appeared at Marilyn's door with the amazing news he'd taken a job at Boston University and was moving from Scotland so he could be with her, Marilyn had been overwhelmed with joy. With Ian she had found, at last, true, abiding—and, oh, yeah, sexually fantastic!—love, something she'd assumed, now that she was fifty-three, she would never have.

Even the mundane complexities of existence seemed to melt into honey in the warmth of their love. The condo she was renting for herself and her vaguely senile mother Ruth proved to be much too small the moment Ian entered, carrying his briefcase and suitcase and baggage claims for the books and other possessions he'd brought. He was to start his professorship in January. He had to have a private study for his books, computer, drafting table, monographs, and professional journals. Besides, Ruth had been agitating for a little attached apartment of her own where she could be independent.

So Marilyn and Ian had phoned a Realtor, toured a series of houses, and rented a charming, narrow, triple-decker row house in Cambridge. After they were married, they'd find a *wonderful* house, one that satisfied all their needs and fantasies. But for now, this peculiar little house was sufficient.

Ruth had her apartment in the basement—the Realtor had called it the "garden floor"—with an intercom in every room, so she could alert Marilyn if she needed something.

The first floor had a living room, dining room, and kitchen, all tidy and modern. The second floor had three bedrooms and two baths. Just perfect. Ian and Marilyn shared the master bedroom, and they each had an office. It meant running up and down the stairs a lot, but they agreed this was a good thing. It would keep them in shape.

They settled in, treating themselves to a handsome new bed, ordering the newest, sleekest, most efficient furniture for their offices, and comfortable furniture in neutral colors for the main floor. Neither Marilyn nor Ian cared much about décor. They were so busy teaching, working on their scientific projects, and making love, they had no time to care whether the sofa coordinated with the carpet.

In her garden apartment, Ruth pottered about blissfully, knitting her endless scarves, laboring over her crossword puzzles, carefully clipping recipes from magazines, pasting them onto cards, and filing them neatly away in cheerful little boxes that often got lost beneath her knitting. She went to the Senior Citizen Center several days a week, and at least once a week she went to dinner or a movie with her eighty-seven-year-old beau, Ernest Eberhart, whom she'd met when he'd asked her to pull up his baggy pants, which he'd been unable to do without taking his hands off his walker. Each day Marilyn made many trips down to Ruth's quarters, to share afternoon tea or a joke she'd just heard, and at night to kiss her mother good night, while surreptitiously checking to be sure the burners and oven were off.

Sometimes, rushing up or down the stairs, Marilyn thought about the wedding. It was the second marriage for both Marilyn and Ian. Still, they wanted an *occasion,* attended by family and friends. There was no rush—at their age, they both agreed they could take their time and enjoy the journey instead of hurrying to the destination. But when? Where? What kind of reception? They never had time to talk about it, busy as they were with teaching, and Ruth, and—

And Ian's son, Angus, who had just moved in with them.

She tapped and softly called Angus's name. There was no response and she didn't hear the tap of his computer keys, so it was possible that for once he hadn't fallen asleep at his desk but had actually slept in his bed. She left the tray outside his bedroom door and tiptoed down to her office on the second floor.

Angus was a genius. At twenty-nine, he'd finished his Ph.D. in computer science. Now he was engrossed in what he called "divide-and-conquer algorithms," which involved "hyperthreading" and "speculative execution," and other incomprehensible electronic acts. Marilyn and Ian had set him up with temporary quarters in the attic. He didn't want much furniture, only a bed, a chair, and a desk for his computer. Now, never caring or even knowing whether it was day or night, Angus hid away in his lair, typing and muttering maniacally, like an oversized, chittering goggle-eyed bat.

Tall and lanky like his father, Angus was a peculiar man with a receding hairline, bad teeth, and thick glasses. He lived so intensely in his head that he'd all but forgotten he possessed a body. He completely forgot to eat unless Marilyn brought him something. He forgot to bathe, change his clothes, or brush his teeth, too, which wasn't a problem of much consequence since he never left his computer. He wasn't exactly homely, but he did look eccentric, with big ears and a head shaped like an ostrich egg protruding from a nest of unkempt brown hair. He'd always been shy, Ian had confessed to Marilyn. Ian and his now-deceased wife had worried terribly about their son, who was desperately shy around people. When, after graduating from college, he announced that he was moving to Sydney with his girlfriend, an equally brilliant nerdy woman named Ursula, Ian and his wife had been thrilled. Someone loved their son!

Unfortunately, she no longer did. That was all the information Marilyn and Ian could get out of Angus, who twitched and stuttered whenever the subject arose.

Poor boy! Marilyn thought. Poor, brilliant boy. She hoped he might take heart from meeting her own son, Teddy, who was also a brilliant science geek. Teddy was married to a gorgeous woman named Lila who adored Teddy; they had a daughter, little Irene. But when Marilyn had everyone to dinner in January, Angus had remained more or less mute at the dinner table, clearly miserable and so intimidated by Lila's beauty that after his first jaw-dropping glance, he never looked at her again. Teddy made valiant attempts to converse with Angus, but Angus only managed abrupt monosyllabic replies.

Angus was sweet, Marilyn thought, from the little she could know of him. He needed to have his self-confidence built up. He needed to be drawn out of himself. But she couldn't do much about that, at least not for a while. She'd taken a sabbatical from MIT, but in January the department head phoned to beg her to teach one of her favorite courses as well as two upper-level paleontology courses. She quickly agreed. For years she'd dutifully taught Introduction to Geology to freshmen. Here was a chance to teach more exciting courses.

The new year, which had seemed on its first day to spread before her like an open diary of days, suddenly pleated up like a folded accordion with appointments and duties. She hired a handsome Jamaican woman to come in five days a week to clean the house, do the laundry, and keep a diplomaticly watchful eye on Ruth. Ian helped her do errands and the major grocery shopping on Saturday. Still, it seemed she had more work to do than hours in which to do it. And planning a wedding? She could hardly find time to brush her teeth!

Her briefcase was on her desk! Hallelujah. She seemed to waste so much time looking for things these days. She grabbed up her briefcase, ran down to the kitchen, poured herself another cup of coffee, and carried it down to her mother's quarters. It was important to her to spend a little time with her mother at the beginning of every day.

"Good morning, darling!" Ruth was snuggled into a rocking chair, watching a morning television show, still in her yellow terry cloth robe. With her white curls sticking out all over, she resembled a big baby chick.

"Morning, Mom." Marilyn kissed the top of her head and settled into a wing chair opposite. "How did you sleep?"

"Oh, beautifully. I always do."

Except for the times you wet the bed, Marilyn thought. Ruth's occasional incontinence was a tricky issue. A rubber sheet or night diapers might be hygienically helpful, but psychologically devastating— for Ruth *and* Marilyn. They both wanted to believe that Ruth wasn't failing.

"Did you hear the news?" Ruth asked, nodding toward the TV.

"No, what's going on?"

"Two peanuts walked into a bar, and one was a salted."

Marilyn laughed. She'd only heard that joke a million times since she was a child, but she appreciated her mother's attempts to be jolly. Ruth didn't dwell on her aching muscles and creaking bones, and Marilyn knew that Ruth's genuine interest in other people was one of the things that kept her going.

"I've been studying the garden," Ruth said now. "You've got lilies of the valley coming up all around the tulips. Whoever lived here before did a lot of landscaping. But all the beds could use a good weeding."

Marilyn suppressed a sigh. One more responsibility for which she had no time. "I've got a full schedule today," she told her mother, "but I'll see about hiring a landscaper."

"We'll need the lawn mowed, too. Unless Ian wants to do it."

"Ian's pretty stressed out with work right now," Marilyn reminded Ruth. "He's the new kid on the block in his department."

"Oh, I understand." Ruth's face grew melancholy. "I wish I could help." Not so long ago, she'd been strong and active.

"You've got so much to do!" Marilyn reminded her. "Are you going to the Senior Citizens Center today?"

Ruth's wrinkled face brightened. "I am. I'll take a cab. Ernest is meeting me there, then he's taking me out to lunch."

"What fun. Tell him hello for me, will you?" Marilyn drank the rest of her coffee and rose. "I've got to go. I've got a nine o'clock class."

"I wonder, darling, could you pick me up some bananas?"

Marilyn swallowed a sigh. With four people to feed, it seemed she was always at the grocery store, and in a busy city like Cambridge, even going through the express lane required a good chunk of time. She tried to make lists so she didn't have to go every single day.

Ruth's voice was apologetic. "I put bananas on yesterday's list, honey, but you bought me grapes."

No, Marilyn remembered, Ruth had not written *bananas* on her bluebird-bordered note paper. She had put *grapes,* because Marilyn recalled standing in the produce section, wondering whether Ruth wanted green or red grapes.

"I wouldn't ask, darling, except without bananas, I tend to get a little constipated." Ruth's forehead crumpled slightly, with embarrassment. She looked like a very sweet, very old, little girl.

"Of course I'll get you some bananas," Marilyn said, forcing a smile. "Anything else?"

"No, that's all, thank you." Ruth brightened. Helpfully, she offered, "Would you like me to call a skyscraper?"

Marilyn ignored the little verbal slip. They were just part of Ruth's speech these days. "No, Mom, I'll ask around for some references today. You just enjoy yourself."

"I will, sweetheart. I always try to remember that today is the first day of my restful life."

4

Polly often wished she were more like Alice. Alice was a lioness. Polly was a possum. Alice was a champion at assertiveness, which was why Alice had been an executive in an enormous insurance company and why Polly had made her living as a seamstress, working by herself and meeting her clients in the security of her own home.

Perhaps, Polly decided, as she returned from The Haven in the early afternoon, perhaps she'd ask Alice how to go about solving her problem. Alice had been head of personnel, and this was a personnel problem.

Or perhaps she wouldn't ask Alice, because Alice was, after all, so close to Shirley and might see Polly's overture as some kind of insult to Shirley.

Perhaps Polly should just get in bed and eat ice cream until she exploded.

When Polly had agreed to supervise the five Havenly Yours employees who made the clever outfits that sold from The Haven's shop as fast as they could be made, she hadn't really realized what an enormous task she was taking on. In the rush of excitement last summer, when she and Faye had designed and sewn the trial garments, Polly had been so exhilarated she'd felt she could do almost anything. As the months went by, the satisfaction of watching a dream come true had buoyed Polly up. They'd put together a business plan, got a loan from a bank, installed industrial sewing machines and fabric-cutting and ironing equipment, and set up a day care for the children of the women workers. Havenly Yours was *happening*. In fact, it was on the brink of expanding.

And the thought of expanding made Polly want to weep with exhaustion. She was tired of spending five days a week at Havenly Yours.

She was crinkled like a potato chip from bending over tables, lifting heavy bolts of fabric, squinting to inspect seams, listening to personal problems and offering creative solutions. By the weekend, she had no energy left to sew for her own customers.

Plus, there was the money thing. She hadn't asked to be paid, and she wouldn't starve without a salary, but without money coming in from her own business, she had to live more frugally than she liked. Alice and Faye had both been in at the start of the business, Alice setting up the bookkeeping and Faye helping with the designs, but now a professional bookkeeper ran that part of the business and Faye had gone back to her first love and real talent, painting.

But Polly had stayed on. And *why*?

At the core of Polly's dilemma was a problem as old as high school: she was the new girl. She was, in fact, the fifth wheel, and what was that cliché? As useless as a fifth wheel? She'd met the four other Hot Flash Club women a year after *they*'d all bonded, and while she felt loved and supported by them, while she never felt at all slighted by any of them, she still felt—well, *expendable*. But she *was* essential to Havenly Yours. She was afraid that if she stopped supervising the seamstresses, they'd have to find someone to take Polly's place, and paying another salary would diminish the profits Havenly Yours was showing.

Really, it wasn't such difficult work, Polly reminded herself. She enjoyed all the women, and she was learning Spanish without trying, and the colors and fabrics were all so luscious.

She parked her car in her drive, grabbed the mail from the box, and entered her house. Her dear basset hound Roy Orbison waddled up to her as fast as his stubby legs would carry him, tail wagging.

"Hello, old friend." Polly bent to scratch him at his favorite spot just above his tail. "Want to go out?"

She led him out to the backyard, collapsing on the porch steps while the dog performed his duties and sniffed the grass for messages. The May evening was golden. Polly should really start weeding around her iris, but she was just too tired.

"Come on, Roy," she said, curtailing his evening's constitutional. "I've got to lie down."

Roy studied her with his soulful eyes, then, with one of his enormous sighs, followed her back into the house. Polly fed him an extra chunk of food as reward for his good-natured acquiescence, and then dragged her exhausted blubber up the stairs, collapsed on top of the bed, and fell asleep at once.

When she woke, she could tell by the way the light spilled through her curtains that it was evening. For a while, she lay there, warm and drowsy, letting her thoughts flow and twine like reeds in a stream. She thought about Havenly Yours, and she wondered whether she ought to have a plasterer in to redo the bedroom ceiling. Over the years she'd become accustomed to the series of wandering cracks, even oddly fond of them, as if they were developing in sympathy with the wrinkles in her own face. She didn't want to change the bedroom ceiling, really. But when did the cracks stop being a superficial problem and become a warning sign that the ceiling might collapse on her at any moment?

Were the cracks becoming deeper, longer? Or was she just so depressed these days that everything took on a more somber cast?

She'd always been an optimist. She still was. Her good-natured acceptance of the inexplicable ways of man had helped her survive the bizarre turn her life had taken when her son David, her only child, had married Amy Anderson, a slender, sweet-faced vegetarian whose will-o'-the-wisp looks concealed a tyrant's might. Amy's family owned a farm west of Boston, where they grew organic vegetables, knit shawls and blankets from the wool of their own sheep, and performed other earth-friendly actions, making them absolutely superior to everyone else on the planet. Especially to Polly, who sometimes had been known to eat steak or wear polyester. David and Amy had a son, Jehoshaphat, Polly's only grandchild, whom they allowed germy, meat-breathing Polly to see about once a month, when she drove out to visit. The occasions were never terribly successful. Polly could not understand her son's complete adoration of his wife, or why he, who had once been a banker, was so happy driving a tractor and pitching hay. But he was happy, and Polly was glad for him.

She tried not to feel rejected, even though she had, in fact, been rejected. She reminded herself, as did her Hot Flash friends, that not every grandmother got to see her grandchildren every day. Faye's daughter and family had moved to California. And Marilyn's son and his family lived nearby, but Marilyn was too busy to see her grandson more than once a month.

Polly turned over on her side, feeling the blubber in her belly and bum shift accordingly. Here was something else to be depressed about— her ever increasing weight. She battled to diet and exercise, and when she still gained weight, she battled to remain philosophical about it. Her Hot Flash friends and their good humor and support helped her here, too. She wouldn't be quite so negative about her aging body if only her beau, Hugh, were just a tad more reliable.

Hugh Monroe, her lover of almost two years, was sixty-three. Hugh was an oncologist, a sympathetic, emotionally generous man whose pa-tients adored him. Rotund and jovial, he lived large. He liked roller coaster rides and scuba diving, he liked adventure and celebration. He was always taking care of other people, never hesitating to interrupt a meal or a movie to rush to the bedside of a good friend, or to the aid of one of his children—*or* to help his perpetually dependent ex-wife, the ir-ritatingly size-six Carol.

Five years before, when Carol left Hugh for another man, Hugh had been relieved. Their marriage had been empty for a long time, and the divorce was amicable. They'd stayed together until their children were through college, married, and with children of their own. Carol had kept their large Victorian house in Belmont, and Hugh moved into a hand-some apartment on Commonwealth Avenue in Boston, close to his hos-pital. The children were shocked but resigned. Hugh slowly entered the dating scene and had just met Polly when Carol's lover collapsed of a heart attack on the tennis court.

A week after the funeral, Carol invited Hugh to dinner at the house where they'd raised their three children. She wanted to get back together, she said. When Hugh gently declined, she burst into tears, crying, "How can you do this to me!" For two years now, Carol had campaigned to get her husband back. It wasn't enough for her that all the Monroes got to-gether on every possible family occasion—birthdays, holidays, even a grandchild's graduation from preschool triggered a family get-together. Carol wanted to get married again. She tried to enlist the services of their three children. The youngest sided with his mother, but the two oldest rebelled enough to tell their mother they thought Hugh had the right to do as he wished.

Last Christmas, when Hugh accompanied Polly and Faye and Aubrey on a Christmas Get-Away cruise to the Caribbean, had been the first time Hugh had not been around for a family event. Polly had had hopes that it was a trendsetting experience. But when they returned to Boston, Carol still phoned Hugh when she needed any little thing, and Hugh dutifully, if reluctantly, went.

Something was always going wrong with Carol. During the last year, she'd suffered from chronic fatigue syndrome. She wasn't eating, she didn't have the energy to go out, she was losing weight. (Losing weight! Without trying to! Polly gnashed her teeth at the thought.) Hugh refused to examine or treat her, but he did begin to visit her again, with his children, and when Hugh was around, Carol perked up, dressed up, and ate the delicacies her children brought. Hugh left Polly alone at the ballet or in her bedroom, rushing off to kill the mouse that turned out to be a beetle or to show Carol how to use the dehumidifier they'd bought years ago. If Polly protested, it only made Hugh miserable. It did not make him stay.

Now and then, Hugh did spend an nice big chunk of time with Polly. When he did, on the rare occasion, ignore his beeping cell phone, Polly envisioned her love life as a holiday feast, with Carol—a wilting, starving, dejected Gandhi-esque figure—staring at them longingly through a plate glass window, ready to smash it at any moment. She was certain Hugh hadn't proposed marriage because no one, not even Polly, wanted to imagine what drastic, dramatic displays of wretchedness Carol would resort to *then*. That was all right. Polly didn't need to be *married* to Hugh. Oh, it would be nice, but she felt fortunate simply to have him in her life. He was such a good, generous, openhearted man. He only wanted everyone to be happy.

But could *she* continue to be happy with this constantly interrupted love affair? She wanted to be able to count on Hugh. More than that, she wanted everyone to know that she was part of Hugh's life. She wanted Hugh to introduce her to his children. She wanted his children to realize she wasn't some sexpot gold digger but a nice, reliable, intelligent, middle-aged woman who gave Hugh the nurturing he'd been missing out on for so long. She wanted, if she were honest, to be married to Hugh, she wanted him to live with her, so they could lounge together in bed, and prepare dinner together the way they sometimes did. She wanted him with her all the time.

But that didn't seem to be what Hugh wanted, or at least what Hugh was capable of giving her, and so her thoughts turned inward like the coils on a snail shell, circling back to her sense of self-esteem, provoking the questions of self-doubt that ran on a loop in her mind. Was she too fat? Was she simply not attractive enough, not sexy enough, for Hugh to want to be with her all the time? She reminded herself that Shirley— skinny, yoga-toned Shirley; sexpot, blubber-free Shirley—had no man in her life . . . though heaven knows, she was trying to change that. So it wasn't just Polly's being overweight that kept her alone in her house, never knowing when she'd be with Hugh.

It wasn't just about her weight, but speaking of what was reliable and ever-present—heaven knew her weight was always with her! Faithful to a fault!

Polly groaned and sat up. It was time to shower and dress for dinner. Hugh had asked if he could spend the evening with her, and she'd bought a couple of nice thick steaks and lots of fresh salad ingredients. The thought cheered her. In the bathroom, she lathered herself with a luxurious perfumed soap. She felt cooler when she stepped out, fresher, rejuvenated. This was more like it! She had to stop lying around grumbling like a beached sea lion. She had to remember to enjoy the pleasures of the day and stop whining about what she couldn't have. Wrapping a towel around her, she padded barefoot into her bedroom. Now what was that joke Shirley had told her? It was a hospital joke; Hugh would love it. Oh, yes! Now she remembered!

The one about a man in a hospital bed with an oxygen mask over his mouth. A young nurse comes in to give him a sponge bath.

"Nurse," the patient asks, "are my testicles black?"

The nurse blushes. "I don't know." She gets busy washing his feet and legs.

"Nurse," the patient repeats, impatiently, "are my testicles black?"

With a sigh of frustration, she lifts the sheet, pushes his gown up, takes his penis in her hand, and leans down really close, carefully inspecting his balls.

"They look just fine," she tells him.

The man snatches the oxygen mask off his face. "Good to know, but could you please tell me, *are my test results back*?"

Polly laughed. It would be such fun telling Hugh—

The red light was blinking on her answering machine—while she'd been in the shower, someone had left a message.

She collapsed on the side of the bed, just staring at the machine. She knew it would be Hugh, canceling. And she knew she'd be so frustrated, she'd go downstairs and eat both steaks plus the pint of ice cream in the freezer.

5

Shirley knew she was a nitwit, as far as men were concerned. She didn't need her Hot Flash friends to point it out to her. She'd been married and divorced three times. She'd had lots and lots of lovers. Which was not to say she'd had lots of *love*.

Although she *had* had lots of fun.

Not to mention, she admitted to herself wryly, quite a bit of heartache.

Part of her problem, she was well aware, was that she couldn't help falling for handsome, younger men.

Now she stepped from the shower, dried herself in a fluffy towel, and rubbed generous dollops of perfumed lotion into her skin. Feet, legs, torso, arms, neck, hands. Really, for a woman in her early sixties, she had a great body. Over the years she'd done zillions of stupid things, but one thing she'd done right was to practice yoga and keep her body supple and slender. Marilyn was slender, too, but she had terrible posture from slumping over textbooks and test tubes or whatever in her labs. Faye, Alice, and Polly, however, were just plain overweight, in spite of their diet and exercise programs. Not that Shirley ever mentioned it— they were all so touchy on that subject.

But Faye, Alice, Polly, and Marilyn all had men in their lives. Men who loved them.

Shirley was alone.

Not that Shirley felt competitive. Well, okay, she *did* feel competitive. She loved her Hot Flash friends, she couldn't live without them, they'd made all the difference in her life. Without them, she wouldn't have The Haven, she wouldn't have any kind of a future.

But they were so *judgmental*.

They would tell her, she just knew they would, that the dress she slid over her head was too young for her. That it plunged too low in front, that the skirt was too short and her heels too high. As she made up her face, she could just *hear* them whispering affectionate, *subtle* suggestions: *Maybe not quite so much mascara, Shirley. Are you sure you want to wear such bright red lipstick?*

"Oh, shut up!" Shirley shouted at the empty room. "I'm going out with the bleeping accountant, aren't I?"

Last fall, when Shirley's lover Justin—her twelve-years-younger, handsome, sexy, charming, knock-your-socks-off lover, Justin—had proved to be a user and a cad, Shirley had broken off with him. She'd been proud of herself, and her friends had rushed to comfort and encourage her. Which was all very nice, except Shirley really, *really* liked having a man in her life. At Christmas, after three months of agonizing celibacy, Shirley had whined to Alice, who was a great problem solver. She'd recommended Shirley try an online dating service.

Shirley took Alice's advice. At first, she was wildly optimistic. She tended to be optimistic, anyway, and she got so many hits, and spotted so many guys whose profiles looked wonderful, she'd thought the problem would be choosing from an embarrassment of riches.

Not.

First of all, very few men were interested in over-sixty females, especially, it seemed, the over-sixty males. The men who did make it past her three-step weed-out—e-mail conversation, phone conversation, Hot Flash Club approval—were all fine on paper but lacking in real life. Her first date, a divorced salesman, was in a contest with a friend to see how many women he could get into bed. Her second date, a garage mechanic, had a great, earthy sense of humor, bad breath, and teeth the color of old bruises. Her third date lived with seven cats. The rest blurred in her memory—for once she was grateful her memory was failing.

Tonight's date was the exception. Stan Elliot was a sixty-three-year-old widower, retired from a lifelong position as an accountant for the IRS. His two children lived in other states; one in California, one in Florida. He owned a handsome little condo near the Belmont Country Club, where he played golf three days a week with friends. He drank, ate, and exercised in moderation. He was not only solvent, he was, as he often told Shirley, so carefully and strategically well invested, he wouldn't have to worry about money for the rest of his life. He had insurance policies in case he'd ever need assisted living or long-term medical assistance, and also for his burial service, so his children would never be responsible for him. He was lost in the kitchen, however, he'd confessed to Shirley on their first date. He missed having a woman around. He was healthy, and pleasant, and kind.

And punctual. Shirley hurried out to her car and zipped off toward Boston. She was meeting him at a restaurant he'd chosen because it was almost exactly halfway between her home and his. She'd met him here for dinner before, and even though Shirley hadn't felt that little *zing* of attraction, she did appreciate his obvious niceness.

His rather *bland* obvious niceness. Stan wasn't a handsome man, but he wasn't ugly, either. He wasn't brilliant, but neither was he stupid. He was kind, clean, inoffensive—perfect, if she wanted to date a Boy Scout.

Still, it gave Shirley a little shiver of pleasure to enter the restaurant in her flirty new dress, to sense people looking her over, and to say, "I'm meeting Mr. Elliott."

"Of course. Please follow me." The maître d' threaded his way through the tables. Shirley followed, feeling just a little bit *onstage,* and quite a bit pleased with herself because the person waiting for her was, for all the room to see, a man. A respectably dressed, very pleasant man. She felt *chosen.*

Stan rose when she arrived at the table. Leaning forward, he kissed her cheek. "Hello, Shirley."

"Hello, Stan." She sank into the terribly comfortable chair and allowed the waiter to slide her toward the table.

"Notice anything?" He cocked his head playfully.

Shirley inspected him. His head was bare except for the toilet-seat-fringe of white hair around his balding pate. He hadn't had a haircut. She thought his metal-framed glasses were the same. Oh! "You wore a purple tie!"

He nodded, smiling. "Had to buy it. Didn't have one."

He did it because she'd said purple was her favorite color. That was just *sweet.* "Well, it looks wonderful on you, Stan. Really becoming."

"Not too gaudy?"

"Not at all."

The waiter interrupted their fashion analysis, took their order, and went off.

"How has your week been?" Stan asked.

"Okay." Shirley sipped some of her sparkling soda. "Actually," she continued, "it's been rather annoying. I'm a creative kind of person, a hands-on person. Remember, I told you, I used to be a massage thera-pist, and I like that personal contact, but now that The Haven's up and running, I spend an enormous amount of time reading boring forms and sitting in on committee meetings."

"Perhaps you should retire," Stan suggested.

Shirley shook her head. "Oh, no. I'm not ready for retirement."

"You might like it. I do. This week for example, I improved my golf game by two strokes." He paused, expectantly.

"Really?" Shirley tried to appear sufficiently admiring.

"Really. As one grows more mature, the quality of flexibility is not as present as it was during younger years, which means that one's swing is thrown off, necessitating a relocation of the wrist hinge. Also, the club rests on the fingers rather than the palm of the hand."

Shirley rested her chin in her hand, trying her best to stay with him, but her mind kept drifting away. Stan's manner of speaking reminded her of her high school geometry class, where the teacher spoke very slowly, pronouncing each word carefully, as if enunciation alone would enlighten his audience.

". . . a ninety-degree angle should exist between the shaft and the left forearm at the top of one's swing . . ."

Good grief, it *was* just like geometry, Shirley thought.

The waiter brought their dinners. Shirley ate like a starving woman, thrilled to have something interesting to do.

". . . if one increases one's wrist hinge for a full backswing . . ."

Mentally, Shirley pulled out her hair. Did the man lack the normal conversational sensors? She didn't think so. He spoke almost *confid-ingly*, as if he were sharing the secrets of his soul. What if he really was? There was a scary thought!

When the waiter arrived with dessert menus, Stan said, at last, "Oh-oh. I have been going on, haven't I? You must think I'm obsessed with golf." Before Shirley could answer, he continued, "My wife would laugh if she were here."

Briefly, Shirley had the unnerving image of his wife at the table with them.

"She used to get on me about how I go at things. I can't help it. Before my knees went, I was a fanatical jogger. I ran two hours every morning before work, six days a week, fifty-two weeks of the year. I found that jogging helped me concentrate later at work. I learned to pace myself . . ."

And we're off, Shirley thought ruefully, listening to Stan present a treatise on jogging shoes, paraphernalia, and lore.

He's not an ax murderer, Shirley reminded herself. During her life, there had been long lonely periods when that was about her only criterion. *He's solvent,* she continued mentally, *he's polite, he's educated, he's kind. He does resemble a big toe, but he can't help that. He talks.* It was hard to find a man who actually talked about what was important to him.

Finally, the evening was over. Stan paid the bill, stood in a gentlemanly way to pull back Shirley's chair, and escorted her through the restaurant and out the door.

"Let me walk you to your car."

"Thanks." It was one of the ten words she'd been allowed to get into their conversation the entire evening. For a moment she couldn't remember where she'd parked. She scanned the lot, thinking. "My brain's clogged," she joked. "I need Braino."

Stan stepped back from her quickly, as if afraid she might detonate. "Are you all right? Do you need an aspirin?"

"No, no, Stan, I was joking. Drano, Braino, get it?"

"Oh." He thought a moment, then produced a dutiful laugh. "Ha, ha, ha."

Shirley spotted her car. "Over there!"

When they arrived at her sporty little convertible, Stan surprised her by putting his hand on her shoulder. He was just her height, so he didn't have to lean down as he kissed her. It was a tidy kiss, with no teeth, lips firmly closed, moderate pressure, and no hand-straying or body-bumping. Shirley bet Stan had calibrated a schedule for his sexual encounters. First date, handshake. Second date, thirty-second kiss. Third date—did she even want to know?

Stan stepped back. "When can I see you again?"

Shirley paused. She *did* wonder how many dates it would take him before they'd go to bed. And she did wonder what he'd be like in bed. Perhaps he'd be methodical, but he also seemed dutiful, so perhaps he'd make sure she was pleased. Perhaps she could do something that would make him deviate from his schedule. That might be kind of fun.

"How about next Friday night?" she said. "Come to The Haven. I'll make you dinner."

As she drove home, she regretted her invitation. He was such a nice man, but how long was she going to live and how much time did she have to spin on a man who monopolized the conversation? Stan hadn't even asked whether she played golf. Probably, it wouldn't have mattered. Shoving her Aerosmith CD in, she let their music make her pulse pound, the first time it had done so all evening.

The Haven was dark when she got home, but a light still shone in the gatehouse where Jennifer and Alan and their baby lived. She knew they wanted to buy a house of their own, and she didn't blame them, but she would miss them when they were gone. Letting herself into the grand old stone building, she thought how incongruous it was that she'd moved from her shambling little house in Somerville to become chatelaine of this magnificent old mansion. Sometimes people rented the other condos on the second floor. Faye had for a while, and so had Star, the yoga teacher, before she moved into a house with her boyfriend. Justin, that creep, had lived with her for a year, and now as she unlocked her door, she felt, as always, a little pinch of melancholy. She'd been lonely so much of her life that loneliness almost felt like home.

The light was blinking on her answering machine. Shirley hesitated. This was her personal number, but people still used it for business purposes. It could be Elroy Morris, the building and grounds manager, about the new septic system. It could be Polly about Havenly Yours. She really had to talk to Polly, who was doing too much, without any kind of a salary, something they had to address at the next board meeting. It might be one of her Hot Flash friends. But it was probably too late to phone them back, unless it was an emergency.

Kicking off her high heels, Shirley hit the play button and collapsed on her sofa, closing her eyes as she listened.

What she heard surprised her so much, she jumped off the sofa and stood in the middle of the room, laughing out loud and hugging herself at the games life played.

6

All the members of The Hot Flash Club loved their monthly dinners at Legal Seafoods. Over the past two years, these meetings had served as psychiatric therapy, vocational inspiration, wardrobe analysis, romantic investigation, and psychic recharging. Plus they got to eat all the chocolate they wanted.

Now they hugged each other with genuine pleasure as they arrived at their table. As they slipped off spring jackets and pulled out their chairs, they admired Faye's new blue topaz earrings which so brilliantly accentuated her eyes, Alice's handsome new chunky amber necklace, framing her long neck, and Polly's pretty spring frock, which she'd actually bought instead of making herself as she usually did. Shirley, who'd just come from a conference with the building-and-grounds guy, wore a business suit they'd seen before, and Marilyn was in her normal intellectual-drone brown. Everyone still told everyone else, "You look great!"

They settled in at the round table, shaking out their napkins and giving their drink orders. Then, catching their breath, they realized with a shock that, on closer inspection, not one of them looked great. Not really.

Alice was never one to beat around the bush. "Well, ladies, I know why *I* look like a cast member from *Night of the Living Dead,* but what's going on with all of you?"

They started to object, then as one, they sighed, and drooped.

"I'll start," Marilyn decided. "I shouldn't complain, not when everything is so wonderful in my life, but . . ." She paused, too guilty to continue.

"But your mother's driving you nuts?" Shirley suggested.

Marilyn frowned. "Not exactly. It's just that I'm so overwhelmed, trying to take care of everyone and do a decent job of teaching my courses and sitting on committees. I *love* Ian—you know I do—and he made an amazing sacrifice, leaving Scotland to be with me. He really is the love of my life. And I like his son, too."

"Is Angus pretty demanding?" Faye asked.

Marilyn shook her head. "Not at all. Just the opposite. He always hides up in the attic, tapping away on his computer. He doesn't even eat unless I take up food and remind him. I worry about Angus."

"So," Alice summed up, "you're taking care of your mother, your fiancé, and his son."

"What else is new?" Polly jested.

"What else is new is that we're older," Alice pointed out. "We've got to meet thirty-year-old demands with our sixty-year-old bodies. We *should* be taking it easy."

"This reminds me of a joke," Faye said. "Why was Jesus a woman?"

They all grinned. "Why?"

"Because when there was hardly any food, he managed to feed a crowd, and even when he was dead, he had to get up because there was more work to do."

"I hear you." Alice shook her head. "Is it worse because we're doing it out of love? I mean, I *adore* my granddaughter. I don't think I've ever loved *anyone* quite so much. I treasure every moment I get to spend with her. And I'm so glad to be able to help my son and Jennifer."

"But you're tired," Shirley said.

Alice pinned her with a glare. "You're saying I *look* tired?"

Shirley often backed down when Alice challenged her. But tonight she had a reason to be forceful. She had news. "Yes, Alice, I am saying you look tired. Exhausted, frankly. I'm worried about you."

Alice gave in. "You're right. I *am* tired. No matter how much aspirin I take, my arthritis makes me ache all the time and gives me muscle spasms that make my whole body fold up like a deck chair. I don't have time to exercise and"—she held out her hand in a *stop* gesture at Shirley—"I'm eating too much and gaining weight again. But I need the fuel for energy, and I just don't have the stamina to stress my body out with a diet."

Faye leaned forward. "Have you mentioned this to Alan?"

"Alan! Of course not. I don't want him to feel guilty. He's got enough on his mind. I'm out there to help them, not worry them."

"Have you considered cutting down your hours?" Polly asked. "Like, just going out three days a week instead of five? That way you'd have two to rest and recoup."

Alice made a face. "I can't do that. They need my help."

"You won't be much help to them if you have another heart attack," Shirley observed quietly.

"I'm not going to have another heart attack!" Alice insisted. "This is *good* stress, after all."

"What does Gideon say?" Faye asked.

The waiter arrived with their drinks, and Alice got busy squeezing the lime into her vodka tonic.

"Right," Shirley said. "So he agrees with us."

"I suppose," Alice admitted grumpily. Looking around the table at her friends, she asked, "But really, what can I do?"

Wanting to perk up the group, Faye leaned forward with a sly grin on her face. "No one's asked me why *I* look tired."

Marilyn obliged. "Tell me, Faye, why do you look tired?"

"Because Aubrey and I finally got around to making love."

"High five, girl!" Alice held up her hand.

"Not so fast, Alice. I haven't told you the whole story."

"He couldn't get it up." Marilyn had dated a man with this particular problem.

Faye shook her head, looking mischievous. "Actually, he could. Without, I might add, any chemical assistance." Everyone knew about the disaster that had taken place when Marilyn's lover had tried Viagra. "No, Aubrey did really well. I mean, he was like Mt. Everest, and I was climbing right up into the rarefied heights." She lowered her voice. "To drop the metaphor, I was on top, and his hands were on my, um, chest, supporting me a little, and things were happening that haven't happened for me in years, and just at the crucial moment . . ." She hesitated.

"Don't stop now!" Polly cried.

Faye laughed. "Those were my thoughts precisely. But he *did* stop—he has bursitis in his shoulder, and I guess my weight was too much for him. He grabbed his arm like I'd shot an arrow into it, clenching his teeth with pain. I felt terrible! He took three aspirins, lay on a heating pad, and had to phone his doctor for painkillers in the morning."

"That's horrible!" Marilyn said. "Poor Aubrey."

"Poor *you*," Alice said, with feeling.

"He's at my house now," Faye continued. "He's basically planted on my sofa, taking Percocet three times a day. He's too drugged out to do more than watch television."

"And you're waiting on him hand and foot?" Shirley asked.

Faye nodded. "Well, I do feel responsible. I *am* responsible."

"We're all at the age when bits and pieces are falling apart on us," Polly mused as she stabbed her fork into her swordfish.

"It can only get worse," Marilyn chimed in. "Mother says when she goes to the Senior Citizens Club, she hears a lot of 'organ recitals.'"

Shirley looked at Polly. "I notice you're not saying a thing, but you look tired, too."

Polly took a sip of wine. "Well, I guess I am in kind of a rocky spot with Hugh."

"Rocky spot?" Alice scoffed. "You and Hugh have his ex-wife at the center of your relationship!"

"I know." Polly looked dejected. "I try to talk with him about it. I told him I don't want to turn this into an ultimatum, either he chooses her or me. I'm not that dumb! I know if he had to choose, he'd choose Carol, because of their three children and all the grandchildren. I'm not asking him to stop seeing her forever. I just want him to get her to back off a bit. I want him to remind her that they're divorced."

Shirley pointed her fork at Polly. "You still haven't told us your *real* problem."

Polly raised her eyebrows. "What do you mean?"

"You're working too hard for Havenly Yours."

Polly's jaw dropped. She didn't think anyone had noticed. "Well . . ." Wriggling in her chair, she debated with herself just how much to say.

"Polly's been at Havenly Yours almost every work day since January," Shirley reminded the others. "Without pay, I might add. The three of you are independently wealthy—"

"Not *wealthy*," Faye objected.

"—so you probably just didn't think about all Polly's doing for free. I think we should give her a break."

"Which means what, in practical terms?" Alice inquired.

"It means we should hire someone to take Polly's place." Before Alice could object, she continued, "Havenly Yours is showing a very slight profit now. It's enough to pay another person full time. Come on, The Haven's never been about profits anyway. It's meant to be *a haven,* for all of us on the board as well as our clients."

Faye put her hand on Polly's arm. "Tell us how you feel about this, Polly. I knew you were working, but I thought you liked it. It never occurred to me you'd be burnt out. Are you?"

Chagrined, Polly felt her lower lip quiver in response to so much concern. "Yes. But I don't want . . ." *to become dispensable to the group,* she thought, but could never have admitted aloud, any more than she could have jumped up and danced a tarantella on the tabletop.

"And while we're at it," Shirley raised her voice slightly, "I'm pretty tired myself. I never realized how administrative duties could weigh you down."

Alice nodded in sympathetic agreement. "Yeah, the papers accumulate one by one. It's like having a few little snowflakes drift down and while you're bending over to pick one up, an entire igloo falls on your ass."

"So should we all make a pact to take things a little easier?" Marilyn asked. She looked worried even thinking about it.

"No, Marilyn, we're going to do a lot more than that!" Shirley wriggled all over like a puppy. Waving her hands to quiet the table, she explained, "You all know Nora Salter, the great old gal I used to give massages to. Well, of course you know her, she's invested heavily in The Haven. Well! Now she's called to ask a favor."

Alice snorted. "Okay, we're all stressed out, and your antidote is to do Nora Salter a favor?"

Shirley's glow didn't dim. "Absolutely. Wait till you hear."

"We're waiting." Alice folded her arms over her chest.

"We're going to spend the summer on Nantucket. Here's the deal. Nora owns a house there. It's been in her family forever. She usually goes there in the summer, but she's got to have an operation—a hip replacement. So she can't go down there this summer, but she doesn't want to leave the house empty. She asked if we all might like to use it."

"Wow." Faye sighed. "I love Nantucket."

"I've never been there," Polly admitted.

"Nor have I, "Marilyn said. "But I'd love to spend some time there. I know the island has an indigenous population of horseshoe crabs, a descendant of the trilobites I study."

"Well, that sells me," Alice said dryly. With a suspicious eye on Shirley, she asked, "What's the catch?"

"Well, Alice, does there have to be a *catch*?" Shirley shot back defensively. Wilting slightly under Alice's steady stare, she confessed, "It's not a catch, as such. It's just that a lot of small, valuable antiques have been disappearing from Nora's house. She's got a friend who checks the place about once a week, and she says there are no unlocked doors, no broken windows, no signs of breaking in. She noticed some stuff missing in February. Nora went down last week. She was stunned at how much had disappeared. Silver candlesticks, cloisonné vases, that sort of thing."

"It's got to be the caretaker, doesn't it?" Faye observed.

Shirley shook her head. "Nora says absolutely not. Kezia Jones is absolutely trustworthy."

"Maybe her children?" Polly suggested. "They'd have access to her keys."

"Kezia's child is about one year old! Come on, ladies!" Shirley urged. "We're talking about a house on Nantucket for the summer for free! And all we have to do is *be there*. Our presence will be enough to prevent anyone from breaking in and taking anything until Nora can get down there."

Leaning her chin on her hand, Marilyn said in a dreamy voice, "The beaches are heavenly there. Golden sand stretching forever."

Shirley told them, "We could swim, bike, take long walks, and get really healthy."

"We could *shop*," Faye added with a gleam in her eye. "I've heard the stores are fabulous."

Alice brought them down to earth. "But none of us can take three months off! Three *weeks* maybe, but even that would be stretching it. We've all got too many responsibilities. We can't just leave everything."

"We don't have to, silly!" Shirley countered. "We don't all have to be there all the time!" Drawing a grid on the tablecloth with her knife, she said, "Five of us, twelve weeks, that's eighty-four days. We'll stagger our schedules so that three, or two, or even one of us is always there, while the rest are up here carrying on."

"But we all five have to be there together *some* of the time," Faye cried. "Think how much fun it will be! We'll lie in the sun, walk by the surf, sip margaritas or"—with a smile for Shirley, who was a recovering alcoholic, she added—"iced tea with mint."

"The Hot Flash Club Chills Out," Polly said. "What a concept!"

"How soon can we go down?" Marilyn asked. "Let's all go together the first time, okay?"

Alice dug in her purse for her Palm Pilot. "Let's find a couple of dates that might work for all of us."

Polly was looking worried, Shirley noticed. "The first thing we're doing tomorrow, Polly, is starting a search for someone to take on your job."

Alice glanced up. "I'll help with that. Now, the weekend is probably best for all of us, right?"

"Not necessarily," Faye said. "The middle of the week works as well for me, and I'll bet the weekends are getting pretty crowded now, with people going over to open up their houses."

"Okay, then. How soon do we want to go?"

"Tomorrow!" Faye cried playfully.

"No, we've got to organize a few things first," Marilyn said.

"The week after next?" Shirley asked hopefully. "That should give us all time to arrange things."

Everyone nodded eagerly.

"This is so exciting," Marilyn said. "I feel better already!"

"I can feel the sand under my feet." Faye sighed.

Alice was less romantic. "I can feel the sand in my bathing suit."

Shirley softly tapped her fork against her glass to get their attention again. "There's one more little thing."

"Oh, boy, here we go," Alice said. "Spit it out."

"It's nothing to worry about. It probably won't even bother us. It may not even exist!"

"What on earth are you talking about?" Marilyn asked.

Shirley hunched her shoulders up protectively and said in a very small voice, "Nora says there might be a ghost."

7

Mother, I'm putting the lists on the refrigerator, okay?"

"Yes, dear," Ruth replied. "On the refrigerator."

"Here's the phone number for the Nantucket house, and my cell phone number is here, and so are Faye's and Alice's just in case mine doesn't work for some reason."

"Darling, I'll be fine."

"Of course you will, but I just want to go over things with you again. Here is Ian's work schedule and his phone number at the university and his cell phone, in case of emergency. We stocked your cupboards yesterday, and I've made some casseroles; the instructions for heating them up are on the list, too."

"I know how to heat food, Marilyn, and you've left enough to feed the Tibetan army."

Marilyn hesitated, wondering whether Tibet even had an army. That just didn't seem *right* somehow, so was this another sign of her mother's increasing senility?

Focus, she commanded herself.

Faye was arriving at any moment to pick up Marilyn for the drive down to Hyannis, which was great for Marilyn since she had only one car, and Ian might need that, even though he, like Marilyn, often commuted to work via the subway. Marilyn had been up since five-thirty, responding to e-mail related to her MIT classes, students, and committees, making lists to leave for her mother and Ian, and, finally, packing for this little weekend jaunt, which turned out to be more complicated than she'd anticipated. Last year, when she'd flown fairly often to Scotland to visit Ian, she'd had her travel kit ready to go at a moment's notice, but of course now that Ian was living with her, she hadn't used the kit. For a while, she couldn't even *find* it, because when she and Ian moved in to this narrow, three-story rental, she'd happily and quickly thrown things into boxes and black plastic bags. Last night, it had taken her one long, muttering, hair-pulling hour to paw through the various boxes and bags at the back of the various closets, an hour she'd planned to use for other things, such as making lists for Ruth.

The beep of a car horn interrupted her thoughts.

"That's Faye!" Marilyn bent over to kiss her mother. "Now remember, Ian's son Angus is living here for a while, so if you hear anyone walking around upstairs, don't be alarmed."

"Darling." Reaching up, Ruth put both bony hands on Marilyn's shoulders, pulling her close enough to give her an Eskimo nose rub. "I'm going to be just fine. I'm snug as a bug in a mug down here."

"Good." Faye had picked up Shirley and Polly first; Marilyn's home in Cambridge was the closest to Route 3, the highway down to the Cape. She didn't want to keep all three women waiting.

Ruth continued, "If I get lonely, I'll invite Ernest over. But I've had a busy week, and I'm looking forward to a nice quiet weekend with my knitting, my television, and my crossword puzzles. So don't you worry about me for a minute! Just have a wonderful time."

"Thanks, Mom." Marilyn appreciated her mother's words, but the little speech took so long, and her mother's hands made her feel so trapped—she felt like an adolescent again, desperate to get away.

Three more toots sounded. Marilyn could tell her mother couldn't hear them. Faye had planned extra time into their schedule for the drive to Hyannis, in case the traffic was heavy; still they had to be there on time or they'd miss the ferry.

"Faye's here! She's honking her horn! Gotta go!" She wrenched herself away.

Just as Marilyn got to the door to the stairs, Ruth called, "Marilyn?"

"Yes, Mother?" She forced brightness into her voice.

"Remember, if you don't fricassee, fry, fry a hen."

"Ha, ha, ha!" Was that a touch of hysteria in her dutiful laugh? "See you tomorrow night, Mother!"

Marilyn raced up the stairs, grabbed her backpack and duffel bag, returned to the kitchen to double-check that all the burners were off on the stove, confirmed that her house keys were in the middle of the kitchen table with a note written in BIG letters telling Angus to use them if he needed to, ran down the hall and out the front door.

Faye's hunter green Mercedes idled gently in the driveway. Faye, Polly, and Shirley waved merrily from the windows. Marilyn waved back, tested the doorknob to be sure it was firmly closed, crossed the porch, skipped down the steps, tripped on the last step, and went sprawling on the front lawn.

"Marilyn!" Unbuckling their seat belts, all three threw open the car doors and jumped out.

Marilyn lay on her side. She'd caught herself with her hands and taken the brunt of the fall on her right hip. For a moment she couldn't get her breath.

Faye knelt next to Marilyn. "Are you all right?"

"Fine," Marilyn gasped. "Must . . . catch . . . breath."

"Take your time," Shirley urged. "We're in no hurry."

That, Marilyn knew, wasn't precisely true. Gingerly, she sat up.

"How do you feel?" Polly asked.

"Like an idiot."

Faye grinned. "She meant, did you break anything?"

Marilyn stretched, taking a mental inventory of her body. "Nope. Only my pride is hurt." But when she pressed her hands on the ground to push herself up, she realized she'd abraded them during the fall.

Faye helped Marilyn up. Shirley took Marilyn's hands in hers and inspected her palms. "Oh, dear."

"Just little scrapes," Marilyn said.

Polly peered over Shirley's shoulder. "Still, you'd better wash them and put some ointment on."

Marilyn turned to go back into the house. "I can't get inside. I left my keys for Angus."

Polly said in a sensible tone, "Well, knock on the door, he'll let you in."

Marilyn shook her head. "Uh-uh. Angus is up in the attic. Besides, he wouldn't hear me if I yelled his name through a loudspeaker. He lives in his own little world."

"Well, isn't Ruth home? Let's go around back to her French doors—" Shirley set off walking.

"Shirley, stop!" Marilyn's voice took on a slightly desperate tone. "Trust me, if we go into Ruth's place, she'll take forever just to get to the door, and then she'll want to cluck over my hands, and she'll have to ask you all how you are, and we'll miss the ferry—we'll miss *all* the ferries." To her surprise, she was on the verge of tears.

"Right." Faye picked up Marilyn's duffel bag and tossed it in the trunk of her Mercedes. "Let's go!"

They all settled into the car, sinking into the luxurious leather seats. As they pulled away from her house, Marilyn felt as if she were on a spaceship, leaving a planet with exceptional gravitational pull. They went through Cambridge, along Memorial Drive, and were through the Big Dig area in Boston before the tug of responsibility finally thinned.

"We didn't pick up Alice," Marilyn noticed suddenly.

"She's flying down to Nantucket," Faye told her. "She's not thrilled about this whole thing, doesn't want to take the boat, thinks it's a waste of time."

"I'm looking forward to it!" Shirley said enthusiastically. "I've never been on a ferry before."

"Neither have I," Polly said. "And isn't it a gorgeous day for a trip!"

They all looked out the window. Along the highway, the tender tips of newly budding trees waved beneath the blue sky like flags of a brand new country.

8

Hyannis was a crowded port. Getting to the ferry and then on the ferry seemed, for a while, a lot like their normal lives—full of schedules, rules, and organization. They found a parking place in one of the lots near the Steamship Authority's terminal, and clustered around to observe Faye putting the receipt in the zipper pocket of her purse, so *one* of them would remember where it was when the time came to reclaim the Mercedes. They lugged and pulled their weekend luggage along the busy street and through the lines of cars to the office, where they bought their tickets.

By the time they joined the line of fellow voyagers standing by the boat slip, the handsome white ferry was making its stately approach. It docked, releasing passengers, cars, and trucks. They handed their tickets to the attendant, tramped up the ramp onto the first deck, and up a set of metal stairs to the main deck with its scores of blue vinyl benches and white tables, all securely fastened down.

"Let's grab a booth," Faye suggested. "We can go out if we want sunshine, but it might be too cool to spend the entire trip outside."

Taking Faye's advice, they claimed a booth, dropped their bags, and climbed another flight of stairs to the top deck with its double smokestacks and rows of seats, where people were already settling, opening picnic baskets, or leaning back to soak in the sun. A male voice came over a public address system, welcoming them to the boat, advising them there was no smoking, and providing information about where to find life jackets, which freaked them all out for a moment, until they noticed that no one else was paying any attention. The boat sounded its horn three times, and with a deep satisfied rumble, pulled away from shore.

The four women stood together at the stern, watching the buildings, streets, trees, and rooftops of the mainland retreat.

"That's the Kennedy compound," Faye told them, pointing toward the shore, her other hand pulling her hair from her face as the wind blew it.

The houses grew smaller and farther away. Gulls swooped through the clear air. Duck couples idled placidly in the gentle swells. The ferry chugged steadily toward the horizon, until it was surrounded by Nantucket Sound, the wind furrowing the blue waters into fields of white-tipped waves. Sunlight struck sparks on the water, as if someone beneath the surface were tossing handfuls of diamonds up into the air.

One by one, the four women separated, silently going off alone to lean on the white rails, gazing out at the dancing azure waters. One by one, they felt the duties of the real world slip away, evaporating into the fresh air. The horizon was empty—almost. Far in the distance, sails cut white triangles in the blue, but for a while they saw no land, no houses, no human edifices, only the eternal expanse of sky and water, impervious to their power and their desires. They didn't notice how their breathing deepened, how their shoulders relaxed, how their blood slowed. The blue waters were hypnotic, allowing a white ship of calm to sail through their minds.

A dog barked. A baby cried. A pack of teenage girls giggled past. The spell was broken. Faye, realizing she was slightly chilled from the breeze, hurried back down to the main deck and bought herself a cup of coffee.

Polly, Shirley, and Marilyn joined her at the booth, which, with their purses, duffels, sweaters, and scarves had become a temporary nest. The boat was in deeper waters now, and waves smashed against the ship.

Marilyn put her hand to her belly. "I think I'm getting a little motion sick."

"Eat something," Faye advised.

"What a good idea!" Polly bent over her duffel bag and brought out a plastic plate covered with foil. She opened it to reveal dark-chocolate fudge brownies, caramel-chip cookies, and almond macaroons. "Made them myself, just for the trip," she told them, with a smile.

"Brilliant, Polly!" Faye exclaimed. "We don't dock until 11:30, we won't get to the house till after noon, by the time we get back into town for lunch, it will most likely be one or after. This will tide us over nicely."

Munching away happily, they gazed out the window as another ferry, a cheerful white, red, and blue, passed them going in the opposite direction. Passengers waved from the upper decks.

"This is the way to travel," Polly sighed contently. "We sit and eat while the scenery moves."

"I can't wait to see the house," Shirley said.

Marilyn asked, "Have you found anyone to take Polly's place at Havenly Yours for the summer?"

Polly nodded, her mouth full of chocolate.

Shirley answered for her. "We think Rosa, one of the seamstresses, can do the job. She's smart enough, works well with the other women, and seems comfortable with authority."

"I've left her in charge before," Polly continued. "Some days I couldn't make it in for one reason or another, and Rosa has always kept things running smoothly. Shirley and I have spoken with her, and told her she's getting a raise and will get another one after the summer, if all goes well."

"Plus, there's always the cell phone," Shirley added. "Faye, how does Aubrey feel about you spending time on Nantucket this summer?"

Faye grimaced. "To be honest, he's become a bit of an old crab. His shoulder isn't healing as quickly as he'd like, and now that he's moved back to his own apartment, I'm not there to fetch and carry for him at the drop of a hat." She stopped, looking startled. "Gosh, that sounded bitchy!"

"You're allowed," Shirley assured her.

Faye made a face. "Well, I feel guilty, but by the way, I'm not the only reason his bursitis is acting up. He admitted that earlier that day he'd gone golfing with a friend and it bothered him then. I was just the straw—let me rephrase that. I was just the elephant that broke the camel's back."

"You're not an elephant!" Polly argued.

"Thanks, Polly." Faye squeezed her friend's hand. "It's funny, isn't it, how quickly we fall back into the role of Florence Nightingale/Mama. I loved being a nurturer when my daughter was young, but *I* was younger then. I had more energy, more stamina. I'm not sure I want to spend the rest of my life nurturing Aubrey. Does that sound wicked of me?"

"Not at all," Marilyn assured her.

Faye folded her paper napkin into intricate patterns. "Aubrey has begun to talk about marriage."

"Oh, Faye!" Shirley, ever romantic, sighed at the fairy tale word.

Faye smiled ruefully. "I'm not sure I want to marry him. I'm not even sure I want to *live* with him. I like my new little house. Now that I've gotten used to it, I like my independence. If I married Aubrey, we'd have to buy a new house and compromise on everything. Aubrey's apartment is overwhelming, in a gentleman's smoking room sort of way, all dark wood and Remington statues of cowboys."

"Goodness, Ian and I haven't even considered *décor*." Marilyn looked alarmed.

"That's because it doesn't matter to you," Faye told her. "Which is fine for both of you. And it's only one part of the equation of marriage. For example, as much as I love Aubrey's company, there are nights when all I really want to do is settle down on the sofa with a thick novel and a bowl of popcorn." Looking at healthy Shirley, she added, "Finished off with a crisp apple."

Shirley weighed in, her face earnest. "But wouldn't it be nice to have someone who loved you to rub your feet? Who brought you chicken noodle soup and ginger ale when you were sick? Who cheered you up at the end of a long day?"

"Is that what you want, Shirley?" Faye asked. "You could have that, if you married Stan."

Shirley's face fell. She stuck her lower lip out in a little pout. "That's mean, Faye."

"Why? I don't mean to be mean!"

Shirley heaved an enormous sigh. "It's not like Stan and I are anywhere close to talking marriage. I'm not even sure that we're seeing each other exclusively."

"Have you slept together yet?" Marilyn asked.

Shirley leaned her elbows on the table and hid her face in her hands.

"That bad, huh?" Polly's voice was gentle.

"Not *bad*," Shirley amended. "Just not *wonderful*. It's kind of like he's operating on a timetable. One compliment, two kisses, three touches, in, out, and we're done!"

"But he could still bring you chicken noodle soup," Faye said. "Or rub your feet. He would be company. You wouldn't feel alone."

Shirley lifted her head and with her fingertips, pulled down the skin beneath her eyes and stuck out her tongue. Everyone laughed.

"Where's the *romance*?" Shirley demanded. "That's what I want to know!"

"Maybe we're too old for *romance*," Polly suggested.

"Oh, easy for you to say, when you've got wonderful Hugh in your life," Shirley huffed, leaning back in the booth and folding her arms over her chest.

"It's not all romantic, believe me," Polly retorted. "Sometimes it is, yes, that's true. Hugh's a wonderful lover. And he's so imaginative and playful. When we go off on trips together, we have a spectacular time! But daily life is—*challenging*. For example, once again, this year we didn't spend Valentine's Day together, because his daughter had one of her intimate family dinners. His children and grandchildren always come first for him, and since they always include his ex-wife, they never invite me. That leaves me alone a lot, and that makes me fret and fume and stomp around feeling rejected."

"And anger gets in the way of romance," Faye said quietly.

"You bet it does!" Polly agreed.

"We know too much," Marilyn said musingly. "We've lived long enough to lose patience with Cinderella stories. I think *romance* belongs to the young and foolish."

"Well, hey, I'm *old* and foolish!" Shirley joked, a hopeful note in her voice.

"Look!" Faye interrupted the conversation, leaning toward the window, pointing. "Land!"

"Ahoy, matey," Polly cried. "Let's go up on deck!"

"Here." Shirley took out a tube of sunscreen and passed it around.

"Shirley, it's only May," Marilyn said.

"Yes, and the sun is strong, and even stronger when you're near water."

So as the four leaned on the railing, watching the island come closer, the scent of citrus and coconut drifted around them, waking up little brain cells that had been snoozing for years. There were no palm trees on Nantucket, but there were long expanses of sand, and dozens of boats bobbing in the harbor, and a stubby little lighthouse nestled on a point. Gliding past it, the ferry entered the harbor, its engines churning slowly, and they saw the town rise before them in shades of gray and lilac and white. Gold gleamed from a church steeple and spring buds filigreed the scene in pale green.

"It's beautiful!" Polly breathed. "It's like another world!" Grabbing Shirley, she hugged her. "Thank you!"

As they watched, the ferry rumbled into its slip. Chains clanked as the ramps were dropped and fastened, and the boat dipped and rose as cars and trucks roared to life and filed out onto land.

"Time to go!" Faye said.

They grabbed their bags, clattered down the metal stairs, and joined the line of passengers disembarking.

And then, there they were, on Nantucket.

9

They scouted the area for Kezia Jones, Nora Salter's caretaker, who had said she'd meet them at the boat.

"Maybe she's over by the luggage racks," Faye suggested.

They followed the crowds across the parking lot to the blue baggage wagons parked near the pay telephones and taxis. Various individuals approached, then passed on to greet someone else. After ten minutes, most of the crowd had dissipated, everyone else off in a car or cab to enjoy the beautiful day. The four friends stood on the dock, backpacks and duffel bags in hand, looking around.

"She said she'd be here," Shirley murmured hopefully.

"Do you have her cell phone number?" Polly asked.

Shirley was digging through her purse when they heard a squeal, and around the corner zoomed a huge silver SUV. It braked to a halt next to them.

Out jumped a slender young woman. Her black hair swung in a high ponytail, her eyes were a dazzling dark blue, her nose and cheeks were sunburned, and her smile was infectious. She wore old leather work boots, shorts, a long-sleeved T-shirt, and a long-billed scalloper's cap.

"Hi, guys! Are you Nora's friends? I'm Kezia! Sorry I'm late! Everything seems to take just a bit longer now that Joe's in my life." She nodded over her shoulder.

The women peered in the SUV's window. Happily ensconced in a car seat was the world's cutest baby, gnawing on a blue vinyl teething ring. Seeing the women's faces, he shrieked with glee and offered it to them.

While the women cooed at Joe, Kezia opened the back of her gigantic vehicle and began putting in the luggage. Her long legs were tanned

and supple, and she swung the bags up as if they weighed no more than
a flea.

"Can you all squash in?" she inquired. "Sorry, but Joe's seat takes
up a lot of room."

"We can manage," Faye affirmed. "Polly, you sit up front. Shirley or
Marilyn can sit on my lap. It's just a short ride, right, Kezia?"

"Right!" She slammed the hatch shut and jumped into the driver's
seat. While the older women got themselves in and adjusted, she turned
to the backseat to flirt with her little son. "Who's Mr. Cutie Pie?" Her
baby chuckled, blew bubbles, and waved. "Ready? All hands on deck?"
With a flip of her ponytail, Kezia faced front and put the car in gear.

In a matter of seconds, they were bouncing over the uneven cobblestones on South Water and Main Streets.

"Did you have a good trip?" Kezia called over her shoulder. They
scarcely had time to respond when she said, "I'll bet you did. It's such a
great day. You'll probably find it a little cooler here than in Boston.
We're always cooler here in the spring, but warmer in the fall. You
guys'll want to get outside today, it's just so gorgeous. Sometimes we get
lots of wind and rain in the spring. We'll probably still get some crazy
weather in June, but today is heaven. B.J.—that's my husband, Big Joe—
B.J. works construction and his crew's getting a pantload of stuff done
with weather like this. He's actually ahead of time!"

As Kezia chattered away, the older women stared out the windows
at Main Street, with its charming brick storefronts. The windows displayed gorgeous clothing and needlepoint and furniture. The window
boxes shimmered with daffodils, lilacs, and tulips. Then the SUV turned
up Orange Street and with breathtaking insouciance, Kezia steered her
huge vehicle into the narrowest driveway in the universe.

They clambered out of the car and found themselves in front of a
tall, gray-shingled house, with white trim and a neat blue front door that
had a brass knocker shaped like a mermaid.

"Good grief!" Shirley looked up and down the narrow street.
"These houses all look alike!"

"Many of them do," Kezia agreed, opening the hatch and hauling
out the luggage as she talked. "We're in the Historic District, so most of
these houses were built over a hundred and fifty years ago, when the

Quaker Society of Friends was centered here. To them, simplicity and plainness were virtues. But don't worry, you'll find plenty of ostentatious homes." Tossing all the luggage over her shoulders, she strode up the sidewalk, up the wooden steps to the small front porch, and jangled a set of keys.

"Here you are, guys!" With a flourish, she gestured to the open door.

They hurried up the steps and through the door.

"I won't come in with you," Kezia said. "Too much bother getting His Highness out of his throne and all that. But here's a set of keys to Nora's house." She handed them to Shirley. "Now if you want to make copies, go ahead, but remember, we're already having some theft in this house and you don't want to go making keys and losing them all over the island for everyone else to find."

"We'll be careful," Shirley promised.

Kezia smiled. She had a gorgeous smile, as wholehearted and carefree as her son's. "Okay. If you need anything, my phone number's on the notepad by the phone. If you have any problems with the house, call me. 'Bye, guys!" With that, she sprinted down the front steps and back into her SUV. She leaned over the seat to give her baby a big kiss, then put the car in gear and roared away.

"What a little powerhouse!" Faye said.

"What I wouldn't give for a fraction of that energy," Polly murmured.

"Hey, *guys!*" Shirley bounced up and down, pretending she was Kezia. "Want to see the house?"

Like kids released from school, they raced off in all directions. Inside, the house was larger than it looked from the street. All the rooms—front parlor, back parlor, dining room, den—were floored with gleaming wide boards. All but the kitchen had fireplaces.

Upstairs were five bedrooms, each with a fireplace, and two bathrooms, one with a claw-foot bathtub and wooden floor, and a newer one, built out on an ell, with ceramic tile and a shower. Stairs at the back of the house led to the second floor and on to the attic, where another bathroom and several more bedrooms were squeezed beneath the eaves. Another set of stairs led down to a dark, uninviting basement. The walls were brick, and from the ceiling beams, bare lightbulbs hung down like the tubers of tulips and daffodils, giving the basement a very under-ground ambience.

"I'm glad the washer and dryer are in the old butler's pantry," Polly said as they scurried back up the stairs.

Throughout the house, the furnishings were mostly antiques of the more sturdy and usable sort, American pine in the kitchen, Empire sofas in the parlors. Many of the chairs had frayed caning or worn needle-point seats, the Persian rugs were thin in spots, and the swooping drapes were faded. But the sofas were deep and comfortable, the beds were firm, and the cupboards were filled with beautiful old embroidered sheets as smooth as silk to the touch.

"Five bedrooms," Faye called out. "Let's each choose one!"

"Shirley," Polly said, "you get first pick, because you're the reason we're here."

Shirley hesitated, then staked her claim. "I really do want this one at the back of the house, because of the ocean view, but when I'm not here, anyone else can use it."

"Who wants the other ocean-view bedroom?" Faye asked.

Polly said, "I don't care about an ocean view. I'd love the little side bedroom with the two white iron beds and the patchwork quilts. There's a cradle in there, too, filled with antique dolls."

Marilyn and Faye inspected the three remaining bedrooms.

"I'll take one of the two at the front of the house," Marilyn decided.

"But don't you want the ocean view?" Faye asked.

Marilyn blushed. "I'd rather have the room with the queen-size bed."

"Aha," Shirley said, "for when Ian visits!"

"Then I'll take the ocean view." Faye stepped into her room and sank for a moment onto the window seat. "Heaven."

"But what about Alice?" worried Shirley. "That only leaves the smallest bedroom at the front of the house for her."

Faye thought about it. "I doubt that Alice will fuss. She doesn't seem very keen on this little enterprise. She probably won't spend as much time here as the rest of us."

As if speaking of Alice had conjured her up, they heard a car door slam, and a few moments later, Alice was knocking on the front door.

All four women clattered down the front staircase to the entrance hall.

"Alice!"

Alice stepped inside, pulling her rolling suitcase with her. Always beautifully, even glamorously, put together, today majestic Alice was disheveled.

"Oh my God!" She returned their hugs only halfheartedly. "Have you ever flown on one of those little toy planes they use to get to this island? Seats about ten? Honestly, I've worn coats bigger than the plane I just flew in!"

"You should have taken the boat with us," Shirley told her.

"I'll certainly take the boat back." Alice dropped her purse on her suitcase and looked around. "So this is it?"

"This is it." Faye held her arms wide. "We just got here ourselves. We've been choosing bedrooms."

Alice strode through the house, scrutinizing it. "Quaint."

"This is your bedroom." Shirley lead Alice into the bedroom at the front of the house. It was very simple, with a spool bed, a wooden rocker, a wooden chest, and a large pine armoire.

"Where's the closet?" Alice asked.

"They didn't have closets when this house was built." Polly had done some reading before she came. "Over the years, closets have been built into some rooms, but this bedroom has this." She opened the armoire to show the wooden rod with pretty padded hangers.

Marilyn opened a window, letting the brisk spring wind whisk into the room. "You'll hear the street noises from this room. Will that bother you?"

Alice shook her head. "Too much *quiet* would bother me. Traffic noises will make me feel right at home." Aware that her friends were rather breathlessly awaiting her reaction, she told them, "This all looks great. And I want to see the town. But first, I want to eat. I'm starving!"

It took about two minutes to walk to Main Street. They passed the bookstore, an antique shop, a couple of clothing stores, and a jeweler that made them pause for a moment of window-shopping. The first restaurant they came to was called Even Keel. They peered inside, studied the posted menu, approved, and went in. Its bustling coffee bar, Internet section, and long chrome counter gave it a chic urban feel. Colorful canvases by local artists brightened the walls. They settled in around a table, and as they ate lunch, they studied the various guides and newspapers they'd picked up, reading the interesting bits aloud.

"There's so much to do here!" Polly chirped. "Plays, museums, lectures at the library."

"Openings at art galleries," Faye murmured, circling dates with a pen. "Lots and lots of art galleries."

"We'll make a list," Marilyn suggested.

"Oh, yum," Shirley cooed. "We're going to have such fun!"

Alice was frowning. "I wonder how Aly likes her other grandmother."

Polly reassured her. "I'm sure she adores her!"

"But not *too* much," Shirley quickly amended, knowing how easily Alice would get jealous.

After lunch, the group decided to go their separate ways. Faye hurried off to check out the art galleries. Polly and Marilyn decided to tour the Whaling Museum together.

Shirley and Alice stood on Main Street, blinking slightly beneath the sun.

"I'm going down to the harbor," Shirley said. "I love looking at the boats, and according to the map, there's a small beach within walking distance. I might get my feet wet."

"The water's going to be cold," Alice warned. She yawned. "You know what I'd really like to do? I'd like to take a nap."

"Then you should do just that." Shirley reached into her purse. "Here's the key Nora gave me to the house. I'll have copies made for each of us."

"Thanks. Oh, man, I can't wait to take off my shoes!"

Shirley studied her guide book. Nothing was more than a few blocks away from the water, so she meandered through town on the way to the harbor. Nantucket center was as neat as a village in a model train set, just a few streets in a tic-tac-toe lattice of cobblestone and brick. Shirley took note of the location of the brick post office, and the magnificent Greek Revival library. She strolled back to Lower Main Street, and down to the Hy-Line docks.

Straight Wharf was bustling with passengers arriving and departing, some with babies in Snuglis, others with dogs on leashes, some with babies *and* dogs, and one woman with a dog in a Snugli. Daffodils, tulips, and hyacinths were everywhere—in pots, in window boxes, on sweaters. The people disembarking from the ferry and those waving hello all looked so healthy, so hearty, so *athletic,* in their khakis and L.L. Bean plaids, their canvas shoes and sneakers, their heads protected by base-ball caps. They looked ready to paddle their own kayaks. Shirley felt a bit out of place in her lavender batik sundress and multicolored shawl, and her stacked high-heeled pastel sandals were definitely unsuitable! She'd been letting her red hair grow out from the tidy businesslike page-boy she'd adopted when she was first starting The Haven. She'd worn her hair long all her life, and now that the wellness spa was prospering, she felt she could relax a bit, even show a bit more of her true inner self.

Perhaps she also secretly thought—and even more secretly, *hoped*—the sign of a slightly wilder Shirley might scare her boring beau Stan away. With her Hot Flash friends breathing down her neck, reminding her constantly how pleased they were that she was finally dating some-one *appropriate,* she didn't dare break off with him. They'd kill her if she did. Alice would kill her twice. So she was resorting to subterfuge. Plus, it felt really nice, the bounce of her long curls against her neck, the flirty swish of it when she turned her head quickly. But here on the wharf, it seemed all the other women wore their hair restrained by a clip, or cut in short, sensible styles that wouldn't blow in their eyes while they were reeling in a bluefish or take too long to dry after a hard day on the tennis court.

Charming little shops with wooden toys and seashell chimes beck-oned enticingly along the brick wharf, but Shirley wanted to find the beach. Spotting an empty bench, she sat for a moment, feeling a bit self-conscious as she studied a map, sure she'd get it wrong. She hadn't had much opportunity to travel in her life. She wasn't even sure how to read a map.

It's all right! she told herself. *Take your time!* It was good for the aging brain to learn new things, she reminded herself, and squaring her shoulders, she chose a direction and set off. If she kept the water on her left, she couldn't go too wrong. The cobblestone road and brick side-walks were so uneven beneath her dainty pastel high-heeled sandals that she tottered and tripped, feeling self-conscious and idiotic.

She hurried to the quiet passageway along New Whale Lane. On her right, fuel tanks loomed behind a chain-link fence, casting the small cobblestone avenue in shadow and providing a contemporary note to the rest of the area, which was probably much as it had been for over a century. At Old South Wharf, a row of fishermen's shacks converted into posh boutiques extended far into the harbor. She passed boats of all sizes bobbing gently in their slips along Swain's Wharf and then, between two small gray cottages, she spotted a bit of golden beach. A few sailboats idled in the shallow waters and a pair of mallards bobbed dreamily beneath the spring sun.

Wobbling along, she made her way past the cottages and onto the sand, which was damper than she'd expected. With a squelching noise, her sandals sank. Shirley extracted her feet, walked to higher and dryer ground, plunked down on the sand and removed her shoes.

When she stood up, the wet sand felt chilly to her exposed soles. She took a few exploratory steps. Well! Walking was easier barefoot. She could expand her stride, she could move with more freedom. Holding her sandals by one finger, she ambled over the beach, testing the feel of the seaweed lying over the sand in clumps—it was slightly rough and tickly, but it provided more give than the sand.

By the time she reached the town pier, she was feeling just a bit like an athlete, or some kind of person at ease with the outdoors. She'd always lived in Massachusetts, but she'd never had the time or money to play by the seaside. She didn't even know how to swim. She knew enough to tell that the boats tied up at the town pier were mostly motorboats rather than sailboats. She hesitated, wondering whether it would be all right for her to walk the length of the pier. Did you have to own a boat tied up here to step on it? She didn't see a No Trespassing sign. She set off. In contrast to the sand, the boards were warm on her feet, and made satisfying thumping sounds as she went. At the end of the pier loomed an eighty-foot-long fishing trawler, magnificently serious among the wastrel pleasure boats, like a Saint Bernard deigning to share space with Jack Russell puppies. Shirley studied it for a while, admiring its sturdy, battered steel hull, its cables, thicker than her wrists, its chains and ropes and masts, all so complicated, so silently self-confident and powerful. *Masculine,* she thought to herself with a smile.

According to the map, the harbor ended a few hundred yards away in a series of salt marshes. She strolled in that direction, idly gazing at the tide lapping the shore in light, lacy foam. High up on the sand lay clusters of overturned rowboats. Gulls squawked and dipped, occasionally landing on the roof of one of the little seaside cottages.

A golden Lab suddenly appeared out of the tall beach grass, galloping toward her with a big grin on its face. Shirley bent to pet the dog, but she didn't want to be petted—she wanted Shirley to throw her stick into the water. Shirley obliged. With great gusto, the Lab plunged into the harbor, swimming out to grab the stick in her mouth and return it proudly to Shirley. She threw it again, and again, smiling at the dog's pleasure. After about seven hundred repeats of the game, she tired, and turned to walk back to town. The Lab bounded through the grass up to the spot where her owner was painting an overturned rowboat a wonderful bright cherry red. He waved at Shirley, who waved back. That much contact—that islander's wave—made her believe she could actually fit in here, even in her inappropriate lavender batik.

This gave her the courage, at last, to dabble her toes in the water. Alice was right. It *was* cold. But it would warm up. Shirley vowed to herself that this summer she would swim in the ocean.

That evening, Nora Salter's house was full of light, movement, and pastel flurries of perfume as the five women got ready for dinner out.

"This is like college!" Wrapped in a towel, Faye left the steamy bathroom and passed Marilyn in the hall, headed for her own shower.

I wouldn't know, Shirley thought, *I didn't get to go to college.* All the other women were better educated. Plus, they all had children. She was the outsider. Still, she reminded herself, they had come here because of *her,* because she, uneducated, childless, thrice-divorced Shirley, had been asked to use the house by Nora Salter, who probably had enough money to *buy* a college. The thought cheered her. Why was she so easily dispirited these days? She didn't used to be so whiney.

"Ready?" Alice called. "I'm starving!"

They gathered up their purses and wraps. Shirley locked the door behind them as they stepped out into the bright spring evening. The day's breeze had grown stronger, making their skirts and scarves flip like kites. They all lurched occasionally as their high heels caught on the uneven paving of the brick sidewalks and the cobblestone streets. Startled, they laughed at their unexpected clumsiness.

"Stop!" Faye giggled. She whispered, "I'm not wearing a pad!"

"Pad!" Alice snorted. "I need a catheter with a hose connected to a bag on my ankle."

This made them all laugh even harder. By the time they arrived at The Boarding House, they were staggering with their knees locked together, bent nearly double.

"Dignity, ladies," Shirley exhorted.

They choked back their laughter as they were shown to their table. The beautiful room's elegance calmed them, and by the time they'd ordered martinis and wine and sparking water for Shirley, they were back in sophisticated mode.

"It's cooler here than I thought it would be," Polly observed.

Alice lifted one eloquent eyebrow. "Oh, and that's why you bought that cashmere shawl?"

Polly laughed. "Isn't it gorgeous? Touch."

Everyone leaned forward to stroke the shawl.

"It feels like spun whipped cream!" Faye sighed.

"Trust you to use a food analogy." Alice laughed. "The quality of the shops here *is* amazing."

"So you're glad you came?" Shirley inquired anxiously.

"Yes, and I'm coming next weekend, if that works," Alice said. "I want to attend The Nantucket Film Festival."

"Oh, yum." Faye licked her lips. "Do tell."

Alice's silver and turquoise bracelets clattered as she waved her hands. "They're showing first runs of new movies, and some directors and actors will be here. Steve Martin, for one."

"I'll come, too," Faye said. "Is it expensive?"

Alice dug in her purse. "I have a brochure here somewhere. Oh, and that weekend there's a performance by that wonderful Asian cellist, the beautiful young woman, oh, what's her name . . ."

Before she could remember, the waiter arrived with their starters. Faye had the mussels in white wine, Alice the grilled scallops in wine sauce, Marilyn, a crepe filled with lobster and cream, vegetarian Shirley a salad of field greens, and Polly the smoked salmon.

Alice took a bite. "Divine!"

"*Too* good," Polly agreed with a sigh. "How can I eat food like this and still fit into a bathing suit?"

Faye grinned. "A man asks his wife what she wants for her birthday. She's our age. She wants to be a little wild, a little daring. She envisions herself in a sporty little convertible, so she hints, 'Give me something that goes from 0 to 200 in 6 seconds!' So, on her birthday, her husband gives her a bathroom scale."

"Oh, no," everyone groaned.

"Look." Alice put on her executive face. "We're supposed to be relaxing here, right? We're supposed to be de-stressing. We've got to have a rule. No dieting on Nantucket!"

Faye lifted her wineglass. "I'll drink to that." She looked over at Marilyn. "Hey, you're pretty quiet this evening. Did you enjoy your day?"

"Loved it!" Marilyn answered.

"Anything here to pique your interest?" Alice asked.

Marilyn said, "Well—"

"Look!" Shirley interrupted. "There's Kezia!" She twiddled her fingers in greeting at the young woman entering the restaurant with three other people.

All the members of the Hot Flash Club stopped to stare. Kezia wore a scarlet tank top ending above her belly button, and an azure silk skirt riding low on her hips, accentuated by a baroque jeweled belt. A slice of her sleek belly showed like tanned satin as she walked. Her thick black hair was free from its ponytail and fell around her shoulders like a gleaming shawl. A necklace of glittering stones lay across her chest. She threw the group a gorgeous smile and waved.

"She looks like a medieval princess." Shirley sighed.

"Is that her husband?" Polly gaped at the tall blond man who pulled out Kezia's chair. "Gosh, he's handsome. They're all so beautiful! So perfect! They look like gods!"

"They're *young*," Marilyn reminded her. "They haven't been marked by time."

Alice raised a critical eyebrow. Quietly, she muttered, "*I* want to know how they can afford to eat in a restaurant like this. They're island people, aren't they? Not dot-com zillionaires."

"Oh, silly." Shirley laughed. "Her husband's in construction. He probably makes eighty dollars an hour."

"Then why is she caretaking?" Alice demanded.

"Why not?" Shirley countered. She turned to Marilyn. "Sorry, Mare, I interrupted you. How do you like Nantucket?"

Marilyn beamed. "It's a scientist's paradise! There are wildflower tours and marine ecology seminars, birding field trips, not to mention the Maria Mitchell Museum."

"Who's she?" Polly asked.

"Maria Mitchell discovered a new comet in 1847. She was Vassar's first professor of astronomy. The science museum here is named after her."

"Still," Faye pressed, "you seem preoccupied."

Marilyn sighed. "Just worried about everyone back home."

"Well, phone them," Alice said sensibly.

"I did, before we came out. It took Mother forever to find her cell phone—she'd lost it in her knitting basket. Ian said he's going to share a pizza with Angus tonight. I just don't want Ian to feel I'm deserting him because his son came to live with us, and I certainly don't want my mother to think I'm running away from her."

"I have an idea," Shirley said. "Why don't you bring Ian and Angus and your mother down here for a visit this summer. I don't mean all together. At different times."

Marilyn nodded. "That will help."

But Faye shook her head. "Marilyn. Look at your hands."

Dutifully, Marilyn held out her hands. Jewelry didn't interest her, so she wore only the pretty diamond solitaire engagement ring Ian had given her.

"Turn them over," Faye ordered.

Marilyn obeyed. The scrapes on her palms from her morning's fall were an angry red.

Faye gently cupped Marilyn's hands in hers. "Only this morning, you fell on your face because you were hurrying. I've been doing the same sort of thing. We're all so busy with our lives at home. I think Nantucket should be just for us, a get-away-from-it-all vacation spot. At least for a while."

"I agree!" Alice looked around the table. "*Plus,* if we've made it a rule that there's no dieting on Nantucket, let's make another rule: no worrying on Nantucket. We're here for pleasure, ladies. We're damned lucky that Nora Salter's letting us have her house for three whole months—do you have any idea what kind of rent someone could get for that here? We couldn't afford it. This is an unbelievable luxury, and I think Fate would be absolutely *offended* if we didn't enjoy ourselves."

Shirley raised her glass of sparkling water. "I'll drink to *that*!"

The others raised their glasses, too.

After dinner, they walked around town, pausing to gaze in the shop windows, wandering down to the waterfront to watch a ferry pull in. Strolling back through town, they passed the Dreamland Theatre.

"The Film Festival will be showing some of its movies here next week," Alice said.

"Cool." Polly drew her shawl around her against the cold sea breeze. "Wasn't there a movie set on Nantucket?"

Faye nodded. "Um, yes, I remember . . . what was it called?"

"Oh, I know!" Shirley wrinkled her forehead in thought. "What's his name was in it."

Faye looked intently at Shirley, as if their joint brains could connect and conjure up the information. "The lead actor had dark hair. Was it George Clooney?"

"No! It was . . ." Polly tapped her lip. "Was it Ben Affleck?"

"No, no, someone older."

"Was it Denzel Washington?" Alice asked.

"No," Faye shook her head. "Let's walk, maybe movement will kick my brain into gear. It was . . . Peter! Peter someone!"

"Peter Sellers?" Alice offered.

"Peter Ustinov?" Shirley suggested.

"No, no," Faye said. "Peter, Peter . . ."

"Peter O'Toole!" Marilyn yelled.

"No, that's not right—Peter Gallagher!" Polly cried, clapping her hands in triumph.

"Right!" Faye gave Polly a high five. "And Michelle Pfeiffer."

"Except she wasn't really in it," Polly continued, as the memory returned, "because she was the wife who died in the beginning. On a boat, right?"

"Right," Faye agreed. "And doesn't the husband see a ghost on the beach—"

"That's enough!" Alice interrupted. "No talking about ghosts before bedtime."

The rising wind drove them back to the house. Except for the occasional restaurant, the town was shut down for the night. Street lamps illuminated the empty sidewalks. The businesses and shops were closed. One lonely truck rattled over the cobblestones and off into the darkness.

"Kind of dead here," Alice observed, drawing her jacket tight around her neck.

"Not in the summer," Faye told her. "I've been here in July. There are street musicians, and the shops are open, and the streets are crowded."

"Hope so." Alice shivered. "It's too quiet for me."

"We're supposed to *enjoy* the quiet," Shirley reminded her.

They'd left a lamp burning in the window, and as they stepped into the Orange Street house, they felt their spirits lift. The old house, in spite of its roominess, was cozy and welcoming.

"Anyone want a nightcap?" Faye asked. "I brought some Baileys Irish Cream."

"You're wicked!" Polly laughed. "But guess what? I brought some, too!"

"Pajama party!" Shirley cried.

"I'll join you in a minute," Marilyn told them. "I've got to phone Ian and Ruth."

"I've got to phone Gideon," Alice said.

"I've got to phone Aubrey," Faye said.

"I don't *have* to phone Hugh," Polly said wistfully, "but maybe I will, anyway."

I could phone Stan, Shirley thought, *but I don't want to.* "I'm going to make myself some chamomile tea. I'll meet you all in the front parlor."

She was curled up on the sofa with a mug on the table next to her and a gorgeous glossy photography book about Nantucket in her lap when the others came down.

"Let's light a fire," Faye suggested. "I'm freezing."

"Do the fireplaces work?" Polly asked nervously.

"I'm not sure." Shirley grabbed a pad and pen lying on the table. "I'll add that to my list of things to ask Nora."

"Surely we won't need a fire in the summer," Alice said.

"You never know," Faye told her. "This island gets lots of wind and fog."

"Well, for tonight, how about turning on the furnace?" Alice suggested.

Shirley flipped through her notes. "There's a thermostat—"

"There!" Faye pointed. "By the portrait of the sea captain."

Alice turned the dial. From deep in the house, the furnace rumbled to life, and in moments warm air wafted into the chilly room.

"That's more like it." Alice plunked down into a wing chair and lifted her legs, resting her feet on the coffee table. "Aaah." She yawned. "I don't know why I'm so tired."

"It's the sea air," Faye told her. "You'll sleep like a baby tonight."

Polly came out of the dining room bearing a tray of small crystal glasses. "Ta-da!" She poured the creamy liqueur and handed it around to everyone but Shirley.

"I was just wondering," Alice remarked lazily, "how much our choice of night wear reveals about our personalities."

"What a funny thought!" Faye cast her artist's eye on the others. "Well, Shirley's sexy little lavender negligee and matching peignoir with ruffled sleeves and neck is exactly what I'd expect her to wear. She's romantic even when she's not with a man."

"You know my motto, Be Prepared!" Shirley joked, tossing her red curls playfully.

"And Alice, as always, looks like royalty," Polly observed.

Alice wore gold and scarlet paisley silk pajamas cut Oriental fashion, with frogs on the asymmetrical closings and a neat Mandarin collar. "Thank you, thank you." She gave them a mock royal wave, Queen Elizabeth style.

"And Faye looks like an artist," Polly said, admiring Faye's yellow silk nightgown and turquoise kimono splashed with flowers and birds. "While I"—with a rueful grin, she held out the cuff of her light fleece robe, which she wore over a heavy cotton nightgown.

Alice searched for a compliment. "You look the most comfortable."

"I thought it might be cold here," Polly explained. "I've read that because the sea is still cold, the island takes longer than the mainland to warm up."

"Very sensible," Faye said.

Polly sighed. *"Sensible."*

"Marilyn wins the prize for *sensible*!" Alice said.

They all focused on Marilyn, who wore faded, old, mismatched sweat pants and sweatshirt.

"They're cozy!" Marilyn protested.

"Do you wear those with Ian?" Faye asked gently.

"Of course." Marilyn looked puzzled. "Why not?"

The other four laughed.

"So much for our ideas about what's sexy," Polly said.

"Well, I'm sure the right clothes make *us* feel sexier," Alice said.

Faye had her head cocked. "I'm thinking. Marilyn, what you're wearing now isn't much different from what you wore in the day. And I'll bet you don't have any saucy little summer numbers to wear on the island."

"Shopping spree!" Alice and Shirley yelled simultaneously.

"I'll drink to that!" Faye raised her glass.

Around midnight they agreed it was time for bed. They carried their glasses into the kitchen, setting them in the sink for a morning washup. They double-checked that both front and back doors were locked. They took turns using the bathrooms, called good night, then sank down into their various beds.

They fell asleep at once, exhausted by the long day and the fresh salt air, and if anything woke them in the night—a noise, a drift of air, a shifting shadow—they simply snuggled more deeply into their pillows, sinking back into their dreams.

Everyone rose early, except for Alice, whose snores from the front bedroom sounded like the purring of a large cat. Shirley went into the front parlor to do yoga. Faye and Polly set off for the Nantucket Bake Shop to buy croissants and bagels and sweet rolls, and Marilyn went in the other direction, down to the Grand Union to buy milk, sugar, coffee, and juice. The four were gathered in the dining room, just finishing their breakfasts, when Alice padded barefoot into the room, rubbing her eyes.

"I can't believe I slept so late!" She collapsed in a chair.

"Coffee?" Shirley poured a cup and handed it to Alice. "We're planning our day. It's gorgeous out there, sunny and warm."

"I want to walk around town some more," Faye said. "The yards are all like little jewel boxes bordered with white picket fences."

"Daffodils everywhere," Polly added.

"Flowering magnolia," Marilyn said.

Shirley wasn't impressed. "We can see those things at home. I think we should go to the beach. I walked down by the town pier yesterday and it was just heavenly."

"Okay, then! Let's do it *all*!" Faye started gathering up her breakfast things. "We don't have to leave until this evening."

"Hang on," Alice grumbled. "I haven't finished my coffee."

"And I haven't finished my croissant," Polly added. "Alice, try the beach plum jam. It's amazing."

As she spread the jam on her roll, Alice looked around the dining room. "What a lot of antiques Nora Salter's got in this house."

Marilyn agreed. "I don't know how she's able to notice that anything's gone missing, there's so much here."

"The scrimshaw alone must be worth a fortune," Polly said. Seeing Alice's raised eyebrow, she pointed to a box on the mantel. "Scrimshaw is ivory with designs etched and inked into it. Original scrimshaw was made of whale's teeth, but now that whales are no longer hunted, people use ecologically approved resin imitations. It's a fascinating, painstaking process."

"What do you think of Nora's paintings?" Shirley asked Faye, nodding toward the landscapes above the sideboard.

"I haven't studied them all closely," Faye told her, "but some of them are by fairly well-known artists. Pretty valuable, I'd say. Not to mention the china. Look at the corner cabinet. Spode."

Polly went over to study the collection. "There's a salt shaker here, but no pepper."

"Maybe that's one of the things that's gone missing," Shirley said. "I'm going to have keys made, one for each of us, but we've got to be supercareful about keeping this place locked up."

Faye stretched. "I can't wait any more! The sun's too inviting. Alice, why don't we meet you somewhere—down by the Steamboat Wharf, in about thirty minutes?"

Alice, mouth full of bread and jam, nodded.

"I'll wait and go with Alice," Shirley decided. "You all go ahead. I'll do the dishes." When the others hesitated, she made a shooing motion with her hands. "Go on!"

Marilyn, Faye, and Polly hurried off. Alice finished her breakfast, then offered to help Shirley wash up, but Shirley, singing as she bustled around the kitchen, told her to get dressed, she had everything under control.

In her tidy little bedroom at the front of the house, Alice pulled on her slacks, sweater, and handsome Italian loafers. She appreciated the Quaker simplicity of the room, but decided she'd bring down a few of her own things to make it less stark. She lifted her watch off the embroidered runner on the dresser and slipped it onto her wrist, and then reached for her turquoise and silver earrings. She stopped, staring in confusion, at the lone earring lying on the cloth. Thinking she must have dropped an earring as she prepared for bed, she knelt on the floor, searching, and found nothing. When she rose, her eye fell on the bedside table. The other earring was lying there, next to her travel alarm clock.

Now why would she do that, put one earring on the bureau and one on the bedside table? Help! She was *truly* getting senile! For a moment she stood paralyzed, trying to remember the night before.

Oh, chill out, Alice, she told herself. It's simply a case of too many nightcaps. Snatching up the earring, she put it on, grabbed her leather jacket and cap, and left the room.

When they all met up at Steamboat Wharf, Marilyn announced that she'd plotted the route and would be the trailblazer, so the others were free to goggle and gawk at the beautiful hotels and houses as they walked along South Water Street and Hulbert Avenue. At Brant Point, they paused to catch their breath and inspect the lighthouse.

"This is the second oldest lighthouse in the country, established in 1746," Marilyn read from the guidebook.

"I'm more interested in the Coast Guard Station," Shirley joked. "You know how I love men in uniform."

"I prefer them out of uniform," Alice quipped.

They watched a few sailboats brave the brisk, chilly winds, then continued on to Jetties Beach.

Here, stiff caramel-colored beach grass waved in the high sand dunes. The tide was in, the dark water lapping at the gray boulders of the Jetties. Toward the west, the beach stretched as empty of humans as a scene from *Robinson Crusoe*. The gray-shingled concession stand was boarded up, the restrooms locked. The women took turns standing guard while they each went behind the dunes.

Alice came out grumbling as she adjusted her clothing. "The outdoor life is not for me. While I was holding my trousers out of the way, I peed on my hand."

Shirley laughed. "Rinse it off in the ocean, silly."

Faye was out on the jetty, arms extended for balance as she stepped from one boulder to another. Polly followed. Marilyn wandered off in the other direction, strolling just at the water's edge, enthralled by the millions of rosy slipper shells scattered on the sand. Black-green seaweed dotted the beach in twisted bits and pieces like arcane calligraphy, or was tossed down in hunks like discarded rags, or combed through the sand in long curling strands like Pre-Raphaelite hair. These were, Marilyn decided, from the phylum chlorophyta with branched thalli. She saw no horseshoe crabs on this beach, but other shells were plentiful.

Alice stood at the water's edge, shivering. Except for the cry of the gulls and the slap of waves against the beach, it was quiet. No roar of traffic, no horns and sirens, none of the eternal rumble of city life. Shirley came crunching over the sand to stand next to her.

"I'm bored and my feet are cold!" Alice grumbled.

"Oh, Alice." Shirley patted her friend's back. "Don't be such a spoilsport. This is exercise! It's good for you!"

"My shoes are filling up with sand," Alice complained. "The wind's whipping my hair into my face. If I'm going to exercise, I want to do it in the comfort of a gym or spa." She glared at Shirley. "Why do you think people love The Haven so much?" Abruptly, she turned, stomped up the boardwalk, and collapsed on the steps of the concession stand. Digging in her purse for her cell phone, she announced, "I'm calling a cab. I'm too beat to walk all the way back."

"Alice—"

"I've walked forty minutes already."

"We've strolled. We've *dawdled*."

Alice started to argue, then changed her mind. Looping her arm through Shirley's, she coaxed, "Yes, and now I want to *stroll* and *dawdle* around the *shops*. Want to come?"

Shirley found Alice irresistible when she was charming. Besides, the wind kept blowing her hair into her face. "Okay. Let's tell the others."

When they met for a late lunch at the Tap Room, they were all in high spirits.

"I'm ordering a cheeseburger with fries!" Polly cried happily. "I deserve it, after all the walking I did today."

"You're a little sunburned," Faye admonished her. "We've got to remember to bring sunblock."

"It's probably windburn," Alice said. "Look what I bought!" She held up her left arm to show off her new turquoise bracelet.

All four women bent to study it.

"Beautiful!" Faye said.

"Look what *I* found!" Marilyn reached into her pocket and lifted out something white. Holding it in her hand like a butterfly that might fly away, she displayed a delicate shell. "It's called Angel's Wings. They're very brittle. It's really rare to find one intact like this."

"Okay," Shirley said, "Polly has a new shawl, Alice has a new bracelet, Marilyn has a new shell, and I found this on the bulletin board outside a gift shop called the Hub—a list of yoga classes taught on the island. I love trying out different yoga classes, and one person offers yoga on the beach. Doesn't that sound heavenly?"

Alice made a face. "Oh, yeah. Can't wait."

Shirley rolled her eyes at Alice. "What did you find, Faye?"

"I found the best thing of all," Faye exclaimed. "I found so many places to paint! The beaches, the lighthouse, the gardens, the doors! I can't *wait* to get back here with my easel and equipment!"

Relaxed and happy after lunch, the group strolled back to Orange Street to pack up their things. As they arrived at the house, the clock at the Unitarian Church struck three. They all paused, looking up at the fine wooden tower. Then they went up the steps to the front door. Like many houses on the street, there was no garden between the building and the sidewalk. All the open space was behind the house, in a small walled garden.

As Shirley dug in her purse for the key, they heard someone say in a loud, imperious voice, "Excuse me!"

Standing on the porch of the house next door was an elegant woman in a marvelous cranberry-colored wool cape. She looked to be in her seventies, but even with the marks of age, her face was beautiful and her clothes were fabulously stylish.

"Oh, hello!" Faye went down the steps, holding out her hand. "I'm Faye Vandermeer. We're going to be living here this summer!"

The older woman recoiled. "You are—*renters*?" She endowed the word with the horror she might give to the word *prostitutes*.

"No, no," Shirley hurried down the steps to join Faye. "No, Nora Salter is a friend of ours. She asked us to stay here for the summer—"

Before Shirley could finish her sentence, the older woman sniffed disdainfully. "She *would*."

Alice drew herself up to her full commanding height. "She's asked us to stay here because she has to have an operation and won't be able to come down." She purposely didn't say that it was an operation on her hip, hoping to shame the old biddy into some kind of sympathy.

But their neighbor showed no compassion or even interest. "I hope you're not bringing *animals*. Or intending to have loud parties. This is the Historic District, and we're very strict about what goes on here." She ran her eyes over all the women, obviously not impressed with what she saw. "I suppose you'll invite all your relatives."

"Yeah," Alice snapped, "especially our teenaged nephews with their saxophones and drums."

The older woman's eyes narrowed and her nostrils quivered. Without another word, she turned her back on them and went into the house.

"Well," Shirley said into the awkward silence, "that was special."

"Who is she?" Marilyn wondered aloud.

"I'll ask Nora when I get home," Shirley said, turning the key and leading them all into the house. "She's so beautiful," Faye mused.

"Too bad she's such an old witch," Polly said.

"Maybe she's lonely," Shirley said. "Maybe when we get to know her—"

"Shirley!" Alice barked. "You are such a *hopeless* romantic!"

"No," Shirley corrected with a smile. "I'm a hope*ful* romantic!"

Faye put her arm around Shirley. "Shirley's right! Come on now, don't let her spoil our mood! We've got to pack and get out of here or we'll miss our ferry."

"I wish we didn't have to leave." Polly sighed.

"I know," Marilyn agreed.

"We'll make plans on the trip back," Alice said executively.

"Great!" Faye said. "Because I can't wait to return!"

It was midnight. Faye lay in her own bed at home, wide awake and on the verge of tears. She was so tired. She was so tired and so virtuous—she'd managed to fall asleep without the aid of any pharmaceutical product. She'd waited patiently for sleep to come, and had finally sunk deep into the sweet healing oblivion of slumber . . . and *boom*! A hot flash hit her body like a thousand volts of electricity. In an instant she was awake, throwing the covers off, desperate to cool down, and emotionally frazzled.

Now she couldn't fall back asleep. She'd exercised today, and eaten healthily, and was physically exhausted, and even so, her body would not *subside*. It was as if she were experiencing premenstrual tension, which was ridiculous, because she no longer had periods. The intense pressure beneath her skin was the same, though, and the irrational desire to scream and throw things. What was even worse was the knowledge that this episode tonight would exact a huge toll on the kind of energy and enthusiasm she would have tomorrow, so she suffered in the present and for the future at the same time.

What was the *point* of this physical mayhem? Scientific Marilyn would say it was the body's way of telling a woman she was no longer of childbearing years, but Faye's body had informed her of this long ago. Couldn't her mind telegraph her body that she'd gotten the message?

But what was the point of anything? Faye wondered now as she lay alone. What was the point of her husband having a fatal heart attack at sixty-three? She wanted, she *endeavored,* to find meaning in the confusing, inexplicable ways of the universe, and many times she felt that while she had not arrived at a state of understanding, she'd come near enough to trust that something—a pattern, a design, a beautifully elaborate plan—existed.

Then she'd be hit by a hot flash and everything would seem simply ridiculous and chaotic.

She pulled on her kimono and slid her feet into her slippers. Sometimes she could trick herself into falling asleep in other spots in the house. Her physician had advised her to sleep only in her bed, to make that the "safe sleeping place," but her physician, a lovely young woman, obviously had never suffered insomnia.

Without turning on any lights, Faye wandered around the second floor. Illumination from the street and the sky turned the guest room and her studio into chambers of gray and navy blue. She leaned against the door for a moment, thinking about the picture still on the easel. She'd just finished it, a commission for the Sperry Paper Company. It was a lush bouquet of red roses, white lilies, and evergreen fronds; the company would use it for their Christmas note cards. Carolyn Sperry, Aubrey's daughter, had asked Faye to paint some still lifes and scenes for a set of exclusive note cards, and Faye had been delighted to oblige. It provided extra income for her, of course, but money was not the primary motivation. She wasn't fabulously wealthy, but Jack had left her well-off, and she didn't have exorbitant desires. She didn't long for trips to exotic places, for designer clothing or fabulous jewelry. Now that her daughter was grown and happy, Faye's greatest joy came from her work—

—and now she remembered the trip to Nantucket last weekend, and suddenly, in the dark hallway, she found herself smiling. She hugged herself, thinking of the Nantucket light. She'd noticed it once before, when she'd visited a friend on the island, but for some reason, this weekend, she'd been struck by it so forcefully it had been a little like falling in love. She supposed the scientific explanation was that the moisture in the air caused the luminous clarity that made everything seem somehow *more* than itself. Of course the ocean reflected back the light, making the translucent air dazzling. But even away from the water, along the side streets of the town, where spring was only beginning to come, the daffodils and hyacinths, the meandering brick walkways, the gray-shingled houses with crisp white trim, all were washed in a kind of brilliance;

where time and weather had worn the paint away on a faded blue doorway, the gentle softness of it struck a note of gratitude in Faye's heart.

She couldn't *wait* to go back to Nantucket to paint.

Yawning, she stumbled back to bed, curling up on her side, remembering her bedroom in the Nantucket house. The cushion on the
window seat had been so soft, its faded flowered cover like a comfortable old friend with secrets. And the view from the window! The
panorama of town, harbor, and the thin streak of golden sand where
Coatue's sandy bars stretched—the tall white lighthouse on Great Point,
shimmering in the sun like a dream . . .

Faye fell asleep.

In the morning, she took a second cup of coffee up to drink as she showered and dressed. She had so much to accomplish today. She'd woken
early, eager to go to her favorite art supply store to purchase paints, canvases, and a lightweight easel to take to Nantucket.

The Hot Flash Club had come up with a tentative schedule for the
month of June. Faye had the most free time during the week. Marilyn
had courses to teach, Alice took care of her granddaughter, and Polly
and Shirley were tied to The Haven—so until something changed, Faye
would be living in the Nantucket house by herself during the week, returning on weekends when the other women would take over. The
thought of being alone didn't trouble her. Since Jack's death, Faye had
learned how to live alone, and she'd always craved great chunks of solitude for her painting. On Nantucket she was going to try landscape
painting, a genre she'd not attempted for years. She knew her days
would be full and stimulating; she'd be content to collapse in solitude in
the evening with a good book.

The phone rang just as Faye was going out the door. She hesitated,
then raced back to the kitchen and picked it up, in case it was her daughter calling.

It was Aubrey, sounding rattled. "Do you have any plans for the day,
Faye?" Before she could reply, he told her, "I was hoping you could drive
me to the hospital."

Faye sat down hard on a chair. "Hospital?"

He chuckled. "Sorry, didn't mean to alarm you. I have to have an MRI. For my shoulder."

"Which hospital?"

"Mass. General."

"Oh . . ." Faye thought fast. Aubrey lived on Beacon Hill, only a few blocks from the hospital. He could walk there easily, and it was a beautiful day. "Aubrey, I've got a business meeting out at The Haven today." That was true. It was in the afternoon, so Faye could *possibly* drive Aubrey to the hospital and back, but then she wouldn't be able to get to the art supply store, and that would mean putting off her return to Nantucket.

Aubrey said nothing. *Funny,* Faye thought, *how silence can carry the weight of disappointment.* She knew she needed to make a peace offering.

"Why don't you let me treat you to dinner tonight? At one of your favorite restaurants!"

Aubrey sighed. "I'm rather tired of eating in restaurants."

"Then come here for dinner."

"I'd rather not drive. My shoulder hurts when I do almost anything."

"Oh! Well . . . why don't I come in this evening and make you dinner at your place?"

"That would be very nice, Faye. If you're not too busy," he added petulantly.

She ignored the last remark. "What time would you like me to come?"

She chatted a little more with Aubrey, infusing her voice with warmth and caring, wondering why she was so reluctant to do such a simple favor as driving him to his MRI. He'd been wonderful to her, after all, the Christmas she sprained her ankle. He'd brought champagne and lobster dinners to her house for New Year's Eve. He'd been absolutely gallant.

But he doesn't have a broken ankle, she reminded herself. He's got bursitis, not a brain tumor. An MRI might be boring or creepy, but it wasn't painful or debilitating.

If she were a man, Faye thought with a twinge of bitterness, no one would expect her to neglect her work. Immediately, she corrected herself: Who was this great "no one" she was getting into such a snit about? It was her own sense of responsibility she had to appease. It had always been that way, she'd always had to divide her time between work and family. But Aubrey wasn't *family*. And the hope of painting on Nantucket pulled at her so powerfully . . . she hurried out the door to buy the paints before the phone could ring again.

Marilyn opened the hatch of her Subaru. For a moment, she just stood there, looking at all the bulging plastic grocery bags. In the past year she'd gone from living alone to living with three other people, all of whom she cared for, all of whom had to be fed daily, and none of whom was ever around to help. Long ago, when she was married to Theodore, and was a mother with a little boy, she'd only had three people to shop for. Plus, she'd been younger, she'd had more energy.

But this was now. And she was a fortunate and happy woman, to have so many people she loved in her life. So she grabbed the first bunch of bags and lugged them into the house.

Back and forth she went. She stowed the groceries for herself, Ian, and Angus, then carried her mother's groceries down to the basement apartment.

"Marilyn!" Ruth was seated in her favorite armchair, still wearing her spring sweater set with the butterflies and lilacs. A matching butterfly pin adorned her white curls. The television set was on, as usual. "Hello, darling! I've been waiting for you! Come over here and see what I've got!"

"I'll just put your groceries away first, Mother." Marilyn worked as she talked. "I don't want your butter to go bad. Or your milk. I got you lots of bananas, I'll put them here in the fruit bowl, okay?"

"Marilyn, sweetheart, you don't need to hurry so. Come over here and sit with me for a while."

I can't sit! Marilyn wanted to shout. *I've got papers to grade, lesson plans to prepare, dinner to fix, and for the first time in my life I have an adorable man I want to spend some time with!* But she knew her mother got lonely down here by herself, and counted on Marilyn's company. Still, today Ruth had gone to the Senior Citizens Center with her beau, Ernest, so Marilyn didn't feel quite so guilty.

"I'll be right there, Mother."

Stashing the plastic bags in the trash beneath the sink, she noticed that Ruth had neglected to sort her trash into the various recyclable bins. Marilyn would have to do that later, when she carried the trash out to the barrels. Or should she do it now? The remains of a can of tuna trailed soggily over the newspapers, and a glass jam jar had shattered and lay in shards among the rest of the trash. Marilyn would have to be careful when she sorted, or she'd cut herself. Of course, she could just cheat, this one time, and not recycle. But she knew so well how important recycling was. How did anyone decide between saving the environment and saving a few moments for one's own sanity?

She shut the door on the trash and washed her hands. "Okay, Mother, now! How are you?" As Marilyn went over to the sitting area, she really *looked* at her mother. Ruth was sitting in a very odd way, hunched over herself.

Marilyn's heart kicked with fear. Had Ruth had a stroke? God, Marilyn would never forgive herself—

But Ruth smiled beatifically. "Look what I've got."

Marilyn came close. Now she spotted it—curled in Ruth's lap was a tiny black kitten. "Oh, Mother! How adorable!" She knelt next to her mother, and gently put one finger onto the kitten's silky head. The kitten responded by lithely twisting around to expose its very fat, soft, furry belly.

"She's a present from Ernest," Ruth said. "He knows I get lonely down here, and he thought she would be good company."

"What a wonderful idea!" Marilyn wished she'd thought of this herself. "What are you going to name her?"

"Marie, I think. For Madame Marie Curie. I think Madame Curie is too much to say, don't you?"

"Marie's a great name."

The kitten, awakened by their attention, mewed, then climbed up Ruth's bodice to her shoulder and licked Ruth's face. Ruth giggled like a little girl at the touch.

"I'm so glad Ernest gave her to you!" Marilyn said.

"Isn't he wonderful?" The kitten was now on the back of the chair, batting at Ruth's wispy white curls. "How was your day, darling?"

Marilyn moved to the sofa, wishing she had a nice glass of wine in her hand. "Busy. You remember how it was, teaching, sitting on committees, dealing with endless memos."

"I wish you didn't have to work so hard," Ruth said sympathetically.

"Oh, but I love my work, Mother," Marilyn reminded her. "Being busy's not a bad thing."

Ruth lifted the kitten off the back of the chair and set her on the floor. "You look a little tired."

"It's just the end of the day," Marilyn told her. "I'll get out of these shoes, have a glass of wine, and relax. I made lasagna last night for all of us. It will take about an hour to heat up. Want to come upstairs and have dinner with us?"

"Could you all come down here? I hate to leave Marie."

"Well, bring her upstairs." Marilyn didn't want to have to carry all the plates, the heavy lasagna pan, the salad bowl, the bread basket, and wineglasses down the stairs and back up again.

"Do you think I should? On her first night? I'd rather let her get used to my apartment first. Maybe later she can come upstairs."

Marilyn wanted to bang her head gently against the wall. "Sure," she said. "We'll bring dinner downstairs." She rose. She'd change into comfortable clothes, drink a glass of wine while she prepared the meal, play a little Bach on the kitchen CD player to revive her spirits—

"Oh, darling, before I forget!" Ruth pushed herself up out of her chair and tottered over to the counter between the kitchen and her living area. "Marie is going to need a few things. A litter box and litter, and food, of course. I made a list. I'd like to get her a collar and perhaps a cute little bed, but that can wait until you can take me to a pet store. But she'll need these things right away. Do you think you could get them before dinner?"

Shirley was a vegetarian, but she didn't force her choices on others, and tonight she was roasting a chicken, because Stan was coming to dinner. She didn't feel too guilty about the chicken; it was cows, with their kind, flower-eyed faces, whom she couldn't easily cook. Shirley wouldn't eat the chicken, and as she prepared it for roasting, she said a little prayer to it, the way she'd read Native Americans prayed to the deer they killed for food.

"Dear Spirit of This Little Hen," she prayed, "forgive me for sacrificing your life so that Stan might have food. Actually, you might never have had a life if you hadn't been bred for human consumption, and according to the packaging, you never had to live in a cage but got to walk on the ground, eating organic feed, so maybe you had a really wonderful little chicken life. I hope so. And thanks."

She slid the roasting pan into the oven, then washed her hands. A fresh salad waited for its dressing. She was making a mushroom risotto for her own dinner and for Stan's, and she'd prepared a bowl of fresh fruit for dessert.

She'd also bought a bottle of red wine. It gleamed temptingly from the table. She'd been in AA for most of her life, and most days now she didn't miss drinking, but during times of stress, her very bones seemed to plead for just one nice hit of alcohol. Plus, all the health experts claimed a drink a day was good for the heart.

Her problem was that she wouldn't be able to limit herself to one drink a day. After one drink, her body, mind, and very soul would be dancing with joy, freeing her from all inhibitions, and coaxing her to have just one more drink . . . and just one more, until she turned into a staggering, yodeling, hiccuping blob.

No. No wine for her. But Stan enjoyed a couple of glasses of wine with dinner, and she rather hoped he'd drink the entire bottle. Perhaps it would relax him. She thought they'd probably make love again tonight, and she wanted to see if she couldn't slow him down a bit, entice him away from his lovemaking timetable. Her Hot Flash friends thought he was such a great catch, and they hadn't liked Justin, who'd turned out to be a complete rat, so she knew she should pay attention to her friends' advice. She really wanted to do her best to make this relationship work.

The buzzer sounded. Shirley skipped down the stairs and across the foyer to open the door. Evening yoga classes were going on, but the students entered at the other end of the building. This door was locked at five, when Wendy, Shirley's assistant, left for the day.

"Hello, Shirley." Stan stood there in a new multicolored cotton sweater. Shirley knew he'd bought it to please her, to show her *he* could be colorful, too. She tried to be fond of him because of this. She tried to ignore that the sweater, splashed with burgundy, brown, and yellow, reminded her of her worst hangovers. Stan held out a box of chocolates.

"Hi, Stan. Well, thanks! Come on in."

"How was your day?" Stan asked, as they climbed the stairs to Shirley's condo.

"It was okay. How was yours?"

"Well, let's see." Stan took the question seriously. "The morning started off well enough, although I was constipated, even though I drank Metamucil last night. Then my breakfast was interrupted by one of those telemarketers. I said to him, 'Look, young man, my toast is growing cold because of you. I'm going to have to throw it away and make myself a new piece. That's just wasteful. If you consider all the toast you're ruining all across the United States as you and your colleagues make these totally unnecessary phone solicitations, you'll realize that you're responsible for an inordinate amount of wasted food, which in the long run is bad for the economy, not to mention the impact on people's dispositions. Why, you could be starting a chain reaction . . .'"

Shirley pretended to be listening as she poured Stan a drink. Setting the chocolates on the counter, she saw the price tag still stuck to the side of the box. They were from a discount house, marked down from ten dollars to two. She shouldn't care. She knew Stan prided himself on his frugality. But she wished he'd removed the sticker. Although perhaps he'd left it there on purpose, as a point of honor.

Shirley lit the candles and carried the food to the table. As they ate, Stan continued to take her through each moment of his day. She was beginning to understand that Stan didn't enjoy conversation; he simply needed an audience for his monologues. All Shirley had to do was say "Oh," or "Ah," at an appropriate moment. She allowed her mind to drift.

She admired the romantic ambience she'd created: the pale lavender tapers on the table; the bouquet of spring flowers she'd bought at a farm market, set in a tall green vase on the coffee table; the overhead lights turned off and only a couple of table lamps and the candles filling the room with a soft, romantic light. She was a spiritual person. She was sensitive, receptive. She wished she could channel Danielle Steel or, better yet, Sawyer from *Lost*.

Last year, when Marilyn was dating Faraday, Marilyn had complained of his impotence problems. Shirley had tried to get Marilyn to slip a few capsules of the Chinese botanical supplement Horny Goat Weed into Faraday's food, but scientific Marilyn tended to scoff at herbal remedies. Shirley had been disappointed—she loved hearing first-hand accounts of the effectiveness of herbal medicines. She was definitely planning to serve Stan some tea with ginseng, which helped boost testosterone, and she'd considered slipping a few capsules of a male libido enhancer made from Chinese herbs, fried antler glue, and mantis-egg-case into his dessert. But Stan's problem wasn't really impotence. Stan was simply not romantic. No herbal cure had been discovered for that.

After dinner, Shirley and Stan sat on the sofa watching a Red Sox game on television. All through the evening, Stan threw numbers at Shirley—each player's RBI stats, the number of times a particular player had hit a home run against one of the opposing team's pitchers, the varying sizes of ballparks. The miles per hour of each pitch was often flashed on the screen—this game was an accountant's dream.

Men all over America were watching baseball, Shirley reminded herself. Plus, many of them were swilling beer and scratching their armpits. Stan was clean and clothed. He was not going to murder her. He was not going to steal her money. He was not going to use The Haven in some disgraceful way. She wanted a man in her life, and here he was. What was wrong with her? Why couldn't she be happy?

16

Ladies!" Alice held her hands up as if she held a megaphone. "Start your engines!"

This Saturday morning was so brilliant with light it seemed the sun was brand new. The Hot Flash Club gathered at the main doorway, clad in easy off-and-on clothes, credit cards poised in their purses next to their shopping lists. They were at the Burlington Mall!

"Our mission, should you accept it," Alice announced, "is to buy as many fabulous summer clothes as possible before lunch." She held up her arm. "Synchronize watches. We meet at the Cheesecake Factory at two o'clock."

"Check," Faye said. "Okay, then, I'm off to J. Jill."

"I'm going to Ann Taylor and Talbot's," Alice said. "Who wants to come?"

"I'm more a Target girl myself," Shirley reminded them.

Alice grabbed her arm. "You come with me." Scrutinizing the group, she said, "Someone's got to supervise Marilyn."

Marilyn didn't object. She knew she had no fashion sense.

"I'll do it," Faye said. "Polly, want to join us?"

"Sure!" Polly was glad she'd be with Faye, who was voluptuous like Polly.

Laughing with anticipation, they bustled through the main door, then went their different ways. They flew through the stores. They purchased beach robes and bathing suits and saucy sarongs. They bought white slacks and turquoise shirts. Lime green sundresses and straw hats with green, white, and pink striped bands. Loose long shirts in deep azure or fuchsia, crisp white nightgowns and fluffy toweling robes.

Khaki shorts and polka dot capris, gauzy gypsy shirts and tees in pastel blue, rose, and lemon. Sundresses with spaghetti straps and soft pashmina shawls. Silk and lace undergarments in playful colors. Thonged shoes with faux gems, and sandals with stacked heels, and striped slide-on sneakers.

Then they went for the jewelry. Had there ever been a summer with more fabulous jewelry around? Chunky turquoise or pink quartz necklaces, wide beaded bracelets, jade and amethyst earrings, and for Marilyn and Shirley, both of whom had nice flat waists, leather belts with elaborate jeweled buckles.

When they met in front of the restaurant for lunch, they were too encumbered with packages to gather at any table, so they raced out to stash their loot in their cars first. Back at the restaurant, they were seated at a round table, and ordered.

"I am so psyched!" Shirley giggled as she held up the bracelet she hadn't been able to resist putting on immediately. "It's like I've been *dying* for turquoise! And I bought the most adorable little beaded shoes. Totally impractical, and completely fabulous!"

"I bought a beaded sweater!" Alice said.

"I bought a beaded skirt!" Faye said.

"I bought a beaded shawl," Polly said.

They all looked at Marilyn.

"Uh . . . I bought . . ." She looked hopelessly at her friends.

"You are so maddening!" Faye said, laughing. "We found Marilyn a cashmere tee as light as a moth's wing and a long, embroidered silk skirt. *Tres romantique!*"

"Well," Shirley announced, "*I've* bought *you* all a present!"

"Oooh, goody." Faye rubbed her hands together expectantly. "I love presents!"

Shirley passed around four little lavender paper bags. Each woman pulled out a key chain shaped like a silver scallop shell. One key dangled from each chain.

"Now we each have a key to Nora's house," Shirley told them.

"Thanks, Shirley!" Alice reached into her capacious leather bag and drew out her electronic journal. "I've made up a rough schedule for June, showing what dates each of us is going to be there. Any changes, let me know."

"Now that Rosa's taking over the supervision of Havenly Yours, I've got loads more free time!" Polly's relief was evident in her smile.

"Cool!" Faye took Polly's hand. "Come down with me tomorrow. I'm going to be there for the week."

Polly chewed her lip. "I don't know whether I can leave Roy Orbison that long. Although the neighbor's boy has dog-sat Roy a lot, and Roy always seems perfectly content there."

"Never mind your dog, is it wise to leave Hugh alone for any length of time?" Shirley wondered. "I mean, out of sight, out of mind, and all that."

Polly twirled her new key chain. "I don't want to live my life that way, afraid I'll lose Hugh if I go out of town. Hugh doesn't seem afraid to lose *me* during all the times he spends with his ex." When the others started to speak, she held up her hand. "I'm not doing this for spite, or to make a point, or to make him miss me. I just want to go to the island and relax. Not worry about Havenly Yours, or Hugh's weird family, or anything. I want to catch my breath."

"I know exactly what you mean," Faye agreed. "I'm tired. I'm *rattled*. I may not look my age, but I certainly *feel* my age. Aubrey's got to have an operation for a torn tendon, after which he has to wear a sling for at least three weeks and not turn or raise his arm or stretch the tissues. He'll need to be driven to physical therapy for several *months*. And while I'm terribly fond of Aubrey, I don't want to become his full-time nurse."

"No reason for you to," Alice remarked sensibly. "He's got plenty of money. He can hire around-the-clock help."

Faye nodded. "True, but he says he doesn't want strangers taking care of him."

"What about his daughter?" Shirley asked.

"Oh, you know Carolyn. She's busy running the company, plus she's got a baby. She's not the caretaking type, anyway." She ran her fingers up and down the cool runnels of the little silver shell. "I love this, Shirley," she said. She smiled. "I'm planning to spend a week on the island. I'm going to rent a Jeep and drive all around the island, looking for landscape scenes to paint. I'll see how I like it there, before I decide how much to take on with Aubrey."

"I'll go with you," Polly decided. "I'll protect you from ghosts—and the next-door neighbor."

"That reminds me!" Shirley leaned in. "I spoke with Nora about that witchy old bat. Nora said Lucinda Payne and she have known each other since childhood, and hated each other every minute of every year. Their families got involved in some feud years ago, and they're still adversaries. But Lucinda's also a snob, turns her nose up at everyone."

"So," Alice pinned Shirley with a glance. "Sounds like none of your 'all you need is love' stuff will charm her."

"I know," Shirley agreed. "I'll just ignore her. She's in her seventies; even at my most optimistic, I don't think I could change her in one summer."

"Plus," Faye instructed sternly, "no one is taking on any more personal responsibilities! Nantucket is for relaxation and rejuvenation."

"And eating chocolate," Polly added.

"I'll drink to that," Alice said, raising her glass.

17

Howling winds and streaming rain beat against the ferry as it bucked and pitched its way over Nantucket Sound. The heaving waves slammed the steamship into the dock. It was still rocking as Polly and Faye staggered down the ramp, clutching their coats and bent nearly double by the forceful gusts.

They hailed a cab, tossed their luggage in the trunk, and squeezed in. Their driver was a genial young Russian whose tag told them his name was Boris.

"What happened to summer?" Polly inquired.

Turning around to face them, Boris nodded fervently. "Yes, yes!"

"Watch out!" Faye called, as the cab missed another car by an inch.

"Yes, yes!" Boris agreed happily. Facing the road again, he drove with operatic flourishes and a jerking right foot over the uneven cobblestones on South Water Street and Main Street, singing loudly in Russian.

Faye tugged on Polly's sleeve. "Don't distract him," she whispered.

Five minutes later, "You here *are*!" Boris announced suddenly, braking so hard the women nearly flew over the seats into his lap. Jumping out, he lifted out their luggage and opened their doors with the élan of a diplomatic attaché.

Faye hurriedly gave him his payment and tip, then she and Polly raced through the rain, lugging their bags up the steps. Polly used her key to let them into the house, where the air was as chilly and almost as damp as it was outside.

"I'll pay for the fuel," Faye announced decisively, turning up the thermostat. "I'm soaked and freezing."

"We could make a fire," Polly suggested.

"Let's wait and do that this evening," Faye told her. "We've got to get supplies before we can settle in."

Polly stood dripping on the front hall rug. "Should we change?"

"We'll only get wet again," Faye said. "Come on, let's brave the storm."

After double-checking their maps, they pulled the hoods of their raincoats up over their heads and set off down Main Street. By the harbor, they found the Grand Union. Consulting their shopping lists, they pushed their carts up and down the unfamiliar aisles, paid for their purchases, then began the return trek home. Polly started a stew roasting while Faye went back out into the blustery day to buy wine. By the time Faye returned, the aroma of garlic, onions, and olive oil drifted through the house.

With a great heave, Faye set the packages of wine on the kitchen counter. "Mmm, Polly, that smells divine."

Polly was staring out the window at the small back garden and the houses beyond. Everything was as blurred and gray as smoke. "Where can we go on a day like this?"

"Well, where's the best place to go on rainy days no matter where you are?" Faye asked. "Let's hit the library."

The wind whipped their raincoats around their legs as they hurried down the brick sidewalks, passing small shops whose windows glowed through the downpour like little golden grottoes. Across from the post office sat the majestic white Greek Revival building, the Nantucket Atheneum.

After being given their library cards, they scanned the new books in the fiction and nonfiction sections, then headed to the Great Hall on the second floor, where the art and history collections were kept. Polly settled in one corner of the room with a pile of books on Nantucket crafts while Faye established herself near a window, poring over books on art. At closing time, they hurried home, juicy new novels clutched to their chests beneath their rain gear.

Still the rain thundered down, veiling the spring evening in gray. The house was warm and cozy, a refuge in the storm. Faye hurried upstairs to shower and unpack while Polly headed back to the kitchen to check on the stew.

Then Polly climbed the stairs, her own luggage in each hand, and finally reentered the small side bedroom with its charming white iron beds and rag wool rug.

Flicking on the overhead light, she looked around the room, smiling with pleasure. It was so clean, so simple, it was a *retreat*.

Then her eye fell on the bed by the window, "her" bed, as she'd come to think of it, and she blinked.

How odd.

"Faye?" she called.

Faye came down the hall, wrapped in her turquoise kimono, toweling her hair dry. "What's up?"

"No one's been in this house since we were all here in May, right?"

"Right."

"No other friend of Nora Salter's might have used the place?"

"Not as far as I know."

Polly rubbed her arms for warmth. She was still in her damp clothing. "Well, this might seem trivial, but the day I left, I put one of the little china dolls from the cradle on my pillow." She blushed to admit something so childish. "And now she's not there."

Faye crossed the room and lifted up the quilt and pillow shams. "Hmm." Pulling the bed away from the wall, she looked down at the floor. "Nothing, not even a dust bunny." She looked under the bed. "Well, there's no doll here—have you looked in the cradle? Maybe you only thought you put the doll there."

Polly knelt by the child's cradle. Four dolls lay propped on a lacy pillow, but not the doll that had been her immediate favorite, a rosy-cheeked girl in a navy corduroy jumper and a red checked blouse. Her doll had brown hair done in pigtails, tied with red ribbon, and carried in her hand a little basket with a blue-and-white checked picnic cloth.

She looked up at Faye. "No, the doll's not here."

Faye stood with her hands on her hips, gazing around the room. "I don't know what to say, Polly. Nothing's missing from my room."

Polly rubbed her forehead. "Gosh, I hope I'm not getting senile. I mean, we all joke about it, but this is kind of worrisome."

"You're not getting senile, Polly!" Faye assured her heartily. "We were all in such a gaggle here, all five of us running around. Why, maybe one of the others moved the doll."

Polly nodded. "I guess . . ."

"Look, get out of those damp clothes and have a hot shower and come down and drink some wine with me. I'll make a fire."

Polly shook herself out of her trance. "Right."

Later, after dinner, they lounged on the sofas in front of the fire, toasting their toes, reading their books, occasionally sipping an after-dinner liqueur. Outside, the wind continued to scream and batter the rain against the windows. It was deliciously snug.

When the grandfather clock in the hallway struck nine, Polly stretched and looked over at Faye. "Good book?"

"Good book." Faye put it facedown in her lap and rubbed her eyes. "Yours?"

Polly pressed the collar of her toweling robe up against her neck. "Good, too."

They watched the fire in silence for a while.

"Faye," Polly said gently. "Would you tell me about Jack?"

Faye looked over at Polly. She smiled, while at the same time, tears came into her eyes. "I was just thinking of him. I was just wishing he were here."

"I know," Polly said. "I miss Tucker. I don't talk about him much with the others."

Faye nodded. "The others are all divorced. They wouldn't really understand. Plus, I'm not sure they ever lived with a man as the center of their lives. Marilyn's so caught up in science, Alice was an ambitious, hardworking career woman, and Shirley . . . well, Shirley is her own special case."

"Shirley's so good-hearted," Polly said. "And she does such a great job with The Haven. I don't know why she has such disastrous taste in men."

Faye shifted on the sofa, rearranging her legs and her kimono over them. By discussing Shirley this way, they were edging toward the unspoken danger zone of their Hot Flash friendship. They'd all agreed they didn't want to have little cliques within the larger group.

"But perhaps that's because there aren't that many really good men around," Polly said, leading the conversation away from Shirley. "My first marriage was a disaster. I was so lucky to meet Tucker and have the years I had with him."

"I feel that way about Jack."

"Tell me about him."

Faye's face softened. "Jack was older than I by ten years. He was a lawyer, and very—oh, I guess morally upright is the best way to describe him. Not that he was a prig. He was just so *good*."

Polly snuggled deeper into her robe. "Where did you meet?"

"At a friend's party . . ."

As Faye reminisced, Polly watched her friend's face change. The years seemed to melt away, and Polly realized what a really lovely woman Faye was. Faye's face was plump, like Polly's, so the skin around her eyes and the two laugh lines around her mouth were the only wrinkles. Still, Faye's face was not young. Her eyelids hung in folds, making her eyes look as if they were slightly different sizes. The bottom half of her face was heavier than the top half, almost jowly. What was it Alice had said the other day? "I know I don't look my age! I know I don't look like a sixty-three-year-old woman! I just look like a really ugly woman in her fifties."

Still, Polly decided, as she listened to her friend talk, Faye was a fortunate woman. She said as much. "You're lucky to have loved a man so very much, and to be loved by him the same way."

"I know," Faye said. Pulling her knees up, she hugged them against her chest. "Gosh, Polly, I haven't talked about Jack like this for a long time. It's nice, you know. It's really nice to talk about him—it's like being there with him again."

"Then tell me more," Polly urged.

As Faye talked, the fire cast flickering shadows through the room. Polly thought of all the other women who, over the past generations, had sat here talking. She felt certain they had spoken of love, of children, men, and marriage, of the unassailable mysteries of life. The andirons, shaped like owls, had glass eyes that glittered as the flames danced, so they seemed almost alive, and alert. *Watching. Listening.* What had they heard over the decades? What grief or joy had filled the air, penetrating the very core of the iron and the bricks? What sympathy warmed the room along with the firewood's heat?

18

The weather continued rainy and cool all week, but the sun came out in a blaze on Friday, when Alice, Marilyn, and Shirley arrived.

"You've brought us good weather!" Polly cried, hugging her friends as they stepped off the ferry.

"I'm dying," Alice moaned. "I'm going to barf."

"Rough ride?" Faye asked sympathetically.

"I didn't think so," Shirley said. "But then *I* took ginger capsules which prevent motion sickness."

Alice glared. "You don't want to be messing with me right now."

Faye laughed. Hoisting one of Alice's bags off the blue luggage rack, she said, "Come on, Alice. A little walk in the fresh air will cure you."

At the house, Alice dragged herself to her bedroom and collapsed on the bed for a nap. Shirley said she couldn't wait to walk on the beach. Marilyn said she wanted to tour the Maria Mitchell Museum; would Faye and Polly join her? They would.

As much as Shirley longed to fit in, to be seen as someone who belonged on Nantucket, it was just not in her character to wear khaki shorts and sporty rugby T-shirts. Besides, in spite of the strong sunlight, the air was still cool. Shirley was glad she'd brought along her quilted jacket, patch-worked in various shades and designs of purple. Her violet flannel yoga pants had no pockets, nor did her side-tie shirt, but her jacket had pockets, and she found herself shoving her hands far down inside them for warmth. It was cooler on the waterfront than she'd anticipated.

She wandered through the village and along the curve of beach until she reached the town wharf. Many more boats were tied up at the dock than had been before. Walking out on the pier, she watched people lifting coolers down into their boats, coiling ropes, bending over charts, and scrubbing the decks. The tide was out, the wind skipping lightly over the water, so she slipped off her sandals and walked barefoot. At a small beach, she had to detour up to the street to make her way around a boatyard and seafood shop. She continued to walk until she found herself at the end of the harbor, where the ocean dwindled into creeks winding through salt marshes.

It was very quiet here. Houses, businesses, and roads, all the edifices of man, were at a distance. Golden sand, wet and spongy, sloped into crystalline water. Looking down, Shirley saw fiddler crabs scurrying over the sand and minnows making little silver hyphens as they flashed from place to place. Grass grew in the marshes, a pale, tender green. Overhead, gulls called and flew, their shadows splashing the water.

Spotting a piece of driftwood, Shirley sat down on it, leaned back, and took deep breaths. The truth was, she felt a little uneasy out here. She'd never had much opportunity to be at one with nature, not real nature like this. She was good with indoor waterfalls and potted plants. Being here, in this new place, made her just a tiny bit—not frightened, but *alert*.

And that was good. She liked that. Perhaps she even needed it. She liked knowing that a safe house and an active town were within walking distance, but here she could see and touch the water that had washed this way from . . . who knew where? The ocean was so vast. Here, where it lapped lightly against the sand, she was not afraid.

She made herself just sit, doing nothing. She made herself just *be*. A plane hummed overhead, gulls cried, and if she tried very hard, she could hear the water making light lapping noises as a boat far out in the harbor sent a wake that reached all the way to this very spot.

She was getting chilled. Rising, she turned back to town, ambling along the waterfront. As she approached the town pier, she heard a loud splashing noise. A golden Lab leapt out of a small wooden sailboat and paddled its exuberant way toward Shirley.

"You again!" Shirley called.

The dog shook itself, dousing Shirley's trousers with a spray of sea water, then dashed up the beach, grabbed a stick and, tail wagging, raced back to Shirley.

Smiling, Shirley threw the stick out into the water. Out in the shallows of the harbor, the dog's owner tied the boat to a buoy, then slid over the side into the water, which came up to his knees, just touching the hem of his canvas shorts. He waded up the beach to Shirley. His feet were shod with ancient leather deck shoes.

"You know she'll never let you stop," he told her, with a grin. "You could throw that until your arm goes numb and you collapse on the sand, and she'll stand over your body begging for more."

Shirley laughed. She threw the stick again, glad to have something to do to hide the excitement that flashed through her body: this man was her age, and attractive! From under his long-beaked scalloper's cap, silver hair curled around his ears and down to his collar. His face was already tanned a deep brown, making his blue eyes glow.

"How do you like the salt marshes?" he asked.

"They're beautiful," Shirley told him. "So quiet. So . . . *serene*." Immediately, she flushed with embarrassment, because "serene" sounded so gooey.

He looked at Shirley curiously. "Not many tourists ever see this part of the island, and it's so near town."

She gave him an arch look. "Is it so obvious that I'm a tourist?"

He shrugged. "Nothing wrong with being a tourist. It supports the island economy."

The golden Lab raced up to her, wriggling with joy. Shirley took the stick and tossed it into the water again.

"Her name's Reggie," the man informed her. "Short for Regina. My little island queen. Certainly the queen of my home."

Shirley wondered if that was a hint that he was unattached? "You live here, then."

"I do." He nodded toward the north. "Over in Polpis Harbor." He held out his hand. "I'm Harry."

"Shirley." Shirley put her own in his. His was warm, firm, hard, and callused. A working man's hand. For a moment, Shirley felt the world tilt. It took all her concentration to seem normal. "Did you grow up here?"

"I've lived here most of my life. I've never much wanted to be any place else."

"Doesn't it get lonely here in the winter?"

"I like lonely."

She studied his face. His skin was weathered and furrowed with laugh lines, but his eyes held a touch of sadness. But whose wouldn't, Shirley thought, by his age. No one gets through life unscathed.

"Where are you from?" he asked.

"Boston. Well, just outside Boston. I'm down here with some friends for the weekend. I own—we own—a spa, and one of our clients is giving us her house for the summer."

"Nice deal."

"I know." They were walking side by side now. Shirley stopped to pick up a shell. "I've never spent time on Nantucket before."

They were almost at the town pier. Someone in a motorboat yelled and waved. The man waved back, and Regina took off galloping down the wharf.

"Well, Shirley, I hope you enjoy your stay." He tipped his cap, then turned to follow his dog.

———

That night the Hot Flash Club went in a group to see an independent film presented by the Nantucket Film Festival. It was shown in a funky old barn called the Dreamland Theatre located between the library grounds and the Easy Street basin. Afterward, they went to the Atlantic Café for drinks and a late dinner, and then they wandered over the cobblestones, back up Main Street, to the Orange Street house.

Saturday, Alice spent the day at the Film Festival, reveling in the sight of so many beautiful people with fabulous urban looks. Shirley meandered around the piers. Polly attended a workshop offered by a scrimshaw artist. Faye set up her easel on Easy Street and began a sketch of the old cottages extending on a wharf into the harbor. Marilyn joined an ecology field trip to the beach, using a seine net to capture—for a harmless moment—some of the various creatures who made their homes at the water's edge. As the teacher discussed in charming detail the activities of fiddler crabs, jellyfish, and scallops, Marilyn gazed down upon each individual animal in her net. Here was one of millions, individual, alive. She loved the sense of being taught again. Even though she knew all the facts, it was still lovely to hear them told, like a favorite fairy tale read by a new voice. Saturday night, the five joined up for dinner and a concert.

Sunday morning, they all read newspapers around the dining room table, then went their separate ways. That afternoon, everyone but Shirley and Alice packed up for the trip home. Once again they met around the dining room table with pads and pens for lists, assigning responsibility for bringing over staples like toilet paper, sugar, and cleaning products. They'd quickly realized how much more expensive even the most modest items were on the island.

"Just one thing before you go," Shirley said. "Since I'm the one Nora Salter spoke to, I feel the most responsible, and so I just want to ask that we all be sure, *every* time we come and go from the house, that we lock the door. And double-check that all the doors are locked." She looked around the room. "I can't be sure, but I think something's disappeared this weekend. Wasn't there a green pitcher shaped like a fish on that sideboard?"

"There was!" Marilyn said. "I'm sure there was. And it's gone. How odd!"

Faye squinted her eyes, thinking. "I know we locked the door when we went out to buy the paper this morning . . ."

"Well, *I* didn't go anywhere," Alice said defensively. She'd spent the morning sleeping in. "And I didn't hear anyone in the house while you were gone."

"But you were asleep, right?" Shirley asked.

"True," Alice conceded.

"And the way you snore, Alice . . ." Shirley grinned. "I can hear you down the hall."

"I think a china doll got taken," Polly told them. "Although I can't be sure . . ."

"Maybe we should make an inventory of all the things in the house," Faye suggested.

"Are you nuts?" Alice waved her hands at the tables and bureaus covered with serving pieces, artwork, clocks, knickknacks, and vases. "That would take us forever."

"Could we put them all in storage?" Polly suggested.

Marilyn winced. "We'd spend the entire summer moving stuff."

Faye brightened. "I know! Let's take photographs! It won't take long, and we'll have a visual record."

"Good idea," seconded Marilyn.

"I'll do it," Alice volunteered. "I'll buy some of those throwaway cameras."

"You're going to have to buy quite a few," Polly said, looking around the cluttered dining room.

Shirley made calming motions with her hands. "I don't want you all to get too riled up over this. We're supposed to be coming here for *relaxation,* right?"

"Right," Marilyn agreed. "And when one or more of us is here every day, that should deter any unwanted guests."

Faye looked around the room. "You know, I can't wait to get back here. This place is so beautiful, and after a few days here, I feel so relaxed."

"When can you come back?" Shirley asked.

Faye made a face. "That depends, I guess, on Aubrey."

19

When Marilyn was in her early twenties, just after she married Theodore Becker, she privately and not unhappily gave up all dreams of ever making a significant contribution to the world of science. For her, being a mother and wife came first, and she considered herself fortunate that she'd managed to squeeze out the time to finish her doctorate in paleobiology and, later, when Teddy started kindergarten, to be offered a position at MIT.

She'd never been interested in fame, anyway; it was the *studying* she loved. It was the sense of connection with the profound and intimate secrets of the universe that thrilled Marilyn to her core and enriched every day of her life. Because of her teaching and family obligations, she'd never been able to do much field work, so she was surprised at how much she had enjoyed her few hours on Nantucket.

The island had such a unique geology—she felt as if she'd just begun to read a mystery. She was eager to return to it. She wanted to study the fascinating terminal moraine, its creation by glaciers, to understand how the flora and fauna came to thrive there. She'd not yet even seen the moors, which spread across the middle of the island, nor most of the beaches. She was especially interested in the one along Coskata, one of the major habitats of the horseshoe crabs, those creatures of venerable, ancient pedigree.

She couldn't wait to tell Ian about Nantucket. Ian, who had a doctorate in paleobiology, was an artist who specialized in drawings of vanished species. How wonderful it would be to spend some time on the island with Ian—walking along the beaches, inspecting the variety of marine and estuarine invertebrates—it would be bliss! Perhaps, when the summer semester was over, she and Ian would be able to spend a few weekends together in a guest house.

Faye's voice broke into her thoughts. "You've been awfully quiet back there."

Marilyn forced herself into the present. She was in the backseat of Faye's BMW as it zipped off Route 93 onto Memorial Drive. Faye was driving her and Polly back home, and as Marilyn's eyes focused, she saw by the congested streets they were almost there.

"Did you fall asleep?" Polly stuck her head around from the passenger seat.

"No. Just daydreaming." Marilyn yawned and stretched. "I love that island."

"Did you sleep well there?" Faye asked.

"Like a baby." Reality struck as they turned down Marilyn's street. "I only hope Ian was able to sleep. We have an intercom set up between Ruth's quarters and ours, in case she needs help. She often wakes up in the middle of the night and watches TV a while before she falls back asleep. She forgets to put her hearing aid in, so she cranks up the volume." Marilyn laughed ruefully. "I was awakened a few nights ago by Ethel Merman bellowing 'There's No Business Like Show Business'."

"You should be grateful she wasn't watching *Scream 2*." Faye laughed.

A few moments later, they pulled into Marilyn's driveway. She grabbed her overnight bag from the seat next to her, leaned forward to kiss Polly and Faye good-bye, and stepped out of the car. It was Sunday evening, almost nine o'clock, but spring light still lingered in the sky.

Good-bye, Nantucket. Hello, real life.

She waved as Faye and Polly drove away, then took a deep breath and entered her house.

Immediately, she noticed a smell. She stood in the front hallway, a backpack in one hand, a duffel bag in the other, and sniffed. The smell was unpleasant, earthy—it smelled a bit like manure. How very odd. Oh, dear, she thought, had her mother's kitten found its way up here and used a rug as a litter box? Well, whatever—she'd sort it out.

Torn between the duty of saying hello to her mother and the pleasure of seeing her beloved Ian, she allowed herself to choose pleasure, and carried her bags up the stairs.

"Is that you, Marilyn?" Ian came out of his study to meet her in the hall. He had the habit of pushing his reading glasses up on his forehead when not in use, making him seem four-eyed, but he still looked like heaven to Marilyn.

"Hello, darling." Marilyn hugged him tightly.

He kissed her thoroughly. "I missed you. Did you have a good time?"

"Oh, Ian, it was great!"

"I want to hear all about it. Tell me about it over a sherry," Ian suggested. "I just want to finish off some e-mail first."

"Fine. I'll go down and visit Ruth for a few minutes."

At Ruth's name, Ian's face changed. "Before you go down, um, I've got to tell you, I think I've caused us a bit of a problem."

What could have happened in two days? Marilyn wondered. "Oh, yes?"

Ian took a deep breath. "I bought Angus a puppy."

"A puppy." The words somehow would not compute.

"You know I've been so worried about him. He won't leave his room, he's in there day and night. I thought that if he had a puppy to care for, he might stop being quite so self-absorbed, plus he'd *have* to go outside, to take the dog out."

Marilyn stepped back from Ian. "I see your reasoning . . . but a dog in the house . . . perhaps that's the sort of thing we should discuss."

"Oh, I know, I know," Ian hurried to agree. "It's just that Brad, who teaches at B.U. with me, told me he had a litter of pedigreed bulldogs, and the runt hadn't sold, and they're moving houses, and he said he'd just *give* me the puppy if I could take it yesterday, it would be a help to them. It all just happened so spontaneously, so quickly . . ."

"I wish you had at least phoned me," Marilyn said.

"To ask your permission?" Ian bristled slightly as he posited the question.

"Of course it's not a matter of *permission*," Marilyn countered. "It's just that bringing an animal to live in the house seems like a major decision, in which we should both participate."

Ian folded his arms over his chest. "Well, Marilyn, your mother brought a cat into this house without my prior knowledge or consent."

Marilyn nodded. "Yes. Yes, that's true." She felt like a piano had just landed on her shoulders. "But a cat is less of a commitment, somehow. I mean, for one thing, cats use litter boxes. They're very clean animals. Dogs have to be housebroken."

Ian looked guilty. "You're right. And I do apologize. Darwin's had a few accidents this weekend."

"Darwin?" Marilyn smiled.

"That's what Angus named him." Ian waved his hands around. "I've done my best to clean up after him. I thought I'd gotten it all."

"Maybe not *all,*" Marilyn said. "The first thing I noticed when I came in was the smell. Has Angus been taking the dog out regularly?"

Ian looked even more guilty. "Perhaps not as often as he should." He rubbed his hands over his face. "I made a big fat mistake, didn't I? I'm sorry, Marilyn."

Her heart went out to him. "Oh, Ian, this is really too bad. I love you so much, and I missed you this weekend, and I have so much to tell you, and I certainly didn't want to walk into the house and get into an argument with you." Closing the space between them, she wrapped herself around him again, snuggling close. "We'll get it all sorted out."

Ian held her close, kissing the top of her head. "We've always had dogs in our family, Marilyn. I think it really might be what Angus needs to bring him out of his isolation."

"I hope you're right. I worry about him, too." His arms were so warm, his body matched hers all up and down. She felt at home with him, right here, right now, in his embrace.

"I wonder how soon we can go to bed," Ian murmured in her ear.

She pressed against him. In many ways, she felt like a young girl with Ian. Certainly she'd never discovered before in all her life the depth of sexual joy she felt with this man. "I wonder if we even need to go to bed," she whispered as her body flushed with sexual heat.

Ian bent and kissed her passionately. "Marilyn." His voice was hoarse with lust.

She unzipped his trousers and reached inside. He groaned. "Let's go in the bedroom," she urged.

He clasped her buttocks with both hands. "Yes. Hurry."

A noise sounded from the upstairs hall. A door opened. They heard footsteps—not the measured stride of a two-legged animal, but more of a breakneck four-pawed gallop, and suddenly a silver-white ball of fur half-ran, half-fell down the steps, landing at their feet in a muddle of splayed limbs, plump belly, and long pink tongue.

"Meet Darwin," Ian said.

"He's adorable!" Marilyn knelt to scratch the puppy's squashed, snorting, pink snout. "Hello, Darwin!"

The puppy rolled on his back, waving his fat little legs in the air, slurping and spitting as he licked Marilyn's hand.

"Marilyn? Marilyn, darling, are you home?" Ruth's voice suddenly blared from the intercom.

Darwin jumped to his feet, shivered all over, and peed on Marilyn's shoe.

20

Monday morning, Alice was awakened from a deep sleep in her Nantucket bed by a slightly off-key but extremely enthusiastic version of "Oh What a Beautiful Morning!" Shirley was in the bathroom, singing. Her lavender perfume drifted down the hall in a cloud. Alice lifted an arm from beneath the quilt, pulled back the curtain, and looked out the window. Rain thundered down, blown sideways by a fierce wind.

"Oh, what a beautiful morning?" Alice pulled her pillow over her head.

A few moments later, Shirley wafted into Alice's bedroom. "Rise and shine! Today is the first day of our new health regimen!"

Alice didn't even turn over. "I'm not walking in that rain."

"Um, yes." Shirley grabbed the covers and pulled them back. "You are."

Alice cracked one eye open. Shirley was already dressed in one of her amazing purple yoga outfits, complete with striped leg warmers. "No one wears leg warmers anymore."

"I do. Now get up." Shirley plunked down on the bed, making it bounce.

"Go away."

"Not going to happen."

"I mean it, Shirley. I'm tired. I need more sleep."

"No. You need to move your big fat butt. Then you won't be so tired."

Alice growled.

Shirley bounced.

"Stop that! You're making me motion sick!"

"Then get out of bed!"

"Fine!" In one angry explosion of movement, Alice turned over, stuck her feet on the floor, and stood up.

"Now get dressed," Shirley said bossily. "I'll go down and make your health drink."

"Oh joy." Alice trudged off to the bathroom.

"Great!" Shirley practically skipped from the room.

How did Shirley manage to get away with it, Alice wondered as she dressed. Sometimes Alice felt like one of those rhinos on the National Geographic channel, with Shirley as the little bird who rode the rhino's backs and pecked bugs from her hide. When Alice was an executive for TransContinent Insurance, no one *ever* treated Alice the way Shirley did. Alice was tall, with wide shoulders and an imposing physique. She carried herself like royalty, and through the years of executive management, she'd developed an expression that was, she knew, absolutely haughty— and that was when she was in a *good* mood. When she was angered, her expression could strike fear in her colleagues' hearts. She could even back Gideon off if she got in one of her worst tempers.

But Shirley had somehow developed a protective barrier—no, it was more than that. Shirley actually bossed Alice around. She was like a border collie, agitating, barking, leaping, herding Alice where she wanted her to go.

Now Alice went where Shirley ordered. She tromped downstairs in her velour track suit and sneakers, tossed down the health drink Shirley had made—it didn't taste half-bad!—pulled on her raincoat and hat, and followed Shirley out the door to begin their morning walk.

"We're not going to walk into town," Shirley told her. "You'll want to look in the windows, and that would slow us down. We've got to keep up the pace. Best watch where you're walking—these brick sidewalks are so uneven, it's easy to trip."

"I can't look up anyway," Alice groused. "Not with the rain blowing in my face."

"It will be at our backs on the way home," Shirley assured her.

"You are such a Girl Scout."

"Look at that door knocker!" Shirley pointed across the street. "It's shaped like a whale's tail! Oh, and aren't those flowers in that window box adorable!"

"Shirley, I'm walking," Alice muttered. "Don't expect me to *enthuse* as well."

But Shirley couldn't stop exclaiming over everything, the picket fences, the slate walks through curved arbors into dollhouse gardens, the hurricane lamps and lacy curtains and blue glass bottles showing through the windows of the houses they passed. It was like taking a walk with a kindergartener. Alice thought she should hold Shirley's hand when they crossed the street.

Yet, in her deepest heart, Alice trusted Shirley. As much as she hated it, and Alice *really* hated it, she knew she had to make some changes if she was going to stay healthy. Shirley knew what Alice needed to do, and for whatever bizarre reason, Shirley was capable of irritating Alice into action. Shirley had created a plan of exercise and diet for Alice. She'd also taken on the job of personal trainer. She was going to weigh Alice, measure her, and whenever possible, supervise her.

The only person Alice ever allowed to know her weight was her doctor, during her annual physical exam. She commiserated with Polly and Faye about extra weight and sagging body parts, but it was only Shirley with whom she felt comfortable discussing the real nitty-gritty. Perhaps that was because Alice had met Shirley when Shirley was in her poor, dithering, befuddled phase, working as a masseuse and only dreaming of larger things. Even though Shirley was the most different from Alice of all the women in the Hot Flash Club, she was also the one Alice felt closest to. Go figure.

They plowed along Orange Street, past the Nantucket Bakery—where Alice cast a longing eye at the door—then turned back, weaving in and out along the narrow one-way streets, until they came out where Pleasant Street met Main, near the Hadwen House, which, Shirley informed her, they were going to visit later.

"Swing your arms as you walk!" Shirley yelled over the roar of the wind. "It will help your heart."

Alice obeyed. She knew she needed Shirley's optimistic attitude to balance out her own more realistic nature. In return, she knew Shirley counted on Alice's opinion for all her major decisions. Shirley often hated Alice's verdicts, especially when it came to men, but they both knew that Alice's instincts about Shirley's love life were always on the money. Just as Alice knew Shirley's concerns about Alice's health were valid.

So here they were, stomping through the puddles down the street together. Alice felt like Shrek with Bambi.

Back at the house, they stripped off their wet gear, pulled on dry clothes, and met in the kitchen for breakfast. Shirley's granola tasted like the crumbs from the bottom of a hamster's cage, which made the fruit and coffee taste even better.

Then Alice went back to bed.

That afternoon, they toured the Hadwen House and the library. They browsed through a few boutiques, attended a noon organ concert, and in the evening, after a healthy meal of Shirley's homemade vegetable soup, they went to a little theater production of a series of one-act comedies.

One afternoon they went through the parlors and the dining room, snapping shots of the various tables, sideboards, and shelves laden with heirlooms and knickknacks. Alice had the photographs developed, labeled them according to room, and put them in a folder. She enjoyed the little task. She was just a little bit bored, although she'd never say so to Shirley. She missed spending time with her granddaughter. She missed sharing an evening drink with Gideon—Shirley insisted she didn't mind if Alice had a drink, but since Shirley was in AA, Alice refrained. She missed the noise and clamor of Boston. She missed her bridge group. She missed her television most of all, although she'd never tell anyone that. There was a TV in the back parlor, but so far no one else had wanted to turn it on. She didn't want to be the TV addict, so she hadn't watched it yet. But she was glad to know it was there.

21

O f the many habits Faye treasured, one of the most pleasurable was wandering around her backyard, still in her kimono, very early in the morning, when the dew still beaded the grass. She carried her mug of hazelnut cinnamon coffee with her, sipping it as she gazed at the perennial beds, idly noting what needed weeding or cutting back. The lilies of the valley were in bloom, their white bells reminding her of the little melody she'd learned so long ago in Girl Scouts. Kneeling, she sang softly.

"White coral bells, along a slender stalk, lilies of the valley deck my garden walk. Oh, don't you wish that you could hear them ring? That will happen only when the fairies sing."

Their troop had learned to sing in rounds, and now in her memory all the sweet voices echoed. For a moment she was suffused with joy as she relived the moment when she was innocent, when she believed in fairies, when she was in awe of their leader, when the achievement of a badge to sew on her green uniform had been a source of enormous pride.

She touched the tip of a dark green leaf, then stood up. Her knees cracked, snapping her right back into the present. These days she often thought of her childhood or adolescent years, or her years as a young wife and mother. The memories arrived intact, a kind of pleasant daydream. Entire blocks of time would disappear—she'd find she'd been staring at the same page of a book as if it were a slide show. Was this a sign of aging? *Another* sign of aging? Should she worry about this? As an artist, she had learned to trust the wanderings of her mind. She wanted to trust the enticements of fate. After all, it was chance that had caused her to meet her wonderful Hot Flash friends, and chance again that sent her to Nantucket, where she'd experienced an almost forgotten sensation—a lust to paint, a craving to be there, painting.

She hugged herself, smiling. What a luxurious summer this was going to be, divided between her garden and Nantucket!

From inside the house came the trilling of her phone. Oh-oh, she thought. That was Aubrey, no doubt. She sighed as she went back inside. What were the final words of the Girl Scout pledge?

I promise to help other people every day, especially those at home.

It was late morning when Faye let herself into Aubrey's condo, using the key he'd given her earlier in the month.

"Hello!" she called.

A muffled sound came from the bedroom.

As she made her way to Aubrey, she noticed that the place was clean—he had a housekeeper come three times a week—but it smelled slightly dusty, as if the windows hadn't been opened all week.

She found her beau lying in bed, staring at the ceiling, his right arm held tight against his chest in a sling. His covers were rumpled, the curtains were closed against the sunny day, the television was on, and he held the remote in his left hand.

In the week since she'd last seen him, he hadn't shaved once.

"Hello, darling!" She bent over and planted a big kiss on his forehead. "I like the edgy, urban beard! Very sexy." With a sniff, she noticed he hadn't bathed for a while, either. "How are you?"

"Not so good." For the first time since she'd met him, Aubrey's voice held a slight quaver of age.

"Poor baby." Faye sank down on the bed next to him. "Does your arm hurt?"

"Yes, my arm hurts. My whole body aches." He shifted on his pillows, groaning just a little. "I'm not sleeping well."

Faye looked around the room. "Have you made yourself some breakfast yet?"

Aubrey shook his head. "It's too difficult, with only one hand."

"Well, then!" Faye said briskly. "We'll get some coffee into you. And what would you like for breakfast? Some nice scrambled eggs?"

Aubrey gave her a brave sad smile, like a Dickensian orphan. "That would be nice. I'm awfully hungry. Carolyn brought me some lunch yesterday, but I didn't really have dinner last night."

This was a needy, invalid side of Aubrey that Faye hadn't seen before. She didn't much like it. Still, she remembered how her husband Jack had turned even a common cold into a Camille-on-her-deathbed performance. "That was silly of you. You can still walk. You still have the use of your left hand. Why don't you come into the kitchen with me now? I'll tell you all about Nantucket while I cook."

"I'd rather stay here," Aubrey pouted. "It hurts to move."

"Aubrey," Faye said bossily. "If you don't move, you're going to get weak."

"Maybe after breakfast," Aubrey conceded.

"Fine." Faye went off to the kitchen, feeling irritated and guilty. She'd planned to spend last week on Nantucket, and she'd refused to change her plans, so Aubrey had been brought home from his operation by his daughter Carolyn, who had stocked his refrigerator with food and his bedside table with books. His housekeeper had come in daily to check on him, and he had a phone next to him, and he had plenty of friends. Still, she told herself as she whisked cream into the eggs, just the way Aubrey liked them, most of his friends were more social than intimate. And Aubrey had always been admired for his elegance, his dapper appearance. He wouldn't want just anyone to see him weak and convalescing. Faye would try to think of this as a kind of honor, a new step in intimacy between them.

She set a silver tray with a small pot of hot coffee, the sugar bowl and creamer, a plate of eggs and toast, a tall glass of orange juice, silverware, and a cloth napkin. When she picked the whole thing up, it was so heavy she nearly dropped it. Her painting arm twinged dangerously. This had to be the last meal she brought him in bed!

Aubrey was still slumped in place when she returned, so she set the tray on a table and plumped up several pillows, positioning them behind his back. With much ado, he scooted up, and she set the tray on his legs.

"I'm going to need you to buy me a bed tray," Aubrey murmured as his tray wobbled on his legs. "To support my food."

"No, you're not," Faye responded. "Because you're not going to get into the habit of eating in bed." She pulled a chair close to him and lifted a mug of coffee she'd made for herself off the tray. "Now let me tell you about Nantucket!"

"I need cayenne pepper," Aubrey said querulously. "I can't eat my eggs without cayenne pepper."

"Right. I'll get it." Faye rushed off to the kitchen. Returning, she set it on his tray, then sat down again.

"Is this cream in the pitcher?" Aubrey asked, peering into the silver vessel. "I don't like cream in my coffee. I prefer two percent."

"But Aubrey, you like cream in your eggs," Faye reminded him.

"Yes, in my eggs, but not in my coffee." He gazed helplessly at Faye.

Faye carried the pitcher back to the kitchen and brought back low fat milk.

"Thank you," Aubrey said. "I'm sorry to put you to so much trouble."

"It's no trouble at all, you know that," Faye told him, settling into her chair. She raised her coffee mug to her lips.

"Oh, am I out of strawberry jam?" Aubrey wondered.

"I don't know. Don't you like blueberry?"

"I'd rather have strawberry." Once again Aubrey made his starving orphan face.

Faye got the strawberry jam.

Finally Aubrey settled down to eat. Faye walked around his bedroom, pulling the curtains and opening the windows to the fresh spring air.

"Don't open the windows," Aubrey insisted. "I'll get chilled."

"No," Faye told him. "You won't get chilled. Because when you're through with breakfast, you're getting dressed and coming to my house."

Aubrey gave a small, satisfied smile.

2 2

O h, Roy, what would *you* do?"
        Wednesday evening, Polly sat at her kitchen table with a glass
        of iced tea nearby, her dog Roy Orbison, all sixty-five lovable
        pounds of him, at her feet, and a deck of cards in her hands.

She had decided to play solitaire. She'd been back from Nantucket
for three nights and two days now, and she hadn't phoned Hugh.

And he hadn't phoned her.

She tried to remember exactly how they'd left things at their last
conversation. It had taken so much courage on her part, to tell Hugh
how she felt about all the attention he paid to his ex-wife Carol, how
much it hurt her when Hugh left Polly to go fix a problem in Carol's life
that anyone else could fix. It had been so hard for Polly to discuss this
with Hugh. She'd felt like a supplicant; she'd been thrown back to childhood, except that when she asked Hugh to tell Carol that he loved Polly,
Polly's body had exploded into a hot flash that would have thrust a mis-
sile to the moon.

On his part, Hugh had grown cool. Polly had actually sensed him
contract away from her. He'd have to think about it, he told Polly, and
his face had been stressed when he spoke. Hugh very seldom looked
stressed. He was a natural optimist, full of energy and good cheer. When
they were together they had really wonderful times. Not for them, sitting
at home in front of the television. No, they went sailing or walking or
they attended lectures and movies. They'd even gone bowling . . . *once.*
Polly's arm had been in pain for days afterward. They'd gone on a
cruise with Faye and Aubrey last Christmas, drinking, dancing, laughing, playing bridge. . . . Polly looked down at the cards in her hand. Back
then, she hadn't expected to be sitting here, alone on a beautiful summer

evening, using a game of solitaire to help her decide whether or not to phone Hugh. When he'd left Polly's house last week, he'd said he'd have to think about everything she said. But he didn't say he'd call her, did he? Had she said she'd call him?

An invisible cloud of gas floated up from where her dog lay. Was this a message from Roy? No. Roy's flatulence was only a function of old age, no omen.

"Oh, for heaven's sake," Polly said to her dog. "What does it matter who calls whom? This isn't high school!" Hugh knew she was going to spend a week in Nantucket. Maybe he didn't know exactly when she'd return. It would simply be *normal* for her to call him.

But would that make Hugh feel as if she were pressuring him?

"Damn it, Roy! The first rule of the Hot Flash Club is Don't let fear hold you back! I'm going to call him!"

Roy shifted position slightly, letting out a low grunt as he moved. Polly chose to interpret this as agreement.

Polly dialed Hugh's number. When he answered, her throat clogged up with apprehension. "Hugh? Hugh, it's Polly."

"Polly!" His deep rumbling voice boomed forth. "Are you back from Nantucket? How was it?"

His friendliness, his *right-thereness* made her sink back into her chair as if it were a bubble bath. "Wonderful. We had a fabulous time. How was your week?"

"Completely boring. I missed you, Polly."

"Oh!" Better and better. "W-would you like to come over tonight?"

Hugh hesitated. "I'd love to. But I have a prior commitment."

Carol, Polly thought, slumping. "Oh."

"There's a Red Sox game on TV tonight," Hugh said teasingly.

"Well, I do have a television set here. And homemade apple pie." There was one in the freezer, just waiting for occasions like this.

"I've got to shower and change, then I'll be right over."

"Lovely." Polly hung up the phone and did a little dance around the kitchen table. "He's coming over tonight, Roy!" As she took out the pie and set the oven to preheat, she sang an old classic: "My boyfriend's back and you're gonna be in trouble!" She'd shower, too, and change out of her frumpy jeans and T-shirt into something more revealing, per- haps her sexy little . . .

Something smelled. She stopped dancing.

What?

Sniffing the air, she looked around, then down, beneath the table.

Roy Orbison lay there, eyes closed, deeply asleep. His long velvety ears splayed out to each side of his head like airplane wings. His tongue hung limply from his mouth. A small puddle of urine spread out from his rounded rear.

"Roy?"

Polly dropped to her knees. Gently, she stroked Roy's head. "Roy? Are you okay?"

The dog didn't respond. She lifted an eyelid. The eye was still, staring. She shook him slightly. He was warm, but limp and heavy.

"No, Roy," Polly whispered desperately. "Not yet." She ran her hands over her beloved fat old friend, trying to find a pulse of life beneath his tan and black hide. But he was gone. He was dead.

"Nooooo," Polly keened. It took all her strength, but she managed to lift her sweet old basset hound into her arms. She cuddled him like a baby, stroking his fat belly, cradling each heavy fat paw in her own hand, kissing the top of his noble head. Her body shook with sobs that should have awakened him, but he lolled loosely in her embrace.

Oh, Roy, her dearest, most trustworthy, most trusting friend! Tucker had given Roy to her when he was only a gawky, goofy puppy who tripped on his ears when he ran but still ran with all the eagerness of hope. Polly had been suffering from empty nest syndrome, her son David off to college, and Roy seemed to understand her unhappiness. Roy had adored Polly, following her from room to room, often accompanying her in her car, his head out the window, long ears blowing backward in the breeze. Roy had been her mainstay when her husband died. Gallant in his youth, Roy became clownish in his old age, as weight and arthritis hampered him; still, he'd followed Polly companionably as she moved through the house. He slept with her at night—his warm, beloved, reliable bulk keeping Polly from feeling the worst of being alone in the dark.

Polly hadn't thought Roy would live *forever*. She knew the average life expectancy of a basset hound was twelve years. Even though Roy was overweight, he'd still lived four years longer than average. . . . Yet could he have lived longer if she'd fed him less? He seemed to share with

Polly a love of food that blocked out all other considerations. Would he have lived longer if she hadn't gone away for a week? No, she refused to believe that. Willy always kept Roy when Polly went away. Roy loved Willy Peck. Willy let Roy sleep with him, too. No, Roy had died of old age, and she was glad for his swift deliverance. He did not suffer, he hadn't had to undergo surgeries or endure unpleasant medications. He'd had a happy life and now he'd had a quick and easy death, and Polly was grateful for that.

But what was she going to do without him? Polly wailed. She cuddled her dog against her bosom and wept.

"Polly?" Suddenly Hugh was there. "Polly, what happened?"

"Roy," she sobbed. Her face and her T-shirt and much of Roy Orbison's long drooping dewlaps were soaked with her tears.

"Oh, Polly." Hugh knelt next to her. "I'm so sorry."

"My poor old boy," Polly cried. "My sweet old buddy."

Hugh went off, returning with a snifter of brandy. He sat down on the floor next to her. "Drink this."

Polly took the glass and sipped. The liquid burned, and she choked, but swallowing made her catch her breath, and Hugh's presence next to her was a comfort.

Hugh didn't try to make her relinquish Roy's body. He didn't point out that her clothes were getting soiled. He put one arm around her shoulder and held her as she grieved.

"How old was he?" Hugh asked.

Polly knew Hugh knew. But it helped to talk. "Sixteen."

"Old for a basset hound."

"Yes. Yes, he had a good long life."

"Remember the night he got a pastry out of the trash and the tape on the pastry box got stuck to his ear? We heard this odd scratching noise, and here Roy came, a little white cardboard box dragging along on the floor attached to him."

Polly smiled. "He was such a clown."

"Take another sip of brandy, Polly."

Polly obeyed. The sharpest anguish was abating as she leaned against Hugh, still cradling her dog in her lap. She was so grateful for Hugh's presence. She was so glad Hugh had gotten to know Roy.

An odd vibration rang in the air. For a moment, Polly had no idea

THE HOT FLASH CLUB *Chills Out* • 1 2 5

what it could be—she was so deeply engrossed in her dog's life and death, she wouldn't have been surprised to see an angel appear to lift the basset hound from her arms.

"Sorry." Hugh took his cell phone from his jacket. He listened, then removed his arm from Polly, stood up, and walked to the other side of the kitchen. "This isn't a good time." He turned his back to Polly, but she could still see him sigh. "Carol, the place was just exterminated. There can't be any bats." He shook his head. "Aren't all the doors locked? The windows? And I personally checked to see that all the fireplace flues are closed." Another sigh. "Okay. I'll be right there."

He knelt next to Polly. "I have to go."

"Oh, please," Polly pleaded, unashamed of her blotchy, tear-streaked need. "Please stay with me, Hugh."

He looked miserable. "I'll be back. Let's phone one of your friends and have her come over. Alice? Faye?"

Not this, Polly thought, not this now. She did not want Carol imposing herself into this sacred hour of Roy Orbison's death. She didn't want her own jealousies to blot and soil the love she felt for her animal companion and the depth of mourning he deserved.

"I'll call someone in a minute," Polly said through swollen, icy lips. "Go on, Hugh. I'll be fine."

Thursday, after her walk and shower, when Alice pulled on her trousers, she realized they were just a fraction of an inch looser than they had been. And today, the fourth day of her regimen, she didn't feel like going back to bed. Lord, maybe Shirley was right. Maybe she really could regain some of her old energy! That was more exciting than the prospect of looking good.

Perhaps her mood was elevated because today, for the first time, the sun was shining. All around Nantucket, flowers were bursting forth with blooms opening to the sun. All the buildings and streets glowed with a fresh-washed shine.

"Come with me on a bike ride," Shirley begged.

Alice shook her head. "I've never been on a bike."

"Then now's the time to start."

"Not today, Shirley. Give me a break, okay?" When Shirley hesitated, Alice said, "You know I wouldn't be able to keep up with you if I came along. Not to mention, I'd probably fall off in the middle of the street, get run over, and ruin your little jaunt."

Shirley grinned. "Well, okay. You have been good." Tying a sweater around her neck, she said, "I'm going to rent a bike at Young's and take along a little picnic lunch. I won't be back till late this afternoon, okay?"

"Okay. I'm going to cruise the shops for some little presents for my granddaughter."

"Great! See you tonight."

Alice watched Shirley hurry away. Bless Shirley, who got so excited about something as boring as a bike ride! Pouring herself another cup of coffee, she went out to the back porch and sank down in one of the inviting wicker rockers that looked out over the small backyard. A bird flitted from tree to tree. Tulips stood erect and blazing in the warm sun. The grass needed mowing. Shirley said Nora Salter had someone who took care of that, so Alice didn't have to worry about the yard. Right now, she didn't have to worry about a thing. She didn't have to be anywhere. She didn't have to feed the baby or rub Gideon's back or review a bill for The Haven. She *couldn't* play bridge. She was absolutely idle.

She wasn't sure she liked it.

Her thoughts drifted back to the days when she was a divorced young woman with two little boys, trying to excel at her job and make decent grades in her night school courses. If anyone had ever told her that someday she'd be here, sitting on a porch in the middle of this WASP stronghold, she would have laughed. But she'd been happy then. That was just the way she was, happiest when she had fifty different things to do at the same time. Shirley told her she had to learn to slow down, to enjoy the moment, to *be here now*. But Alice found that when she sat still for long, her thoughts scrolled back through the past . . . or forward, to the future. And what could her future hold? She was sixty-three. She was almost *old*. She'd had so many wonderful things in her life, how could she expect anything more?

A movement from the yard next door caught her eye. A wooden fence divided this yard from the other, but here on the porch, Alice was high enough to be able to watch that old biddy—what was her name? Oh, right, Lucinda someone. Lucinda Snot Nose, that was it—come toddling out along a little path. The older woman wore baggy canvas trousers, rubber gardening clogs, a loose denim shirt, canvas work gloves, and a floppy straw hat. She carried a basket of tools which she set down next to her. She knelt—it took her forever to carefully, carefully, fold her body down to the ground—then took a while to inspect the ground in front of her. Finally, she reached out, took hold of a weed by its stem, and pulled. The plant resisted. Lucinda pulled harder, not in one fierce tug, but with a slow, steady, relentless effort. When the weed finally surrendered, Lucinda said, "Aha!" and held it up triumphantly, like a prize. She did this over and over again, placing the derelict plants in a neat little pile by her side.

Alice had never done much gardening. She'd never had the time. Now she lived in a condo on the Boston waterfront, so her gardening was limited to watering a few houseplants—when she remembered. Lucinda seemed to be in what Shirley would call "the zone." But it wasn't much of a thrill to watch. Alice lifted her cup to her lips, but it was empty. Time to go shopping for baby gifts.

The truth was, Shirley hadn't been on a bike since she was a little girl on a tricycle, except for the exercise bikes she'd tested when they were installed in The Haven.

Every time she'd come to Nantucket, she'd noticed people spinning effortlessly past on their beautiful, sleek machines. They'd looked so healthy! So athletic! So absolutely *superior* as they glided down the street, arms extended to the handlebars, legs working in an almost musical rhythm, sunlight gilding their skin. She admired the striped spandex racing outfits of the serious bikers, but when she spotted a woman on a sky blue bike with a wicker basket on the handlebars and a bouquet of daisies in the basket, she developed an instant passion to be just like that.

Young's Bicycle Shop insisted she wear a helmet that rather ruined her dream image—she wanted to sport a straw hat with a pink ribbon trailing down her back. But she took their advice about safety seriously and promised to wear it. She asked for the least challenging bike they had, confessing that she hadn't ridden for "a while." A nice teenage guy who worked there took her across the street to the long parking lot where trucks waited to board the steamship and let her practice riding up and down until she got the hang of the hand brakes. She studied the map he gave her, memorized his instructions about signaling, and then, with her heart thumping in her chest, she set off.

It was a good time for a novice, he had told her. Mid-June and the island traffic wasn't crazy yet. Midweek, and there weren't as many people out. If she went along North Water Street, she'd have several blocks of the uneven spine-wobbling stones to cross, the boy told her. He suggested she bike up Broad Street to Center Street and then across to Orange. That way she'd just have the cobblestones of Main Street to deal with. She followed his advice. As she went past Nora Salter's Orange Street house, she flicked her eyes sideways, hoping she'd see Alice—hoping Alice would see *her,* pedaling along on her cute silver bike, all ease and coordination, as if she'd been born playing tennis, sailing boats, riding bikes. But Alice wasn't there, and she was afraid to take her eyes off the road for more than a second.

Really, it was surprisingly easy. Shirley liked the way her pumping legs invigorated her, the way the street unrolled under her slender wheels, and the houses wound past, windows reflecting the sunlight at her like dozens of little lighthouses. She wasn't even winded when she reached the Rotary, but she was intimidated by all the traffic, so she dismounted and walked the bike until she got onto the 'Sconset Bike Path. A short way down, she walked her bike again, as she crossed the road.

Now she was on the Polpis Road Bike Path. She passed forests and houses tucked behind flower beds, a car dealership, and Moors End Farm, which in August had, she'd been told, the best corn on the planet. She began to puff as she struggled to pedal up a hill, and from here she saw the island spread out in all directions. This was a very Zen activity, Shirley decided, as she rolled along. Every part of her body and brain was in use, she was breathing deeply, she was focused, she was conscious of the roll of the land, the curve of the path, the spots on the path where trees cast shadows, like pools of coolness, as Shirley zipped through. The moors, she knew from maps, were on her right, a rolling landscape of greenery in an amazing variety of shades. Occasionally, a trophy house loomed up, perched like a bloated toad on the horizon. She kept pedaling, past pine trees and twisted scrub oak nestled among Scotch broom covered with yellow buds. Silvery beach grass was tangled with the dark green of rosa rugosa and a shrub covered with white flowers blazed everywhere. Vines curled around trees and fence posts and a mysterious sweet fragrance occasionally greeted Shirley as she sped past.

It was thirst, not exhaustion, that made her finally stop. She hadn't thought to bring lunch or even a bottle of water. Stupid. Pulling her bike off the path, she collapsed in the shade of a juniper tree. Leaning against its trunk, she let her legs rest on the ground and discovered to her surprise that they were trembling. Had she overdone it? Probably. She had no idea how long she'd been biking. She had no idea how far she'd come. Now that she'd stopped, she realized she was not only thirsty and tired, she was starving. Well, she'd give herself a nice long rest, then bike back to town, right to Orange Street.

Her pulse slowed and her breathing returned to normal. It was very quiet here. She could hear the birds sing. She could hear rustlings in the bushes. She could almost hear the sun shine. It was a cool day, perhaps only about seventy degrees, but she'd sweated through her lavender spandex pants and her loose tee. She'd have a shower when she got back, and a huge lunch. Her stomach growled at the thought.

She'd only been biking for about an hour, she thought. She'd bike faster on the way back, push herself a bit, get home sooner.

She jumped on her bike and headed back toward town.

But something was wrong.

For some reason, she couldn't match her former pace. It was as if an invisible opposing force were pushing her backward. Then she suddenly understood: an invisible opposing force *was* pushing against her—the *wind*. No wonder she'd biked along so effortlessly. She'd had the wind behind her! With it facing her like this, it was as if she were trying to bike through some kind of clear marmalade, some substance that slowed her down and would not yield. Her thighs burned with the effort. She could feel her heart churning. Her breath pounded in her ears. The slightest incline down felt like a blessing, and the slightest incline up, a curse.

After a few moments, she wondered if she were going to be able to make it. Her face was hot with exertion, her mouth uncomfortably dry. It was like a terrible nightmare, where the harder she pedaled, the slower she went. Suddenly all the "cute" sayings she'd heard about "Let the wind be at your back" made sharp, brutal sense.

She could hear a vehicle coming down the road. Wanting not to appear as completely out of shape as she obviously was, she tried to sit back on the bike, instead of leaning nearly collapsed over the handlebars. She still had that much vanity left. An old red truck rattled past her.

To her surprise, it turned in a driveway and came back, pulling onto the verge, parallel to the bike path.

"Hello, there!"

Shirley could not summon the coordination to keep pedaling while looking away from the path. In a clumsy flurry of movement, she squeezed the handlebars, stopped the bike, and staggered to a stop. Then she focused on the red truck. A golden Lab stuck her head out the passenger window and barked a greeting.

"Reggie!" she cried with delight. "Harry!" How lucky was this, that the one person she knew on Nantucket had appeared at this particular moment in time! Gosh, it was like Fate!

"You're working pretty hard against that wind." Harry grinned.

"I'm an idiot!" Shirley told him, embarrassed by the way her chest was heaving as she tried to catch her breath. "I never thought about it!"

"Would you like me to drive you back to town?"

"Oh, would you, *please?*"

Harry turned off his engine, climbed out of the car, and came over to the path. "People always forget about the wind here. Well, the first couple of times they do." Effortlessly, he hefted the silver bike up and laid it gently in the bed of his truck. Then he opened the passenger door. "Scoot over, Reggie. We've got company."

Shirley climbed up into the cab of the truck and collapsed on the seat. "Oh, man, does this feel good."

Harry got in on his side and slammed the door. "Where were you headed?"

"Oh, I don't know. Everywhere!" Shirley waved her hands. "It's so beautiful here."

"Would you like me to drive you home through the moors?"

"Sure, I guess, if you have time."

"I've got all the time in the world." Harry put the key in the ignition and the truck rumbled to life.

They followed the main road for a few minutes, until they came to a dirt road nearly obscured by bushes. Harry turned off onto it, and soon they were bumping along a rutted track, away from civilization, into a sweeping sea of green.

"It's not like the mainland here," Shirley remarked. "Everything's so low to the ground."

"That's why it's called the moors," Harry said. "Forests grew here once, centuries ago, but all the trees were cut for timber for houses, then sheep were pastured here, and they destroyed the vegetation. What you've got left is heath land and some hearty wild plants, and also a lot of endangered flowers. Later, in the summer, the sweetest wild blueberries grow out here, and beach plum, too." He braked to a stop and pointed out the window. "See that patch of white flowers, low to the ground? They're called Quaker-ladies."

Shirley smiled. "I've been reading about the Quakers on the island."

He raised an eyebrow. "Have you?"

"Yes, and I want to go see the Quaker meeting house, later on in the summer, when I have more time. There's so much to see and do here."

He set the car in motion again. "True. Though most tourists stick to the beaches."

Shirley studied his profile. "Why do I get the feeling you don't approve of 'most tourists'?"

"Because most tourists litter the beaches and trample endangered vegetation. They drive monster SUVs and destroy the environment." He flashed a grin her way. "I've become an obstreperous crab in my old age."

"You're not so old," Shirley told him. Neither was she, she thought, with her heart going wild in her chest. Harry's sideways smile had kick-started a little engine in her torso. Her body was flooding her with a wonderfully pleasant sensation. Her cheeks tingled, and so did—oh my gosh!—her belly, way down low. She looked out the window, letting the breeze cool her burning skin.

Harry steered the car over a grassy track and onto another dirt road that plunged downhill past a small pond. A short distance on, he pulled off the road and turned off the engine. "Let me show you something few people see."

Shirley hopped down from the truck and followed Harry and Reggie. Through a gap in tall bushes, she saw a round blue pond, its waters shimmering beneath the sun.

"We call this the doughnut pond," he told her, pointing to the small island in the middle.

Shirley surveyed the area. The pond was ringed with grasses, shrubs, and trees. "Over there!" she whispered excitedly. "What is it?"

Harry smiled. "White heron."

"Oh, she's so pretty! Like a painting."

Harry looked down at her. Shirley could feel him studying her face. She felt a warmth emanating from him that was setting the tingling in her body to a full boil.

"You really like it out here," Harry remarked.

Shirley moved away from him, pretending interest in the pale green grasses, striped, threaded, and wound with darker plants and vines. It was either move away, or jump the guy. "Do I? I guess so," Shirley responded honestly. "I've never spent much time in the country. I run a wellness spa, The Haven, about thirty miles outside Boston. My condo's there, too. We do have a large grounds with space for badminton and croquet and a woods with a walking path. Still, it's all part of, well, *civilization*." She sat down on a hillock of tough moss, linked her arms around her knees, and stared out at the water. "Just think, all this is here, all the time, while we go on with our busy lives."

Harry sat down next to her, not too close, but not too far away. Reggie went sniffing off into the high grass ringing the pond. A large bird flew overhead.

"Hawk," Harry told her.

"Wow."

"Yes, this place is a real bird sanctuary."

"And other animals, too?" Shirley pointed to a set of tracks in the sand near the water.

"Deer come here to drink. Yes, we've sure got deer. Too many of them. And rabbits."

"Oh, I love rabbits. I hope I see some."

Harry laughed. "You won't be able to miss them." He pointed to a long-stemmed plant with a tiny blue flower. "Blue-eyed grass."

Shirley laughed. "What a great name. As if the grass can see."

"Not necessarily. I mean, we say the 'eye' of the storm. Meaning the center of something."

Shirley sat in silence for a while. "I think . . ." she said musingly, ". . . I think I ought to come out here by myself now and then. And maybe my friends should, too. I mean, it seems to me that nature like this"—she waved her hands around—"without any sign or evidence of humans, is like a kind of halfway house between life and death. What we construe as death. I mean, there's life, but not *human* life. You can hear the birds rustling, and sort of sense the, well, the *alertness* of the plants, and so you think, hey, it's really okay, it's different, the natural world, but still so *vivid*, and it will be okay when you die and leave your human body, because there's all this to get to be part of."

Harry didn't reply, but Shirley could feel his eyes on her.

She looked at him. "I know. I'm so weird. I'm sorry."

"No," he protested. "Please don't apologize. I like what you said. It was interesting. I'm just thinking about it." He reached over, putting his warm hand on her wrist. "I think you've articulated something I've often felt."

His touch made something inside Shirley melt. Their eyes met and held. Gosh, he was good-looking. Shirley felt her lips part. Harry seemed poised—was he going to *kiss* her?

An explosion of noise made them turn. The golden Lab came bounding out of the pond, her coat wet and slimy with weeds, a filthy stick in her mouth. With an expression of great pride, she presented it to Shirley.

Shirley laughed, stood up, and threw the stick for the dog, who plunged happily back into the water. They played the game about a dozen times.

Harry finally stopped them. "Come on, Regina, you spoiled old thing. Let's go."

The dog obviously understood. She lunged through the grass to the truck, pausing to shake the water from her coat.

"Have you seen 'Sconset yet?" Harry asked as they settled in the truck.

"Not yet," Shirley told him. "I'd like to. I've seen pictures of the lighthouse and those little fishermen's cottages."

"Let me take you out there someday," Harry said.

"I'd like that," Shirley said.

She noticed, as they drove back into town, how Harry stopped to let other vehicles turn out onto the street. "You're a polite driver," she told him.

"We've all got to be, in the summer. It gets so crowded. If we aren't courteous, we get all riled up over something that in the scheme of things is absolutely infinitesimal."

Shirley smiled. She liked that he used the word *courteous*.

"Now where are you living, exactly?"

When she told him the address on Orange Street, he gave a little snort of surprise. "You're staying at Nora Salter's house?"

"I used to be her masseuse in Boston. We became friends, and she's one of the investors in The Haven." She glanced at him. "And you know her?"

Harry pulled his truck up onto the sidewalk in front of the house. "Oh, yeah. Used to come to her house, back when I was on the cocktail party circuit. Never saw a place crammed with so much stuff." He jumped out of the truck, unlatched the tailgate, and lifted her bike down to the ground.

Shirley took hold of the handlebars. "Harry, thank you so much for taking me through the moors. I loved it."

"My pleasure."

For a moment, they just stood there, smiling at each other.

"I'll call you." Harry dipped his head in a kind of salute, then jumped back in his old red truck and rattled away, leaving Shirley so giddy she had to restrain herself from hugging her bike.

On the last Thursday in June, it was finally warm enough on the island to cast off sweaters and long pants. Shirley, in a swirly summer dress, and Alice, chic in a black linen shift, strolled along Straight Wharf, idly gazing at the sleek yachts and pleasure boats docked in the harbor. The day was warm, bright, and mild, the water a dazzling blue.

"There they are!" Shirley cried, pointing to the Hy-Line catamaran as it rounded Brant Point. "Oh, I just love these boat trips. It makes everything so celebratory!"

As the ferry glided near, people on the upper deck waved. Alice and Shirley waved back. The boat drew to a stop. The deckhands set the ramp in place and the passengers filed down to the cobblestoned dock. Alice and Shirley hurried to greet their friends. They all hugged and talked at once as Polly and Faye grabbed their luggage off the blue luggage trolleys. Marilyn had only a small canvas purse; she was just here for the day. She'd driven Faye and Polly down, left her car in a Hyannis lot, and would drive Alice and Shirley home.

"We're having lunch at the Ropewalk." Alice led them over the bricks to the restaurant at the water's edge. "That way Marilyn, Shirley, and I will be right here to catch the boat back."

The host met them on the patio. "Inside or out, ladies?"

"Inside, please, but could we have a table by the water?" Shirley requested sweetly.

"Absolutely." He led them into a large room with a bar along an inner wall and tables on the far side, overlooking the docks where smaller craft bobbed gently in their berths. Gulls swooped overhead, and a pair of mallards paddled idly near the pier, waiting for a bit of bread to drop. A beautiful young couple in bathing suits sunbathed on the deck of their polished teak sailboat. Farther out, a fabulous private yacht slid majestically into the harbor.

"This is too blissful," Faye said, looking around with a sigh. "I'm going to go wild and order a drink."

"We make dynamite strawberry daiquiris," the waiter informed her with a wink.

"Fabulous!" Faye clapped her hands together. "*So* healthy!"

Everyone else ordered one, too, except Shirley, who asked for a cranberry juice with lots of ice.

"Now," Alice said, "tell me. How's life in the real world?"

Marilyn, Polly, and Faye exchanged glances.

"We talked nonstop on the ride down," Marilyn informed Alice and Shirley. "We still haven't solved our problems."

Polly had dark circles beneath her eyes. Quietly, she said, "And isn't there a rule that we can't worry when we're on Nantucket? Because if there is, I've got nothing to talk about."

"Okay, okay, rule rescinded," Alice said quickly. She put a hand on Polly's arm. "What happened?"

Polly's eyes filled with tears. "Roy Orbison died." She covered her face with her hands. "Sorry. Sorry. Don't mean to be so emotional."

Faye patted Polly's shoulder. "Polly loved that old dog so much. Plus, he was sort of the last tie she had with Tucker."

"And to add insult to injury," Marilyn added, "Hugh came over to be with Polly when the dog died, but then Carol phoned him and he went off to help her deal with a rat or a bat or something."

The waiter brought their drinks, tall, frosty glasses filled with frothy pink liquid, topped with a dollop of whipped cream and a strawberry. Shirley's cranberry juice was adorned with an orange slice. They toasted and, instead of taking dainty sips, pretty much slammed back their drinks.

Polly played with her straw, stirring it in the pink drink. "Well, he did come back . . ."

Faye shook her head angrily. "Yeah, *three hours later*. Polly had phoned me, and I drove over to be with her. We wrapped Roy's body in one of Polly's homemade quilts."

"And I phoned my son." Polly sniffed. "David drove over to see him. He was sad, too. He put Roy's body in his truck and told me he'd bury him on his farm. I didn't especially want Roy out there, since my daughter-in-law makes me feel about as welcome as the chicken pox, but David had always loved Roy so much. I guess Roy's spirit would be as happy to be there as anywhere."

"You've had to deal with so much death in the past few years," Shirley said sympathetically. "Your husband. Your mother-in-law. Now your beloved dog."

Polly nodded, letting the tears spill down her face. "That's true. But you know, it's all part of the cycle of life. I understand that. I accept that. It wouldn't be so bad if I felt like I was *somehow* part of the future. I mean, it's nice to know I have a grandson, but Amy keeps him sequestered out there on the farm. I'm not really part of the little boy's life. I'm not part of my son's life, either. You're so lucky, Alice, and you are too, Marilyn, because you've got grandchildren who live close to you, whom you get to see whenever you want."

"But my grandchildren live in San Francisco," Faye reminded her.

"And I don't have children or grandchildren," Shirley said.

"Well, you have a boyfriend," Polly told Faye. "And Shirley, you do, too."

Shirley made a face. "I don't think I'd call Stan a boyfriend." She snorted. "Believe, me, he's certainly no antidote to the thought of death."

"Stan's honest, reliable, and trustworthy," Alice told Shirley.

"So was Roy Orbison," Shirley shot back.

"Maybe you should get a new dog," Faye suggested to Polly.

"Maybe I should," Polly agreed.

"Maybe," Shirley joked, "*I* should!"

The waiter came, took their orders, and went off.

"Because," Polly continued, "I'm going to end it with Hugh."

"Oh, Polly," Shirley cried. "Are you sure?"

Polly nodded. "It's just too insulting, the way he leaves whenever his ex-wife calls. I'll never be part of his complete life. I can't share a future with him. I haven't even met his grandchildren, and he dotes on them, goes to their recitals and games. I'm treated like a mistress, even though he's no longer married."

"Well, now, hang on." Faye folded her arms on the table. "Think about it, Polly. What's so wrong with being a mistress? What's so wrong with just having fun with him? Because you do have a wonderful time with him."

"True," Polly conceded.

"We're all older now, and we should be able to define our relationships differently from how we did when we were young and wanted to have homes and children and all those complications. Perhaps you could just have fun with each other."

"Yeah!" Shirley liked that idea. "Stay in a kind of perpetual state of romance! Like you're always dating. So you don't have to argue about utility bills or who should put gas in the car."

Polly shook her head. "That seems so *incomplete*. I want the whole thing, the 'for better or worse' bit."

"Think about that seriously," Faye warned. "I can tell you, I'm not so sure I like the 'in sickness and in health' part at our age."

Alice turned to Faye. "How *is* Aubrey?"

"Driving me out of my mind." Faye tossed back the rest of her drink. "He *loves* being an invalid. I swear, I sometimes think he is truly regressing mentally. They say people become childish when they grow older, but Aubrey's only in his early seventies. He wants to be waited on hand and foot, and he needs constant coddling, and the part of being with him that I loved has just vanished into thin air! He's not charming, he's not interesting, he doesn't care how I feel. It's completely about taking care of him. And it's not like he's got a terminal illness! He's just got a wonky shoulder!"

Sentimental Shirley asked, "But what if he were Jack?"

"If he were Jack," Faye said, "we would have already gone through scores of years of give and take. Jack would have taken care of me, and I would have taken care of him. Besides, Jack would never have been such a *baby*."

"But we're all older now," Alice pointed out sensibly. "We're sliding out of our 'Golden Years' into our 'Rusty Years.' Maybe in another year, Aubrey will be taking care of you."

"Yeah," Shirley agreed, nodding her head. "Remember, Aubrey was pretty sweet to you when you were down with your ankle and neck over Christmas."

"Not *this* sweet," Faye argued. "He came over a lot, brought me flowers and food, but *I'm* fixing all his meals, running all his errands, adjusting his pillows, I'm his constant nursemaid. And I *know* I *thanked* Aubrey when I was down. He's gotten so petulant and cranky, he never thanks me. He just gets irritated if I don't read his mind and bring him his ice pack the moment he wants it."

"Women are more nurturing by nature." Shirley looked uncomfortable. "I know that's not a feminist position to take, but I think it's true."

"Fine," Faye said. "But believe me, I've done more than my share of nurturing this guy."

Alice looked thoughtful. "It's not like he's going to be down with his shoulder forever, Faye."

"No," Faye agreed. "Only over this summer, when I want to be here, landscape painting." She looked around the table. "Come on, if I were a man, no one would expect me to give up a chance to start painting seriously again in order to stay home taking care of Aubrey. I mean, he's not even really sick. If he were, then I do care about him enough to nurture him. But he's not seriously ill. And I'm seriously *excited* about getting back into my work! And I am getting older, I don't have that much time left."

The waiter brought their lunches. They all tucked in with delight. After a few bites, Faye's mood lightened.

"So Alice, tell me, how was your week here?"

Alice shot a triumphant look at Shirley. "It's been great! Shirley has kept me on an exercise plan, and I haven't weighed myself, but my pants are just a tad bit looser."

"And we've gone to some fun plays and concerts," Shirley chimed in.

"And I've done a bit of shopping for my granddaughter," Alice added. "I can't wait to see her. And Gideon, too."

Faye looked at Shirley. "What about Stan? Are you looking forward to seeing him again?"

Shirley yawned.

"Now, Shirley," Alice interrupted. "Stan's a good man."

"Yeah, but life with him would be like one long dental appointment," Shirley shot back. "Might be good for me, but it sure wouldn't be fun."

"Maybe you'll meet a man on Nantucket!" Polly suggested.

A waitress passing by overheard. "You know what they say about meeting a man on this island? The odds are good, but the goods are odd."

The Hot Flash Club laughed. Shirley laughed the loudest. She couldn't stop thinking of Harry, but she wasn't ready to tell her friends about him yet. And really, there wasn't much to tell.

Alice looked mischievous. "Nantucket women have a history of being satisfied without a man. They had to be inventive—so many of their husbands were away for years, off at sea hunting whales. So they created a little, um, *device,* out of baked clay, as a substitute. Shaped like a phallus and called a 'he's-at-home.' "

Shirley giggled.

Faye was astonished. "Good grief, Alice, where do you find information like this?"

Alice smiled. "I read an article by Tom Congdon in *Forbes FYI,* entitled 'Mrs. Coffin's Consolation.' "

"What's *Forbes FYI*?" Polly asked.

Alice looked slightly abashed. "A supplement to the business magazine. I glance at it occasionally."

"I'm sure women have invented sexual substitutes since the beginning of time," Marilyn said.

"Well, *you* don't need one," Shirley pointed out. "You've found a good guy!"

"True." Marilyn smiled, looking smug. "Ian is wonderful. I do love him. And I want to marry him. But at the same time, Polly, I can see how having only a good-time relationship might not be a bad idea."

"Is his son a problem?" Alice asked.

"Well . . ." Marilyn leaned back in her chair, ignoring the french fries that had come with her sandwich. "I guess Angus is no more a problem than my mother. Life is just so messy. Especially now that Angus has a puppy whom he keeps forgetting to house-train."

"Oh boy." Alice pinched her nose.

"You got it," Marilyn told her.

"Oh, Polly," Shirley said. "I just can't stop thinking about you breaking it off with Hugh. I think you should give that careful thought."

"I will, this week," Polly said.

The waiter came up. "Coffee? Dessert?"

Everyone ordered coffee.

Marilyn looked at her watch. "Our ferry should be here any moment."

"Anything we should know about the house?" Faye asked Alice and Shirley.

"We've left a lot of food and toilet paper," Alice told her.

Shirley leaned forward. "You might want to be very careful with any precious jewelry. I don't know what's going on, but I think the house has a pack rat. I've now lost two different earrings."

"I've lost an earring there, too," Faye said, then shrugged. "But they're so easy to lose. They get caught when we take off our shirts, they fall out when we walk—the cobblestones here are so uneven."

"I'm just saying," Shirley insisted. "Be careful with good jewelry."

"Do you think there's a ghost in the house?" Marilyn asked, looking amused.

Everyone turned expectantly to Shirley.

Shirley looked apologetic. "It was probably just noises on the street. You know the Orange Street house is so close to other houses and to the road, and I'm used to sleeping out at The Haven, which is so quiet. . . ."

"Go on," Faye insisted.

"Two nights ago something woke me up. Sounds. Some kind of—*thumps*. And some, I don't know, some sort of shuffling noises, as if someone were walking around downstairs."

"What time was it?" Polly asked, eyes wide.

"About three in the morning."

"Did you hear the noises?" Marilyn asked Alice.

Alice shook her head.

"Please. Alice snores too loudly to hear King Kong fart in her ear," Shirley joked. "So anyway, I decided to go downstairs to investigate."

"Brave of you!" Polly declared.

"Well, I feel a responsibility to Nora," Shirley said. "I'd like to find out who's taking things."

"Did you see anyone?" Marilyn asked.

"No." Shirley leaned forward, a new urgency in her voice. "But we think a little Fabergé box disappeared from the front parlor table."

Alice added, "You know those photos I took? I compared them with what's there now—not an easy task, let me add. And I didn't get as close up as I should have. I'm going to take more photographs with more detail. But anyway, there is a little box missing."

"I wonder whether anyone on the island buys antiques," Polly said. "Maybe I'll check around, see if I can spot any of her pieces."

"Good idea," Alice told Polly.

"Here comes our ferry!" Marilyn cried.

They paid their bills and hurried out to the dock where they all hugged once again. Marilyn, Alice, and Shirley headed up the ramp and onto the boat. Polly and Faye stayed on shore, waving until the boat left the dock, and with three blasts of its horn, sped out into the harbor and around Brant Point, out of sight.

When Faye and Polly arrived at the Orange Street house, they saw Kezia's silver SUV parked in the driveway. They discovered Kezia herself at the back of the house. Her baby Joe was stashed in a backpack, a teething ring in one hand and his mother's thick black braid in the other.

"Hi, guys!" Kezia greeted them with a big smile. She glowed with a healthy tan and energy. "Sorry to barge in on you, but I thought it might be a good time to come take your trash. You've all done such a *good job* sorting it!"

"Thanks." Faye found herself both amused and vaguely insulted by the younger woman's compliment. They'd read the instructions Kezia'd left for them in the kitchen, and they weren't quite so senile they couldn't differentiate among the bins set on the back porch stating in clear large print: *Glass. Misc. paper. Garbage. Plastics. Aluminum cans.*

Perhaps Kezia felt Faye's coolness. "I'm sorry if I came at a bad time. I just don't know when you guys are here. Want to set up a pickup schedule for me? Or you can phone me."

Polly suggested, "Could we schedule it for some afternoon? I want to be able to wander around in my nighty with a cup of coffee in the mornings."

"Good idea," Faye agreed.

Kezia pulled a tiny electronic toy from her back pocket. "Wednesday afternoons are free for me and Joe."

"That works for us," Faye said.

"Great!" With surprising ease, Kezia hefted four sagging trash bags out of their bins, bounded out the back door and down the back porch steps, and disappeared around the corner of the house. Faye and Polly heard her singing, "Giddy-up horsie!" to her little boy.

A few seconds later, Kezia bounded back up into the kitchen. "That's that!" She went to the sink and vigorously scrubbed her hands. "Now!" Turning to face them, she asked, "Is there anything I can do for you?"

"Actually," Faye said, "if you have time, could you drive us out to the airport? We've rented a Jeep for the summer and we want to pick it up today."

"Cool! Let's go!"

Polly sat in back so she could play with baby Joe. Faye took the passenger seat in front. "Were you born on Nantucket?" she asked Kezia.

Kezia tossed back her head and laughed. "I wish! No, I was born in New Jersey, came here during college to make some money waiting tables one summer, met B.J., and fell madly in love. With him and with the island. Joe and his family are natives, and so is little Joe."

"But Kezia's an island name, isn't it?" Faye inquired.

Kezia gave Faye an admiring glance. "You've been boning up on island history! Yes, Kezia's an island name. My given name was Kathy, and I just felt it was so boring, and Kezia's so unusual, I legally changed it. I've never met another Kezia! Plus, it makes me feel more linked to the island. I'm just dotty about the place."

"Do you own a house here?" Faye asked cautiously. "I mean, I know how expensive they are."

"We do own a house!" Kezia nodded so enthusiastically her braid bounced. "It's just a tiny little thing, not at all like Nora's grand old heap, but we own it. Out in Tom Never's Head. My clever ol' husband built it with his own hands. Our mortgage is humongous, but we've got about a thousand years to pay it off, so that's all right. Once we build another room on to it, we're going to have another baby!"

Braking exuberantly, Kezia pulled up in front of the airport's doors. "Car rental agency's right in there."

"Thanks, Kezia." Faye was very aware of her own size and speed next to Kezia. She couldn't *jump* out like Kezia. She felt like a lumbering old mastodon as she eased her bulk down from the high SUV seat. When Polly extracted herself from the back and joined her on the sidewalk,

Faye was grateful for her company. She felt less of a circus fat lady with Polly there.

The two of them waved as Kezia sped away.

"I need a nap," Polly said, only half-joking, to Faye. "Did we *ever* have that kind of energy?"

"Did we ever have that kind of body?" Faye wondered in return. "I don't think I did. She's so slim!"

"She's young." Polly and Faye were quiet for a moment, as if paying their respects to their own lost youth.

Then Faye cheered up. "Come on. Let's get our car!"

At the rental counter, they handed over their driver's licenses, signed papers, and were duly given the keys to a four-wheel-drive Jeep. They whooped when they saw it—it was as red as a hot flash! Faye played chauffeur on the trip back to town, driving slowly as Polly navigated. There was no garage attached to the Orange Street house. They were fortunate, they'd been told, even to have a shoebox-size brick parking spot squeezed between their house and the one on the left.

"Good grief!" Polly shrieked as Faye carefully inched the Jeep into place. "One millimeter wrong and you gouge the house with the side mirror!"

"This will teach us patience," Faye muttered. When she'd parked the Jeep successfully, she unfastened her seatbelt. "What next?"

"Let's go everywhere!" Polly suggested.

"Excellent idea!" Faye fastened her seatbelt again.

All afternoon they toured the island, rattling over cobblestones, making paper-clip turns from one narrow lane to another, shrieking with laughter when the side mirrors almost touched the walls of houses built right next to the street. They exclaimed with pleasure as the landscape opened out on the long road to Madaket on the far western tip of the island. They sighed with admiration for the romantic mansions along the Cliff with its stunning view of the harbor and Nantucket Sound. And they were stunned into silence by the old-fashioned beauty of the little village of 'Sconset at the eastern edge of the island, with its wide, elegant, tree-shaded avenue.

Here they stopped at the 'Sconset Market, an old-fashioned store with wooden floors and delicious ice cream sold at new-fashioned prices. They each bought a cone to lick as they strolled along gazing at the old fishermen's cottages now transformed into miniature fairy-tale homes. They drove back into town, went around the rotary, familiarized themselves with the area where Stop & Shop and other stores were located, then rode out past the schools all the way to Surfside Beach.

Here, the land sloped down to a long golden curve where the waves soared and dropped, churning the water with sand and foam. Sun-bathers in swimsuits, with towels and sweatshirts pulled around them to block off the breeze, were making their way up the hill in the late afternoon light, past the gray-shingled concession stand, and back to the parking lot.

Polly leaned out the window, looking. "We should come here some evening with a little picnic."

"Good idea," Faye agreed, then added, "Why not tonight?"

Polly jumped out of the Jeep and stood in the open air. "It's kind of breezy."

Faye jumped out, too. "We'll bring sweaters."

They raced to their house to equip themselves, then hurried back to the shore. It was just past the summer equinox, so the sun was still high, but the late June water was still too cold for most swimmers and the evening air too cool for sunbathing. The beach was almost deserted. Snug in quilted jackets and scarves, they established a little nest between the dunes, and laid out a blanket. Faye opened a bottle of wine while Polly made a plate of cheese, crackers, and dark, oily olives.

"They say if you sail from here in a straight line, the next land you hit would be Portugal," Faye mused.

"We should come out here some morning to watch the sun rise," Polly suggested, leaning back on her elbows and stretching out her legs. "Oh, it's so peaceful here." She turned to Faye. "Did you see any places you'd like to paint?"

"I saw a hundred places!" Faye told her. Waving her hands, she said, "Just look at the light! Sometimes it's diamond sharp, sometimes the mist diffuses it into a kind of illuminated net. I'm going to paint tomorrow." She hugged her knees. "I can't wait." Glancing over at Polly, she asked, "What will you do tomorrow?"

Polly thought a moment. "I'll make us a wonderful dinner."

Faye frowned. "Polly, you don't have to do that."

"But I want to," Polly insisted. "I love to cook. And it will be nice to have someone to cook for. I'm in such a funny mood. I never know what's going to make me start crying. If I see a dog, I think of poor old Roy. If I see a man, I think of Hugh, and when I see couples together, I think of Hugh and his ex-wife!" Tears sprang to her eyes. Polly angrily wiped at her cheeks. "Damn it! I promised myself I was not going to loom around you like Eeyore." Pushing herself up, she announced, "I'm going for a walk."

Faye watched her friend stride off, down to the water's edge where the tide chased lacy waves up onto the sand, then sank back, hissing. Polly headed to the west, so Faye decided to take a little walk toward the east.

Polly moved rapidly along, hands shoved deep into the pockets of her jacket, the tip of her scarf flipped by the wind against her cheek. She was angry with herself for being such a blubbery wimp, for spoiling a lovely evening by the sea for herself and Faye. But her entire body seemed to be swollen to overflowing with the salt water of tears. She wanted to cry. She needed to cry. And here on the edge of the island, just now, just this moment on this evening, she allowed herself to weep, for the death of her loyal old dog, for the death of her beloved husband, for the loss of her son to a woman who, for whatever reasons, kept him separated from Polly. And last, for a romance with Hugh that was as lovely as that streak of rose light glowing along the horizon—and as steadfast.

The sand was pocked with footprints from earlier walkers. The tide rushed up, filling in the hollows, carelessly erasing all signs of human presence. By the shelter of a dune, she came upon a heart drawn into the sand, complete with an arrow through it and the inscription *Andrew loves Jenn forever!* Polly stood a moment, her sobs lost in the pounding of the surf. *Forever.* Andrew and Jenn had to be young, and powerful with the hope of the young. For them, their love was larger than the ocean, their lives as bright as a summer day. When you are older, Polly thought, you know that life really is an island, and to be old is to be like this, perched alone on the edge of the land, knowing that *forever* was as cold and uncaring as this ocean, eternity as dark and unknowable as the swirling jade waves.

Faye ambled along the golden beach, picking up and discarding shells, skipping out of the way of an unexpected rush of surf, gazing right toward the gray-shingled cottages set back among the beach grass and dunes or left, out to the ocean, infinite, mysterious, and radiantly blue beneath the sinking sun.

Her mind teemed with thoughts of Winslow Homer's seascapes, and Childe Hassam's rainy day Nantucket scenes, and of the way George Inness caught the mess of daily life in a moment of radiant beauty. She meditated on the genius of Eastman Johnson's Nantucket painting "The Cranberry Harvest." She thought of color and light and line, of shadow and darkness.

Then, from nowhere, completely unexpected, came a hot flash, whipping through her body like a creature escaped from a cage, blanking all thoughts from her mind in an inferno of discomfort. Only with great effort did she restrain herself from simply plunging into the ocean, whose waves offered such cool deliverance. She untied her scarf, yanked off her jacket, and still bursting with heat, she collapsed on the sand, untied her sneakers and tore off her socks. She dug her feet into the sand, which felt deliciously icy next to her burning skin.

She thought as she sat there how her hot flashes were like warning lights, like the flashing lights on streets or the beacons from lighthouses, or the blaze of color in autumn leaves, reminding her that she was approaching the end of her particular travels, that unavoidable dangers loomed ahead, that she should declare her talent *now,* while she still could. She was falling in love with this island, with its infinite variety of beautiful views. She was eager to paint, not so that she would have the paintings, but so that she would once again be immersed in her work, in the mysterious alchemy Fate had delivered to her between the world, her eye, and her hand. She was falling in love with herself as a woman of a certain age, alone.

26

Thursday afternoon, Marilyn was pleased with herself. She was in one of those rare periods when, somehow, she'd managed to arrange to facilitate all the actions necessary for the happiness of her family.

The first part of the week had been chaotic. Because Marilyn had spent the day going to Nantucket to have lunch with her Hot Flash friends, Ruth had missed her weekly Saturday-afternoon outing, when Marilyn drove her to the library, grocery store, and pharmacy. Ruth was too sweet to complain, but Marilyn knew her mother missed that little island of togetherness in the midst of the solitude of Ruth's life. In order to make it up to Ruth, she'd taken her out to have a little meal and do errands on Tuesday night, which meant that Marilyn didn't get all her papers marked for her Intro to Geology class, which meant she either had to stay up until early morning to get it done, or neglect something needing doing in the house, like harassing the landlord from whom they were renting the condo to get the broken central air conditioning fixed or, more importantly, the toilet in the third-floor bathroom unclogged. Marilyn had no idea what had gone wrong with the toilet, but it intermittently overflowed, sending rivulets of water down the wall in Ian's study and causing the plaster ceiling to bulge ominously. Ian had had to move his desk and drafting table to the center of the room, which made for an unsettling ambience and no doubt threw what Shirley called the feng shui into negative overdrive. Angus had to use the second-floor bathroom that Ian and Marilyn used, and Angus, absentminded about everything, seemed especially clueless about bathroom etiquette. Angus forgot to put the toilet seat down. Worse, he often forgot to flush. What adult, Marilyn thought, wanting to shriek and pull her hair, forgets to flush?

She remembered when her son was a toddler being toilet trained. It had seemed for a few months that the core of her life revolved around feces. But that was nothing compared to what was going on now. Not only was Angus forgetful about himself, he still couldn't seem to remember to take his puppy out. Darwin was adorable, a comedian of a bulldog, good-natured and earnestly eager to please. No, it wasn't Darwin's fault that he had "accidents" in the house.

This afternoon, neither she nor Ian had scheduled classes, so they planned to spend a couple of hours by themselves, discussing wedding plans. But Ruth received a phone call from the daughter of her beau Ernest, telling her that Ernest had had a minor stroke and was in the hospital. So Ian and Marilyn had spent the afternoon with Ruth, calming her and escorting her to the hospital to see her ailing gentleman friend. Afterward, they gathered up Angus and his dog and drove everyone to the Boston Common, where the trees provided wells of cool shade and the dog could get some exercise and Angus could get some sun on his wan, pasty face.

For a few moments, it was a pleasant family outing. Then Darwin, still in his clumsy puppy phase, raced away from Angus, dragging his leash behind him. Angus yelled, "Come back!" Surprising them all, Darwin obeyed, turning on a dime, then galumphing back. In a flurry of doggy delight, the puppy tripped over his own feet and tumbled into Ruth. Arms flailing, Ruth tottered backward. Ian grabbed her in time to save her from falling. Darwin got up, shook himself, and staggered around in a flash of puppy fur, twining his leash around Ruth's ankles, paralyzing her, while Angus bumbled around trying to grab the dog and the leash and tripping over his own feet. It was funny, really, and everyone laughed, but Marilyn's heart had flip-flopped dangerously when she thought her mother might be knocked off her feet. Marilyn could imagine Ruth breaking a hip, and then being hospitalized like Ernest, and then becoming depressed and ill . . .

But everyone was fine. They drove to Memorial Drive, bought sandwiches and sodas to enjoy while they sat on benches watching the sailboats skim along the Charles River and the roller skaters glide along the sidewalks. Angus fed Darwin a sandwich, and the puppy, full and exhausted, collapsed at their feet for a snooze, so the humans had almost thirty minutes of peace.

And now here they were! Home, with no broken bones! Ruth retired to her ground-floor hideaway, happy to be back with her kitten and her television shows. Angus led his adoring pup up the stairs to the attic and reimmersed himself in his computer world. Ian and Marilyn spent a couple of hours on necessary household and university matters, and then— could it be? It was only ten o'clock at night, and they still had enough energy for a bit of bedroom romance.

They locked the door and turned off the lights. They snuggled up close to one another on the broad bed. The house was quiet around them. Ruth was asleep. Angus might be sleeping or he might be on his computer, but he was engaged. Because the air conditioning was broken, the windows were open, but the night air was muggy and thick, so they'd set an oscillating fan up in one corner of the room. It whirred gently back and forth, wrapping them in a kind of cotton wool of sound. Marilyn burrowed her face into Ian's chest and for a few moments indulged in his wonderful clean Ian smell. Ian ran his large hand down her back and over the curve of her hip and buttocks.

He was already erect, but he whispered into Marilyn's hair, "Let's take our time. Let's pretend we have all the time in the world."

Marilyn loved the idea of taking time during lovemaking. Her daytime life was lived at such speed, with so many distractions, so many minutes and hours of multitasking, that bringing the rush and roar of life down to this peaceful secret moment seemed like bliss. Because Marilyn and Ian knew and revered the pace at which the planet polished its stones and frilled the slightest ripple of its seas, taking time seemed to be the way the universe loved its humans to make love. And this was what it was all about, really, what books and sonnets and songs were written for, and movies made and beautiful clothing donned and beds created—for two people to lie together, heart to heart, mouth on mouth, bodies cleaving and souls expanding. This was the golden nugget at the core of the universe, this was the radiance spun, like gold from straw, from the bulk of two human beings.

Ian kissed Marilyn's mouth softly. He kissed her neck, her collarbone, her breasts, and she did not mind that they were flattened and flaccid from age, she felt beneath his breath how perfect a thing her body was, that the simple touch of hydrogen, carbon, and oxygen could magic its way from the surface of her skin along her nerves until her entire body unfolded like a flower. She ran her hands over his torso, so warm, so full of power and life, until she felt the curly bristle of his pubic hair. She touched his penis. Ian's groan was like a rock parted by the green insistence of a plant to reach through and to the sun.

Everything fell away. The university, her mother, Angus, dogs and cats, computers and laboratories, cars and television sets, age and fear of dying, they all fell away, leaving Marilyn and Ian floating in a sea of sensation, the only sound their exhalations, the only sight each other. Ian raised himself up above her, resting on his elbows, not yet penetrating her but caressing her belly and thighs with the length of his penis. Marilyn put her hands on his face and looked into his eyes, which shone in the dark like lamps.

"Oh, Ian, I love you," she said.

"I love you, Marilyn." He lowered himself to kiss her. Their bodies trembled against one another, urging for completion. The slightest movement of their legs or torsos shot through them like earthquake tremors.

"Ian," Marilyn said urgently. "Don't make me wait any longer."

Ian smiled. Lifting himself up again, he poised himself just on the brink of entering Marilyn, and his slightest push set pleasure and need radiating through her thighs and groin. He pushed again, entering her just a little. They both groaned then. Marilyn closed her eyes. She tilted her hips, urging him to come further, and slowly Ian did so, pushing into her like a bore into a vein of gold.

"Oh, Ian," she cried.

Ian drew back—

The phone rang, startling them out of their mood like an alarm clock blasting them out of a dream. They stared at it as if it were a rabid dog.

Ian slid off Marilyn, resting on his side. "Who would call this late at night?"

"Only family." Marilyn sat up in bed, terrified. "Teddy, about Lila— or the baby!"

Ian tried to soothe her. "It's probably just a wrong number."

Marilyn snatched it up. "Yes? Yes, he's here." She handed the phone to Ian, then sat with the sheet clutched to her chest as she watched him talk. An expression of dismay fell over his face and stress threw him into Scottish dialect Marilyn couldn't understand. "Brae dinna thole merrit oor awfy," he seemed to blather, punctuated by the occasional, "Ach, Lassie, iss terrible." She did manage to understand that he was agreeing to fly back to Scotland immediately. Who could it be? Both his parents were dead. His sister and her family were often in touch via e-mail and all seemed to be well there.

Ian finally hung up the phone, his face drained as he said, "My best friend, Tam Muir, died tonight. That was Fiona, his wife." He buried his face in his hands.

Marilyn put her arms around him. "Oh, Ian."

"I've got to fly over there on the first plane I can catch," Ian said. "I've got to help her with the funeral, and she wants me to speak at the service."

"Of course. What can I do?"

Ian was pale, stunned. "I-I don't know."

"Well, look. You pack. I'll phone the airlines and get some information. You know there's a morning flight to Edinburgh."

"Yes, yes, thank you, Marilyn." But he didn't move. In only minutes, he'd become an old man. His face was haggard.

Marilyn's heart ached for his sorrow. "Ian, tell me about Tam."

Ian smiled. "We were best friends since we were five years old. His parents had a wonderful estate with a trout stream. We used to fish, swim, ride ponies together. It was paradise. We went to university together. Tam went into the medical profession, practiced general medicine in Edinburgh." As Ian continued to talk, something loosened inside him, and tears welled in his eyes, then rained down his face. He broke down, heaving great wracking sobs.

Later, Marilyn fetched him a brandy, and helped him pack, and phoned the airlines and made the reservation. By the time she set the alarm for five o'clock, it was already two in the morning. They didn't sleep, but lay curled together on the bed, just trying to rest. When the alarm sounded, they dressed, and Marilyn drove Ian to the airport.

She didn't stay to watch the plane take off. She had a class to teach at ten. She drove back home with her head dizzy and stuffy with lack of sleep, scarcely aware of the brilliant summer day and the explosion of flowers everywhere. As she walked from her car to the house, she was vaguely aware of the perfume of a neighbor's clematis, and the hot beat of sunshine on her shoulders. Her mind churned with thoughts of love and sex, of death and sorrow and aging.

She was so completely fatigued! Her head ached. She was so shaky, fitting her key in the lock took several tries. She didn't have the energy to climb to her bedroom. She'd just collapse for a brief nap on the living room sofa. Finally she opened the front door and stepped inside the front hall.

"Marilyn! Marilyn! Help! Help!"

Ruth.

Heart lurching, Marilyn raced down the stairs to the ground floor. "Mother?"

Her mother stood in front of the sofa, wringing her hands. She was still in her pink flannel robe, which was wet and stained with coffee. "He won't stop, I can't get him to stop!" Ruth cried.

Darwin, the adorable fat bulldog, had Marie, Ruth's kitten, trapped in a corner. The little kitten was arched and hissing like a teapot. The bulldog was barking so hard he nearly rose off the floor with each yelp. His tail wagged back and forth like a frantic metronome.

Marilyn hesitated. Darwin was only a pup, but his massive head and powerful jaw filled Marilyn with trepidation. If he bit her, if he only *nipped* her, he could do substantial damage, couldn't he?

"Stop! Bad dog!" Ruth cried. "Oh, my poor little kitten."

Marilyn had to do it. She plunged in, grabbed the dog by his collar, and yanked him away so hard that they both almost fell over backward. Darwin didn't try to bite, but did struggle to get back to his prey as Marilyn hauled him across the floor and up the stairs. When she even slightly relinquished the pressure of her hold on his collar, he would flip, with surprising agility for such a fat little butterball, and try to go in the opposite direction. Bent nearly double, her fingers hooked tightly around his collar, Marilyn half-carried, half-escorted a barking, wriggling, tail-wagging, slobbering Darwin up three flights of stairs to his master's room.

Angus's door was partly open.

"Angus?" Marilyn called.

No answer.

She pushed the door open and dragged Darwin inside. Angus was sound asleep in front of the computer, his head resting on the desk, his arms hanging down limp.

"Angus!" Marilyn slammed the door behind her and released the dog, who raced around the room, yipping triumphantly.

Angus continued to snore.

"Angus!" Annoyed, Marilyn shook the young man's shoulder.

Finally he opened his eyes. "What."

"Angus, wake up. Angus, listen to me. You didn't latch the bedroom door properly. Darwin got out and went down to my mother's quarters and terrorized her kitten."

Angus yawned and rubbed his eyes. "Ach, he was only playing with her."

"Well, he *acted* like he wanted to eat her. The point is, he frightened my mother, who is eighty-seven years old. She could have had a heart attack. She could have tripped over the dog. You have got to keep him under control if you're going to have him in this house."

"Fine," Angus said. "Sorry."

"Angus, come on," Marilyn pleaded. "Look at your pet! He needs to go out! He's full of energy. And I'm sure he has to pee." She glanced across the room, where a water bowl sat on some newspapers. "Angus! Darwin's water bowl is dry! Really, that's cruel. You've got to keep it filled! What's the *matter* with you! I don't care if you waste your life away hiding up here like an albino vampire, but I do care that you neglect your animal!"

Darwin, startled by the sharpness in Marilyn's voice, quivered and peed on the floor.

"Oh, for God's sake, Angus!" Marilyn screamed. "You have got to get yourself in control!"

27

Alice rose early Thursday morning, sliding quietly from the bedroom where Gideon remained snoring. She showered and dressed, scribbled a note for Gideon, and hurried down to her car.

She wanted to get out to The Haven early, before Jenn and Alan opened their bakery, so she'd have a few moments to talk to them.

She had to do it today, *immediately,* before she lost her nerve. Her five days on Nantucket had brought home quite clearly how tired she was, and how much more she enjoyed her life when she wasn't frantic and rushed. Saturday night, she and Gideon had played bridge with friends, and for the first time in a long time, Alice had been able to *focus.* She'd played like a champ, her happy mind clicking away memorizing the other players' bids, the cards they'd played, figuring out who had what king, queen, or jack, and she'd won almost all the games, except for the one where she and Gideon were both dealt hideous hands. Afterward, she'd felt absolutely exhilarated. Sunday, she and Gideon had taken a long, slow stroll through the city, holding hands and talking, and Alice didn't feel exhausted, but invigorated by the walk. Gideon had seemed so much more charming to her, so much less irritating, and when she mentioned this to him, he'd said, with a rueful smile, "Alice, I'm the same as I always am. It's you who've changed. You're more relaxed."

It was true. The five days on Nantucket had worked like a stay at a health spa. Her heart hadn't acted up once. Her senses were sharper. Food tasted better, flowers were more fragrant, and Sunday afternoon, when she and Gideon attended a concert, the music had sent her spirits soaring.

So she was determined to change her life. She'd talked it over with Shirley and her Hot Flash friends and with Gideon. She'd given it serious thought. She would tell her son and his wife that she couldn't babysit every single day for darling baby Aly. She'd continue for a week or so, until they lined up a replacement. She'd remain available in an emergency. She'd even babysit one or two days a week, regularly, so she could have time with her granddaughter. But she just couldn't keep doing it every day.

Now Alice parked at the front of the gatehouse and let herself in with her own key. Alan and Jenn kept the front door of their home locked, so customers wouldn't wander in.

The small living room was cozy, cluttered today as it was every Monday morning, with the debris of a lazy Sunday. Newspapers hung over the coffee table, and baby paraphernalia was scattered everywhere. It was only a little after eight o'clock. The shop didn't open until nine, but Jenn and Alan would have been up since five-thirty, baking. Aly might be asleep in her cot in the private kitchen, or lying there, blowing bubbles at the brightly colored plastic mobile hanging above her. Alice didn't call out because she didn't want to wake the baby.

She headed toward the kitchen.

And stopped dead.

"I can't do it anymore, Alan!" Jenn's voice was shrill. "I'd rather get divorced!"

Alice's heart shot rockets of fear through her body. Her fingertips and lips went cold. She grabbed the back of the sofa for support.

A door slammed. A few moments later, Alan's bakery van raced around the side of the gatehouse and out to the main road.

Jennifer walked into the living room, holding the baby in her arms. Aly was awake, her lower lip protruding, obviously on the verge of tears.

"Alice!" Jennifer jumped.

"I didn't mean to eavesdrop," Alice hurriedly informed her daughter-in-law. "I came early. I wanted to talk with you and Alan. I'm sorry if I intruded."

"Oh, it's all right," Jennifer said. "Look, Aly!" With a false smile and a forced chipper voice, she plunked down on a chair, holding her baby up. "Alice is here!"

Alice waved her arms and smiled. Alice took the baby from Jennifer and sat down on the sofa with her, cooing to her and nuzzling noses in the way that always made the baby laugh.

"I was going to talk with you about it, anyway," Jenn said in a martyred tone. She leaned back in her chair, closing her eyes.

"What's going on?" Alice asked.

Tears rolled down Jenn's cheeks. "Alan. He's gotten so *weird*. He's not the man I fell in love with. He's not the man I married. He's sullen, and negative, and so easily offended. We seem to fight all the time."

Alice lay the baby on her back along the length of her legs. Aly's diaper was full, she could tell by the smell, but this was no time to interrupt Jenn, and the infant was content, blowing bubbles as Alice bounced and cooed.

"You're both overworked," Alice began.

Jenn shook her head. "We're not working any harder than we were a year ago."

"But you have a baby," Alice pointed out. "A new baby in the house always complicates everything." Smiling down at her granddaughter, she said in a singsong voice, "And she's such a perfect little baby, too!"

"Yes, she is, but she still won't sleep all night." Jennifer gave way to full-force sobbing. "I'm so sleep deprived."

"When your mother was here—" Alice began.

Jenn cried harder. "Oh, she was wonderful with the *baby*, but she kept comparing my life to my sisters'. *Their* babies are all perfect. *They* don't have to work, so they can keep the house in order. And my brother's wife has a full-time live-in nanny!"

Anger stung Alice. Jenn's mother clearly disapproved of Alan as father and husband. Because of Alan, Jenn had to work. Because of Alan's lack of financial success, they couldn't afford a full-time nanny.

"Well," Alice thought aloud. "What if you stopped working for a year or so? Until you thought Aly was old enough to spend some time in day care? If you stopped working—"

"If *I* stopped working, we'd have to hire someone in my place, and pay a salary and we'd never save any money toward a house of our own!" Jenn dug in her pocket for a tissue and noisily blew her nose. "Alan certainly couldn't manage without my help. He's hardly doing his part as it is, and he's gotten so sluggish and *pathetic* about everything.

He's just *dragging* himself through life, and he's pulling me down with him."

"Oh, Jennifer." Alice hated the sound of condemnation in her daughter-in-law's voice. Yet she understood Jennifer's impatience. Alan had been a "moody" child. A couple of years ago, after a failed marriage, Alan was diagnosed with depression. It worked on him silently, gradually, he told her. It was not abrupt, not like being hit by lightning. It was more as if, normally, his good spirits flowed through him like a recirculating fountain, until something, some rogue chemical in his brain, pulled the plug. Slowly, gradually, relentlessly, his energy, love of life, and optimism were drained away, leaving him empty and emotionally weak. The illness was sneaky, too. He never knew it had hit him until he was sapped and strained, and after his medication kicked in and his good spirits recovered, he couldn't believe he'd ever been as despondent as people told him he was.

"You know," Alice said slowly, "Alan does have a problem with depression."

Jennifer sniffed. "I can't tell my mother that. She'd freak out."

"Depression is nothing to be ashamed of," Alice reminded her. Yet as she spoke, she knew she was being hypocritical. Ever since Alan had been diagnosed with depression, *she*'d felt ashamed, and *guilty*. Didn't everything in Alan's personal makeup come from either nature or nurture? And wasn't she responsible for both? *She* had never had depressive episodes, but her ex-husband Mack, the boys' father, had been a charming womanizer, capable of great highs and also great lows that sent him off to neighborhood bars and other women's beds. Perhaps Mack had a problem with depression, but back then, no one ever called it that. But Alice had married Mack, which made her responsible for the genes that created Alan. But would Alan be *Alan* without his depression? Certainly he wouldn't be who he was if she'd married someone else.

"Maybe not to *you*," Jennifer said sulkily.

Alice was surprised by Jennifer's tone. Jennifer was usually such a sweetheart, so good-natured, so buoyant. "Jennifer," she said softly, trying not to upset the baby, but putting a warning in her voice, "*you* went through a pretty bad postpartum depression after baby Alice was born."

"Great, throw that in my face!" Jennifer snapped. "*I* had a *reason* to be depressed, I'd just nearly died with preeclampsia, I was bloated and my blood pressure was all over the place. There was a physical cause for my depression."

"That's true," Alice said softly, conciliatorily. "And as I recall, Alan was wonderful then. He was solicitous and caring. He ran the bakery and pampered you. Perhaps he's tired. Perhaps your mother's disapproval hurt him and—"

"Oh, fine, blame it on my mother!" Jennifer began to sob again.

The baby's little face scrunched up in a pre-tear pucker. Alice hoisted the baby to her shoulder, stood up, and walked around the room, bouncing Aly, holding her so she could see the gleam of light on a brass candlestick, one of her favorite sights. The baby cooed at the candlestick, waving her arms in excitement.

"Jennifer," Alice said softly. "Why don't you go lie down for a little while?"

"I can't!" Jennifer's voice was shrill. "I've got to be in the shop. Alan's off on a delivery."

"I'll man the shop," Alice said.

"How can you do that and take care of Alice?" Jenn demanded. "Believe me, she's not going to fall asleep."

"Look, your shop is not exactly Au Bon Pain," Alice pointed out sensibly, which only made Jenn cry harder. "I mean, you're out in the country here. I'm not going to have to feed the multitudes. Most of your drop-ins are people from The Haven wanting a cake or a loaf of bread, right? Some mornings you hardly have any drop-ins at all."

"No," Jenn refused, wiping her eyes. "No, you've got enough on your hands with Aly."

"If the shop gets busy, I'll phone Shirley and ask her to come help," Alice said. "Now go on, grab a nap while you can."

"Well . . . okay then." Jenn wobbled off into the bedroom.

Alice put a fresh diaper on Aly, then carried her through the bakery kitchen and out to the little shop. Already her shoulders ached. With relief, she spotted the playpen in the corner, behind the display case and next to a small desk where they answered the phone and typed orders into a computer. She settled the infant on her back in the playpen. The baby waved her legs and smiled at her mobile.

The phone rang. Alice picked it up and took an order for a birthday cake to be picked up on Friday. As she tapped the information into the computer, she glanced at Aly. The baby had fallen asleep, her long eyelashes slanting against her chubby cheeks, her perfect mouth making sucking motions, as if she were dreaming of her bottle.

Alice looked around the shop. All was quiet. Everything was clean and shining. Clearly Jenn and Alan kept their place of business in perfect order, even if their home was in chaos. Alice slipped into the kitchen, poured herself a cup of coffee, and returned to the shop. From here she could see cars going up the drive to The Haven. It cheered her to know that Shirley was so nearby. Maybe she'd phone Shirley, invite her down here for a little chat . . .

. . . and maybe she wouldn't. Shirley would be sure to remind Alice that Alice had decided to stop working so hard, to start taking care of herself. Shirley would remind her, and so, when she returned home this evening, would Gideon, and so would her other friends when she spoke to them, that Alice had planned to tell her son and his wife that they needed to make other arrangements, so she could stop making the daily drive out to help them.

Well, obviously, she couldn't let her son and his family down now. Alice sipped her coffee, her thoughts racing. When Alan returned from his delivery, she'd have a little heart-to-heart with him. She'd suggest he go back on his medication. If he did that, his temperament would improve rapidly, within a month or so. She could continue to help out here for at least another month.

Her heart did a triple somersault worthy of a carnival acrobat. Rubbing her chest, Alice blamed it on the caffeine in her coffee.

28

Friday afternoon, Shirley drifted through The Haven. In the hopes she'd look professional and administrative, she carried a clipboard, but really she was just trying to inhale some of the stimulating, relaxing, life-affirming scents, sounds, and vibrations from all the various rooms.

Star was leading a yoga class in the smaller workshop space. Her voice was so full of warmth and serenity, Shirley wanted to unbutton her tight jacket, lie down on the floor in her business suit, kick off her heels, and let herself drift.

In the gym, several women were spinning away on their stationary bikes, singing along to headphones, really caught up in the movement. A blonde's long ponytail bounced to the beat, reminding Shirley how she used to jog to Aerosmith, filling her lungs with good clean air while her spirits soared on the wings of Joe Perry's guitar.

She didn't jog anymore. She hadn't mentioned it to her Hot Flash friends, but her right knee was sort of falling apart. She tried to stay healthy with regular yoga exercises, but her running days were over, and she'd been informed by her doctor that knee surgery was in her future.

Laughter and chatter flew like bright birds around the locker room. Women rushed in and out, showered, dressed, or undressed for a massage, or an aromatherapy session, or a soak in the Jacuzzi. Shirley stuck her head into the aromatherapy room and took a long inhalation of the scent wafting through the air—thyme, she thought, and perhaps grapefruit?

She went up the back stairs to the second floor, her knee twinging with each step. Beth Young stood in front of a classroom of fourteen women, teaching a seminar called "Medieval and Modern Women: How

Different Are We?" Shirley smiled and leaned against the door jamb for a few moments, listening.

A petite brunette, Beth had once been shy to the point of invisibility. She'd first come to The Haven because her boyfriend's family was superathletic, while the heaviest thing klutzy Beth ever lifted was an anthology of English literature. Slowly and steadily, Beth had developed, if not muscles, then the belief that muscles could exist on her slight frame. More importantly, she'd increased her self-esteem. She'd married her boyfriend Sonny, finished her Ph.D., and made close friends with three of the women she'd met at The Haven. Her life was full, and Beth was flourishing. She'd even gained some badly needed weight. It was as if she had become substantial to herself.

A success story. One of many. Shirley allowed herself a moment of pride at the thought. Then, because she didn't want Beth to see her lurking out there, she moved on down the hall. The other rooms were empty at this hour. Faye had once taught art therapy here, and a new teacher had taken Faye's place, but she could teach only on Saturdays. Justin, Shirley's vile ex-lover, had once taught creative writing here. No one had replaced him, which was okay for the summer months when fewer people signed up for indoor activities. She'd find someone to teach starting in the fall, when, as the days grew shorter and colder, people sought out classroom endeavors.

Shirley loved that Beth, once a student, now taught at The Haven. There was something fluid, circular, and whole about it, something taken and given back. This was exactly the sort of thing she'd always dreamed of achieving: creating an atmosphere where women could be soothed, healed, and rejuvenated.

Shirley was only now admitting to herself that the success of her dream had grown past her original dream. The Haven was a thriving establishment. Its membership was steadily increasing. And so were Shirley's responsibilities.

Because Shirley was the director of The Haven, and because it had originally been her idea, she was always the one who met personally with every new client, interviewing them over herbal tea, filling out a form and jotting down notes about what courses and programs she thought would best serve each individual. During the last week of June, she'd interviewed eighteen new clients, which was wonderful, a sign that The Haven was becoming increasingly popular and profitable, but also, for Shirley, just a tad bit exhausting, because she had to schedule the interviews in among so many boring administrative details.

The interviews were her only real contact with her clients. The rest of her workday was spent in her office, dealing with hundreds of details—salaries, additions to the personnel handbook, health and accident insurance, building and grounds maintenance—something always needed repairing, the storm windows, the hardware on the doors, the faucets. Some days seemed to be spent entirely on the phone chasing down the men responsible for keeping the gym equipment or the Jacuzzi or the locker room toilets in good working order. Meetings with the accountant for The Haven were almost the worst of all. Shirley had never been interested in money, and it cramped her style and crimped her brain to concentrate on his numbingly dull, finite, black and white figures.

She passed through the connecting doors between the classroom wing and the long corridor with four private condos. Star, the yoga teacher, lived in one of the condos. Shirley lived in the largest one, at the far end, and she unlocked the door, went in, and collapsed on her sofa. She kicked off her heels and unbuttoned her jacket. Curled on her side, her head resting on one of her purple velvet pillows, she stared at all her beautiful, inspirational possessions, her statue of the angel and the unicorn, her Tree of Life banner, the mermaid figurine, her labyrinth hanging, her "jewel"-encrusted goblets etched with dragons, Celtic crosses, ravens, and fairies. They sustained her. They had always sustained her. She believed in them as much as Marilyn believed in the Loch Ness Monster. She believed magic existed in the world, that humans only saw one tenth of all the miraculous network around them.

Now she sensed a kind of magic on Nantucket.

And she wanted to slap herself upside the head for thinking that that guy Harry was part of the magic.

Hadn't she learned enough hard-knock lessons about men and magic? Hadn't she allowed herself to trust her feelings, her instincts, about men, and hadn't she, every single time, been wrong? She'd been married and divorced three times. Three times! She'd need an abacus to list all the short-term romantic liaisons that had started like a violin concerto and ended like a car crash. Her last and truest love, Justin, would have given her a royal screwing, and not the sexual kind, if Alice hadn't stopped him.

She was in her sixties, for heaven's sake! She ought to be grateful simply to be alive. She *was* grateful to have such wonderful friends, and she would never stop thanking the universe for making her dream of The Haven come true. If she felt overwhelmed by boring practicalities of running the place, tough toenails! This was real life. How many people got to have their dreams come true, after all? She was almost unique!

If only . . . if only her personal life held just a *touch* more romance. She knew she should respect her Hot Flash friends' advice and be glad to have such a reliable, honest, earnest man as Stan in her life. Hell, she should be glad to have *any* man in her life at her age.

A breeze drifted through her open windows, tinkling the wind chimes and dappling coolness through the hot room. It was almost the Fourth of July. Last year, Shirley had had a wonderful Fourth of July picnic here at The Haven. It had been a perfect day. She'd had red, white, and blue decorations everywhere, even her earrings had been like little firecrackers, and sweet little old Ruth had worn a red, white, and blue sweater with a matching bow in her white curls. All her friends and their beaux had come, and Alan and Jennifer had announced that they were married and Jennifer was expecting.

Shirley wasn't holding a picnic this year. First of all, Faye and Polly were going to be on Nantucket. Second, she suspected Alan and Jennifer were too beat and overwhelmed to want to help cook for a large group. Third, and mostly, Shirley just didn't feel up to it. Maybe she'd ask Stan if he'd like to go to the local baseball field for the fireworks display Monday night. That could be fun. Shirley had always loved fireworks. The thought of them bursting out in blossoms of color against the night sky, the designs they made, the excitement of the explosions—it invigorated Shirley. She got up to change clothes for her date with Stan.

———————————

Promptly at six-thirty, Stan appeared at the main door of The Haven. Shirley let him in and together they went up the stairs to her condo.

"Something smells very nice, Shirley," Stan said as they entered her living room.

"Thanks. It's lasagna."

Stan removed his sports jacket, opened the closet, and hung it inside. As Shirley watched, a slight trickle of alarm tingled through her. This was the third time he'd been to her place, and already he was acting as if he belonged here. He irritated her further by immediately sitting on the sofa, picking up the remote, and clicking on the TV.

Don't be so contrary, Shirley admonished herself. She'd set a board of cheese and crackers on the coffee table. Just like last time, they'd have a drink and watch the news before dinner. What did she expect? That he'd throw her on the rug and ravish her?

She asked, "Would you like a glass of wine?"

"I'd prefer a gin and tonic, actually." He was settling into the sofa, stretching both arms proprietarily out over the back.

"I don't keep hard liquor here, usually, but I bought a bottle of wine because I know how much you like it with your meal."

Stan peered at her over the top of his eyeglasses. He thought for a moment, then patted the sofa next to him. "Sit down for a moment, Shirley."

She sat.

Putting his hand on her knee, Stan smiled. "You're a wonderful girl, Shirley. I really enjoy being with you, and I don't think I'm wrong believing you like me, too. So why don't we just go on and get some things out of the way. I don't mind that you're a recovering alcoholic—"

"You knew that about me before we met," Shirley reminded him. She'd told him that when they were in the first e-mail stage.

"That's true, that's true. But if you and I are going to have a lasting relationship, we're going to have to make some compromises. For example, you're going to have to start stocking hard liquor. I'm hardly an alcoholic, but I do like my evening drink. It's part of my routine, and I like my routine. If you can keep away from wine, I expect you can resist the temptations of gin."

It wasn't *what* he was saying that irritated her so much, Shirley thought. It was the *way* he expressed himself. He was prissy, and he was condescending. He was just like her geometry teacher.

"And we might as well address the matter of your vegetarianism," Stan continued. "I'd bet ten dollars your lasagna is meatless."

"You're right," Shirley told him. "It's got mushrooms, and zucchini, and—"

"But I like meat, Shirley. If we're going to continue dating, I'll expect you to provide me meat."

"Well, I did roast a chicken for you last time," Shirley reminded him.

"True, and a very nice job you did of it, too. So why did you have to cook vegetarian tonight?" He didn't wait for her to respond. "After all, when I take you out to dinner, I allow you to eat whatever you want."

"But isn't it a bit different when you or I actually cook the food?" Shirley asked. "I mean—"

Stan looked impatient. "I've already told you I don't cook. I think we should alternate eating out and your cooking for me. That's fair. I pay for one meal, and that's always more expensive than your cooking at your own home. You cook next, and it's only fair that it should be something I like, don't you think? Then I take you out for the next meal. And so on."

Shirley squirmed on the sofa. "Doesn't that lack a little . . . spontaneity?"

Stan smiled kindly. "At our age, we don't really need spontaneity, do we? At our age, I think security is much more important."

Shirley's brain whirled. Of course security was important, she knew that! Still . . .

"I'll pour your wine," she said, wanting to get away from him.

By the time she returned from the kitchen with his wine and her cranberry juice, Stan was engrossed in the news. Shirley returned to the kitchen, put the bread in the oven to warm, and tossed the salad.

As they sat at the table, eating her meatless lasagna, Shirley said cheerily, "Shall we plan to do something fun for the Fourth of July?"

Stan was busy cutting his lasagna into ten pieces of the same size and shape. "Sure. What do you suggest?"

"I'm thinking of going to one of the local baseball games, where they have fireworks after."

Stan shook his head. "That wouldn't be a good idea, Shirley. Anyplace where they set off fireworks is a potential disaster scene. Fireworks are dangerous."

Shirley opened her mouth. "But—"

"There will be fireworks on television if you want to see them. Besides, I don't attend minor league baseball games."

"But I thought you loved baseball!"

"I enjoy watching the Red Sox. I'm familiar with their players and their statistics. But I don't go to their games, either. I'm very uncomfortable in large crowds, and I very much dislike the difficulties of getting out of congested parking lots."

Shirley slumped. "You play golf . . ."

"Of course, but I choose times when the fairways and the club houses aren't busy."

Be creative, Shirley told herself frantically. Just because he liked routine didn't mean she couldn't propose stuff she'd enjoy. "Well, then, Stan, how's this for an idea? I'll put together a picnic for the Fourth of July. I'll make ham sandwiches, or roast beef, whatever you want. And we'll go to Walden Pond and have a picnic!"

Stan looked pained. "I've never enjoyed eating outdoors, Shirley. The food attracts insects of all kinds. As for swimming—I can only imagine how many other people will be in the pond, half of them urinating children."

"Oh. Well . . ." Defeated, Shirley picked at her salad. "What would *you* like to do for the Fourth of July?"

"Well, there's a Red Sox game we could watch on television." Stan brightened. "I know what! You make your little picnic, and we'll eat it in the living room, watching the Red Sox game!"

———————

After dinner, Stan and Shirley watched an old black-and-white movie on television. It wasn't particularly interesting, but Stan objected to renting movies from video shops on the grounds that it was a waste of money when so much was available for free on TV. When the movie ended, Stan clicked off the TV with the remote control and turned toward Shirley.

"Shall we retire to your bedroom?"

"All right."

They didn't turn on the lights, but left the door open to let light shine in from the hall. While Shirley turned back the covers, Stan undressed, carefully folding his clothing and draping it across a chair. They took turns in the bathroom, then slid into bed next to each other.

"You are a beautiful woman, Shirley," Stan told her as he turned on his side and pulled her against him.

This was nice, Shirley thought. Nice to be called beautiful, nice to be held. Nice to feel a warm male body.

"You're still pleasantly slim," Stan continued, running his arm over her back. "I really admire the way you haven't let yourself get fat like so many other women your age."

Well, that might not be the most romantic thing she'd ever heard, but it was a compliment. Shirley purred, "You feel good, too, Stan."

He kissed her mouth. He kissed each of her breasts. He patted her crotch as if it were an obedient pet. He pulled away in order to slide on his condom.

Shirley took Stan in her arms and into her body. It wasn't unpleasant. It didn't hurt. But she felt disconnected. She caught herself looking over at the clock—she'd bet Stan wouldn't take long.

He didn't. Afterward, he hurried off to take a shower. Shirley lay there, remembering Justin, whose lovemaking had been masterful, ecstatic, sublime. He'd brought her to such extremes of joy she'd lain weeping in his arms afterward. Even Jimmy, her beau before Justin, Jimmy, who drank too much and had bad grammar and worse manners, Jimmy, who certainly had no sexual *technique,* Jimmy had still had a kind of primitive, physical, caveman appeal. He'd worn jeans and a studded black leather jacket—that had been as good as foreplay for Shirley. He'd been huge, strong, heavy, and vigorous, and when they were through making love, Shirley had felt wonderfully *used up.*

But Jimmy had left her with a pile of unpaid bills, riding off on his motorcycle at a moment's notice and never looking back. And Justin had done much worse than that to her.

Shirley sighed. Stan came out of the bathroom, fully dressed. Shirley pulled on a robe and accompanied him to the door.

Stan put his hands on her shoulders and gazed affectionately down at her. "I know you want to have a little more fun, Shirley. I can sense that about you, you know. I'm a sensitive man. I had an idea in the shower. I know what we'll do for the Fourth of July!" Stan looked very pleased with himself.

She couldn't help it. She perked up. "What will we do?"

"I'll bring over a jigsaw puzzle! A nice, complicated one, at least a thousand pieces. I won't bring one of my old ones, either. I'll buy something new. I'll surprise you."

"Well," Shirley said weakly. "I'll look forward to that." No fireworks, she thought sadly, this Fourth of July.

Polly woke in her sweet twin bed with the ornate white iron head- and footboards, beneath a hand-sewn pastel quilt patterned with girls in sunbonnets. She lay there gazing at the other twin bed with its wedding-ring quilt, and at the small wooden cradle where antique dolls lay propped on lace pillows.

Life was so strange, she thought. This room brought back memories of her childhood dreams. She had planned to have daughters, and make all their clothes! As a teenager, while others were listening to Elvis Presley, Polly was designing matching mother-daughter dresses with pinafores. She could remember the exact details—the smocking, the heart-shaped pockets, the lace trim.

Instead of three daughters, life had given Polly one son. Of course she wouldn't trade him for anything, but just for this very quiet moment, she allowed herself to remember the sweetness of her childhood dream. She planned to braid her daughters' hair and tie the braids with grosgrain ribbons. To make clothes for their dolls to match their own clothes. To make dollhouses, with curtains, and tiny beds and tiny pictures on the walls.

Now her son was grown and married and had a child. A son. Polly loved Jehoshaphat, as much as she was allowed to, but she didn't see him often. If David and Amy did ever have a daughter, Polly doubted that she'd be very much part of the child's life. Amy and David were so inaccessible. . . .

Now her thoughts were turning gloomy, so Polly threw back the covers and put her feet on the rag rug.

"Oh, gosh," she said, looking at the clock on her night table.

It was almost ten o'clock! She shook her head in disgust. She was sure Faye had already gone off. Lucky Faye, to be obsessed with her work! Polly felt a bit untethered. This week, while Faye rose early to slip out of the house to paint, Polly had toured all the antique shops, "browsing," and surreptitiously checking to see if the missing Fabergé box had turned up anywhere. She didn't spot it, which made her feel she'd wasted her time, even though all the other Hot Flash Club women thanked her for her investigative work. It would have been such a coup to discover it! It would have been a little success, at a time in her life when she felt just a bit like a failure.

She did make wonderful meals for her and Faye every night, but while Faye retired to the front parlor to read, Polly slumped like a big fat blob in the back parlor, watching any old thing on TV. And last night, after Faye said good night and went up to bed, Polly had cut herself another slice of her homemade chocolate fudge cake and eaten it while watching *An Officer and a Gentleman,* where Richard Gere, in that snow white uniform, had swept Debra Winger up in his arms and carried her away. Oh, how Polly had blubbered at that part! She'd wept because life never gave you such a perfect moment, and she wept for the loss of her husband, and for the loss of her youth, and for the loss of her dog.

She hadn't gone to bed until two.

In the bathroom, she peed, then exchanged grim glances with her reflection in the mirror. She looked like a depressed porpoise.

She had to snap out of this despondency! She was on Nantucket! She owed it to herself to enjoy herself!

But she couldn't tear her eyes away from the mirror. The day was overcast, the sky threatening rain, and the dismal gloom from the window mingled with the utilitarian glare of the overhead light to spotlight her aging face. Her fair Irish skin had always been lightly freckled, but now some spots were for whatever bizarre reasons growing darker than the others, forming little constellations, Orion on her right cheek, the Big Dipper right in the middle of her forehead. The skin on her chin had a texture different from the rest of her face; it was pebbly, porous, and stippled, like the surface of the moon. When she lightly drew her fingers over the sides of her face, she felt tiny bumps beneath the smoother skin, little volcanoes preparing to erupt.

She couldn't erase the creases in her forehead or the rings around her neck or the U-shaped rolls of flesh cradling her chin, making it look as if her jawline was supported by a series of rubber bands. But she could use the expensive skin creams she'd bought on sale a few weeks ago. She *should* use them! What else did she have to do today? Already rain was spattering the window.

She padded barefoot downstairs to the kitchen. Faye had brewed coffee, and the pot was half-full. Polly tested the side of the pot with her hand, decided it was warm enough, and poured herself a mug, adding plenty of milk and sugar. Carrying it back up the stairs, she unpacked the many shimmery bottles and tubes, setting them out on the bathroom counter, sipping her coffee while she read the directions. As she did, an old, almost atavistic, thrill awoke within her. She was shot through with sensations wrought from a lifetime of faith in the alchemy of beauty lotions and potions. She was a little girl again, watching her mother carefully paint her face before going to a party. She was a young teen, experimenting with makeup, covering her childish freckles with a smooth makeup base. She was a college student who wanted to lose her virginity, rouging her mouth in a flamboyant creamy red.

She tied her auburn and white hair back with a band, rinsed her face with water, then applied the first coat for deep cleansing. After the requisite ten minutes, she wiped her face clean with soft tissues, then opened the second jar, the extravagantly expensive gold jar full of "micro-encapsulated nanosphere" ingredients that would provide deep exfoliation, leaving her skin smooth and radiant. The cream quickly hardened into a bright orange mask from which her eyes peeked out like someone in a state of shock. She would have laughed, but she didn't want to break the mask. She wished Faye were there to see her.

She had to wear the mask for thirty minutes. It wasn't spread on her lips—her mouth required a different cream—so she padded back down the stairs to refill her coffee. She was pretty sure she could sip coffee if she did so slowly, without moving her jaw.

Carrying her mug with her, she wandered through the big old house, admiring the various antiques, wondering what some of the odder bibelots were, checking her reflection in every shining bit of silver. At the front of the house she looked out at Orange Street, its colors muted by the streaming rain into an array of grays. The pavement was pewter, the sky dove, the shingled houses granite. The only spots of color were from the petunias and pansies in the window boxes, and even their cheer was dimmed by the downpour.

A big black SUV rolled up the street, its lights blurring in the rain. Just at that moment, a small tabby cat streaked out from under a rhododendron, racing into the street. The SUV slammed to a stop, but its front wheel had made contact with the cat.

"Oh, no!" Polly raced out the front door, down the steps, and out to the street.

The driver, a young woman, had already jumped out of her vehicle and was bending over the cat. "Oh, God! Oh, God! I didn't see her coming." Her face was white with shock.

"She ran out in front of you," Polly assured her. "You couldn't have known."

They squatted next to the injured animal. The young woman wore a raincoat, but Polly and the cat were quickly sodden as the rain streamed down. The cat wasn't bleeding, and hadn't lost consciousness, but when it tried to rise, its right hind leg wouldn't support it. It looked at Polly and made a pitiful meow.

"I'll take it to the vet." The young woman's hands were trembling—her whole body was trembling.

"I'll get a blanket to wrap it in." Polly rose.

"Wait, I have one in the car."

The rain soaked Polly's back and snaked in rivulets around her neck and down the crease between her breasts. She reached out a tentative hand to pat the cat. "Poor kitty, kitty. You'll be okay, kitty, kitty."

The cat lay still on the cold, wet street, regarding her with trusting eyes. Polly stroked its head and neck, murmuring comforting words. The cat had no collar, no ID tag. The young woman returned with a plaid wool blanket. Carefully they arranged it so they could lift the cat onto it, then they folded the blanket around the animal, who didn't object or fight or try to flee but only mewed feebly. Polly opened the door, and the young woman laid the cat carefully on the backseat.

"Would you like me to go with you?" Polly asked.

The other woman looked surprised by Polly's offer. "No, no, thank you. You're kind, but I think we'll be fine. I should just hurry and get her there."

As the SUV thundered off, Polly went back to the house. No wonder the young woman didn't want her company, she thought, with a shaky laugh. She was still in her robe, which was drenched and sticking to her skin. Her face was orange. Heaven only knew what her soggy hair looked like! Time for more coffee and a hot shower!

Energized, she turned the knob on the front door, pushed, and—nothing happened.

She pushed again.

The door was locked.

"You idiot!" Polly hit herself on her forehead, forgetting to worry about cracking the mask. "You unbelievable ninny!"

Moving as fast as she could without slipping on the soggy ground, she hurried around the side of the house and up the back porch steps. The back door was locked, too.

"Damn!" She stomped her foot, then looked around helplessly. If she could get to a phone, she could dial Faye's cell and ask her to come home and let her in. Slogging through the rain, she returned to the front of the house and, because she was such a big fat dope, tried the front door again. Still locked.

No lights showed in the houses across the street. Just a few feet away, all the shops on Main Street were open, but she could hardly wander down there in her soaking cotton robe and nightgown, her face a cracking mask of orange.

She could wait on the back porch. She'd be sheltered from the rain, and it was warm today. She wouldn't catch pneumonia. But the thought of sitting in wet clothes for endless hours didn't thrill her.

There *was* a light on next door, at the aptly named Lucinda Payne's house. Even if the cranky old bat didn't like her, surely she would allow her to use her phone.

What other choice did she have?

Polly trudged across the sidewalk, up the steps, and knocked on the door.

After a few moments, the door was slowly pulled back, revealing the owner of the house, fully clad in alabaster silk slacks and matching shirt. Pearls hung at her neck, and pearl earrings gleamed from her ears, making her white hair luminous and accentuating her brilliant green eyes.

Her expression as she took in the sight of Polly in her wet robe and orange mask did not change except for a slight, disdainful, pursing of her lips.

"Yes?" Her voice was cold.

"Mrs. Payne? I'm Polly Lodge. I live next door. Well, I don't live there, I mean my friends and I are staying there as guests of Nora Salter . . ." Polly stumbled on the name of the woman who was known to be Lucinda Payne's enemy. The older woman did not react. Polly bumbled on. "I did a foolish thing. I dashed out of the house like this because I saw a car hit a cat right in front of the house—"

The older woman leaned out into the rain to survey the street.

"She's okay, the cat, the driver took her to the MSPCA, I think maybe the hind leg was broken, but the thing is, I've managed to lock myself out of the house. I mean, I didn't even think to grab the keys or to check that the lock was off, so I'm wondering, could I please use your telephone? I'd like to phone my friend and ask her to come let me in."

Lucinda Payne looked Polly up and down with the scrutiny of an airport security guard. Obviously she didn't approve of what she saw. Still, she opened the door wider.

"Come in. But please stay in the hall until I've brought you a towel."

"Thank you. Thank you *so* much." Polly shivered now, and hugged herself as she looked around. The wide board floors of the hall were bare, the walls ivory, the only furniture a small chrome table with a Nantucket lightship basket centered on it, holding letters.

The towel the older woman brought her was thick and soft, more luxurious than some of Polly's best clothes. She dried her hands and dabbed at her hair, but hesitated to touch the towel to her orange face— she didn't know whether the chemicals would stain the towel, and she didn't want to sink any lower in Lucinda Payne's estimation. Finally she dried her neck and draped the towel around her shoulders for warmth.

Lucinda had gone off again, leaving Polly standing in the front hall. Leaning forward, she peered into the parlors on either side, surprised by the modernity of the furnishings. This house had the same basic architectural style as Nora Salter's—the wide board floors, the plaster rosettes centering the ceilings with lighting fixtures, brick fireplaces, and six-over-six paned windows. But unlike Nora Salter's, the furniture and decorations were new. Everything was cream, with a few spare touches of navy blue. The mantels and tables held no clutter, simply a few vases with fresh flowers, a magazine or a book, candlesticks, and a clock. The result was a remarkably fresh, young, almost urban ambience, surprising from a woman Lucinda Payne's age.

"I've brought you the phone." Lucinda Payne handed the portable handset to Polly. Quickly she punched in Faye's number—winging a silent prayer to thank the gods that she'd *remembered* Faye's number!—and explained her problem to Faye, who promised to come back immediately.

Polly handed the phone back to Lucinda. "She's on her way."

"Where is she?"

"She's out in 'Sconset, having a cup of tea in the café there. She's an artist, and she's been working on a landscape out that way, and she thought the rain would clear, but obviously it hasn't."

Lucinda looked at Polly, calculating. Polly looked back at the older woman, teeth chattering.

Lucinda sighed and resigned herself to the obvious demands of normal human etiquette. "You look cold. Come into the kitchen. I'll make you some tea."

"Thank you *so* much."

Polly eased off her slippers and dried her feet thoroughly before padding down the hall. As in Nora Salter's house, the kitchen was at the back of this house, but unlike Nora's, it had been modernized. Everything was white and gleaming chrome, except for the teak table and chairs centered on the black-and-white tiled floor. Next to a lone placemat lay a book of crossword puzzles, a dictionary, and a pen.

Delighted to have a neutral topic of conversation, Polly remarked, "Ah, you like crossword puzzles!"

"They serve to keep one's mind sharp," Lucinda said. "Earl Grey?"

"Perfect, thanks."

The older woman took two cups and saucers from the cupboard and set them on a tray. She brought out two teaspoons and lay two cloth napkins beneath them. She poured milk into a small pitcher and set that on the tray. She worked in silence, moving with arthritic stiffness and elegant, rigid posture. Finally she carried the tray to the table and sat down to pour the tea.

Even though the silence was uneasy, Polly waited until the little ceremony of tea serving had been performed and the other woman seated before speaking.

"You have a lovely home."

"Thank you."

Okay, Polly thought, so this is going to be work. At least I'm drying off.

"How old is this house?"

"It was built in 1840 by a whaling ship captain."

"Ah, like Nora Salter's house, then."

Lucinda's face darkened. "This house is *two* years older than the Salter house."

Polly sidestepped to a neutral subject. "There's so much history on this island."

But Lucinda wanted to make a point.

"It's unusual for houses to remain in one family through the generations. My father, Wetherford Payne, inherited the house from his father, and so on, back to 1840."

"Did you grow up here?"

Lucinda sniffed. "Of course not. My father was a banker. This was our summer retreat. I grew up near Boston."

Polly frowned. "Your last name is Payne?"

"I reverted to my maiden name when I was divorced."

"And your children?"

"I had two sons. They're both deceased." Lucinda glared at Polly, as if she were responsible.

"I'm so sorry."

Lucinda nodded. "I wanted more children, but I had several miscarriages, unlike that breeder next door. Nora has three children, but what good has it done her? They've all moved to the west coast." Icicles dripped from her words.

Polly smiled. "Children do go off on their own. I have one son, and he lives in Massachusetts, but his wife tends to keep him to herself."

"How *is* Nora?"

Slightly thrown by the quick change of subject—and then realizing that as far as the older woman was concerned, the subject hadn't changed; Lucinda could care less about Polly—she replied, "I don't know Nora well. I've met her at a couple of events. She's the friend of Shirley Gold, who owns The Haven, a spa outside Boston."

"But Nora's not coming down at all this summer?" Lucinda's green eyes bored like diamond drill bits into Polly's.

"She has to have an operation."

Lucinda's eyes took on a gleam of pleasure. "A *serious* operation?"

Polly was reluctant to give the other woman the information. But she was horrible at pretense. "I believe she's having a hip replaced."

Lucinda smiled slightly. "Ah." More to herself than Polly, she murmured, "Total anesthesia is always dangerous for one her age."

Well, you're a charming old ghoul! Polly thought, bristling. "Her daughter's coming back from California to take care of Nora after the operation." The light went from Lucinda's face. *Damn,* Polly cursed silently, *why did I let myself get caught up in this bizarre competition Lucinda seems to have going with Nora?*

"How fortunate for her." Lucinda's voice was etched with acid. "And when she dies, her children will inherit the house. It will be passed on to other Pettigrew descendants. While this house"—she lifted her arm, languorously waving it to indicate the room and the rooms around it—"is willed to the Historic Preservation Association, which will, no doubt, sell it to some millionaire who made his money with a national cesspool-equipment company and use the revenue to buy open land."

There were so many land mines of toxic subjects in that little speech, Polly had to struggle to come up with a dispassionate reply.

"Your house is in beautiful condition. And so . . . uncluttered."

It was the right thing to say. Lucinda's despondency lifted. She smiled, ever so slightly. "Unlike Nora's. What a pack rat."

Geez! Polly felt as if she were in a tug-of-war. Loyally, she countered, "She has accumulated an enormous variety of possessions, true, but they all look old and valuable. Perhaps they're family heirlooms."

"Perhaps." Lucinda's elegant head lifted. "Someone's at the door."

"Oh! That will be Faye!" In her eagerness to jump up, Polly hit her knee on the underside of the table. She cursed inwardly, but outwardly remained—she hoped—calm. "May I help you clear the tea things?"

"No, go on." The older woman made a little shooing motion with her hand. "You must be eager to get into clothes, since it's almost noon." *You lazy cow,* her tone of voice implied.

"Thank you so much for allowing me shelter," Polly said formally, and sincerely.

Lucinda simply nodded her head, in majestic acknowledgment of her benevolence.

"Perhaps you'd allow me to take you to tea sometime," Polly offered. "Or have you to tea at Nora's house."

Lucinda shrugged. "We'll see. I'm very busy."

"Yes, of course. Well, thanks again." Once again Polly hurried down the hall, her bare feet making slapping noises on the floorboards.

She flung open the door. Faye saw Polly's orange face and burst out laughing. Standing there in her cherry red raincoat, laughing, Faye looked like heaven to Polly.

On this warm July morning, Faye woke with the sun. She jumped from bed, hurriedly dressed, and tiptoed down the stairs to the kitchen to make coffee. She filled a traveling coffee mug, grabbed the juice, sweet roll, apple, and sandwich she'd prepared the night before, and rushed out to her Jeep. By five o'clock she was on her way.

The light. The light! No matter where she set up her easel, there was the light, as clear as a spotlight, or shimmering with humidity, or softened by clouds to a veil of gray, and always firing the landscape with a heart-stopping incandescent reality, a kind of visual *truth*. Here was the world, budding and ripe together, past, present, and future, consecrated by the sunlight. The light fell down from the heavens like psalms.

Some days she returned to a site to finish a complicated painting that took several days. The scenes by the harbor, with the verticals of sailboat masts and the shifting iridescence of the water, were the most challenging. Some days she woke knowing she wanted to go to the moors to paint the delicate pink and yellow blooms of Goat's Rue, or the grasses around the ponds. Other days, her subconscious informed her she needed to paint a particular Nantucket house, one she'd passed while driving off to get groceries or strolling around town.

Today rain threatened as clouds rolled overhead, making the light fickle. She drove just a few blocks, to the cross street near a house that had most recently caught her eye. She parked the red Jeep on Fair Street, because the house she wanted to paint was on a narrow lane with no sidewalks or room for parking.

The house itself wasn't unusual; it was much like many others on the island, over a century old, gray shingled, and modest. Its two and a half stories squarely faced the street, its chimney rose straight from the middle of the center-ridged roof. What set it apart was its oddly romantic state of dilapidation. The white trim around the windows was weathered to a mottled, almost feathery softness, like a pigeon's breast, as was the picket fence dividing the small garden at the side from the street. A luxuriant New Dawn rosebush scaled the side of the house, smothering most of the windows with a fairy-tale abundance of fragile pink flowers. At the front, the branches of a holly tree, thick with shiny, prickly leaves, stretched across the front door like a barricade. The windows at the front of the house were swathed with pink and purple clematis, while hollyhocks stood at attention like sentinels in the small space between the house and the street. The grass behind the picket fence was unkempt, uncut, and twined with weeds.

The curtains were all drawn. They never seemed to be opened. Faye assumed the house was unoccupied.

She walked back and forth, trying to find the right spot to set her easel. The houses on either side were higher, casting the smaller house in shadow. She established herself at the end of the small brick parking space across the street from the house. She adjusted her floppy sunhat, set up her easel, took out her palette, and began.

As she worked, the world woke up around her. Birds flashed back and forth in the trees, greeting the day and ordering one another around with bossy little chirps. Down the lane, a front door slammed, and a few moments later a young woman jogged past Faye, sleek in spandex, encased in headphones. She waved at Faye. A while later, another door shut and a boy biked along, the cards in his spokes clattering. She heard windows open. Scents of coffee and bacon drifted out into the morning air, and from behind her floated the measured, pleasing notes of someone practicing scales on a piano.

The front door opened on the house to the left and a young father and mother emerged, shooing their brood of children in front of them, all clad in bathing suits, carrying towels, a picnic basket, beach bags. Later, when Faye stopped to drink coffee, the side door of the house on the right opened and an older gentleman, dapperly clad in white flannels and a peppermint-striped long-sleeved cotton shirt, appeared. He had thick white hair, a dashing white mustache, and sparkling blue eyes. An elegant white poodle accompanied him with such élan it seemed *she* had *him* on the leash.

"Lovely morning," he said to Faye. "Mind if I look? Oh, very nice, very nice. Get away, Mitzi. I know, I know," he said to Faye, as if she'd made a remark, "man with a poodle, a bit tiddley. Mitzi belongs to my wife, don'tcha see, and my wife's a bit under the weather, so I've got the dog-walking duties. Yes, yes, off we go, good-bye, good-bye."

Later, Faye sensed someone watching her. Looking around, she spotted an orange-striped cat sitting on the picket fence, still and vigilant as an owl.

But for most of the morning Faye was alone. Occasionally a car slowly went down the lane, but most of the time people passed on foot or bike. Hidden away from the beaches, shops, and wider avenues, this lane was a real little pocket of peace, an island on an island.

By noon, Faye was tired and hungry. She began to organize herself to leave.

"Hello, my dear."

She looked up. A door at the side of the house she'd been painting was open now, and a little old woman stood in her garden, leaning on a cane.

"Oh! Hello!"

"I see you're painting my house's portrait." Gingerly, as if each step hurt, she progressed through the tall grass. "May I look?" She had white hair pulled into a bun at the back of her head, and several wobbling chins. She seemed very plump, but that might have been because she had so many different sweaters and shawls draped over her faded cotton dress.

"Of course." Faye lifted the canvas from the easel and brought it across the lane.

The older woman's neck emerged from its draperies like a tortoise's from its shell as she leaned forward to peer at it. "My, that's lovely. Just lovely."

"Thank you." Faye set the painting on the ground, leaning against her leg, so she could hold out her hand. "I'm Faye Vandermeer. I live in Boston, but I'm visiting here for the summer."

The older woman peered up at Faye through very thick glasses. "I'm very pleased to meet you. I'm Adele Spindleton and I've lived here all my life."

"You have a beautiful home."

"Yes, that's true. Although, sadly, I haven't been able to keep up with it like I used to." She cocked her head. "Would you like to see the inside?"

"Oh, I'd love to!"

Faye set her paraphernalia just inside the fence, went through the gate, and followed Adele Spindleton into the house. It was so dark, it took a few moments for her eyes to adjust.

The kitchen they stepped into hadn't been renovated since the forties. The floor was wide boards, aged to a deep bronze. A porcelain sink was set in a metal cabinet, and the refrigerator was a short, stocky Amana with rounded corners. The kitchen table was wooden, covered with a checkered tablecloth.

"If you'd like to see the dining room and parlors, be my guest," Adele told her. "I'll just wait here." She collapsed in a wooden kitchen chair. "Don't get around as easily as I used to."

"Oh!" Faye didn't want to intrude, but she did want to see the house. "Well, I'll just peek."

"Take your time."

The kitchen opened onto a dining room, which in turn opened onto a short hall and two front parlors. The ceiling plaster was crazed with cracks, as were some of the walls. Wallpaper had peeled in places, and much of the trim on the doors and windows was chipped. The hearth in the left parlor fireplace was missing a few bricks, and cobwebs laced the corners of the rooms, but clearly this was a fine old home. Family photos were everywhere, hanging from the walls, standing on mantels, tucked up in the bookcases. The floors sloped slightly, warped by age, but their lilt seemed pleasing to Faye, appropriate—it was like being on board a ship. In the right parlor, a recliner was situated in front of a television set, a crocheted afghan neatly folded on its side. Stationed nearby were a TV tray set with a glass of water, a remote control, and several pill bottles. Faye imagined this was where the old woman spent much of her time.

When she returned to the kitchen, she found Adele Spindleton dozing in her chair, her chin resting on her bosom. Faye hesitated. She didn't want to wake her—

As if reading her thoughts, Adele opened her eyes. "I'm awake. Do you have time to make us some tea?"

"Yes, of course."

Faye moved around the kitchen, pleasantly surprised at how tidy and efficient it was. When she remarked on this, the older woman said, "When I turned ninety, I had my children come take everything they wanted, every heirloom, every valuable thing, and the rest of it I donated to the thrift shop. I'd like to remain in my own home as long as my old bones will allow, which means I had to pare my life down to the essentials. Meals on Wheels comes by every day, and the young people next door pick up anything else I need."

"You still have pictures around," Faye remarked.

"Yes, yes, I'm so glad you noticed those. Yes, I kept the old photo albums and pictures. I love to look at them. It's like visiting the past."

Faye brought the teapot to the table, poured the tea into mugs, and helped Adele to milk and sugar. "Did you ever know Nora Salter? We're living in her house on Orange Street."

"Nora Salter. Nora Salter." Adele tapped her temple, as if trying to nudge a memory from its place. "Oh, yes! Yes, of course. Beautiful woman, much younger than I. She's a Pettigrew, you know. Very fine island lineage. Pascal Pettigrew, her father, was born on the island, and so was her mother. Pascal's grandfather had been a whaling ship captain. Oh, yes, lots of history in that family. And so much drama! Oh, my dear," Adele's laugh tinkled like bells. "I haven't thought of them in years!"

Faye was fascinated. "What kind of history?"

"What kind would you like? When you get a family going back for generations, you can take your pick." Adele sipped her tea and her cheeks grew rosy. "He was such a scamp, that Pascal Pettigrew! I'm six years younger than he was, but I heard all about him when I was a child. He was legendary. He and Ford Payne. What they got up to!" Adele cackled and clapped her hands on her knees.

Faye leaned forward. "What sorts of things?"

"Well, for one, when they were kids, they liked to tip over outhouses on Halloween." She peered over her glasses at Faye. "As you can tell, this was a long time ago. At the beginning of the last century. What else? Let's see. If they didn't like their teachers, they'd fill May baskets—people don't do this anymore, but back then, we used to leave May baskets filled with flowers or cookies to celebrate May Day—only they'd put a layer of flowers on top and dog manure beneath!"

Faye tried to organize this history. "Ford Payne would be Lucinda Payne's father?"

"That's right. I haven't seen Lucinda in ages. She's such a beautiful young woman, but rather uppity."

Faye raised her cup to her lips to hide a smile she couldn't suppress when Adele called Lucinda a *young* woman. Of course, Adele was in her nineties, while Lucinda was only seventy-three. Youth was relative. "We met Lucinda Payne briefly. She didn't seem pleased to know we were spending the summer in Nora's house."

Adele waved her hand. "Oh, nothing about *Nora* could ever please Lucinda. By the time Lucinda was born, the scandal had happened. The Pettigrews and the Paynes hated one another. Lucinda and Nora were *raised* hating one another. Oh, they were all so stubborn. Neither family would sell the house that had been handed down over the years, and I can understand that, yes, I can. Still, to live side by side with your arch enemy has got to be difficult."

"*Scandal?*" Faye thought she could actually feel her ears strain forward like a bat's.

Before Adele could reply, a volley of bangs sounded nearby. Adele frowned. "What was that? Thunder?"

"Firecrackers, I think," Faye assured her. "Tomorrow's the Fourth of July."

"Oh, of course." Adele shook her head. "They always have such a fine display down at Jetties Beach. I assume they still do. I haven't seen the fireworks for years."

"Polly and I are going," Faye told her. "Would you like to come along?" When the older woman looked puzzled, she said, "Polly's a friend, another of the five us of who will be spending time in Nora Salter's house this summer. She's my age. You'd like her."

"Well . . . my sake's. Goodness." Adele seemed absolutely stumped by Faye's invitation. "I can't walk very far, you know. And I can't sit on the ground like I used to."

"We'll bring beach chairs. We'll pick you up in the Jeep and drive you as close as we can get to the beach."

"What a kind offer!" Adele's face grew rosy. "You know, I'd love to come! Why not? If you two girls don't mind being saddled with an old nag like me. . . ."

"The fireworks start at nine. We'll pick you up at eight-thirty," Faye told her. "I'll drive the Jeep right to your door."

"Wonderful! Thank you!"

Faye washed the mugs and teapot, then let herself out of the house. As she carried her easel and painting to the Jeep, she realized that in the excitement of planning for tomorrow, she'd forgotten about the scandal.

It was a perfect night for fireworks, clear, warm, and dry. At eight-thirty, Faye and Polly arrived at Adele's house. Faye made the introductions, and they helped Adele through her yard and into the front passenger seat of the Jeep, a challenge for the older woman, who could not lift her leg high enough to set it on the Jeep's sandy floor.

"Would you mind giving me a little push?" she asked. "Don't be shy. You can't hurt me. Can't embarrass me, either. At my age, I've been poked and prodded everywhere. Just go ahead," she chuckled, "and wedge me in."

It took more than a little push to boost the roly-poly older woman into place. By the time Polly and Faye had finished, all three women were dissolved in giggles.

They drove through town toward Jetties Beach, joining the parade of cars and people headed the same way. On Federal Street, they passed Kezia in her huge silver SUV. She was going in the opposite direction, against the tide of traffic. Pleased to see someone she knew, Faye waved, but Kezia didn't see them.

Faye glanced over her shoulder at Polly. "I wonder why Kezia's not going to the fireworks."

"Her baby's probably too young to enjoy them," Polly said. "David was afraid of the noise until he was eight!"

When they turned on to South Beach Street, Adele gasped. "I'm astonished at the number of people going to the beach. I knew the summer population had grown. But to *see* it like this—it just makes my head whirl!"

By the time they reached Easton Street, the crowd was so dense the Jeep could only inch forward.

"Can you put this in four-wheel drive?" Adele asked Faye.

"Sure."

"There's a public way on the right. Few people know about it. It's a perfect spot for watching the fireworks."

Other SUVs were already on the beach, but Faye steered over the sand until she found a spot. She parked, rolled down the windows, turned off the lights, and then the ignition. At once, the scent and sound of the sea swept into the car. The harbor was dotted with boats of all sizes, waving flags, decorated with red, white, and blue banners and flowers. As the sun set and the sky turned from dusky to complete black velvet, horns from boats and cars honked, eager for the show to begin.

Adele decided she would remain in the car to watch the display; it was just too much work to get out and back in. Polly opened the picnic basket next to her on the backseat and handed around a plate of brie and crackers and, to Adele's delight, glasses of champagne.

"Champagne! I can't remember when I last had it!"

Suddenly a bolt of gold streaked through the sky, blossoming into multicolored tendrils of light. The show had started. Polly got out of the backseat and stood in the sand for a better view, but Faye remained in the Jeep with Adele. She was having as much fun listening to the older woman as she was watching the fireworks. So many new kinds of patterns had been developed since Adele last saw them; she was as thrilled as if the planets themselves were putting in an appearance. Out in the harbor, the boats honked and whistled as fountains and pinwheels and volcanoes of light burst through the sky, trailing silver dots that exploded into their own colorful shows. Screamers streamed upward in crazy zigzags, pinwheels threw out silver minnows of light that undulated through the dark before fading. The calm waters of the harbor reflected the display, and the oohs and aahs of the crowd rolled through the night in waves.

Finally the show was over. Polly got back into the Jeep and replaced the empty champagne glasses and the plate. Faye put the Jeep in gear and joined the line of traffic headed away from the beach. Adele fell asleep, head leaning against the window frame, oblivious to the bounces and bumps as they rolled over the sandy ruts. Faye met Polly's eyes in the rearview mirror; they agreed soundlessly to remain quiet, so they wouldn't wake Adele.

The older woman's eyes popped open just as they turned onto her street. Carefully they helped her out of the Jeep, across the grassy yard and into her house.

"I'm fine now," Adele said as they stood in her kitchen. "You girls are so wonderful! That was a treat!" She turned to Faye. "Will you be painting my house again tomorrow?"

"If it doesn't rain," Faye told her. "I'll let you know."

"Lovely. Thank you again, girls."

Driving back to Orange Street, Polly remarked, "We certainly seem to be running into a lot of little old ladies around here."

Faye shrugged. "All the little old men have already died, I guess. Men do die younger."

"Speaking of men . . ." Polly's voice was wistful. "I don't know what to do about Hugh."

"I know. I don't know what to do about Aubrey."

"Have you spoken with him recently?"

Faye waited to reply until she'd carefully steered the Jeep into its tiny space next to the house. "No. I haven't phoned him and he hasn't phoned me. He's angry that I came here instead of staying and taking care of him. His daughter's not thrilled with me, either."

"What if he finds another woman?" Polly asked.

Faye stared out at the dark night. "In all honesty, I just don't know."

Polly sighed. "Well, *I* know Hugh's going to remain attached to his kids and Carol for the rest of his life. He's not going to change. I guess at our age, change isn't easy."

"I'm not so sure about that," Faye argued. "I mean, Polly, I think I'm still capable of changing. *Really* changing. I think we all are! I mean, we've changed our homes for the summer. And in the past couple of years, you've changed from working as a seamstress to running Havenly Yours. Who knows how you might change again?" Faye grew serious and animated. "I stopped painting when Jack died. I thought I'd never paint again. But I *did*. Plus, *now* I'm doing landscapes, outdoor scenes—I *never* used to paint those. I pretty much stuck with still life and a few portraits. I'm learning so much about myself, my style, my abilities, I'm so excited about painting on the island! I feel—I know this is odd—but I feel *young* again, Polly! Remember that feeling, when school starts in the fall, and you buy new notebooks and pencils and your erasers are pink and clean and sort of spongy in your hand? And you've got a new Black Watch plaid dress for the first day of school? That's how I feel about painting! And I love this island!" She threw her arms out so enthusiastically she hit the roof. "The more I see of it, the more I want to see. I love it here! In fact, I can't wait to go to bed so I can get up in the morning to paint!" She looked at Polly suddenly, puzzled. "I think I got off the subject. What we were talking about?"

Polly laughed. "I think the topic was men."

"Right." Faye turned toward Polly, her face glowing. "I've been thinking so much about all this, Polly. It's all tied together—work, and Aubrey, and aging, and my weight. Let me see if I can articulate this clearly. I not only think we can change, I think we *have* to. At this age. At this age, if we're reasonably healthy, we should get to make some decisions about our lives. Oh," she waved her hands in the air, "you have no idea how much I've been pondering these things. First of all, every moment of every day, it seems my first thought is about dieting. Even when I was watching those gorgeous fireworks and sipping champagne, a little voice in the back of my mind was nagging at me: *Don't drink that champagne! You'll gain weight!*"

Polly nodded. "I've got the same little voice."

"So . . . to come back to *men,* to be frank, it's partly because I like being with a man that I work so hard not to gain any weight. I do try to be healthy, Polly, you know that. I'll always eat plenty of broccoli and fresh salads and fruit. But if I eat one piece of bread, or one cookie, or drink a glass of champagne, with my metabolism the way it is—and I *exercise,* I walk almost every day!—I gain weight. I've figured out that the only way I can lose weight is to limit myself to eight hundred calories a day, day after day. Anything over twelve hundred calories and I gain weight. Oh," she hit the dashboard with her fist, "I'm so disgusted with myself! I'm so sick of obsessing about weight all the time!"

"I know," Polly murmured. "Me, too."

"The *point* is, I'm fighting my body every day, and guess what? I'm getting older anyway! And *rounder!* I've got to believe there's a genetic clock in my DNA that is telling my entire body that it's time for me to stop with the vanity, and get—well, *jolly!*"

"I've been 'jolly' all my life," Polly commented.

"No, that's not true. I've seen photos of you, Polly. You were slim once, and even if you were curvy, you weren't like you are now, and I hope I'm not ruining our friendship by saying this, but you are like I am, you are just getting *round*. We once were more linear, like willow trees. Now we're sphere-shaped, like . . ."

". . . like snowmen," Polly finished for her.

"Snow*women*," Faye corrected with a grin. "Right. Now here's my choice: I can continue to obsess about my weight so I can fit into beautiful clothes—and that's another subject entirely, beautiful clothes shouldn't be only for skinny women—I can continue to obsess about my weight so Aubrey will be proud of me when we go out in public. I know how vain Aubrey is. I've met some of the women he's dated. They all are bone thin and elegant." She interrupted herself with a question. "Can a woman be elegant and plump? I don't know."

"*You* are!" Polly insisted heartily.

"Thanks, but . . . anyway, I see continuing my relationship with Aubrey as *work*. Partly because I'll have to continue dieting strenuously to keep in shape for him, and partly because I'll have to stop painting and spend my time taking care of him. I'm just not sure I want to do that."

"*Or*," Polly prompted.

"Or what?" Faye asked, puzzled.

Polly chuckled. "You said you feel like you have a choice. First, keep dating Aubrey and trying not to gain any more weight. *Or . . .* what?"

Faye bonked her head lightly against the back of her seat. "I guess that's what I don't know. Oh, Polly, I'd imagined this stage of my life as one full of peace. I'd travel with Jack and spend lots of time with my grandchildren. But Jack died, and my grandchildren live on the other side of the United States. I've thought about moving to California, but I really don't think Laura would like that. She's very happy now, so capable, she's found her strength. She needs me on the periphery, not in the inner circle. So I have to reinvent my future."

"Well, I'm with you there, too. I lost my husband, and I'm certainly not in the inner circle with my son and his family."

For a while, they sat in silence, contemplating all Faye had said.

Then Polly turned to the backseat. "I think there's some champagne left in the bottle. We don't want it to go to waste."

"Right." Faye dug the glasses from the picnic basket and Polly poured.

"For the rest . . . well, first, Faye, you always look beautiful. Your clothes are always beautiful, especially the ones you make yourself, like the Havenly Yours clothes, layered in different colors. True, you don't look forty anymore. But you do have beautiful clothes, and you did before Aubrey and you will whether you're with him or not. Second"—she stopped to catch her breath and sip some champagne—"are you so sure Aubrey cares about how much you weigh? I mean, after your fall last Christmas, you packed on the pounds, and then gradually lost them again, and as far as I recall, he never showed any signs of wanting to end your relationship because you'd gotten fat, and you know I'm using 'fat' as a relative term!"

"You're right," Faye murmured. "Aubrey's never been bothered by my flab."

"So your quandary about Aubrey isn't about your weight. And it shouldn't be about his health, either, I don't think. He's in his early seventies, true, but for heaven's sake, he's only got bursitis, not a terminal illness! And you have fun with him, I know you do. We had a fabulous time on our Christmas cruise a year ago! You and Aubrey were gorgeous on the dance floor! And he can be so witty. I think the real question, Faye, is whether you love him or not. Not how long he might live. I mean, come on, at this age any of us could go at any moment."

Faye sighed. "Everything you say makes sense, Polly. The truth is, I don't think I know whether or not I love Aubrey. Or whether he *loves* me. Or even if love is important at our age."

Suddenly, from one of the neighboring yards, came a series of pops, shrieks, and laughter, as kids set off firecrackers.

"How apropos," Faye said.

Polly laughed. "The AMA should do one of their famous studies: How Important Are Fireworks in an Over-Fifty Relationship?"

"Love and sex are two different things," Faye reminded her. "Man, look at the time. We've been sitting out here for over an hour. Let's go in."

They gathered the picnic basket and empty bottle and glasses and went through the dark, warm night into Nora Salter's house.

"Maybe I'm thinking about all this because it's Independence Day," Faye told Polly, half-joking as they unpacked the basket in the kitchen. "And I have to say one last thing: If I were a man, and if I wanted to concentrate on painting for the rest of my life, my partner would adjust her life to mine. If I were a man, and my wife had bursitis, I wouldn't be expected to drop everything, I wouldn't have to give up my work—"

"Faye," Polly interrupted, "wasn't there a little silver pheasant up there next to the champagne bucket?"

Faye frowned. "Silver pheasant?"

"Maybe it was a peacock," Polly blithered. "A bird with a long tail . . . not a swan, not a parrot . . . no, I'm sure it was a pheasant."

Faye yawned. "I didn't see anything like that."

"I noticed it when I climbed up on a chair to get the champagne bucket down. I remember thinking it should be in the dining room, not the kitchen, because it's ornamental, not functional, and perhaps it was put in the kitchen because there's just too much stuff in the dining room. I'm sure it was there, Faye. And now it's not." She shuddered. "Someone's been in the house!"

"Polly, hon, that's not possible. I distinctly remember locking the door when we left, and I'm one hundred percent certain I had to use my key to get in just now."

"Right. Still . . ." Polly walked over and tested the back door. "This is locked, too." She put her hands on her hips as she scanned the kitchen. "When Alice took those photos, she forgot to photograph the kitchen. I'll get a camera and do the kitchen tomorrow."

"Good idea," Faye said. "And you know what? Let's have copies made of all the pictures, and we'll put a copy on each table and bureau, so that if anyone *is* sneaking in and stealing stuff, *they*'ll know *we* know, and furthermore, that we have a record of it."

Polly considered this. "That might work as a preventative measure. . . ."

Faye could tell Polly was uncomfortable. "For now, let's look through the house, see if anything else is missing."

"Or if someone's here," Polly whispered.

Faye humored her. She opened a cupboard and took out a flashlight. "For closets."

"Should I take some kind of weapon?" Polly asked. "A knife, maybe?"

Faye's laughter had a bit of hysteria in it. "Polly, I just can't imagine you stabbing someone, not even a burglar hiding in a closet!"

"You're right, I probably couldn't. But I am going to take a fireplace poker!"

Together the two women went through the house, dining room first, so Polly could grab a poker. Since there were about one zillion objects, they couldn't notice any single thing missing. Polly was more concerned about someone being in the house, so they looked through all the closets, behind all the curtains, and beneath the various sofas. As they crept up the stairs to the second floor, Polly gripped Faye's hand for comfort. They flicked on all the lights as they went—not an easy task, because none of the rooms had overhead lights with wall switches just inside the door. They had to walk through the room to the bedside table or the bureau to turn on a table lamp. But a thorough check, under every bed, in every corner of every closet, including the linen closet, revealed no signs of intruders. The door to the third floor was locked.

"Maybe someone got in the first-floor window," Polly suggested.

"I don't think so," Faye argued sensibly as they went through the first floor one more time. "Remember, the windows are a good twelve feet from the ground. We have to climb ten steps or so to get to the front door. Someone would have to put a ladder or stand on a stool at least, to get in through the windows."

Polly nodded. "You're right. I must be mistaken." She returned the poker to the fireplace equipment.

In the kitchen, Faye put the flashlight back in the drawer.

Polly stared up at the shelf. "One good thing. Whoever is stealing stuff doesn't seem violent."

"True." Faye yawned. "I'm beat, and I want to get up early to paint."

"I'm ready to go up, too."

They went through the house together, turning off the lights. They climbed the stairs and called out to one another as they got ready for bed. Finally they settled in for the night in their separate bedrooms. Faye turned off her light immediately. Polly plumped up her pillows and tried to focus on a book, but she couldn't stop straining to hear an unusual sound and her thoughts kept wandering off the sentence on the page.

Finally she relaxed. After reading a few pages, she was drowsy. She took off her glasses, folded them and set them on the bedside table, turned off the lamp, and snuggled down beneath the silky cotton sheet, letting the book fall next to her on the bed.

At least she thought that was what she did. She was surprised, when she woke the next morning, to find her book placed neatly on the table, bookmark inserted between the pages. When she told Faye about this little oddity, Faye assured her she had probably moved the book herself during the night. After all, people did a lot of odd things while they were sleeping.

It was the first weekend after the Fourth of July, and Marilyn was try-ing very hard not to feel sorry for herself. Alice and Shirley had left Friday night for Nantucket. Now, Saturday morning, they were probably sitting around the kitchen table with Polly and Faye, dis-cussing, complaining, planning, laughing. Marilyn missed them terribly. She needed them. She felt she missed and needed them more than she missed and needed Ian. Only at this age in her life was she coming to re-alize how much the happiness of her relationship with the man she loved depended, at least in part, on how much time she got to spend with her friends. The scientific part of her brain wondered whether this concept had ever been tested and charted. Was it possible to come up with a ratio—thirty minutes of conversation a week with friends equals a thirty percent improvement in personal affairs? Because it wasn't just Ian for whom she felt more fondness after she'd had a good session with the Hot Flash Club. She also had more patience for her mother and for Angus and his lovable, uncivilized dog.

Ian was still in Scotland. He'd been there ten days now, and still had no plans to come home. Fiona's children had come for the funeral, but returned to their busy lives and jobs. Ian had stayed behind to help Fiona pack up Tam's belongings and help her think about her future. Marilyn didn't begrudge him his time away; how could she, when she valued her time with *her* friends so highly?

Still, she kept thinking of a silly joke someone had told her recently. *What is a honeymoon sandwich? Lettuce alone.* Now all the trips she and Ian had made back and forth between Boston and Edinburgh seemed imbued with radiance and romance. They'd had so little time to-gether, they'd spent it making love, talking, constantly focused on one another. Now when they were living together, it seemed they had less time together than when they were living apart.

Oh well, she couldn't change things, not this weekend. This weekend Ian was in Scotland, her friends were on Nantucket, Angus and Darwin were in the attic, and her mother and Marie were in the garden suite. Marilyn poured herself another cup of coffee and went down for a morning chat with her mother.

Ruth sat in her armchair, her kitten curled on her lap. She wore a rainbow-colored housecoat and pink flip-flops. She was watching television, but when Marilyn entered, Ruth aimed the remote at the TV and clicked it off.

"Good morning, darling!" Ruth held up her arms for a kiss.

"Morning, Mom." Marilyn bent to embrace her mother. She gave Marie a little pat. The kitten stretched and rolled on her side, showing off her fat belly. "What are you up to this morning?"

"I was listening to PBS. They were performing Andrew Lloyd Wright's music. Such marvelous tunes!"

Marilyn ignored her mother's malapropism as she settled on the sofa across from Ruth. "You know, we could buy you a little CD player and some of his CD's. Or even check one out at the library. Then you could play music down here whenever you wanted."

Ruth frowned. "I'm not sure I could figure out how to operate one of those new machines."

"Mom. You're a scientist. You're a teacher. You can learn how to push a couple of buttons."

"I suppose." Ruth didn't look entirely convinced.

"Are you up for a little jaunt this morning? We could go to the library and the pharmacy. We could go out for lunch."

"I'd like that, dear." Ruth stroked the kitten with her age-spotted, veiny hand. "Have you heard from Ian?"

"Not today." Marilyn hated the melancholy in her voice. "But he'll either e-mail or call. Anyway, let's go out, okay?"

"Give me about an hour to get ready. I've had breakfast, but I want to shower and dress."

Marilyn chewed her thumbnail. "Do you suppose I should ask Angus to go with us?"

"If you want to. I can't imagine the boy would enjoy being with a doddering old crone like me, going to the library and the pharmacy. You know, Marilyn, Angus really needs to make some friends his own age."

"I know he does. But how can that happen when he's always in his room?" She rose. "I'm going to dress, then I'll see if I can 'encourage' Angus to take his dog out, and I'll ask him if he wants to go with us." Marilyn felt like her entire body was weighted with chains as she dragged herself across the room.

"Marilyn?" Ruth said in a sprightly tone.

Marilyn turned. "Yes?"

"What do you see when the Pillsbury Doughboy bends over?"

Marilyn grinned. "I don't know. What?"

"Doughnuts."

Marilyn laughed. "You guys are pretty saucy down at that Senior Citizens Center!"

She was smiling as she climbed the stairs. *Look on the bright side,* she admonished herself. The electrician had finally come and the central air was working. The plumber had come and the toilet was working. Ian would be home soon. She'd probably be able to go to Nantucket next weekend.

As she set her foot on the first step to the third floor, she heard Darwin's excited yip and by the time she reached Angus's door, Darwin was in full-scale scratch and bark mode. The miracle was that Angus seemed able to sleep through the puppy's noise. Marilyn pounded on the door.

Finally the knob turned. Marilyn steadied herself for the onslaught as Darwin threw himself at her, exuberantly boinging up and down, as if he were on an invisible pogo stick, as he tried to get to her face to give her a kiss with his long pink tongue.

Angus was still wearing the clothes he wore last night—jeans and a T-shirt.

"Time to take the dog out, Angus," Marilyn told him. She learned that simple commands were the most efficient. "Darwin needs to pee. You've got to give him a little walk."

Angus scratched the top of his balding head. He yawned, exhaling noxious fumes into the air. Marilyn took a step back. As she watched, Angus looked around him, puzzled.

"You don't need your shoes," Marilyn told him. "You'll be fine barefoot. It's hot out, and you don't have to walk far."

Slouching, Angus found the leash, fastened it on Darwin's collar, and followed the eager puppy down to the front door. There, Marilyn handed Angus a plastic bag. "You know the drill. Any doggie poo has to be picked up." How many times had she told Angus this? Twenty? Thirty? But if she didn't remind him, he'd ignore the dog's droppings, and the angry glances of people passing on the street didn't faze him— he didn't even notice them.

"And Angus, I'm taking Ruth out on a little excursion this morning. We're going to the library and the pharmacy. Maybe out to lunch. We'd love to have you join us if you'd like."

Angus flicked a shy look at Marilyn. "Um."

Okay, Marilyn thought, I've given him too many decisions. "Walk your dog first, Angus. We can talk about lunch when you get back." As an added incentive, she said, "I'll have a fresh cup of coffee waiting for you when you get back."

Angus shuffled off down the sidewalk, his puppy straining at the leash.

Marilyn watched from the kitchen window. Angus wouldn't be outside long, not even on a sunny day like today. He didn't seem comfortable anywhere except in front of a computer. Sure enough, he returned within five minutes. Marilyn handed him a mug and repeated her invitation.

"Um, I think I'll stay here. I've got work to do."

"Fine, but you know you'll need to take Darwin out for a long walk today. He's a puppy, he needs lots of exercise. Perhaps later this afternoon I can drive the two of you to a park."

Angus looked miserable at the prospect, but nodded his head dutifully. "Perhaps."

As Angus and his dog headed back up the stairs, Marilyn went into her bedroom to dress for the day—an easy task. She wore khaki shorts, a blue T-shirt, and sandals. Summer was so blissfully easy! She pulled her long hair into a loose tail to let air flow against the back of her neck as she went into her study.

She had an e-mail from Ian!

Perching on the edge of her chair, she opened it.

Marilyn, my love, I miss you. I'll phone you later, around four or five your time, but the thing is, I'd like to bring Fiona over to the States with me for a while. She's lost without Tam. This is such a terrible terrible tragedy. Whenever she walks from one room to another, she breaks into tears—everything reminds her of Tam. She's so grief-stricken she can't make a single decision. She doesn't know whether to give Tam's clothes and books away or keep them, whether to sell the house, where she would move if she did sell, and so on. She's just overloaded. Doesn't the sofa in the living room open into a bed? If she stayed with us for a while, maybe a complete change of scenery would help her regroup. I think it might. I'll ask her today and let you know when I call tonight. This makes me realize each moment how fortunate I am to have you in my life.

Love, Ian

On this hot Tuesday afternoon, Elroy Morris, the building and grounds manager of The Haven, was presenting his report. The words, cast in his high-pitched, nasal voice, circled Shirley's ears with the persistence of a starving mosquito. Elroy looked like a beaver. He wore brown coveralls and had buck teeth, shaggy brown hair on his head, face, and all over his arms, and a slow, shuffling way of moving.

Shirley tried to pay attention, but it was hard. Her thoughts kept drifting back to Nantucket. Right now she could be walking barefoot on the beach, letting the breeze cool her skin and the salt air work its magical aromatherapy. Instead, she was here at work, trying to comprehend and organize a bunch of essential but mind-numbing information to be presented next week at the monthly meeting of the board of directors of The Haven.

Her mind kept floating back to Nantucket. She'd had a blissful weekend on the island, lazing about with all the Hot Flash femmes, except for Marilyn. She'd dragged Alice along with her on a walk on the moors—Alice had not been thrilled. They'd all gone together to a play Saturday night, and Sunday they sat in their robes and talked and nibbled on a feast of leftovers until it was time for Alice and Shirley to catch the ferry back. Shirley hadn't caught sight of Harry. She hadn't even thought of him—well, not *constantly.*

"For storms and screens for all windows in the upper and lower floors of the main building $26,342 . . ." Elroy droned.

The three of them—Shirley, Alice, and Elroy—were in the conference room, so they could spread their papers out across the big mahogany table. Alice sat across from Shirley, looking distracted and uncomfortable. Usually Alice, who had the acumen and experience with these sorts of practical matters, knew exactly what questions to ask and how to sort through the whirlwind of facts to glean the necessary elements by which to steer the board of directors to a decision.

But Alice had baby Aly on her lap.

And Aly was teething. The infant squirmed in Alice's embrace, fussing and drooling, occasionally pacified by chewing on a brightly colored puffy object, but always managing to drop the teething ring just when Alice had gathered her thoughts and started to speak. Alice had confided to Shirley that Alan and Jennifer were having problems, and Alice donated all her time and expertise to The Haven free of charge, so Shirley felt guilty for feeling impatient and resentful of Alice's divided attention. But without Alice's input, this meeting was a waste of time.

With each passing day, Shirley sensed how little time she had left to waste. It was ironic. She had had a dream *come true*. She had dreamed of, and yearned for, and then, with the help of her friends and some investors, created this place, The Haven. But in many ways it was no haven for her, and there were even times when her dream had the qualities of a nightmare.

" . . . also, in light of the additions and changes to the building, we'll need to review the insurance policy . . . ," Elroy Morris continued.

"Urglelblah!" the baby screamed.

My thoughts precisely, Shirley thought.

The baby arched her back angrily in an attempt to launch herself off Alice's lap and wailed like a siren.

"I apologize," Alice said. With one hand, she held on to the shrieking baby. With the other hand, she gathered together her papers and stuffed them into her briefcase. "I'll take her home so the two of you can concentrate."

Don't leave me!, Shirley wanted to weep. *I can't understand this stuff!*

"That pretty much concludes my report, anyway." Elroy Morris pushed himself up from the table. "If you have any questions, you can e-mail me."

Aly's face was turning purple as she shrieked at hurricane force. As Alice carried the baby out of the office, all she could do as a way of saying good-bye was to waggle her eyebrows and mouth "Later" at Shirley.

Elroy followed Alice, and Shirley gathered her papers and left the conference room, too.

She smiled briefly at her secretary—Wendy, who deserved a huge raise, something else to bring up at the next meeting—and stepped into the peace of her office. No, Shirley decided, not peace. It was quiet in here, but not peaceful. How it could it be *peaceful,* when her desk was piled high with incomprehensible forms needing to be read, digested, and acted upon?

As she collapsed in her chair, her thoughts turned to Alice, who had looked unusually frazzled this morning. Shirley knew how much Alice loved her son and his family, but she also knew about the osteoarthritis that caused Alice crippling pain. She knew how much time Alice needed to spend exercising, paying attention to her diet, taking care of herself— and she knew full well how Alice was ignoring her own health in order to help her son. Alice adored her granddaughter. The little girl's birth had been a kind of miracle for Alice, who had spent so much of her life climbing the spiky ladder of corporate politics that she'd almost lost touch with her soft side. Alice was in a kind of love, but the practical everyday operations of that love were wearing her down. When they were on Nantucket, Alice had a chance to catch her breath. She slept a lot, and ate what Shirley suggested, and went on walks, and began the first steps to getting back in shape. But when she returned to real life, her granddaughter and all the complications of reality sucked her up like a cosmic vacuum cleaner.

But what could Shirley do? She felt guilty, because she relied on Alice's precise executive mind for The Haven. *She* needed Alice, too.

Her phone buzzed. "Shirley?" It was Wendy. "Your eleven o'clock appointment's here."

"Great. Thanks." She picked up her clipboard and pen. This was the part she liked about being director of The Haven. Meeting a new client, assessing her, chatting over a cup of tea in the beautiful lounge, suggesting a plan of therapy that would suit each individual need—that was Shirley's forte. Helping people feel better. That was her gift.

At least it used to be. She wasn't sure how effective she was these days.

She stepped into the staff bathroom in the back corridor to check her hair and makeup. She'd once had long fluffy red curls. When she became director of The Haven, she'd had her hair styled into a more elegant chin-length bob to go with her new tailored—and she felt, completely un-Shirley—suits. Over the past couple of years, as The Haven flourished, she'd allowed herself to soften her look. She'd grown her hair out to her shoulders and let some of the white as well as some of the curl return. She wore her tailored suits only when the board of directors met. Today she wore a summery swirl of lavender silk and lots of amethyst jewelry. She blew a kiss at herself in the mirror. Really, she was looking pretty good for a gal her age.

She went back through the corridor, out to the front lobby, and into the lounge. The prospective new client was gazing at the art hung on the walls, which gave Shirley a moment to study her.

Shirley kind of wished she'd worn the tailored suit.

Usually the women who came to the spa, no matter what their income or social status, showed some signs of personal chaos. A torn hem, slumped shoulders, tightness around the mouth.

This woman looked like she'd just walked out of an ad for a Jaguar. She was trim and blonde, encased in a perfectly fitted black suit. She wore the kind of high black heels Shirley hadn't been able to wear for years. When she turned to look at Shirley, she showed a flawless face. Big blue eyes, peaches-and-cream complexion, and the kind of makeup that looked like none at all.

Shirley gulped. A woman like this always somehow brought Shirley back to her early insecurities, the sense of worthlessness that had once driven her to alcohol. Not every flawless young woman made Shirley feel this way—Carolyn Sperry looked just as gorgeous as this creature, but when they first met, Carolyn had come as a client, with a slight air of vulnerability. This woman looked invulnerable.

Shirley sucked in a deep breath, held out her hand, and crossed the room. "Hello. I'm Shirley Gold, director of The Haven."

The blonde smiled her million-dollar smile, every tooth perfect and dazzling.

"Eden Morton." Her hand in Shirley's was cool and soft.

Of course your name's Eden, Shirley thought. "Let's sit over here."

Shirley sank onto a sofa. "Someone will be bringing tea in a moment." Shirley had instituted this ritual herself. She liked the sense of intimacy it gave. It made the whole process seem more homey, less businesslike. "Peach tea, iced, no caffeine."

"How nice." Eden seemed completely uninterested.

Shirley crossed her legs and rested her clipboard on her knee. "Now. Let's talk about what The Haven can do for you."

Eden arched a perfect eyebrow. "Oh, you must have misunderstood. I'm here to see what *we* can do for *you*."

Great, Shirley thought, another sales rep. She didn't have time for this today. "I—"

Eden cut her off. "I represent Rainbow." She beamed smugly. "The Rainbow Corporation." Reaching into her briefcase, she pulled out a brochure and handed it to Shirley.

Shirley took it with fingers that were quickly going numb. She didn't need to peruse the brochure. She'd heard of Rainbow. *Everyone* had heard of Rainbow. It was like the Vatican of spas. Started ten years ago in California, it had exploded under the leadership of a young, ambitious married couple, Rain and Richard Bow. He was in pharmaceuticals, she was in advertising. Together they'd created an empire.

Shirley's mouth had gone so dry she couldn't speak. She nearly fell on her knees with gratitude when Wendy arrived, carrying a tray with tea. "Thank you, Wendy," she managed to squeak. She didn't dare pick up a glass and expose her shaking hands.

Eden Morton seemed used to this kind of reaction. She waited until Wendy had left the room, then said in a low but authoritarian voice, "We—Rainbow—would like to purchase The Haven."

Feeling flooded back through Shirley in a rush. "Oh, no." Shirley shook her head. She even smiled—an effortless, even triumphant little smile. "Sorry. That's not going to happen. We're quite happy with The Haven."

"Yes, I'm sure you are. You have a wonderful location, a great building, and a growing clientele. Otherwise Rainbow wouldn't be interested."

"Thanks, but *we're* not interested."

"Perhaps you should consult your board." Eden Morton handed Shirley a slip of paper with a number written on it. "Show them this. It's what we're prepared to offer."

Shirley looked down at the figure. It began with a dollar sign. It was a very large number. She almost fell off the sofa in shock.

"I . . ." She cleared her throat. "I see." She stared at the paper, half expecting the numbers to rearrange themselves into something more reasonable. "Well, as I said, Eden, we're not interested, but since you've gone to the trouble to come here personally, I will present this offer to my board of directors. We meet next week."

Eden held out another piece of paper. "My business card. Perhaps you'll phone me after the meeting?"

"Of course." Shirley rose. Once again they shook hands. As she escorted Eden to the main doors, she sent a silent prayer of thanks to the goddess above for the gift of legs that supported her, when she felt like they were made out of pudding.

Overnight, something clicked in nature's thermostat, and when New England residents woke on that July morning, the outside world was one giant sauna. The temperature climbed into the high nineties, and the humidity was in the nineties, too. Air-conditioning units chugged laboriously and still couldn't make the interiors of houses and apartments really comfortable.

The heat made Alice lethargic. Unfortunately, it made Aly irritable. Or perhaps the tension between Alan and Jennifer was effecting the baby. The experts said that babies and children picked up on things adults weren't aware of. Even Alice couldn't miss the clipped words and abrupt looks passing between her son and his wife as they went about their daily business in the bakery. Fans were set up all over, and there was central air conditioning, but with all the ovens going, the heat ruled. Probably trying to cool the place was a simple waste of money, yet it was just so miserably hot and humid they craved even the smallest alleviation.

With the humid heat and the hostility between Alan and Jennifer, Alice found the atmosphere almost unbearable, so she took the baby up to The Haven for a change of scenery. Often the new faces and rooms proved a diversion for Aly. Certainly they cheered Alice. She walked up the long white gravel driveway with the baby safely tucked into a clever backpack. Aly was grizzling again, cranky from the heat and her teeth. By accident, she found Alice's shoulder and began to gnaw on it, finding comfort as her gums touched the bare skin, and it felt so funny Alice laughed aloud, her mood lifting in spite of the heat.

The inside of The Haven was cool and dry—bliss. Alice decided to drop in on Shirley. She didn't do this very often—she knew Shirley had a lot to prepare for the board meeting—but perhaps she might be up for a break, a glass of iced tea. Alice stopped at the secretary's desk to chat a moment with Wendy, then tapped on the door and stepped into Shirley's office.

Shirley was bent over a yellow legal pad, scribbling numbers on it. When she saw Alice, she actually jumped, and she looked oddly *guilty*.

"Hi, Shirley. Sorry to bother you. Just thought we'd stop by to say hi."

"Hi!" Shirley said brightly. She pulled a pile of papers on top of the yellow legal pad.

Alice felt as if she were *invading* Shirley's space, an unusual and uncomfortable feeling. "Actually," Alice tried to sound jokey, "I just wanted to show you that even in this wretched heat I'm exercising. I walked all the way here with this little weight on my back."

Shirley came around the desk to kiss the baby on her nose. "Hello, dolly." Stepping back, she looked Alice over. "How's your heart?"

"Fine. It's fine!"

"Well, Alice, don't get all crabby. You really have to remember, you've got high blood pressure and a wonky heart. This terrible humidity will make you retain water. Are you taking diuretics?"

Alice snorted. "You bet I am. I pee like Niagara Falls. In fact, now that you mention it—want to hold Aly for a moment?"

Alice bent down so Shirley could lift the baby out of the backpack. Alice went out to the restroom. When she returned, Shirley was waiting for her in the corridor.

"Let's go down to the lounge. It's cooler there."

Alice gave Shirley a look. "Are you hiding something from me, girl?"

"*Me?*" Shirley's eyebrows were always a dead giveaway. When she lied, they shot up to her red hair like a pair of caterpillars squirming for cover. Quickly, she changed the subject. "How's Alan?"

Lifting fussy Aly into her arms, Alice sighed. "Low. I'm worried about him. He really needs to get back on an antidepressant."

"Did you give him the Saint-John's-wort and the ginseng?" Shirley held the door open and they went into the lounge, which was blissfully cool.

"Of course." Alice sank into the sofa. She lay Aly next to her, and for a few moments the baby was distracted by the new light and colors around her. "Whether he's taking it, I couldn't say. But he was like this when he was divorced from his first wife, and it was really a prescription antidepressant that brought him out of it. It doesn't help that Jennifer is so unsympathetic, but she's whipped herself."

Shirley sat on the other side of Aly, lightly stroking her fine baby hair. Shirley studied her friend. "Alice, you look *so* tired."

Alice opened her mouth to argue, then slumped. "I *am* tired. And you don't need to remind me, Shirley, I know I've gained back the weight I lost when I was on the island, and I know I'm not exercising as much as I should, but when I get home after taking care of Aly, I'm just too beat to move."

"Why don't you step back?"

"Because Alan and Jennifer—not to mention my granddaughter—rely on me. I don't know what they'd do if I didn't help them!"

Leaning over, Shirley put her hand on Alice's arm. "What would happen if you couldn't help them *ever* again?" That got Alice's attention. "If you don't take care of yourself, Alice, you're going to have another heart attack, and you know it."

To her enormous embarrassment, tears sprang into Alice's eyes. Quickly she closed her eyes before Shirley could spot them. She leaned her head back against the sofa, and for a moment she thought she could fall asleep right there. "All right. I'll think about it."

Barefoot, Shirley idled along the beach, stopping to toss a rock into the water or inhale the fresh salt air. Mentally, she felt like those sandpipers, running back and forth frantically at the water's edge. What were they looking for? Clams? Worms?

Shirley was looking for Harry.

She had awakened this Friday morning, depressed and absolutely *weary,* wondering how she was going to survive another date with Stan. She took an extra dose of omega-three capsules and ginseng, but her spirits wouldn't lift. Then she phoned Nantucket to see how Polly and Faye were doing, and Polly told her she was coming back to Boston to deal with some necessary errands. Well! It seemed just logical for Shirley to hurry down to Nantucket so Faye wouldn't be alone in that big old house. After all, it was because of Shirley that Faye was there. Although Faye insisted she felt safe by herself. And since Polly and Faye had put out the photos of Nora's objects, the thefts had stopped. Still, it just seemed companionable, to go down to stay with Faye. She knew Marilyn couldn't go—Marilyn's fiancé and his best friend's widow Fiona were arriving today from Scotland. Alice was all tied up with her granddaughter. Shirley had some paperwork to catch up on, but that could wait. She'd worked her ass off this week, and she deserved a little break.

She packed a bag, left a message on Stan's machine, grabbed a bus down to Hyannis, and jumped on the first plane she could get to the island. She took a cab to the house, arriving in time to chat with Faye, who was dressing for an evening cruising all the openings at the various art galleries. She invited Shirley to join her, and Shirley said perhaps she'd catch up with her later, but first she needed to go to the beach. She didn't tell Faye why she was so eager to get there. Probably the less her Hot Flash friends knew about her romantic dreams, the better.

She'd been on the beach for about an hour now, and no sign of Harry. Downhearted, she collapsed in the sand, crossing her legs yoga-style, trying to center her thoughts. It was idiotic to expect Harry to show up on the beach just because Shirley was here. He could be any-where on the island! He could be on the moors. Or at his house. Or at another woman's house! She hadn't told him she'd be here this evening. They hadn't made any plans to see each other again—although he had said he wanted to show her 'Sconset. So she wouldn't feel too shy to phone him—but how could she phone him? She didn't have his phone number! She didn't even know his last name!

A burst of laughter sailed over the harbor from one of the larger sloops anchored there. Bright summer light illuminated all the people relaxing on their yachts and sailboats, drinking, talking, laughing, en-joying this golden evening. Everyone was part of a group.

Shirley slumped. She knew she was the most romantic and least realistic of the Hot Flash friends. Alice often told Shirley her thought processes were bizarre, the triumph of optimism over experience. But Shirley had found that Fate often left unexpected little presents on the pillow of her life, and after all, life itself was a gift.

So she sat on the sand, and then she walked up and down the beach until the summer sun finally began to sink toward the horizon.

The next morning, Shirley rented a bike and pedaled her way out to the moors. This time she'd packed a lunch and two bottles of water, plus a handsome little book about the wildflowers of Nantucket. Her knowl-edge of plants was pretty minimal, which was odd, really, since she knew so much about the various herbal remedies and supplements which came from plants. Faye sometimes called plants flora, a Latin name, an *intel-lectual* name. Shirley was going to try to become familiar enough with the flora that she could casually drop the word into one of her cocktail party conversations. She'd often felt less cultured than her Hot Flash friends, and it was never too late to change.

She didn't hurry as she spun along the bike path. It was too hot to push herself, plus she wanted to remain near the road as long as possible, to increase the chances of seeing Harry's red truck. But she'd biked for what seemed like hours without a sighting, and her trembling legs begged for mercy, so when she came to a dirt road leading into the moors, she got off the bike, took a big swig of water, and walked it in.

It was damned hard work! The bike did all right when the dirt was hard-packed, but occasionally she hit a patch of soft sand, and then she could barely move it. She gave up, locked the bike to the trunk of a sapling, and hiked on into the interior of the moors. The land rose and fell in a sweeping vista of greens as far as she could see. Here and there brown ribbons of road curled up and across, and she knew from a map that somewhere around here were some ponds, where she'd love to dip her exhausted feet.

It was very quiet. Occasionally a bird called or a bush rustled—she jumped, wondering if there were mice out here. But mostly the land lay still and hot under the summer sun. No trucks rumbled over the roads. Not even another biker was in sight. Every sensible person was at the beach, Shirley decided, with a rueful laugh at herself.

For a while she turned her attention to getting to know the plants. The flora. The mealy plum bearberry was easy to spot because there was so much of it. She liked the pasture thistle, standing tall and independent, with its little purple bristle like a flag. She spotted the blue-eyed grass Harry had told her about.

But she didn't spot Harry.

Soon she felt too tired to continue, so she found a rock protruding from a carpet of velvety moss and settled on it to eat her lunch. Refreshed, she wandered up and down a hill, keeping an eye out for a pond. She felt very proud of herself, rather brave, to be out here alone like this. She had always been a city girl. Now she felt that she had some stuff to tell Marilyn that scientific Marilyn might actually find interesting.

The sun rose higher. The greenery seemed to steam. She hadn't worn her watch, so she didn't know what time it was when she finally decided that enough was enough. It was too hot to stay out here, and she hadn't seen another person, and she wanted to go home to take a cool shower and a nap.

So she turned around to retrace her steps.

And realized she was lost.

She seemed to be at the bottom of a bowl. Dirt roads coiled uphill in all directions—but which one led back to her bike?

Figure it out, Shirley, she told herself. What would Marilyn do?

She'd follow her own footprints in the sand! Just like Hansel and Gretel following a trail of breadcrumbs! Relieved, Shirley began walking.

But when she came to a crossroads, she found one of those sandy patches, too deep to hold footprints, and when she inspected each path leading away from the intersection, she discovered that they *all* had footprints, *lots* of footprints.

"Damn!" Shirley stomped her foot, put her hands on her hips, and glared around. What was she going to do? Was she going to die out here, dehydrated and starved, her body turned into a weathered piece of driftwood? Why had she ever come out here alone? She was a *moron*! She was no Girl Scout, she'd never *been* a Girl Scout! She was just an idiotic recovering alcoholic with brains fried by the sun. She was just *silly*. She thought she'd find the one attractive man she'd met in the past year by wandering around this big empty island with her head up her ass! She should have stayed with Stan, she *deserved* Stan, Stan was what Fate had put on her pillow, not some gorgeous sexy outdoor guy from this island paradise. What if she couldn't find her way out? Could she really *die* here? Was she the stupidest sixty-two-year-old on the planet? Yes, definitely!

Angry tears spilled down her cheeks. She'd seen enough survivor shows on television to realize she would only hasten the dehydration process by crying, so she sucked back her sobs, took another big gulp of water, which helped calm her down, and made a plan. She would climb to the top of the highest hill, which would be easy, because the hills were really tame. From there, she'd be able to spot the two main roads bordering the moors. She'd head for the Polpis Road, but just in case she was turned around, which most likely she was because she was such a dunce, she'd be glad to be on any paved road. She could find her way back to town, and when Faye came back from painting, they could drive out to pick up her rented bike, which Shirley never wanted to ride again as long as she lived.

She had to pee.

Oh, good, she was going to die of dehydration, and she still had to pee. Briefly she entertained the notion of saving her pee in a cup—didn't some survivor do that in order to have some liquid to drink to keep from dying? She decided she couldn't go to that extreme. Behind her in a little basin was a thick cluster of evergreen shrubs. Shrubs were everywhere, actually, but Shirley eased her way through the scratchy branches until she felt she'd achieved some modicum of privacy. She eased off her gorgeous spandex biking pants, snorting at herself as she did for buying them, dreaming of becoming a jock. She squatted. A branch from a shrub scraped her bare bum.

"Ouch!" Angrily, she snapped the branch in two, then hated herself for destroying the poor plant that was just being there where it belonged.

It felt weird to have her bum exposed out here in the middle of nowhere, but it was such a relief to pee!

Something in the distance grumbled and roared. Shirley nearly leaped out of her skin. Were there coyotes on the moors? Bears? Of course not, she knew that! The noise came nearer—oh, it was a car or a truck, a vehicle driven by a human being! Shirley wanted to run out and flag it down, but she couldn't stop peeing! She clenched her muscles, but the flow continued. What if the person drove by without seeing her? For that matter, what if the person drove by and *saw* her! How embarrassing would *that* be?

Finally, she was able to pull up her tight pants. She crashed her way out of the brush, knowing she was getting cuts and scrapes on her legs and not caring. She burst out onto the road just as the vehicle came over the hill and down toward the intersection.

It was a red pickup truck.

Saturday afternoon, as Polly waited for Hugh to arrive at her house, she *fretted*—a good, old-fashioned word, *fret,* capturing exactly how she felt. Irritated, peevish, nerves on edge. Much of the lace her mother-in-law had bequeathed to her, which Polly used on the Havenly Yours clothes, was fretwork. The pattern was ornamental, yet rigid—a series of small, straight bars intersecting one another at right angles. Guitar strings were pressed against frets, she recalled, and her nerves felt just like plucked strings.

Probably she should have waited until tomorrow to see Hugh. She still was tired from her trip. Friday morning had been fair and bright, but so windy the ferry bucked and shuddered, making Polly nauseous. She'd dragged her luggage with her up to the nearby bus station and taken the bus to South Station and a cab from there to her house. She hadn't had enough energy even to go for fresh milk and groceries for herself. She took a nap, then phoned Hugh. He'd been his normal warm self. He'd agreed to stop by to see her today. Together they'd plan what to do that evening.

She'd taken a lasagna from the freezer this morning, in case they stayed in tonight. It was just after lunch, so she arranged a platter of cheese, crackers, and crisp veggies—she'd nibble on the veggies while they talked. Nerves always made her eat. Well, anything made her eat. As she moved around the kitchen, the memory of Roy Orbison moved with her. Now there was a constant and loyal companion! God, she missed him. Tears sprang to her eyes. She closed them tight and clenched her fists, willing the sorrow to retreat. She had to be upbeat, not gloomy, when she saw Hugh.

For she wanted to have it out with Hugh once and for all. She didn't want to be like Shirley had been with her former boyfriend, Justin, pathetically eager to do *anything* to keep the relationship alive. She wanted marriage, a shared life. She wouldn't press Hugh for that right away, but she did need to know whether or not that was a possibility in their future.

The doorbell chimed. She checked her reflection in the mirror—she looked good, tanned from the week on the island, feminine in her green flowered shift which set off the green of her eyes. Hugh had told her many times how beautiful her eyes were. She was glad she'd taken it easy last night; she looked rested.

"Polly." He wore a light summer suit and carried a bottle of wine.

"Hello, Hugh." God, those blue eyes! She kissed his lips lightly in greeting, then led him back to the sunporch. "Come in. How's your day been so far?"

Hugh took off his jacket and tie and unbuttoned his shirt collar as Polly opened and poured the wine. As they chatted, she smiled to herself, thinking how, in many ways, they were already such a *couple,* familiar with each other's rhythms and habits, comfortable together. When they both had their glasses, they settled on chairs across from each other.

"You look great, Polly," Hugh told her. "Island life becomes you."

"Thanks." Her heart did jumping jacks. Now she could broach the subject. Or she could just let it go. . . . "Hugh, can we talk seriously for a moment?"

He frowned. "Sure. What's up?"

Polly took a deep breath. "I need to know where you think our relationship is going."

He looked puzzled. "*Going?* I don't understand. Why should it go anywhere?" Lightheartedly, he waggled his eyebrows. "I rather thought we had already arrived."

Could he truly be so *clueless*?

"I guess I'm talking about marriage," Polly admitted. She looked him straight in the face.

"Oh, Polly." He heaved a huge sigh and shook his head. "*Marriage?* I don't think I'll ever want to marry again. And why should I? It's not like I'm going to have any more children. I wouldn't have thought you cared about legalities and formalities."

Polly leaned forward. "I don't. What I care about is *sharing* a life. What I care about is coming first in *your* life."

Hugh looked away. "I'm sorry about leaving you when your dog died."

"That really hurt me," Polly told him frankly.

He shifted guiltily. "I did come back, Polly. I did spend the night with you."

"Yes, but you left because your ex-wife thought she had a bat in the house. If there were ever a time when I needed you to stay with me, it was then. And you chose to go to Carol. You've done this over and over again, Hugh, but when Roy died, why, that just broke my heart! You've told me you love me. You know I love you. But you make me feel second place, or if we include your children, even further down on your list of priorities."

"Love doesn't come in lists," Hugh said quietly.

"Oh, don't be so sanctimonious!" Polly exploded. "Of course it does. When you have to choose where to be at any given moment, it does. And you always put me last. You always drop me, no matter what we're doing, if Carol or one of your children calls. We—"

Hugh raised a weary hand. "Polly," he said softly, "I wish you knew how many times Carol scolded me just as you are now. Not because I was with another woman, because I never was. But because I was with my patients. Perhaps I do 'choose' my children or Carol over you, but if I do, it's because I'm trying to rectify a lifetime of letting them down. I'm committed to attending all my grandchildren's events, because I missed all those recitals and baseball games when my own children were growing up. I'm an oncology doctor, I'm on call, I have to go to my patients when they need me, and that's often during a holiday, or in the middle of dinner, or in the middle of the night." Taking off his glasses, he rubbed his eyes. "All I've wanted to do in life is to help people, and yet with those I love the most, it seems that all I do is let them down."

"Oh, Hugh." Polly felt nearly ill. "I didn't mean to *scold* you. I didn't realize—I hadn't understood how things were with you and Carol and the children. What you've just said—well, it helps me understand your actions a little better. But still—I mean, there are other things, Hugh. Like, will I ever be part of your whole life? I mean, will you ever invite me to one of your grandchildren's games?"

His expression gave her the answer. "I think it might upset my children. I mean, Carol is usually there."

Polly nodded. "So I'm always going to be sort of on the sidelines of your life."

Hugh shook his head. "Well, Polly, I don't know. I mean, the grandchildren will get older. Perhaps Carol will meet someone else. Things change. And really, is being 'on the sidelines of my life' such a dreadful place? You're so active with your work and your friends . . ."

"True, but I'd like you, us, *us as a couple,* to be the center of my life, Hugh. I'd like us to live together. At least I'd like to know whether or not we have a future together."

His voice was gentle. "Polly, at our age, we can't say for sure if we're going to wake up the next day. I don't want to worry about the future. I want to enjoy the present. And I do enjoy it, with you. Can't that be enough?"

Polly couldn't prevent the tears streaming down her face. "I don't think so, Hugh. I'm sorry. I want to come first with a man. I want to be married again. I want to share a bed and a home and a life, not exist off to the side waiting for you, always longing for more."

"Oh, Polly." Hugh rose and came to kneel next to her chair. He took her hands in his. "Polly, we have such fun together."

"I know we do." She pulled her hands away and grabbed a cocktail napkin to wipe her nose.

"Not everyone has that. And we do love each other. Just because it's not legalized, is that any reason to throw it away?"

She smiled bitterly. "You do know how to charm a girl. But give me credit here. I haven't been just talking about 'legalizing' our relationship. I'm talking about the real essence of it." Reaching out, she stroked his warm, ruddy face. "I think what it comes down to, Hugh, is that I need to be with you more than you need to be with me."

He caught her hand and kissed the palm. "I do need to be with you, Polly. I truly do. But I have to honor my prior commitments. That's the kind of man I am."

"And the kind of woman *I* am needs to come first. Or at least alongside." Gently she pulled her hand away. Nothing could be said now to rectify the situation. "Hugh, I think I want you to go now." Rising, she left the sunporch and went down the hall to the front door.

Hugh followed, carrying his jacket and tie in his hand. "I'm sorry, Polly."

With her hand on the doorknob, Polly said, "You know, I'm going to see other men now. So you're free to see other women, too."

"I don't want to see other women."

Polly managed to smile. "Sure you do. You might meet someone willing to be on the side." She opened the door. "And I might meet someone willing to be part of a couple."

Hugh opened his mouth to speak, then shook his head. He went out the door. "Good-bye, Polly."

Polly shut the door. She leaned against it until she heard his car pull out of the driveway. Then she slid down onto the floor, laid her head on her arms, and wept.

Shirley pinched herself *hard* just above the elbow.

Ouch! That hurt!

Okay then, she wasn't dreaming. She was really here, sitting on Harry's deck looking out at the shining water, while he fixed dinner.

But the day had been such a fantasy, how could she believe it was real?

This morning, rattled and thirsty and just a little scared, she'd yanked her spandex tights up as she thrashed through the bushes, flailing her way out to the dirt road to wave down the red truck, the first sight of humanity she'd seen for hours. She'd hoped it was Harry's, but she would have been grateful to see anyone who could help her find her way back to the main road.

"Shirley?" Harry's tanned face had lit up in a smile.

"Harry! Thank heavens! Harry, I'm lost!"

"Well, jump in. Reggie, scoot over."

She knew she looked red-faced and disheveled as she climbed into the truck. The golden Lab helped complete her toilette by giving her face a thorough licking, which succeeded in plastering quite a bit of her hair to her cheeks and forehead.

Harry gave her an appraising glance. "You look hot and bothered. Why not let me take you out to my place for a sail to cool you off?"

"Oh, Harry," she confessed, "I don't know how to sail."

"Well, Shirley," he told her with a grin. "I do."

She explained that she'd lost her bike, and Harry laughed, put the truck in gear, and bounced them along over the dirt roads. Very quickly he found her bike.

Once again he tossed it in the back of the pickup. Then he turned onto Polpis Road and sped away from town. At an unmarked dirt path, not even a road, more like a pair of ruts worn between scrub brush and heathlands, he turned again. They bumped along through a thicket, and suddenly the vista opened up, exposing a small lawn and a modest one-story cottage looking down a slope to the water.

"Polpis Harbor," he told her.

The water lay before them like an enormous blue platter full of light. On the other side of the harbor, in the distance, the rooftops of other houses could be spotted, but the curve of the land around the house in an expansive open roll of natural heath gave the illusion of protected isolation. A nearby shed, where Harry kept his sailboat in the winter, was actually bigger than the house, which, he told her, had been built in the sixties as a summer house.

Harry led her into his house. "You won't want to wear those shorts sailing. Go on into the little bedroom at the back. Some old bathing suits are hanging on a hook behind the door. One of them's bound to fit you okay."

The cottage was very male, natural and unfussy. The wooden floors and walls had been left unpainted to darken naturally. Only the plaster between the beams on the ceiling had been painted white. The old buoys hanging from the walls in the living room brightened the place. His sofa was deep and worn, but his television was new, and his tables were covered with an array of books and magazines. On a desk in the corner a laptop sat blinking.

The only bathing suit Shirley's size was a two-piece, and even as slender and fit as she was, her pale white abdomen, dotted with the tiny moles that had sprouted all over her torso during the past few years, had the pasty, loose look of bread dough—sprinkled with rye seeds—set aside to rise. So she pulled on an ancient striped blue Speedo that hung on her. For a moment she stood paralyzed, afraid to let him see her exposed like this, her limbs pale and scrawny, her neck wrinkled, her makeup washed away by that morning's tears.

"Find everything okay?" he yelled.

Well, she couldn't hide in the room for the rest of her life! "I did!" She forced herself to leave the room.

Harry had also changed into a bathing suit and a faded polo shirt.

He wore a scalloper's cap with a long bill, and he grabbed another one from the back of the door and plunked it down on Shirley's head.

"You'll need this, too." He handed her a tube of sunblock. "You can put it on while I'm rigging the boat."

She followed him outside and down to the water. They waded through the reedy shallows to a small rowboat, which Harry rowed out to *Serenity,* his catboat. It seemed to Shirley a pretty little boat with its single mast and curving lines. The golden Lab swam out, too, got a lift into the sailboat by Harry, and established herself next to Shirley, resting her head on her knee. Shirley watched as Harry raised the sail and did mysterious things with the ropes.

"This is the boom," he said, touching the long heavy horizontal pole. "It swings back and forth when I tack, so when I tell you to duck, duck."

She wanted to say, jokingly, "Aye, aye, Cap'n," but at that moment the boat, with a little shiver, took off, racing away into the wide waters. Shirley swallowed as the safety of shore receded. Harry flashed her a smile. She laid her hand on the dog's strong golden head and was reassured. Soon, lulled by the heat of the sun and the hypnotic beauty of the shoreline, she relaxed.

It was so quiet, sailing! No engine, no background grumble. Only the splash of the waves and the cry of the gulls. She and Harry were quiet together—at first, that felt awkward to Shirley, who called out, "Beautiful!" and "Wonderful!" to show her appreciation of the land, the water, and the boat Harry so obviously loved. But Harry merely responded with a nod and a smile, and soon she forgot about manners and obligations and did what she was always telling people to do—*Be here now.*

It was like being in a bottle of champagne when the cork pops and that first delicious foam spills over. The light, the air, the atmosphere were effervescent and crystal clear. They sailed through a narrow cut between two shoals and were out in the larger harbor, sailing to the long spit of golden beach called Coatue. The warmth of the sun was better than a sauna, the slight breeze cool and refreshing. Light dazzled across the water, tossing diamonds here and there, and in the distance the town rose like a dream.

She couldn't help looking at Harry. His limbs were tanned and strongly muscled, scarred here and there, like those of one who's done lots of physical labor. Vaguely she wondered how he could afford a house on the water; but that kind of thought didn't belong in this kind of day, so she let it drift away.

She liked the way he moved. Economical, efficient, steady, he seemed to anticipate the demands of the water and wind. They anchored near Coatue. When Shirley followed his lead and jumped out into the cold water, her feet just touched bottom, so she felt safe as they waded up to the shore. He spread out an old blanket and opened a small cooler, handing her a bottle of seltzer and an apple. They lay around for a while, talking idly, then went for a long walk. Harry regaled her with information about the island, but Shirley was so dazzled by her increasing sense of desire for the man that he might as well have been speaking in Martian.

On the way home, Harry gave Shirley a sailing lesson. She loved the tug of the sheet and the immediate response of the catboat as it lifted or listed or turned, but Harry's proximity tangled her thoughts. She felt so attracted to him—she felt that intense surge of lust and excitement she'd felt with her old boyfriends Justin and Jimmy, but she also felt oddly soothed by his presence. It had been a long time since she'd felt so alive.

When they returned to the house, it was evening. In spite of the sunblock Harry had given her, Shirley felt slightly stupefied by the sun and the motion, and she was delighted when he suggested she take a cool shower while he threw together some dinner. She couldn't help it—she snooped in his bathroom. No signs of a woman—good! A few bottles of pills. The same blood pressure medication Faye took, and Lipitor, which made her wonder. How could a man as fit as Harry have high cholesterol? It was a genetic thing, no doubt. She pulled on a terry cloth robe hanging on a hook on the back of the door and padded out barefoot to find the table on the deck already set with cheese and crackers and a plate of raw veggies.

Harry handed her a glass of iced water. "Nantucket has the best water in the world," he told her.

"Thanks!" She leaned back in her deck chair and looked down the slope of lawn and brush to Polpis Harbor shimmering in the evening sun.

"What do you think?" Harry asked.

"I think I've died and gone to heaven," Shirley answered.

Even now, at seven in the evening, sailboats glided past, their sails as proud and white as swans, long ripples flowing behind them like trains on a wedding gown.

"It *is* a little paradise here," Harry agreed, crossing his bare feet and resting them on the railing of the deck. "I think that every single day, even in January gale force winds." Beside him, Reggie thumped her tail in lazy agreement.

"Don't you ever get lonely?" Shirley swept her arm in an arc. "No houses nearby, and you can't even see town from here."

"Sure, I get lonely," he replied honestly. "But I've come to treasure my isolation. In my earlier days, I spent enough time with people to last me forever."

"What did you do?"

"Oh, what everyone else did. Had a corporate job, married, had two kids, traveled, then got divorced, drank too much, ate too much, screwed around too much." His eyes rested on the water as if he were seeing his past floating there. "The only place I've ever felt at peace has been on this island. So a few years ago I retired here. And even at my loneliest, I don't regret it."

Shirley nodded.

"What about you?" Harry asked. "You told me you run a spa, right?"

"Well, I kind of own it. With the investors and the bank. Nora Salter's one of the investors. I know her because I used to be her massage therapist. I've given massages all my life, but in the past few years, with the help of some friends, I started The Haven. I'm up to my ears in mortgage, but I'm living out a dream I've had all my life—to run a wellness spa."

"Wellness spa means what, exactly?"

Shirley hesitated. Growing up, she'd been taught that if she wanted to keep a man's interest, she had to get him to talk about himself, not dominate the conversation with her own interests. So her reply was brief, but Harry asked a question, and then another, and the sun slipped lower as they talked. She followed him into the kitchen and talked while he fixed their dinner. He respected her vegetarian beliefs, and made a simple pasta tossed with olive oil, fresh broccoli, garlic, cauliflower and tomatoes. He put a long baguette on a cutting board with several blocks of cheese, and carried it all out to the deck.

They ate in companionable silence, watching the water reflect the changing colors of the summer sky. He spoke about his childhood summers on the island, and how he'd tried to recapture that for his own children when he and his family summered here. He spoke about his children and grandchildren and stepchildren and step-grandchildren—he'd been married and divorced twice. Shirley told him she'd been married and divorced three times and had no children, and felt the loss. He nodded, understanding.

They carried their dishes into the kitchen where Harry washed and Shirley dried them as they waited for the decaf to drip into the pot, and then they fixed their mugs and took them back out to the deck. Shirley had never felt so at home with a man before. It was rather like being with a woman, except that as the sky drifted into a soft violet-gray, iridescent and indigo-streaked, like the inside of a mussel shell, she felt more and more sexually awakened. She felt like a night bird—an owl? A nightingale? The deep resonance of Harry's voice warmed her, and when his eyes met hers, something sparked inside her; not just sexual desire, but also a kind of odd hope. She felt like a lost ship, and the blue flash of his eyes on hers flared like a beacon on a lighthouse, beckoning her toward a safe harbor.

When the sky had deepened to black velvet, Shirley said, "I'd better go." Reluctantly, she rose. "Oh." She looked down. "I've still got your robe on."

Harry rose, too, and stood in front of her, just inches away. "Why don't you take it off?"

Heat flooded through Shirley. Desire made her tongue-tied. "I—I'll change back into my shorts."

"That's really not what I meant." He put his hands on Shirley's shoulders. He moved closer, so his chest almost touched hers and she felt his breath when he spoke. "Why not stay the night?"

"Um—Faye might worry?" Her voice came in a squeak.

"Phone her. Tell her you're staying here tonight."

She swallowed. She hadn't experienced sensations this intense for months, if ever. Would she seem easy? Would she—

"I'll respect you in the morning," he said jokingly. "If you'll respect me. Besides, you haven't lived until you've watched the sun rise from my deck."

She was trembling all over. His warm hands steadied her. *I'm old,* she wanted to warn him. *When I lie down, my breasts look like a couple of dead jellyfish.*

"I'm kind of scared," she whispered.

"Don't be," he told her. He drew her against him, wrapping his arms around her, and kissed the top of her head. "You can trust me," he said. Then he kissed her temples, very gently, and each of her eyelids, and the tip of her nose and each of her cheeks. He kissed the top of one ear, and the lobe of the other ear, and breathed warmly against her neck. He kissed her jawline, her sagging jawline, he kissed her chin. He took her head in both his hands, and softly, and for a very long time, he kissed her mouth. It was all Shirley could do not to knock him onto the deck and crawl all over him. She longed to let go of her fears and her vanity and her doubts, and trust him. And so, she did.

Just after noon on Sunday, Marilyn parked her Volvo in the lot nearest the International Terminal at Logan Airport, dropped her keys in her purse, said to herself, "I am dropping my keys in my purse," then hurried into the terminal. She checked the display for the flight number and gate—yes! Ian's flight was on time! She dashed into the restroom for a pee and a quick check of her reflection. She'd gone to the trouble of applying the various bits of cosmetics the Hot Flash Club had helped her buy and taught her to use. She supposed she looked as good as she could; she only hoped her lipstick wasn't too bright—she seldom wore makeup, so when she did add some color to her face, she was afraid she looked like Bozo the Clown.

By the time she arrived at the gate, the passengers from the British Airways flight from Edinburgh were already streaming out of the customs area into the main terminal. Several rows of people loomed between her and the gate. She stood on tiptoe, watching for Ian.

And there he was! God, her heart *thumped* with joy at the sight of her skinny, balding, spectacled, geeky lover. He stooped as he walked, just the way Marilyn's friends told her she stooped, no doubt a consequence of all the hours spent peering into microscopes. In his brown and green tartan long-sleeved button-down shirt and khakis, he looked ready for the lab or field work.

Next to him, her hand clutching tightly to Ian's arm, was the woman Marilyn had to assume was Fiona. Marilyn's breath caught in her throat. Ian hadn't told her his friend's wife was beautiful.

Fiona was tall and buxom. She wore a simple black silk dress that flowed against her generous curves as she walked. No makeup, no jewelry—and she didn't need any. Her thick black and silver hair was pulled back in one of those effortless buns which allowed a few strands to escape, floating in curving frames around her face. Her eyes were deep blue beneath the most exquisitely arched black velvet eyebrows Marilyn had ever seen.

Well, Marilyn thought guiltily, perhaps Fiona had bad teeth.

She didn't. When the introductions were made, Fiona's sad smile revealed flawless white teeth and—oh, God! Kill me now, Marilyn thought—adorable *dimples*. Her eyelashes were thick and black. She was a freaking goddess.

Ian hugged Marilyn to him briefly and kissed her firmly on the mouth, then made the introductions. They found Fiona's luggage with its distinctive tartan tags and lugged it to the car. It seemed only right for Ian to drive and Fiona, who had never been to Boston before, to ride in the front passenger seat. Marilyn sat in back, trying not to feel left out. Fiona and Ian tossed conversational bits over the seats, laughing together as they described their trip, the food they were served, the clever way the flight attendant had dealt with an obnoxious family. Occasionally Ian interrupted their travelogue to point out a bit of scenery he thought Fiona might find of interest. The Charles River. The Museum of Science. MIT.

When they went into the house, an unusual noise exploded from the top floors, and to Marilyn's amazement, Angus came stampeding down, his clumsy bulldog close at heel. Angus had bathed and shaved and dressed in clean clothing, a near miracle.

"Auntie Fiona!" he cried, and bumbled into her warm embrace.

Fiona ruffled Angus's already tangled hair. "Ach, my darling, you're a sight for sore eyes."

"I'm so sorry about Uncle Tam," Angus said. "It's a terrible thing."

"It is," Fiona agreed, her eyes filling with tears. "It's a terrible thing."

Ian quickly moved to take Fiona's arm. "Come into the living room and sit down, Fee. How about a nice cup of tea?" He looked over the top of her head at Marilyn, who nodded and hurried off into the kitchen.

Marilyn made tea for four, set the tray with pot, mugs, napkins, sugar, creamer, plate of cookies, and spoons. When she lifted the tray, she nearly dropped it, it was so heavy. She thought of asking hulking young Angus to carry it for her, but decided not to, and was glad she hadn't, because when she entered the living room, Angus was sitting on the sofa, holding Fiona's dainty white hand and listening to her account of her husband's death.

Marilyn poured the tea and handed it around.

"Thank you, Marilyn," Fiona said. "And thank you for taking me in like this. I'll try not to be a bother—"

"You're never a bother, Fee," Ian hurriedly interjected.

"—but I'm just so lonely, so terribly lost without my Tam, and you see"—she leaned forward and took Marilyn's hand in hers—"Ian and Angus are like my own family. I just couldn't get through this without them."

"I'm sorry we don't have a better guest bedroom to offer you," Marilyn told her. She gestured helplessly around the living room. "Ian and I are only renting this until we can find a house we both like, and of course we've been so busy teaching, we haven't had much time—"

"Oh, my dear, I do understand. It's going to be a challenge, isn't it, finding a home as comfortable as Ian's Edinburgh townhouse." She shook her head, smiling sadly at Ian. "I do wish you hadn't had to give that up. You had it fixed up just the way you liked it."

"Oh, well," Marilyn said brightly, "I'm sure we'll eventually organize just as comfortable a home here." She hoped she didn't sound competitive. She couldn't point out, after all, that they did have a guest room in the attic—and Angus was in it. "Anyway, this sofa makes into a comfortable bed, and there's a full bathroom just on the other side of the hall, and a closet near the bathroom for winter coats, which we don't need now, so it's empty for your things. And the kitchen's just down the hall, and of course you must help yourself to anything whenever you want it."

"You're very kind," Fiona said bravely. "I would like a shower, and actually a little nap." She looked down at the sofa as if it were an object she'd never before encountered. "I'm not quite sure how to arrange this into a bed."

Angus sprang to his feet. "We'll do it for you, Auntie Fee."

While Fiona showered, Ian went into his study to check his e-mail and phone messages. Angus and Marilyn opened the sofa and spread it with clean sheets. Fiona came down the hall clad in a thick terry cloth robe, her black hair loose, curling over her shoulders and down her back.

"I'll take Darwin out for a little walk," Angus told her, "so he'll get tired out and won't wake you barking."

"You're a dear boy," Fiona said, and hugged Angus again.

Ian came down the stairs from his study, a clutch of papers in his hand. "Do you have everything you need, Fiona?"

"I'm fine, my darling," Fiona told him. "I just need a little sleep."

"We'll have dinner when you wake," Ian told her. "Something hot and nourishing."

We will? Marilyn thought. Because it was summer, her refrigerator was full of salad ingredients and cheese. She'd have to run out to the store.

"That will be wonderful," Fiona said. "I find warm, nourishing food very comforting these days." She clasped Marilyn's hands in hers. "Thank you again, Marilyn. I'm so grateful to you for taking me in like this."

"You're welcome," Marilyn told her. "We're glad you're here."

Why, Marilyn wondered as she spoke, *do I feel like the truth is I'm not glad at all?*

Angus took his dog off for a walk. Marilyn and Ian spoke for a while, organizing the rest of their day, and then Marilyn headed down the stairs to see Ruth.

Her mother was changing out of her church clothes into a house-coat. No other creature on the planet shows its age as much as homo sapiens, Marilyn thought as she looked at her mother's arms, the bones and veins and muscles clearly visible beneath the papery, spotted skin, as if ready to break free of this personal bond and return to the elements. The limbs of youth had a unity, they looked like one thing, an arm, a leg, but the limbs of age exposed the increasing disintegration, bone from muscle, vein from skin. Animals had fur which disguised this aging process. Perhaps the purpose of man's bareness was to make him aware of his aging, his forthcoming death, so he could prepare for it.

"Darling!" Ruth stumbled as she turned to greet her daughter. "Did Ian get back all right? And have you met Fiona? Such a pretty name, Fiona."

"They're here. Fiona's lovely. She's taking a little rest and I'm going off to the grocery store to buy a nice roast. Would you like to come with me?"

"Thank you, dear, no." She collapsed in her chair. Immediately her cat jumped into her lap. "I'm exhausted from church and my lunch with the girls." She grinned. "Bettina wore such a cute heart-shaped brooch. It said, 'Let me call you sweetheart. I can't remember your name.'"

Marilyn laughed. "I can sympathize with that!"

"What will you serve with the roast?" Ruth asked. "It's so hot today."

"Ian thought a hot meal would be comforting to Fiona. After the flight, and because she's in mourning. What do you think?"

"That's very thoughtful of Ian. I suppose he's right. A nice roast and baked potatoes and carrots, oh, and nice hot rolls with butter. Nothing's as soothing as a hot roll with butter."

"Good idea."

"And why not make one of your chocolate pudding cakes for dessert? With vanilla ice cream. Soothing and cooling."

"I don't think I'll have time to cook today, Mother. I'm just going to buy a pie. Will you eat with us?"

"I'll come up and sit with you. But I doubt if I'll eat much. I had such a big lunch. We decided to try that new Chinese restaurant. I had Moshe Dayan, very tasty, chicken with bits of cashews and celery and an unusual spice. With rice, of course . . ."

Marilyn opened her mouth to correct her mother, then closed it. Why interrupt her now, when she was so obviously enjoying the memory of her delicious lunch?

"Afterward, Sonya's daughter drove us through Mount Auburn cemetery so we could see all the trees and flowers. It's so beautiful there. And have you ever read the lines inscribed above the sundial? John Greenleaf Whittier wrote them—no one reads him anymore, do they? He was a bit of a windbag, I think, but this little verse touched me so deeply. I scribbled it down to be sure I had it right for you." She bent over, found her purse, and began to search through it.

Marilyn suppressed a sigh of impatience. She hated it when she felt like this, trapped by her mother, as edgy as if she were sitting on tacks. But she had to get to the store and buy a roast, then return and start roasting the roast, and she wanted to spend some time alone with Ian, and she hadn't prepared her lessons for tomorrow . . . life pressed in on her from all sides, and it didn't help that her sweet old mom was bumbling around like this.

"What?" Ruth was patting the sides of her head. "What's happened?"

"You've put your reading glasses on upside down," Marilyn told her.

"Oh, dear!" Ruth clapped her hands and laughed and laughed. "Silly me! Wait until I tell the girls about this one!"

"I'd better get off to the grocery store . . ." Marilyn rose from the sofa.

"Wait, dear!" Ruth waved a piece of paper. "I found it. Let me get my glasses on the right way and I'll read it to you." Carefully adjusting the stems over her ears, she pressed the frame firmly against her nose, then cleared her throat. "This is over a sundial, now, remember." She read:

> "With warning hand I mark time's rapid flight
> From life's glad morning to its solemn night.
> Yet through the dear God's love I also show
> There's light above me by the shade below."

Marilyn said, "That's lovely, Mother."

"I thought you'd like it, dear. Actually, I thought I might give it to Fiona. Perhaps it will bring her some comfort. The image, I mean, the metaphor."

Tears stung Marilyn's eyes. How sweet of her mother to think of consoling this woman she'd never met. Why couldn't Marilyn be more kindhearted, more sympathetic?

Ruth's face creased as she broke into an enormous yawn. "I'm sleepy now. I'll see you later. Thank you for visiting me."

Marilyn felt oddly cheered as she climbed the stairs, found her purse, and organized a shopping list. When she was younger and married to Theodore, they'd had one son, Teddy, and their house and her life had been full. Now she lived in a house with four other people and an omnivorous bulldog, two of whom she sort of wished would go away. And yet, this was *life*. All too soon her mother would be gone, evaporated into the mysterious elements, perhaps into the heaven in which she believed. All too soon Marilyn herself would disintegrate, finding a peace and silence like no other.

But for today, she had lots of food to buy and cook. She'd open a couple of bottles of good red wine. And later, when she was alone in bed with Ian . . . She smiled in anticipation.

39

In Nantucket, Faye sat next to Adele Spindleton on the older woman's ancient sofa in her living room. They were looking at Adele's photograph albums and scrapbooks from the early part of the twentieth century. Outside, a summer storm rained down, churning the roads by the harbor into rivers, drenching the summer flowers, and making landscape painting impossible. Faye was quite content to put aside her work for the day. She loved spending time with Adele. It was a kind of stepping back in time.

"And here I am with Roger, on our way to the theater. We had wonderful live theater out in 'Sconset back then, you know."

"Oh, Adele, you look so glamorous!" Faye touched her fingertip to the faded black-and-white photo of Adele in a long summer dress and her husband in a straw boater.

Adele laughed. "Youth has its own glamour. Now here we are with our first baby, Morris . . ."

As Adele talked about her children, their birthday parties, their high school graduations, Faye's mind drifted back to her own life and its celebrations. Her daughter's life and the lives of her grandchildren were being recorded in photographs and on videotape, or DVDs. Technology had changed, but the important occasions were the same.

"Oh, how pretty!" she said, touching a photograph of the garden of Adele's house. Paper lanterns hung from lines strung from tree to tree, and the flames of candles burned from a long picnic table covered with flowers and food.

"My fiftieth birthday," Adele told her. "Just think, almost half a century ago! I've been so fortunate to remain in the same house all my life. My parents gave us this house when we announced we were going to have our first child. Well, they lived with us for a few years, and that was very helpful, what with the way the babies came, one two three!"

As Adele rambled on, Faye thought how different their lives were in one respect. Adele had lived in only one house, while Faye had moved houses often, especially in the last few years. And even though she loved the new little house she'd settled in, just the right size for a widowed woman, with a guest room and a room that became her studio, she didn't miss it while she was on Nantucket. She was quite happy to have her temporary residence in Nora Salter's grand old mansion.

She was quite happy to be here, on this island.

Strange, how she felt so at home here. The beauty of the land was so generous, the light that revealed it so haunting. She felt she could paint every day of the rest of her life and not exhaust the varied glories of this island. Slowly, she was getting to know other artists and gallery owners. Every Friday night the galleries held openings and the level of the work was exceptional. Many of the artists exhibited in New York or Boston, many had homes in Nantucket and also in Santa Fe, or France, or in the Caribbean. Two of the gallery owners had expressed interest in Faye's work, which both thrilled and terrified her. She had told them that her pictures were shown at the Guild of Boston Artists on Newbury Street, which was, after all, an achievement of some magnitude. And she could show them her older paintings. They were good. But what would they think of her new landscapes? This had become one of the most important questions in her life. She thought about it all the time, although she wasn't ready to show anyone her new work.

"My husband had just turned sixty when he passed away," Adele was saying. "This is the last photograph taken of us together. I'm glad I arranged such a grand party for him. It always was balm to my soul to think that he knew how many friends he had, how many people loved him." She opened a new album, full of photos of that particular birthday party with its crowd of people in pointed birthday hats.

This made Faye think of her Hot Flash friends. Perhaps she shouldn't be surprised that Shirley was in love again. Shirley was the most romantic of them all. She'd spent the weekend at the home of her new beau, Harry, coming in briefly this morning to bundle up a set of clean clothes into her duffel bag.

"I'm not going back to Boston until tomorrow night," Shirley told

Faye. "The Haven will manage just fine without me for a day or so. You know it's always slow in the summer. Oh, Faye!" She'd hugged herself gleefully, looking like a little girl at Christmas. "Harry is so wonderful! He's so handsome! He's so—*delicious*! Faye, we are just so comfortable with each other. I mean, we can just sit and do nothing and not even talk, and we're still *connected*. Wait until you meet him!"

"I can't wait," Faye had said truthfully.

Her opportunity came when Harry returned from doing errands to fetch Shirley. She rushed out to his red truck. Faye had followed, and Shirley made the introductions. Harry was handsome, in a craggy, weathered way, and Faye was reassured to see that he was as old as Shirley. His golden Lab Reggie was adorable, and she liked men who had such happy dogs. But his truck was ancient, the back filled with oily wrenches, toolboxes, fishing poles, and rags. A working man, then. Might he assume Shirley was wealthy because she was staying in this fabulous house?

As the red truck rattled away on Orange Street, Shirley leaned out the window, waving good-bye, smiling from ear to ear. Faye had winged a silent prayer to heaven: *Don't let this man break her heart, too.* She wondered as she returned to the house just how she would describe Harry to the other Hot Flash friends.

Especially to Alice.

"Now what's in this one?" The older woman's quavering voice brought her back to the present. With arthritic, crooked hands, Adele lifted another scrapbook from the cardboard box. She opened it and studied the photos. "Oh, goodness! Here's an old photograph of a picnic I went on when I was younger, and look! Here's Nora Salter when she was a girl! She was Nora Pettigrew back then. And oh, my goodness. Look here!" She stabbed a photograph with one plump finger. "Here's Lucinda Payne."

"You were going to tell me about a scandal between them," Faye remembered.

"You're right. I was." Adele leaned back against the sofa. "I wonder if you'd mind making me a nice glass of iced tea first. Talking this much gives me a dry throat."

Faye went into the kitchen, took a pitcher from the refrigerator and the ice tray from the freezer, and prepared a glass of iced tea for them both. When she returned to the living room, she half expected to find

Adele asleep. The older woman nodded off so easily. But she was rejuvenated by the photos of earlier years, and after a good long swallow of the tea, she began to tell her tale.

"Nora Pettigrew Salter, your friend, is the child of Amelia and Pascal Pettigrew. The house you're staying in was built by the Pettigrews around 1845. The Paynes, as you know, own the house next door to the Pettigrews. Both the Paynes and the Pettigrews are old Nantucket families, you see, having inherited their houses from whaling ship captains. Now, around 1908, the Paynes had a son named Wetherford. Everyone called him Ford. Pascal Pettigrew was born in 1908, too. Ford and Pascal were best friends. They did everything together, and, oh my dear"— Adele chuckled—"they got into quite a lot of mischief when they were youngsters. Even when they went off to separate colleges, they were still best friends; they were like twins even in their twenties. *Then.*"

Adele took a dramatic pause. Leaning forward, she sipped her iced tea, patted her chest, closed her eyes, and took a deep breath.

"Then," she continued, opening her eyes, "then Amelia arrived on the island. She was a stunning beauty. I can find a picture of her in here—" She bent toward the albums.

"No," Faye forestalled her. "Show me her picture later. I want to hear about the scandal first!"

Adele giggled. "I don't blame you. All right. Amelia was a bit of a rascal. She allowed both Pascal and Ford to court her, and she led them both to believe she would marry them. I believe she enjoyed playing them off against one another. I was fifteen years old when Amelia arrived, and she was such a figure of glamour to me. Oh, how excited I was just to catch a sight of her in her beautiful clothes! Everyone talked about Amelia and which man she would choose. She was our own Elizabeth Taylor!" Adele's memories brought back a blush of youth to her face, making her cheeks rosy and her eyes shine.

"Go on," Faye urged.

"Well, in the end, she chose Pascal. They had a stupendous wedding, the most expensive, gorgeous occasion we'd ever seen on this little island. She had ten bridesmaids! And the flowers! Oh, my. Of course, the marriage caused a break between Pascal and Ford. After the marriage, Ford just hated Pascal. Ford married a local woman, Cornelia, who was pretty and sweet, but no match for Amelia. Pascal was a lawyer, who set up his practice on the island. Ford was a banker, and he became *obsessed* with making money. He was determined to be richer than the Pettigrews. He'd lost Amelia, so he was going to *have more* financially. He amassed quite a fortune. Pascal and Amelia had two sons, Sylvester and Frederick. Ford had *four* children. Double Pascal's, don't you see. Ford moved his family to New York but they kept their house on Orange Street for the summer. And then—"

Once more Adele paused to take a drink. Her cheeks were flushed.

"And then," Adele continued, "one summer, Amelia and Ford had an affair!" She fluttered her hands in the air. "Such a to-do it caused! It was 1930, the year I was married, so I remember it well. They had their rendezvous in various 'secret' spots on the island, but of course they were seen and people began to talk, and then everyone was on the look-out, and by August everyone but poor Cornelia and Pascal knew about the affair." She shook her head sadly. "That Amelia. She was a trouble-maker. But such a beauty."

"What happened?" Faye prompted.

"Well. Pascal and Cornelia found out. The affair ended. Ford moved his family back to New York. They kept the summer house, but didn't come back to it for years. The married couples made up with their spouses. Amelia had a daughter, little Nora. So of course Cornelia had another child, Lucinda." She sighed, and the gleam in her eyes faded. "It's sort of terrible, how someone else's love affair can be so *entertaining* to outsiders. Really, it just deepened the hostility between the Pettigrews and the Paynes. All those children grew up side by side in the summer, all those healthy children with all the wealth in the world, and they were all taught to hate each other."

"So the Paynes and the Pettigrews never made amends?"

"Never. Now, of course, all those children have grown up, had their own families, and 'gone aloft.' Of all her siblings, only Lucinda Payne is still alive. What's sadder, Lucinda's two sons—she had just the two children—are both dead. While Nora's two children are alive and flourishing. So I suppose Nora Pettigrew Salter is the 'winner' in the competition between the two families. Which is, no doubt, one of the reasons Lucinda is so bitter."

"How sad," Faye reflected. "To hate someone because of their parents' animosity."

"Yes, and they never got to know one another as individuals." Adele shook her head. "It's the way of the world, I suppose."

Faye could see the older woman was tired. "I should go. Let me put these albums back in the box for you."

"Thank you, dear. I am ready for a little nap. Can you can see yourself out?"

Faye rose. "Of course. Can I get you anything first?"

Adele waved her hand. "I'm fine. I appreciate your coming and listening to an old woman's ramblings."

"It was fascinating," Faye assured her. "Every moment." And she meant it.

40

The July meeting of the board of directors of The Haven finally ended. Most of the directors left, hurrying to enjoy the summer evening.

The Hot Flash Club, all of whom were on the board, remained seated around the conference table. Every single woman looked miserable.

Shirley unbuttoned her suit jacket. In spite of the air conditioning, she'd been stifled in the stiff, severe garment. She wore it because she needed to look corporate and capable, and because the heavy fabric hid her nipples, which tended to poke out like a couple of metaphorical exclamation marks when she got nervous.

"Well!" she said, forcing a smile. "I'm glad that's over!"

Alice pounced. "I can't *believe* you want to sell The Haven." She was so angry her head ached.

"I didn't say I *want* to," Shirley reminded her with teeth-gritting patience. "I only presented the offer the Rainbow Group made. What would you want me to do? Pretend it didn't happen?"

"But you *do* want to sell, don't you?" Alice prodded. "You didn't need to *say* so to make it apparent."

Shirley unscrewed the lid on her bottle of water and took a hearty swallow. "Alice, it's a very exciting offer, financially speaking. And—"

"But The Haven is your baby!" Alice cried. "Your dream come true!"

"That's true. And I'm very proud of what I've accomplished. And it means the world to me. But Alice, give me a break. I never thought it would require so much administrative work. Just because I've managed to do it doesn't mean I *like* doing it."

"Yes, well, that's certainly been obvious the last two weeks. You've hardly been here."

Faye, Marilyn, and Polly silently watched the discussion between Shirley and Alice, their heads flapping back and forth like fans at a tennis match.

Faye broke in. "Alice, it's summer. The Haven's membership isn't nearly as active in the summer. Plus, there's Nantucket. When will any of us ever again have the opportunity to stay, rent-free, in a Nantucket house in the summer? And we owe that to Shirley."

Marilyn, emboldened by Faye's remarks, straightened in her chair. She looked especially disorganized today in lemon and lime dotted silk trousers with a worn red plaid L.L. Bean shirt, the sleeves rolled up. "Now that we're alone, I'd like to say that I'd be *delighted* to sell my share of The Haven. When I came aboard, I hadn't met Ian, I was separated from my husband, I was at loose ends. Now I've got more than I can handle. Even a monthly meeting is too much for me, especially with all the reports we have to read." She gestured to the piles of paper in front of all the women.

Faye said, "I agree, Marilyn. I'm thinking of renting a house on Nantucket for a year or so, and I won't be able to make the meetings . . ."

"Faye!" Polly looked shocked. "I didn't realize you wanted to live on Nantucket! What about Aubrey?"

"I don't think we should discuss personal matters during a board meeting," Alice said grumpily.

"The board meeting has been adjourned," Shirley snapped.

"And our personal matters impinge directly on our relationship to The Haven," Faye reminded Alice in a firm but gentle voice. "They always have."

"Time out!" Shirley looked at her four friends. "I think Alice is right, and Faye's right, too. I think we all have a lot to discuss, but we shouldn't be doing it in this"—she gestured wildly at the room—"this *cell*. It's summertime, for heaven's sake. It's a glorious summer evening."

"You're right," Faye agreed. "Let's go to dinner!"

Marilyn looked at her watch. "I don't know . . ."

"I do!" Alice shot Marilyn one of her looks. "Everyone at your house is an adult. If they're hungry, they can order a damn pizza."

Marilyn smiled wearily. "You're right. I'll just phone them and tell them I won't be home till later."

The Italian restaurant near The Haven was just starting its dinner service. They were escorted to a table set with a snowy white cloth, sparkling glasses, and a low bowl of summer flowers. The air was redolent with aromas of garlic and simmering tomato sauce.

Shirley said, "I can feel my blood pressure drop."

"Mine, too," Marilyn seconded. "It's so nice to be in a room I'm not responsible for, getting ready to eat food I didn't buy, lug into the house, and cook."

"You seem a little overwhelmed," Polly gently observed.

"I'm exhausted!" Marilyn ran her fingers through her hair, which needed a good trim.

"What's going on?" Faye asked. She had only arrived from Nantucket this morning.

The waiter, a young George Clooney look-alike with thick black lashes and a long slow smile, appeared at the table to take their orders for drinks. When he left, Marilyn confessed, "It's like I'm caught in a nightmare! People just keep coming to live with us! You know Ruth has the basement apartment, and she's adorable, but she's eighty-seven, she needs companionship and I have to check up on her fairly often. I love Ian—or I would if I ever got the chance to see him alone. Angus and his bulldog bumble around the house like a pair of laughing hyenas. *Now* the beautiful Fiona, wife of Ian's best friend, has come from Scotland 'for a while' because her husband died and she's grieving. Not to mention, Ian and I have both been teaching summer courses, which—thank heaven!—finished today. I'll have to read the exams and get the grades in next week and then I'll be through and I'll have the month of August free!"

Alice patted her on the back. "Honey, you're wound up tighter than an eight-day clock."

The sympathy made Marilyn's lower lip quiver like a child's. "I know. It would help if Ian and I had any time to be together."

"Well, don't you share a bedroom?" Shirley asked.

"We do, but it's right over the living room where Fiona sleeps in the foldout bed, and Ian just doesn't feel right having sex while she's down there alone and might be able to hear our bed creak." Marilyn gave a little snort. "I was filling out a form the other day, and where it said 'Sex,' I felt like writing in, 'Not recently.'"

Everyone laughed.

Shirley asked, "What does Fiona do all day while you and Ian are teaching?"

"She watches television!" Marilyn waved her hands in the air. "She sits there all day long and watches the most *stupid* TV shows! She never tries to help cook or buy groceries. It's like she's in some kind of trance."

Faye and Polly exchanged glances. "She *is* in some kind of trance," Faye said softly. "After Jack died, I couldn't pick up a paint brush for nine months."

"I watched a lot of television after Tucker died," Polly admitted. "It seemed so . . . companionable . . . and yet it didn't expect anything of me."

"Still," Marilyn argued, "Fiona could stay in her own home and watch TV."

"Then someone else would probably move in," Alice predicted gloomily. "Honestly, I just don't know, do we ever reach a perfect state? I mean, you, Faye, and Polly, seldom get to see your grandchildren, and that makes you sad. I get to see my granddaughter daily, and it's wearing me down."

The gorgeous waiter returned, setting their drinks before them. He moved with such sensual languor, the table fell silent. They all watched, relaxing, smiling as he moved. The day's discontents were forgotten in the momentary rush of seeing his classic profile, glossy black hair and thick eyelashes. His English was heavily accented, giving him the exotic air of a Latin lover, and as he took their dinner orders, he focused his total attention on each woman, lingering on words like "cream sauce," turning the process into a kind of courtship.

When he walked away, Alice fanned her face. "Lordy! That's the best sex I've had in months!"

Polly's cheeks were flushed. "His eyelashes should be registered as lethal weapons."

Faye pressed her water glass to her flaming face. "I got a hot flash when he looked at me."

"You know what we need?" Polly asked.

"Oh, yes, honey, I do," Alice said in a tone that made everyone laugh.

"A good movie!" Polly wriggled with enthusiasm. "We all need to go together to see some fabulous romantic, sexy movie! Like—like *The Bodyguard*!"

"Oh, yes!" Faye pressed the glass to the other side of her face. "That scene where Kevin Costner picks up Whitney Houston and carries her off the stage just about made me faint!"

Marilyn leaned forward. "What about Richard Gere picking up Debra Winger in *An Officer and a Gentleman*?"

"Uh-uh." Alice shook her head. "I get too nervous when a man has to pick a woman up. I cannot relate to that! Any man who tried to pick me up would incur an instant hernia! Besides, it doesn't have to be a romance to do me some good. I mean, sometimes all it takes is a man with a wonderful smile."

"You're right!" Faye agreed. "Funny, I can watch the goriest serial-killer movie ever made, but if Denzel Washington's in it and he smiles just once, I'm happy for a week."

"Like that movie"—Shirley cut in—"With Reese Witherspoon, and that man who's got the sexiest smile God ever gave a human being."

"What's the actor's name?" Polly asked.

Shirley frowned. "I don't know—is it Russell Crowe?"

"Uh-uh," Alice said. "I've seen every one of Russell Crowe's movies. *Twice.*"

"Why, Alice," Faye teased, "sounds like you've got a little obsession going on."

"I like a manly man," Alice admitted with a grin.

Shirley was still wondering. "Was it Hugh Grant?"

"No, but that was another sexy movie, that Bridget Jones one," Polly said.

"Lucky Renee. She got to choose between Hugh Grant and Colin Firth." Alice sighed. "What a choice."

"What was that actor's name?" Shirley pinched the bridge of her nose.

"What was the movie?" Faye asked.

Shirley squeezed her eyes tight as she thought. "Something about a

Southern girl who makes it big in New York, and then goes back to Alabama . . ."

"*Sweet Home Alabama!*" Alice trumpeted.

"Right!" Shirley hit a high five with Alice. "I can't remember the actor's name, but I'll never forget his smile."

"You know, Polly," Marilyn said, "I think you're on to something. Thinking about those movie moments makes me feel as good as if I'd just eaten a box of chocolate."

"*Romance,*" Shirley sighed. "We never stop needing it, I guess."

"Plus, movie romance doesn't have consequences and complications," Alice added.

"I know," Marilyn agreed. "Getting out my tube of K-Y jelly sort of dims the glow."

"Not to mention, let's see, how do I put this?" Polly tapped her lip. "With senior sex, any vigorous activity usually makes romance *Gone with the Wind.*"

"I hear you," Alice said, laughing.

"Books are good, too," Faye observed. "Now and then a nice juicy romance novel really just hits the spot."

"So to speak," Alice wryly added.

Polly said, "When I was a teenager, I could get absolutely lost in a romance novel. It's more difficult now that I've lived with a couple of men and know what they're really like."

"Even if the man is lovely, real life has a habit of getting in the way," Marilyn agreed.

Alice said, "I haven't read a romance novel in years."

"You probably think you're too smart for them," Shirley commented bluntly.

Alice made a face at Shirley. "I just haven't had time to read!"

"I read a statistic somewhere," Faye said, "that romance readers are happier than other people."

"That makes sense," Shirley said. "Because look, falling in love feels *wonderful.*" She hesitated. Should she tell them about Harry now? No, this wasn't a good time. She and Alice were too cranky with one another right now. In fact, Alice was giving her one of her suspicious eagle eye glares. Shirley tried to speak in general terms. "Commitment feels good, too, and living with someone is also wonderful, but in an entirely different way. That falling-in-love thing—it's like looking at that waiter. It's physical and—"

"Mental, too," Polly cut in. "Or emotional. I mean, I get a romance buzz reading a novel or seeing a movie, but sometimes I can just put on one of my old favorites, like Barry Manilow singing 'Mandy,' and I'll dance all around the room by myself, I'll feel like I'm *soaring,* like I'm completely in love with the universe and it's in love with me! I'll play the same song over and over and weep and be full of joy at the same time."

"I know just what you mean," Shirley agreed.

"Barry Manilow?" Faye arched a critical eyebrow.

"Who does it for you?" Polly demanded. "Pavarotti?"

"Since you ask, yes, actually." Faye grinned. "I don't dance around the room, but I do feel that soaring thing you're talking about."

"For me it's U2," Shirley told them. "Bono singing 'One' makes me soar. What a rush."

"I'll take Ray Charles," Alice said. "And you know the weird thing? When I'm *there,* in that zone you're describing, I'm not thinking about any one specific man. Maybe I was when I was a teenager, but now it's like I'm just riding a surfboard on an ocean of feeling, and no other person's involved."

"I know! I know!" Polly hugged herself. "It's like being in love with love. I mean, when I get in that state, I could look at a head of cabbage and think it's the most beautiful thing on the planet."

Marilyn cocked her head. "I wonder why humans are wired like that."

"I think it's just one of nature's gifts," Shirley mused. "I mean, life is so full of daily banalities. Answering the phone. Paying bills. Lugging in groceries. Unclogging the toilet. And that's when there's no big trouble to deal with. Maybe our ability to have these perfect moments helps us deal with everything else."

Marilyn nodded. "That makes sense. Evolution would build in something to flood us with endorphins even if we weren't of childbearing age, to keep us around to do some of the chores of keeping the new humans alive and well."

Alice snorted. "Thank you so much, Dr. Strangelove, for that totally scientific observation."

"Well, let's be brutal," Marilyn argued. "How many times does the average person get to fall in love in her lifetime?"

"Three?" Polly guessed. "Four?"

"Um—thirty-two?" Shirley offered, only half-joking.

Alice chortled. "Shirley throws the statistics off."

"For some people it's only once. But let's be generous," Marilyn continued. "For the sake of argument, let's say four times. And that falling-in-love rush can't last more than—let's be generous again and say four months. So sixteen months out of a lifetime of eighty years, which is 960 months, means that 944 months of your lifetime you're not going to feel that romantic, life-enriching surge."

"God, that's *depressing*!" Shirley wailed.

"Cheer up," Alice told her. "Here comes Romeo with our meals."

41

The group watched, mesmerized, as the handsome waiter approached, thigh muscles swelling against his crisp black trousers. With smooth, sinuous movements, he set a plate before each woman, reciting the name of each dish with his deliciously embellished accent, smiling into each woman's eyes.

"Would anyone like fresh ground pepper?" With both hands, he held out the world's longest, most phallic-looking pepper mill.

Shirley crammed her napkin in her mouth. Faye turned crimson. Polly's jaw dropped. Marilyn smiled appreciatively. Alice said, "Thanks, honey, no. We're fine."

When he was out of earshot, they all burst out laughing.

"I'm giving that young man a big tip," Faye said.

"He'd like to give you a big tip," Alice quipped, sending them into more gales of laughter.

"I predict he'll go far," Shirley said. "I admire anyone trying to make a home in a foreign country."

Faye dabbed her white linen napkin against her throat. Her face still glowed from her most recent hot flash. "Sometimes I feel like *I'm* entering a foreign country. And *not* by choice."

"I know just what you mean," Shirley agreed. "We are leaving the comfortable world of youthful sexuality for a whole new world."

"A new continent of incontinence," Alice quipped.

Polly leaned forward. "We have to abide by new laws. Like we don't dare sneeze or laugh unless there's a bathroom nearby."

"Not to mention living by new diet rules," Faye added. "Plus, we have to learn a new language. Words we never needed to know before, like estrogen."

"And for the men," Alice cut in, "prostate."

Faye nodded. "We have new officials. Physicians. Physical therapists. Dieticians."

"What I hate," Polly said, "is the embarrassment of it. I mean, people write books and appear on TV shows talking about their alcohol or drug addictions, about going cold turkey, and they're respected for it. But talking about menopause is humiliating, as if we're doing something shameful on purpose, like, oh, I don't know, exposing our bums."

Alice laughed. "I know! There are days when my involuntary withdrawal from estrogen makes me feel like I'm going cold turkey."

Faye said, "It's sort of like the opposite of being a teenager. Remember when we were in our early teens? Boys' voices dropped and their skin broke out. We started our periods and developed breasts. It was all normal, but hideously embarrassing to talk about."

Alice nodded. "Except then we could anticipate learning about sex. Now we're leaving sex behind us and only have old age and death to look forward to."

"Oh, stop!" Shirley slapped Alice lightly on her hand. "We're not decrepit yet! I, for one, don't intend to give up sex for a good long time!"

Alice gave Shirley a knowing stare. "I knew you had something going on down on the island."

Flustered, Shirley hurried to point Alice's eagle eye elsewhere. "And look at Marilyn! She's having fabulous sex with Ian!"

"It's true," Marilyn agreed. "Or I would be if we were ever alone."

"And Polly," Shirley babbled, "you're having fun sex with Hugh, right?"

Polly laid her fork down and patted her lips with her napkin. She held her head high. "I've broken off with Hugh."

The four other women looked stunned.

"When did this happen?" Alice asked.

"He came to my house Sunday evening. I pretty much gave him an ultimatum. I told him I had to come first, I wanted to be married, I wanted to go to his grandchildren's recitals, I didn't want to be on the side. He told me he can't commit to anything more than what we've got."

"Oh, Polly." Marilyn reached over and hugged her friend. "I'm so sorry."

"This is terrible!" Shirley was dismayed. "Why didn't you call me? Or any one of us?"

Polly stared down at her lap. "I guess I just wanted to get through it by myself. I don't want to be dependent on anyone."

"Nonsense!" Alice was angry. "We all are dependent on one another, for heaven's sake. You shouldn't have had to deal with this by yourself. That stupid man. That stupid, stupid man!"

Faye cleared her throat. "I can kind of understand Hugh." She gestured, "Wait!" with her hand aimed at Alice. "I'm pretty much breaking up with Aubrey, for similar reasons. I mean, for reasons that probably seem selfish to everyone else. I don't want to be married to him. I just can't put Aubrey *first* in my life."

"Have you spoken to him about this?" Alice asked.

"We've talked on the phone. We haven't finalized things officially, but he knows I want to spend more time on the island. As I said, I'm looking for a place to rent for the fall and winter." Her face lit up as she talked. "The art on Nantucket is just spectacular. There's a marvelous group of artists working there, and several first-rate galleries, and I can't tell you how excited I am about painting landscapes there!"

Alice shook her head. "I hope you're not sorry about giving up Aubrey." She turned to Polly. "I just hope you've done the right thing breaking off with Hugh."

"From my perspective," Marilyn put in, "I think you might be a little impatient. I mean, no one our age gets to have someone without any previous connections. I mean, Ian has to deal with Ruth living with us, and I've got to deal with his son, his son's dog, and now Ian's best friend's widow. It's difficult, but—"

"But Ian wants to *marry* you!" Polly reminded her. "Hugh *doesn't* want to marry me. Ian has you involved with his son's life. Hugh doesn't want me doing anything with his kids or grandkids."

Alice made a discreet, judgmental little snort. "You know about the three rings of marriage, right?"

"What are they?" Polly asked.

"Engagement ring, wedding ring, suffering."

"Oooh, Alice," Shirley protested. "That's so cynical!"

Alice shrugged. "I guess I'm feeling cynical these days. You all know how I worried when Alan and Jennifer got married. Then I fell in love with little Aly. For a while, the world was absolutely rosy. But now Alan and Jennifer are arguing constantly. They're worried about money, they're exhausted from taking care of the baby, and to be completely honest, I'm exhausted, too!"

Marilyn put her hand on Alice's arm. "I know exactly how you feel, believe me."

For a few moments, the table was quiet.

Then Shirley spoke up. "You know how when we all first met, we decided we could solve each other's problems? And we did?" When the others nodded, she continued. "Looking back on it all, don't you think we were kind of brave and crazy? I mean, Marilyn, you pretended to be a secretary in a huge corporation, and Faye, you acted like a house-keeper, and I spied on Jennifer, and Alice rearranged my entire financial life. Well, do you ever think we're all a little—*bossy*?"

Everyone laughed.

"Hell, yes, we're bossy!" Alice was emphatic. "And I'd do it again. Our motto is, after all, *Interfere*! I'd do something now if I could help you, Marilyn, but I've got my hands full with the baby."

"And maybe you shouldn't," Faye suggested softly. "Maybe what Shirley's suggesting is that you should step back and let Alan and Jennifer solve their own problems."

Annoyed, Alice demanded, "Yes, well, what would happen to them if I did?"

"I don't know," Faye replied logically. "No one knows. But remember when you were younger, Alice? As I recall, you were a single mother who managed to take college courses and work for TransContinent. I think, sometimes, being, well, *stretched* by life can be good for us. I know I had more energy and enthusiasm for painting after my daughter was born. Maybe Jennifer and Alan need to dig deep within themselves to discover just how much stamina they have."

Shirley was nodding. "I'm totally with you, Faye."

Polly added, "Me, too."

Faye held out both hands, palms down, to silence the table. She cleared her throat. "We all have a lot to decide, personally and as direc-tors of The Haven. When we first met, we all brainstormed, and we came up with some pretty great ideas—"

"And we made some pretty big mistakes!" Alice reminded her.

"Yes, but in the end, everything turned out really, really well. This summer we've spent very little time together as a group. I think The Hot Flash Club needs to spend one entire week together on Nantucket. To chill out, let the dust settle, brainstorm, and gain a new perspective on our futures."

The others were quiet, thinking.

Alice took a deep breath and exhaled loudly. "Okay, Faye. I think you're right. I agree."

"Me, too," Polly added.

Marilyn looked downhearted. "You all don't have a house full of people dependent on you."

"But you don't have courses to teach in August, do you?" Faye pressed.

"And neither does Ian, right?" Polly added. "Let Ian take care of everyone for a week."

Marilyn squelched her face up tight. "I don't know . . ."

Shirley reached over and took both of Marilyn's hands in hers. "What is the very worst thing that could happen if you spent a week away from your home?"

"Well, for one, my mother could die."

Alice shook her head. "Ruth's as healthy as a horse. She's got her own friends, she's got a way to get to that senior citizen's club of hers, and if you leave, there will still be two—or three, if you count Angus as a grown-up—adults to listen to the intercom and check on her."

Marilyn sighed. "I suppose." But she didn't look happy.

"What else worries you?" Faye prodded.

"Well . . ." Marilyn flushed deeply. "What if," she said, in a very low voice, "Ian falls in love with Fiona? What if he sleeps with her while I'm gone? She's so beautiful."

"*Honey,*" Alice was very forceful now. "If Ian sleeps with Fiona while you're on Nantucket, he would sleep with her while you were at the grocery store. If he doesn't love you, if the man can't be faithful to you, better learn about it now, before you make the mistake of marrying him."

"Oh, dear." Tears welled in Marilyn's eyes.

"That's the worst case scenario!" Shirley hastened to remind Marilyn, at the same time shooting an exasperated glance at Alice. "You don't know that's what's going to happen!"

"She's right," Polly said. "When Tucker died, the last thing I felt like was having sex with anyone."

Faye nodded her head. "If Fiona loved her husband, and from all you've said, it sounds like she did, she won't want to have sex with Ian. From what you've said, Fiona can't do more than watch television."

"Besides," Shirley added, "remember the first rule of the Hot Flash Club. *Don't let fear rule your life!*"

Marilyn wiped the tears from her cheeks with her napkin. "Okay. Okay, I know you're all right. Okay, *yes,* I'll come spend a week with you all on Nantucket!"

"Excellent!" Faye and Polly gave each other high fives.

"Shirley." Alice aimed a level stare at her friend. "You can tell the Rainbow wheeler-dealers we can't give them a decision until the middle of the month. If they don't like it, tough."

"Fine." Shirley was trying her best not to look nervous or guilty. She couldn't wait to be on the island again, but having all her friends there was certainly going to complicate matters.

Faye had pulled a small leather daybook out of her purse. "Let's give ourselves next week, the last week in July, to organize ourselves. We'll all go down to Nantucket next Sunday and spend the first week in August together!"

"Sounds like a plan!" Polly grinned.

Marilyn was smiling. "I think we ought to celebrate this decision with a nice round of chocolate desserts."

"Absolutely!" Alice agreed. "Let's get Romeo back here, one more time!"

Sunlight woke Shirley. She stretched with luxurious indolence, each muscle of her body loose and warm, her heart thudding deep and slow within her like the wing beat of a powerful bird just beginning its journey home.

Harry wasn't in bed with her. She stretched out her hand and felt the pillow next to her. It was still warm. She heard the toilet flush. She checked the clock. Not quite five in the morning! Well, they'd gone to bed early last night. Although, she remembered with a smug smile, they hadn't gone to sleep for quite a while.

Friday night, when she returned home from dinner with her friends, she'd felt mellow and optimistic, as she always did after a good Hot Flash session. But when she went to bed, her bed had seemed vast and cold, and when Harry phoned early Saturday morning to ask her when she was coming back to the island, it had seemed absolutely right to say *immediately.* She'd packed in an instant, driven into Logan, and spent an unconscionable amount of money on a flight from Boston to Nantucket. Harry met her at the airport, and they'd spent a fabulous lazy island day together, and an even more delicious night.

Shirley couldn't believe how easy they were with each other. She felt like salt who'd finally found pepper. She didn't feel she had to flirt, flatter, babble, or squeal—well, at least not any more than she did normally. The thing was, she didn't try to pretend to be younger than her age. Perhaps this was because Harry was the first man her own age she'd dated in a while. Well, except for Stan. Turning on her side, Shirley burrowed her head into the pillow and revised her thought. Harry was the first older man she'd been *attracted to* in more years than she could count. He made no attempt to pretend he was younger, either. He was honest about his various aches and pains and the frustrating diminishment of his strength. But, Shirley thought, with a little frisson of fear, Harry was in amazingly good shape for a man his age. He'd have no trouble attracting much younger women.

Now he came into the bedroom. "Good morning." He was completely naked, as was Shirley. Approaching the bed, he bent to kiss her.

"Mmm." The kiss was brief, but he hugged her to him for a long time. His bristling morning beard rasped against her cheek.

"Come on," he said, taking her by the wrist. "We're going for a swim."

Shirley balked. "I don't have a bathing suit."

"You don't need one." Harry grinned and tugged her out from under the covers. "We're going au naturel. No one will see you, except maybe a few ducks."

"Let me just use the john," she told him.

In the privacy of the bathroom, she peed, then took a moment to glance at her reflection. Big mistake. Her skin was pale and blotchy, and the clear morning light illuminated every long wrinkle.

Harry was out on the deck, still naked, stretching in the warm glow of the sun. The thermometer mounted on the deck showed the temperature nearing a tropical seventy-eight. The calm waters of the harbor were a deep, vibrant blue. In the distance, a gull called.

"Harry." Shirley hugged herself. "I can't swim."

Harry ruffled her hair as if she were a kid. "Then it's time you learned."

Hand in hand, they walked along the sandy path through the green grass and tangled brush down to his dock and the water's edge. Still holding her hand, Harry led her into the shallows. A few shells lay in the sand, glimmering through the transparent water. Shirley got her feet wet, then her ankles, then her knees. The water was warm. When she was in up to her thighs, Harry said, "Now lie down, and I'll hold you."

She cocked an eyebrow at him and joked in her best Mae West voice, "Now there's an offer I can't refuse." She was trying to be brave, but the beat of her heart had tripled with her trepidation.

"Face down," Harry instructed. "Arms up."

She hesitated, then just did it. When her torso hit the water, she gasped. She turned her head sideways to keep her mouth free for air. Her system went on red alert: she was on overload! Harry's arms, solid and warm around her waist, provided enough sensation all by themselves to send her over the edge, and of course the little demonic neurotic Shirley who lived in her head screamed in her ear, "What are you *doing*? He can see your naked old butt! He can see your naked, wrinkly thighs!"

"Get your face wet," Harry instructed. "Get your entire head wet. I'll hold you."

Shutting her eyes tightly, she obeyed.

"Now turn on your back." Harry's hands helped. "First thing you need to learn is to float. Kick your feet a little. Relax. Come on, relax. The water will hold you. Good."

He removed his hands and backed away. Shirley lay on her back, blinking beneath the sun. It was an odd experience, like lying on an air mattress. If she stopped moving her feet, her legs began to drift downward.

"Now stretch your arms up and back, one at a time, like this." Standing next to her, Harry demonstrated.

Shirley did as he said, and to her amazement, slowly wafted a few feet away from him.

"Now roll over, and keep moving your arms up and back, one at a time. And kick your feet."

Shirley panicked. "Um . . ."

"Pretend you're a seal."

No one had ever said that to her before! Shirley thought of seals with their silly amiable faces and their blubbery bodies. She tried to roll over in one sleek move, but her arms and legs got out of sync and for a few moments she found herself snorting water, spitting it out, and flailing her limbs desperately. When she shook her hair out of her face, she found that she was several feet away from Harry, who stood near the shore, his hands on his hips, smiling at her.

"Well done. Now swim back to me."

She thrashed her arms and legs, exploding the water around her, until to her amazement, she bumped into Harry. "Is that swimming?" she asked.

"That's swimming."

Putting his hands beneath her arms, he helped her stand. Her toes curled gratefully into the sand. She was huffing away like a marathon runner, and her eyes stung from the salt. Water drizzled down her face from her soggy hair and tickled her shoulders and back. Naked, helpless, and dripping, she felt like the world's most ancient infant. Her nipples had puckered into raisins, but now she realized that while the air dried her shoulders like a soft terry cloth towel, her legs and hips, still immersed in the water, seemed stroked by shimmering silk.

"Now swim next to me." Deftly, Harry glided away.

"I—"

Harry moved through the water as if he were part of it. Beside him, Shirley felt like a battery-operated windmill. She slapped the water and gasped and sputtered and kicked and gulped and lurched and tilted. Harry slid through the cool element like an otter. Shirley heaved and wobbled and snorted, as awkward and out of place as a camel.

Accidentally, she flipped over on her back. She decided to stay there a while to catch her breath. She kicked her feet, but let her arms drift. She closed her eyes. In a matter of moments, the sun dried the beads of water from her face. Little by little she caught her breath, and her heartbeat slowed. She stopped struggling. The warm water embraced her. It supported her. She felt safe.

"Hungry?"

Opening her eyes, she found herself staring upside down at Harry. Clumsily, she righted herself, glad to find purchase on the sandy bottom.

"Starving," she said truthfully.

Harry smiled. "There's nothing much better in the world than a big breakfast after a wake-up dip." Wrapping his arms around her, he said, "Well, perhaps there's one thing better." He bent and kissed her, his mouth cool and fresh.

Shirley hugged him against her, kissing him back. She felt his penis stir against her belly. *I look like this,* she thought, *with my hair tangled and clumped and every mole and crease and physical flaw glaringly exposed by the sun, and this man is kissing me, this man is sexually attracted to me. Is this all for real?*

I'm ready!" cried Adele Singleton as she opened her door to Faye's knock. She wore green silk trousers and a green sweater embroidered with daffodils. Faye said, "Adele, you look fabulous."

"Oh, well." Adele giggled. "I've got to put on the dog for tea at Lucinda's! Now where's my cane?"

Faye spotted it hanging over the kitchen chair, a green ribbon decoratively tied around the head. "I'll get it."

She placed the cane in the older woman's hands, then took her elbow and slowly escorted her out of the house and down the path to her Jeep, where Polly waited. With much giggling and shoving, they helped the older woman up into the passenger seat, and finally Adele was safely wedged in. Faye went around to the driver's side and slowly steered the Jeep through the narrow lanes back to Orange Street.

Adele was babbling with excitement. "I couldn't sleep last night, I was so excited! I don't know when I last saw Lucinda. We served on several committees together, for the Musical Arts Society and the church, but that was at least a decade ago! And I've never been to her house!"

"Never?" Faye was surprised. These two women had lived all of their lives just blocks away from one another.

"Well, don't forget, dear, I'm twenty-one years older than Lucinda. And I certainly didn't belong to her social set. If I hadn't met you and Polly, I would never have been brave enough to phone Lucinda to ask her to tea."

"Yes." Polly leaned over the seat back. "Isn't it odd that she insisted *you go there*?"

"I don't think so. I just said how much I enjoyed meeting the two of you, and how I wanted to have a little get-together, and how you like the island and would enjoy hearing some of the island's history, and so on. She knows I'm ancient and crippled and bungling. So she said it would be a pleasure to have us at her house. And I agreed it would be easier for me. And now, don't you see, as hostess, she'll be in control, and Lucinda likes control."

"Goodness," Faye said. "Such Byzantine maneuvers!"

"Oh, life in a small town is never without its politics," Adele agreed. "I'm sure Lucinda is as curious about you and Polly as I am to see Lucinda's house. Plus, I have no doubt Lucinda wants to hear about Nora, although she'd never admit it."

When Faye pulled into the Orange Street driveway, Polly bustled around to help Adele down from the Jeep and together the three women went down the sidewalk and up the path to Lucinda's home.

The moment they tapped at the door, it opened. Lucinda Payne stood there in her pewter silk skirt and matching sweater, a vision of ice on this hot day. As always, pearls were at her neck and ears. Her green eyes were cold, but when they lit on Adele, they warmed slightly.

"Adele. How nice to see you. Do come in."

"Thank you, Lucinda. And of course you know your neighbors, Faye Vandermeer and Polly Lodge."

"We've met," Lucinda responded briefly, and unenthusiastically. She led them into her living room, where several minutes were spent getting Adele comfortably settled in a wing chair. Lucinda had had her cleaning lady make a pitcher of iced tea, which was positioned on a silver tray next to a silver ice bucket and four tall etched crystal glasses. Tea and crisp damask napkins and bakery cookies were handed around.

"I can't get over how tidy your house is!" Adele said, with the innocent charm of the very old. "My house is cluttered with memorabilia."

Lucinda inclined her head in acknowledgment of the compliment. "I have never allowed mess. I'm far too busy to accept the interference it causes."

"Are you still on the library board?" Adele asked.

Lucinda said she was, and for a while the two older women discussed how the town's institutions had changed over the past few years. Polly and Faye listened quietly, sipping their tea, feeling just a bit like children who were in their proper place, being seen but not heard.

Faye hadn't been in the house before, and enjoyed examining the interior of this house, built at the same time as Nora's, with many of the same architectural features. While Nora's house was furnished with period antiques and crowded with a century's worth of keepsakes and heirlooms, Lucinda's décor was spare to the point of sterility. Faye supposed the monotone grays and cream of the walls, woodwork, and furniture could be considered serene, but it came off as chilliness, no doubt expressing the owner's temperament.

Adele brought them into the conversation. "Polly and Faye use the Atheneum quite a lot, you know. And Faye has fallen in love with Nantucket. She's thinking of spending the winter here."

Lucinda looked doubtfully at Faye. "I'm afraid you'll find yourself terribly bored. It's very quiet here in the off season."

"I'm an artist," Faye said. "I need peace and quiet. And I've been painting landscapes. I'd like to paint in the off season as well."

"Ah. Will you be staying in Nora's house?" Lucinda inquired idly, stirring her tea.

"I doubt it. I haven't discussed it with Nora. And it's such a large house. I'm sure the electric bills are enormous."

Lucinda looked pleased. "It's true. I live in my house year round, and it's costly. Perhaps more expensive than Nora's budget will allow."

Faye gazed around. "Your house and Nora's are about the same size."

"Mine is larger," Lucinda corrected quickly, "because of the addition on the back. Also, when my sons were younger, we had the basement fitted out as a den for them, with a billiards room and a TV room. Nora's basement is just dirt. Just a place for the furnace." An odd expression—sadness? guilt? discomfort?—shadowed her face. "Of course, I haven't used the basement for years, and I don't bother to heat it."

"I pretty much live in two downstairs rooms of my house," Adele said. "I can't climb the stairs any longer. But I have what I need all around me."

Lucinda studied Adele. "You must be in your nineties now."

"I'm ninety-five!" Adele bragged.

"And still living on your own. That is impressive. Have you considered moving into Our Island Home?"

Adele's face fell. "I'm sure the day will come when I won't be able to live alone."

Lucinda looked back at Faye and Polly. "How long do you intend to remain in Nora's house?"

Polly replied. "Through August, for sure."

"I might stay on through the fall," Faye continued. "I'm looking for a small house to buy or rent."

Lucinda arched an eyebrow. "And Nora?"

"She had her hip operation," Polly replied. "She came through with flying colors, but she's got a long recuperation ahead of her, and physical therapy after that. She wants to try to come down sometime in September or October, with one of her relatives, so she can spend some time on the island this year."

"The fall is Nantucket's best season," Lucinda said.

"I think I'd like it here in the winter," Faye said. "With howling winds and guttering candles. I could walk on the beach during the day, then curl up with a mystery by the fire at night."

Polly shivered. "Not me, thanks. I'd be afraid of ghosts."

"Oh, that's right!" Adele wriggled enthusiastically. "Nora's house has a ghost, isn't that right? Have you girls seen it?"

"We haven't *seen* the ghost, but we've seen signs of it," Faye told her. "A few things have disappeared, although not in the past couple of weeks."

"Oooh." Adele looked worried. "Are you frightened?"

"I suppose I am, a little," Faye said honestly.

"Me, too," Polly agreed. "Although before we came here, I didn't really believe in ghosts."

"Many of Nantucket's older houses have ghosts," Lucinda informed them in a matter-of-fact tone. "Restless spirits who are not satisfied with the way things were when they left this sphere of existence."

"Really?" Faye was fascinated to hear the practical older woman verge into shady territory. "Does yours?"

Lucinda shrugged. "Of course not. Why would it? No one in my family died dissatisfied."

Faye and Polly exchanged glances and held back smiles. So Lucinda was competitive even with those who had, in Adele's words, "gone aloft."

The conversation moved on. They discussed the more famous ghosts on the island, and some of the island's history, and then Adele's teacup began to rattle in its saucer.

"Oh, dear. There's a sure sign I need a nap." Adele smiled regretfully. "I do seem to run out of steam easily at this age."

Polly and Faye helped Adele to her feet. At the front door, Faye thanked Lucinda for a lovely afternoon. "We'd love to have you over for tea some afternoon."

Lucinda looked distinctly uncomfortable. "Perhaps," she replied vaguely. She waited graciously as the three slowly descended the front steps, then shut the door firmly behind them.

Faye and Polly drove Adele back to her house. They helped her out of the car, across her yard, and into the safe haven of her chair. When they arrived back at their Orange Street home, they found Kezia Jones's silver SUV parked in the narrow driveway.

"What do we do now?" Polly looked up Orange Street. As always, any parking places near town were filled.

Faye frowned. "It's not Wednesday. Wednesday was the day we agreed Kezia would collect the trash."

Someone behind them honked his horn, so Faye slowly drove up the street, looking for an empty space. There wasn't one. Perturbed—they both had to pee—they drove around the long narrow block. When they returned to the house, Kezia was just backing her SUV out of the driveway. Spotting them, she stopped. Faye pulled up on the curb as everyone did in this town. Kezia leaned her glossy head out the window and tossed them a radiant smile. At the same time, she automatically lowered the window behind her, so little Joe could see them. He squealed with delight and extended a chubby fist full of cracker.

"Sorry to take your space! I just had to run to the bank, and there wasn't any parking available. I thought you all would be at the beach today, anyway. I hope it wasn't a problem!"

Faye leaned out the window. "No problem," she called.

Polly leaned out her window. "Hi, Joey!" She waved at the little boy.

Faye put her Jeep in reverse and backed down the street so Kezia could give up the parking space for them. "Oh, Polly." She sighed. "Every time I see Kezia, I feel so old. She's so energetic and young!"

"Just compare yourself to Lucinda and Adele," Polly suggested. "That way *you*'ll feel young and energetic!"

"I suppose. It's sort of like seeing the Ghosts of Christmas Past and Christmas Future," Faye remarked.

"And this is Christmas Present," Polly reminded her. She laughed at her pun. "It really is like a Christmas present, having the summer on this island."

"You're right," Faye agreed, as she followed Polly into the house.

44

The Boston area was hit with record heat and humidity during the last week in July. Tempers flared, electrical usage soared, and fuses blew. Overtaxed machinery went on strike.

At The Haven's gatehouse cottage, one of the two complicated commercial ovens died. The electrician's answering machine informed Alan and Jennifer that there was a long line of clients already, but to leave their name, number, and the nature of the problem. They did, and tried to use the small oven in their little cottage for the most pressing orders, and there were a lot of pressing orders, since no one wanted to bake in their own homes in this weather.

Alice arrived at the gatehouse in the morning to find her son and his wife rushing through the door between the domestic quarters and the commercial kitchen, bumping into each other or lifting trays high as they tried to pass. It looked like a badly choreographed French farce, and was almost funny, until, from the other room, the baby woke and began to cry.

Alice raced to greet her granddaughter. Aly lay red-faced and squawking in her crib, dressed in pink cotton pajamas and covered with a light cotton blanket. Alice had advised Jennifer that in this heat the infant didn't need to be covered so thoroughly, but Jennifer obviously hadn't heeded her advice.

"You poor hot little baby!" Alice cooed.

Babbling baby talk, she carried Aly to the change table and stripped off her wet diaper. She fastened on a dry diaper and snapped on a loose cotton T-shirt. By the time she'd finished, Aly was bright-eyed and smiling. Alice carried the baby to the kitchen, grabbed a bottle of formula from the refrigerator, and settled Aly in her fancy little stroller, where she cooed with pleasure at the sight of the musical mobile hanging just above her.

Jennifer and Alan were still running back and forth, carrying baking sheets and mixing bowls. Alan had a portable phone clutched between his left shoulder and his ear. He was pleading with an electrician to come repair the oven.

Alice called, "I'm taking Aly with me to The Haven."

"Thanks!" Jennifer cried over her shoulder as she rushed back to the commercial kitchen.

Alice wheeled the stroller outside. The sun blazed down, the air simmered. It was so hot! In just minutes, sweat glued her shirt to her back. The straps of her sandals cut into the tops of her swelling feet and the waistband of her loose cotton trousers—the *elastic* waistband!—was too tight, pressing uncomfortably against her back. The damp heat smothered her in its inescapable embrace. She wanted to shove it away, and frustration welled inside her at her inability to control it. She felt just completely irritable as she pushed the stroller up the long curving drive.

Finally she reached The Haven. There was a handicap ramp at the other end of the building, but she didn't want to have to stay outside one more moment, so she lifted the baby from the stroller and lugged her up the steps, not even stopping to let Aly check out the stone lions that lay in grand attendance on either side of the steps.

Inside, it was blissfully cooler, and dryer. The downside of this, she knew, was that The Haven's electric bill would skyrocket this month.

She entered the lounge, which was vacant. She lay Aly on her back on the sofa and sat next to her, catching her breath and cooling down. She had to remember, when she returned, to tell Alan and Jennifer that she couldn't babysit next week, that she would be on Nantucket for the entire week. Her stomach pinched with worry for them. They were already so pressured, so frantic. But her Hot Flash friends were right, they were adults, and needed to learn how to deal with the stresses of life. Even if Alice wanted to fix everything for them, she couldn't, and she shouldn't.

Aly was fussing with boredom, so Alice picked her up and carried her up the wide staircase to the second floor and Shirley's offices. When she entered, Wendy jumped up from her desk—nearly jumped *over* her desk—babbling at Alice so fast Alice could hardly understand what the other woman was saying.

"Oh! Alice! Thank GOD you've come! I don't know what to do! My computer has just eaten everything, and I tried to recall it on Shirley's, and the same thing happened there, and I've phoned our computer guru but she's on vacation, and look at these manuals, they're incomprehensible! I promised Shirley I'd get the figures printed out and a report made for those Rainbow people, and now I've gone and messed everything up! What am I going to do!"

"Where's Shirley?" Alice asked, bouncing the baby in her arms.

"On Nantucket. She'll be back Friday."

Conflicting emotions surged through Alice like an internal tornado. Shirley hadn't told her she was going to Nantucket. Why did she have to go this week? She was going to be there *all next week* when the Hot Flash Club had their vacation together. And Shirley left the running of The Haven in Wendy's hands? Well, Wendy had been with The Haven for a year now, and she was a good receptionist and secretary, but still, it wasn't very responsible of Shirley to go off like this.

At the same time, Alice's old professional temperament perked up. She'd always enjoyed cleaning up a business glitch.

She handed Wendy the baby. "Hold her. I'll see what I can do."

As Alice settled into the office chair behind the desk, Wendy cuddled Aly, chattering away nonstop. "I phoned Shirley on Nantucket, the number she gave me, I mean, and Faye said Shirley's out for the day, unreachable. Shirley has a cell phone, but she must have it turned off, it will only take messages. I've left several messages for her, and I did explain the problem to Faye, but of course Faye doesn't know anything about computers. She suggested I phone Julie Martin, you know, she's one of the main investors in The Haven and apparently quite proficient with computers even though her field is really investments . . ."

"Fine!" Alice snapped. "I'm sure you did what you could, Wendy. Now take Aly into the other room. I can't think with you blathering away in my ear."

Wendy whisked the baby into Shirley's office, shutting the door behind her.

For an hour Alice sat at the computer, patiently, steadily, painstakingly, attempting to retrieve the lost information. It was a hopeless task. Something had clearly gone wrong with the computer; it had indeed, as Wendy said, eaten everything. The longer Alice persevered, the more frustrated she got. There was something almost human about the computer with its eagerness to obey human directions that made it seem absolutely *hostile* when it didn't obey, until Alice felt she was in a kind of war of wills with the machine. And the manual had clearly been written by a gang of sadists. She found herself cursing at the equipment, calling it names she hadn't spoken in years, and she even slapped the monitor. That hurt her hand, while the monitor remained impassively blank.

At the point of tears, she shoved back her chair and stomped into Shirley's office.

"Let me look at her computer," she directed.

Wendy was lying on the floor playing with the baby. When Alice came in, she started to get up, but Alice waved her back down.

"No, no, you're fine. Just keep Aly happy."

She plopped down into Shirley's office chair and wriggled the computer mouse. The screen woke up, and Alice began to type in commands, but nothing happened.

Both computers were alert, alive, but intractable.

Alice found the phone book. "What computer services did you phone?"

Wendy named three. "No one's available for at least another day or two."

Alice tried phoning the ones Wendy hadn't tried, but they were not regular servicers and all they offered was to put The Haven on a waiting list.

"I have an idea," Alice said. Snatching up the phone, she punched in Marilyn's number. "Marilyn? Is Angus there?"

One of the things Polly liked best about being a seamstress was its measurable reliability. If she were careful and paid attention, she could make a dress that fit a woman perfectly. She could work from a pattern, and she could count on the pattern not to change, unless she changed it.

Real life was much less reliable. If her patterns were like real life, she'd walk into her sewing room to find the pattern laid out on the fabric, with the right arm attached at the left hip and the neckline dangling from the waistband. Sometimes it seemed there was just no rhyme nor reason to real life.

Before she'd met The Hot Flash Club at The Haven, Polly had met another group of friends there, all stressed out, as she had been, from problems with difficult relatives. She'd become closest with a younger woman, Carolyn Sperry, who was pregnant with her first child. Carolyn's mother had died when she was younger. Polly had only one child, a son who had married a woman so entrenched in her own family's life Polly couldn't find a way in. It had seemed natural—it had seemed *heaven-sent*—for Polly and Carolyn to become close friends. Carolyn had asked Polly to be her daughter's godmother, and Polly had been thrilled and honored. She adored little Elizabeth, who had turned two in April. She tried to see her every week. This Friday evening, Carolyn had invited her for a casual family dinner, and Polly arrived early, so she had some time to devote to Elizabeth.

Tonight, Polly wore white silk trousers and a silk tunic top in a vivid shade of turquoise, an unusual color for Polly, who tended to stick to pastels. But her pale, freckled skin had a burnish to it that allowed the turquoise to work, and she'd playfully tied a turquoise scarf around her fading red and white hair.

She felt almost glamorous as she entered Carolyn's handsome modern home.

"Polly! You look fabulous!" Carolyn, as usual, was running late. "I just got home from work. Hank's not here yet. Would you mind . . ." She waved her hand vaguely in the direction of her child, who toddled up to Polly, crying gleefully, "Pony ride!"

Polly swooped down, picked up the little girl, and kissed her. She smelled so fresh and looked so darling in her little pink sundress.

"Pony ride, Pawee!" Elizabeth insisted.

"All right, Elizabeth." Polly surrendered. "Pony ride!"

She kicked off her shoes, lay on her back on the family room rug, and bending her knees, pulled the toddler up onto her shins, Elizabeth's fat little diaper-padded bottom resting on Polly's feet, her chubby hands held in Polly's. Polly bobbed her legs and sang a little song. Elizabeth squealed with glee.

"Hello, Polly!" Elizabeth's grandfather, Aubrey Sperry, came in through the side entrance that opened right onto the family room. He looked dapper in a lightweight wool cream summer suit, pale blue shirt, and striped red tie.

"Ooof!" Polly's knees were touching her chest as she bounced Elizabeth, which meant that Aubrey had a clear view of her enormous bum, the size emphasized, of course, by the white slacks. In a moment of panic, Polly wondered whether the light days pad she wore showed. She carefully lowered her legs to the floor, holding on to the toddler protectively as she moved. "Look, Elizabeth! Grandfather's here!"

She was grateful for the commotion Elizabeth made as she scrambled to her feet and rushed to grasp her beloved grandfather around his legs. Polly knew her face was red from exertion, not to mention her hair had come loose from the scarf and no doubt looked like a tangle of yarn. It was hard not to feel like a peasant around Aubrey Sperry, with his elegant manners and heirloom ways. Aubrey Sperry came from a family who had started a paper company over a hundred years ago, on the banks of the Rock River. The company had supported a community; an entire town had been named Sperry in its honor. Aubrey had run the company until his daughter took over, and he still showed up for festive and commemorative occasions, standing erect in the spotlight as Sperry Paper contributed a nice fat amount to a local charity, his thick silver hair gleaming like a knight's helmet.

Polly had always thought Aubrey and Faye made a perfect couple. They were both so good-looking, so distinguished, and, just slightly, to Polly's way of thinking, so formal. Faye had a way of drifting away mentally, no doubt pondering her paintings, while maintaining a pleasant smile on her face. Faye never seemed to babble or dither like Polly did. Faye would never have let herself be caught with her bum up in the air!

Polly rose, smoothing her white trousers down over her backside and adjusting her turquoise tunic. "Carolyn's in the shower," she told Aubrey. "Since I arrived early, she took a moment to dash in and cool off. And Hank will be home any moment."

Aubrey's face was flushed. "Would you mind?" He inclined his head toward his granddaughter, who was trying to clamber up his legs into his arms.

Polly swooped over. "Grandfather can't pick you up, Elizabeth, Grandfather's got a wonky arm."

She settled the little girl on the sofa. Aubrey slowly lowered himself next to the child. Elizabeth climbed in his lap, put a hand on each side of his face, and gave him a big wet kiss.

"Could I fix you a drink, Aubrey?" Polly inquired.

"I thought you'd never ask," Aubrey jested, and they both laughed. "Gin and tonic. Strong."

"Oh, is your arm still bothering you?"

"It is. I thought the operation was supposed to help, and it did, but the physical therapy is almost worse than the original injury."

Polly lifted the lid on the ice bucket and began to prepare their drinks, glad to have something to do while Aubrey talked. She'd never been quite at ease with this man, partly because his daughter Carolyn had tried for so long, and in so many ways, to force Polly and Aubrey together when Aubrey was dating Faye and Polly was dating Hugh. A year ago at Christmas, the four of them had gone on a cruise together, and Polly's tension level had increased whenever she'd been alone even for a moment with Aubrey. This past Thanksgiving, she'd made a most un-Polly-esque fuss when she refused to go to London with Carolyn, Hank, and Aubrey, telling them all in no uncertain terms that Faye was Aubrey's companion, while Polly was attached to Hugh.

Now Polly was unattached. And Faye had made it clear to Aubrey that she wanted an independent life.

Polly brought Aubrey his drink and lifted Elizabeth off his lap. "Let's color," she suggested, organizing the child with a sketchpad and crayons. "That's terrible," she commiserated with Aubrey, who was continuing to discuss, in microscopic detail, his shoulder injury. She took a sip of her own vodka and tonic. The tang of lemon and the zing of cold lifted her spirits. She was quite happy right now, this was really what she was good at, *multitasking,* she supposed younger women would call it, keeping a toddler and an older man satisfied at the same time. She felt efficient, and just a little charming.

"Hello, everyone!" Hank came in, loosening his tie with one hand and dropping his briefcase on a chair with the other.

Elizabeth shrieked with glee and raced toward her father, stumbling over her own feet in her excitement. A moment later, Carolyn entered the room, a tall, lean, blond vision of perfection in her chic floral Lily Pulitzer sundress. Together Polly and Carolyn set the table and tossed the salad while, outside, Hank grilled the swordfish steaks and Aubrey one-handedly helped Elizabeth build a castle in her sandbox.

At the dinner table, Carolyn said, "Polly, this is a great rice and bean dish! Thanks for bringing it out."

"You're welcome." Polly smiled, pleased to be complimented. "I'm trying to cook beans more often. I've read that eating beans four times a week protects against colon cancer."

"Really?" Aubrey perked up at this preventative health flash. "What sorts of beans?"

"Any kind," Polly assured him. "Lima, green, string, red—"

"Jelly?" Aubrey joked.

Polly laughed. "Why not?"

The conversation turned to the stock market and the paper company, interspersed with exclamations of delight at how well Elizabeth ate her food. Afterward Carolyn and Hank went off to give the toddler her bath and read her a book before bed. Polly and Aubrey cleared the table and cleaned the kitchen in easy consort, chatting comfortably, both at home with the cupboards and drawers. Polly brewed a pot of decaf and she and Aubrey settled down in the family room, as comfortably as if they were a family, and in a way, they were, even if Polly was only the godmother.

"How do you like Nantucket?" Aubrey asked, leaning back in the chair and pinching the crease in his trousers as he crossed one handsomely shod foot over his knee.

"I love it," Polly said honestly. "Not as much as Faye, I suppose . . ." *There,* she thought, *I've just done and gotten it out in the open. If he wants to ask me how Faye feels about him, I've opened the door.*

"Well, Faye loves painting there, I know," Aubrey said reasonably. "What is it specifically that *you* love about it?"

Polly glanced at Aubrey. He looked as if he were actually interested in what she had to say. As if she weren't only an interpreter, a messenger, from Faye.

She thought a moment. "It's the crafts that fascinate me. Like sailor's valentines and lightship baskets, beautifully intricate, painstakingly detailed objects that carry with them the history and legends of the sailors who began the tradition."

"A sailor's valentine?" Aubrey stirred his coffee and set the spoon carefully in the saucer. "What's that?"

"It's a sort of picture made of seashells," Polly told him. Pulling over Carolyn's pad of papers and crayons, she drew a quick illustration.

Aubrey leaned forward to study her drawing. "Looks rather like a kaleidoscope."

"Yes, right. Lots of tiny chips arranged to make a pattern." With a flourish, she finished the sketch.

"Must take a long time to collect shells that match."

"Oh, yes. And even longer to put them in place. I've read that people use dental tools now, but heaven only knows what they used two hundred years ago."

"I don't have the patience for that kind of thing." Aubrey smiled. "Although I suppose it's a matter of interest. Somehow I have the patience for a game like golf."

"Games, yes. Have you ever played 'Shut the Box'? It's a game played with numbers and dice, something else sailors have done for decades to pass the time." Polly spotted the box on the shelves of children's books and games. "I brought Carolyn and Hank one. It's easy, and so much fun it's kind of addictive."

"Really? Show me."

In a matter of moments, they were back at the table, seated next to each other, coffee nearby, heads bent together as they rolled the dice. Occasionally Aubrey's arm touched Polly's. She didn't move hers away.

Yellow sunlight melted down on the Hot Flash Club as they lay in the sand like five pieces of warm toast fingers soaking in butter, their toenails as pink as strawberry jam. Nearby, the waves of the Atlantic Ocean flounced her turquoise skirts, flashing white lace-trimmed hems. The sweet smell of coconut lotion steamed off their bodies. The murmurs and laughter of other sunbathers floated through the hot humid air. Near the sudsy waves, a girl in a peppermint-striped suit helped a little boy build a sand castle. On their left, a pair of lovers lay twined and drowsing. On their right, a group of gorgeous college boys played Frisbee, easily jumping and running, their limbs so brown and supple it was hard not to stare. Music from someone's radio tinkled in the distance. It was as if they were drifting in a dream.

Then Alice sat up. "I'm hot. I'm hungry." She tugged on the legs of her black bathing suit.

"Me, too." Slender in her purple bikini, Shirley flipped over like a young seal.

Marilyn stirred into action. "I'll put up the beach umbrella. You can set out lunch, Alice." She'd smeared her forehead, nose, cheeks, and chin liberally with protective white foam.

Faye laughed, "Ha! Marilyn, you look like someone just smashed a cream pie in your face!"

Marilyn shrugged good-naturedly. "I've got to protect my skin. I burn so easily."

"I'll unfold the beach chairs." Shirley stood, brushing sand off her thighs.

"Oh, man," Polly sighed as she pushed herself into a sitting position and adjusted the straps on her green one-piece tank. "I was having the best dream. A young lifeguard was rescuing me. Crashing surf, strong legs, muscular tanned arms . . ."

" . . . flowing cellulite, drooping breasts . . ." Faye jested. Sitting up, she grabbed her sun hat and put it on, then added her sunglasses.

Marilyn stabbed the end of the beach umbrella deep into the sand. The Hot Flash Club had contributed jointly to buy this festive work of summer art. Its canopy was in triangular stripes of primary colors, red, yellow, and blue, and their long, thick, thirsty beach towels coordinated. The clever little beach chairs Shirley was setting into the sand in a circle were part of the set, made of chrome and red, blue, or yellow canvas, the backs stamped with bright blue icons of buckets, seagulls, and margarita glasses.

"Ta-da!" Shirley waved her hands like a game hostess. "Instant party scene!"

Alice pulled her chair farther into the shade, opened the cooler, and handed items out to Faye: heavy red plastic paper plates and cups, plastic utensils, Tupperware containers of salads, olives, and cheeses, and sandwiches of watercress and butter, cucumber and butter, chutney and cheese, trimmed of crusts and daintily cut into triangles.

Shirley reached into the cooler and brought out a small plastic bowl filled with red and white carnations. She put it in the middle of the red and white checked tablecloth spread among their chairs.

"A centerpiece!" Faye clapped her hands. "How elegant, Shirley!"

Shirley beamed, pleased. "I've got another surprise." Reaching in, she lifted up a plastic container. Inside was a chocolate cake. "Dessert."

"Oh, yum." Polly smiled. "You really know how to plan a picnic."

"Well, I wanted to bring something special for today," Shirley told the group. "I know you were thinking of bringing a bottle of champagne."

Faye shook her head. "One sip of alcohol in this heat, and I'd pass out."

Marilyn reached into the cooler next to her and lifted out cool bottles of clear water. She passed them around. "In this heat, it's water our bodies need."

They filled their plates, then settled back in their chairs to enjoy lunch. As they ate, they surveyed the scene around them: the crashing surf, glittering in the sunlight, the toddling children, the handsome young men jumping for the Frisbee. A pair of beautiful women strolled past in thong bathing suits.

"Look at that," Alice chuckled. "There's more material in my grand-daughter's diaper."

"I wonder how much more of the human body young women are going to expose," Faye mused.

"I'm baring more than they are!" Polly pointed to her wide thighs. "Because I've got more to bare."

Alice poked her own expansive thigh with her long red fingernail. "It's not the amount of flesh you show, it's the quality of what you've got to hide that matters."

"Right." Marilyn's face was thoughtful. "You could call me emaci-ated, or you could call me slim. Really, I'm just old and scrawny. If I wore a suit like that, I'd be arrested for indecent exposure."

"Marilyn, that's a terrible thing to say about yourself!" Faye scolded.

Marilyn was philosophical. "Perhaps. But true. And it doesn't bother me. I have no desire to attract strange men."

"That's because you've got Ian," Polly told her.

Marilyn looked doubtful. "I hope I've got him. I'm a little worried about being down here for an entire week, leaving him alone with the beautiful Fiona."

"Oh, stop it!" Alice said. "That man left his *country* for you! He took a job at B.U. You two have the most romantic real-life relationship I've heard about for years! Now tell me, are you making any plans for your wedding?"

"We haven't had a chance to plan anything," Marilyn answered. "It's all we can do to keep the house going, with Ruth, Angus, and now Fiona living there. Just buying groceries, cooking, and doing the laundry is overwhelming." She looked guilty. "I really shouldn't have left Ian with all that."

"Nonsense," Faye told her. "You filled Ruth's freezer with a week's worth of food, right? The other three are all adults who can take care of themselves. You deserve a break."

"You're right, I suppose. Still . . . you haven't seen Fiona. She's our age, but she's so voluptuous."

"And she's recently widowed," Polly reminded her.

"But she's not an independent kind of woman," Marilyn said. "I mean, she makes it clear she needs a man in her life. I'm afraid she wants Ian. He was the one she phoned when her husband died. She didn't stay in Scotland with all her other friends. And she's always reminding Ian of all the fun things they did together when they were younger. . . ." Marilyn broke off, looking out at the horizon with a frown on her face.

"Well, then." Alice straightened in her seat. "If you're serious about this, we've got to take it seriously, too. Call Ian and invite him down here."

Marilyn shook her head. "No. This is supposed to be a Hot Flash week. And if I can't trust Ian with Fiona for a week, I'd better learn about it now."

"I think you're right, Marilyn," Faye agreed.

Alice rolled the cold water bottle over her chest. "Here we are, in paradise, and still worrying. You're worrying about Ian. I'm worrying about Alan and Jennifer. Polly's sad because she broke off with Hugh, and Faye's feeling guilty because she's drifted away from Aubrey. And Shirley . . ." She looked quizzically at Shirley, who suddenly got very busy cutting the chocolate cake. "Shirley, you're looking kind of marvelous these days. What's going on?"

"Oh!" Shirley concentrated fiercely on putting the dessert on plates. "I'm just having such a wonderful vacation here. All the sun and fresh air!"

Alice looked suspicious, but allowed herself to be distracted by the nice big slice of chocolate cake Shirley handed her.

"I know what you mean about worrying," Faye said to Alice. "I've been thinking about it a lot since I've been on the island. I think I'm insulated from anxiety about my grandchildren because they're so far away, out in California. I remember how much I used to worry whenever my daughter had a slight cold or cough—I immediately feared she had some serious disease. Oh, Lord, I spent so much of my life *worrying*. Now that I've finally got time and space to myself, I don't want to worry about anyone else."

"Like Aubrey," Marilyn said.

"Like Aubrey," Faye agreed.

"But Faye," Alice said. "If you don't stay with Aubrey, then who's going to worry about *you*?"

Faye smiled. "Women live longer than men. If we're lucky, we'll all live into our nineties. Which means, at least statistically, at some point, we'll end up alone even if we were with a man, because the man would die sooner. I don't mind being alone, and I'm not going to constrict my life now to live with a man in order to have someone take care of me when I'm ancient."

"I think you're right," Shirley said. "You don't want to be with a man just to be with a man. It has to be the right man."

"Listen to Ann Landers here," Alice scoffed. "As if she's ever met the right man in her life."

"Don't be mean, Alice!" Shirley shot back. "Just because Fate dropped lovely Gideon in your lap, that doesn't mean the rest of us are idiots because we haven't found the perfect guy."

"No," Alice agreed. "But some of us are better at making choices. Some of us don't take such risks."

Shirley flushed angrily. "I would think by this age you'd realize we can't see into the future. By now we all know how life sweeps us in strange directions. I think life's a lot like tacking. Harry says life's like sailing. Sometimes you have to go sideways"—she made a zigzag motion with her hand—"to get where you want to go."

"Sometimes," Polly mused, "life seems like it's all tacking."

Alice's eyes bored into Shirley's. "Who's Harry?"

Oh, shit! Shirley thought, mentally slapping herself upside the head. Well, she had to tell them now. She girded her proverbial—and very happy—loins, and waded into battle. "He's an absolutely wonderful man I've met here on the island." She glanced around at the other women, summoning moral support.

"Oh, yes?" Alice grimaced. "And what does Harry do?"

"He's retired. He sails and putters and stuff."

"He lives here all year?" Alice asked. "Does he own his own house?"

"Yes," Shirley answered. "And yes, he does." She always had trouble lying to Alice, and now her face took on the guilty cast of a kid fibbing to her parents. If Alice saw Harry's tumbledown shack of a home, she'd have a fit.

Alice demanded, "What's it like?"

"It's small . . . humble. Oh, damn it, Alice, he doesn't have much money, all right? But he's so interesting, and so much fun, and he's nice to me."

"This is why you want to sell The Haven!" Alice's face looked like thunder. "So you can come down here and spend the profit you make on yet another good-looking cad?"

"He's not a cad!" Shirley protested.

"How do you know?" Alice countered. "Who are his friends on the island?"

Shirley chewed on her thumbnail. "We haven't spent much time with his friends."

"Have you spent *any* time with *any* friends?" Alice persisted.

"No," Shirley said in a very small voice. "But Alice, he does own a house and it's on the water, and he owns a boat. He's *not* a bum!"

Faye waved her hands like a choir director. "Calm down, you two. It's too hot to get so bothered! We can talk about this later tonight, okay? For now, let's enjoy this gorgeous day. We're so lucky to be here."

"Actually," Polly whispered, leaning forward. "I have to pee."

Shirley could have kissed Polly. It was the perfect distraction. They all had to pee. They always did.

"There's a restroom up by the parking lot," Marilyn told her.

Polly stared up the long long path through the dunes. "I don't know if I can make it that far."

"Then let's all go for a swim!" Faye suggested.

"You mean, I should pee in the ocean?" Polly looked scandalized.

"Oh, come on," Shirley told her. "Everyone does. It's a great big ocean out there."

Polly scanned the shoreline. Hundreds of people floated, swam, and played in the waves.

"It's really all right," Marilyn assured her. "After all, the sea weed."

Polly chortled. "Oh no! Don't make me laugh!" She stood up, hands on either side of her face to block the view of the others. If she saw them, she'd be unable to stop laughing. "When I laugh, I turn into an automatic sprinkler!"

Faye rose, too, and grabbed Polly's hand. "Come on. I'll go in with you."

"Okay," Polly said. "But for heaven's sake, don't run!"

Shirley looked worried. "Should we swim so soon after eating?"

"We're not going to swim," Alice told her. "We're just going to cool off."

The five women stepped briskly over the hot sand. When they reached the moist shoreline, a wave brushed up, swirling cool liquid over their ankles. They hesitated.

"It's cold," Shirley said.

"No, it's not," Faye insisted. "It's perfect! Come on. All together now!"

The five women joined hands and raced into the water. Screaming with shock, they danced on the tips of their toes as the glittering waves splashed up past their waists, then their bosoms, then their necks. Polly broke away from the group to swim a few feet away, where she treaded water, smiling blissfully as bubbles rose to the surface.

"You look pleased with yourself," Alice said when Polly swam back toward them.

Polly giggled. "I'm just remembering that children's nursery rhyme, 'The Owl and the Pussycat went to sea in a beautiful pea green boat.' Now I understand it so much better!"

Tuesday evening, in the privacy of her small bedroom on Orange Street, Alice pressed her son's number on her cell phone.

She'd been away from Alan, Jennifer, and baby Aly for four entire days now. Saturday she'd spent packing and organizing her house for a week's absence, and Saturday evening she'd spent with Gideon. She'd almost forgotten how much she enjoyed just hanging out with the sweet man. Sunday she'd traveled to the island with the other Hot Flash femmes, Monday they'd all gone to the beach, and today, thank heavens, it had rained, so they'd gone their separate ways. Tonight Faye and Polly were in the kitchen, preparing a Nantucket dinner for them all. Shirley was still not home from wherever it was she biked off to—no doubt a rendezvous with that dubious character, Harry. And Marilyn was soaking in the tub.

So it was a good time to call her son and his family. For this event, Alice had allowed herself, since it was after five o'clock, a nice tall gin and tonic. She hoped the alcohol would help slow her racing heart. She really did not want to have another heart attack. But no matter how many deep breaths she took, her concern about her son and his family set her heart galloping every time.

"Hello?" A strange voice answered.

"Oh." Alice was puzzled. "I must have the wrong number. I'm looking for Alan Murray."

"He's here. Hang on, I'll get him."

When her son's familiar voice came on the line, Alice asked, "Who was that?"

"That's Greg, Mom." Alan's voice was more buoyant than she'd heard it for months. "Jennifer's cousin, remember?"

"Um . . ." She closed her eyes, trying to conjure up an image. Vaguely, the acne-spotted face of a hulking kid in a striped rugby shirt swam across her vision.

"*You* know," Alan was saying. "Greg graduated from high school this May, and he didn't want to start college yet, so he's at loose ends. We asked him to come help us this week, and wow, is he a dynamite worker! I think he's got Jennifer's baking genes."

"Oh," Alice said again, faintly. "So he's helping?"

"Helping! I don't know how we managed without him. He's so strong, he's got so much energy, he can do twice as much as Jennifer, and he's a quick learner, so basically he's helping me in the bakery and Jennifer's having a chance to spend time with Aly and just be a mom. Greg is . . ."

Alice took a hearty swallow of gin and tonic as she listened to Alan enumerate Greg's endless talents and strengths. Not only was the young man physically powerful and mentally adept, he was fascinated by the baking business, and already they were thinking about arranging for him to work full-time.

"This is wonderful news," Alice said, when her son finally finished praising Greg.

"I know it is, and for you, too," Alan told her. "We know we've overworked you, Mom. We've worried a lot about your heart. This way we won't need you to babysit so much, and you can really enjoy Aly. How's your vacation, by the way?"

Alice had to work hard to summon up convincing enthusiasm. "It's swell. We spent all day yesterday at the beach and today I just sort of loafed around."

"That's exactly what you should be doing, Mom!" Alan sounded like he was praising a five-year-old. "I'm so glad you're taking care of yourself."

"Thanks," Alice said weakly. "But if you need me, I can be there in only a few hours . . ."

"Don't even think about that!" Alan laughed. "We've got it all under control. You just enjoy yourself."

When Alice hung up the phone, she felt like an hourglass whose middle had expanded—a painfully appropriate metaphor. All the sand wasn't *trickling,* it was *gushing* to the bottom. She was glad her son was working things out. She was glad he'd found the solution to their various problems. She was really, truly, glad that finally she was free from that exhausting drive out to The Haven.

But she hated this feeling of being dispensable. Unnecessary. Put out to pasture. *Old.*

In the middle of the night, Marilyn lay on her enormous queen-size bed, tossing and turning and feeling terribly alone. She missed Ian's presence in the bed with her. She missed the slightly operatic crescendo of his snores and the way he reached out for her at odd times in the long night, to clutch her shoulder or arm, as if even in his deepest sleep he needed to know she was there. She missed his warmth. Even though it was a hot August night, she missed his particular warmth.

She'd spoken with him by phone earlier this evening. Their conversation had been pleasant, but brief, and for Marilyn, unsatisfactory. She was glad to know that Ruth was well and happy and she *should* be glad to know that Fiona had broken out of her paralysis long enough to prepare dinner for Angus, Ruth, Ian, and herself, but it hadn't been a real source of pleasure to hear how delicious Fiona's lamb casserole was, how rich, juicy, just like *home*. Marilyn had never been a gourmet cook. Now she felt inferior and slightly alarmed. What if the way to a man's heart really was through his stomach?

This was nonsense. She couldn't sleep, she shouldn't just lie here wallowing in her misery. She would creep downstairs, fix herself a mug of warm milk, find a novel, and read in the living room. After all, she was on vacation. She could read all night and sleep all day if she wanted to.

Her choice of night wear was simply an extra-large T-shirt that hung almost to her knees. She felt around on her bedside table for her reading glasses, stuck them on top of her head, and padded barefoot out of her room. Quietly, so she wouldn't wake the others, she sneaked down the stairs, tiptoed down the long hall into the kitchen, turned on the light—

And screamed.

"AAAHHH!" Marilyn stumbled backward, clutching at her throat, into which her heart had leaped like a mouse for a hole.

"AAAHHH!" screamed the intruder, so stunned by Marilyn's sudden appearance that she dropped the flashlight and the silver pitcher she was holding. They banged on the floor, rolled against the stove, and clanged.

"Oh, my God!" Marilyn cried. "*You're* the thief!"

"Nonsense," scoffed Lucinda Payne. She was very regal as she stood there in her ancient taupe crepe de chine negligee. Every white hair was in place.

"But you *have* to be the thief," Marilyn pointed out sensibly, as her heart slowly descended back down into her chest. "I mean, it's three in the morning, and you're in our kitchen."

"What's going on?"

Alice stormed into the room, waving an umbrella she'd grabbed from the stand in the front hall. Faye, Shirley, and Polly followed, and they all crammed into the kitchen behind Marilyn to stare at Lucinda Payne. The kitchen windows, blacked by night, reflected their images back to them: wide-eyed, their hair shooting out in all directions, as disheveled and disoriented as a pack of lunatics who'd just broken out of the asylum and then forgotten what they were doing.

"Oh, my God!" Faye exclaimed. "You're the thief!"

"I am not." Lucinda was indignant. "I was only returning this silver ice bucket I borrowed a while ago." She glanced down at the container, glittering forlorn next to the stove.

Alice put her hands on her hips. "You can't be *returning* that. We used it last night!"

"This is wonderful!" Shirley cried. "We found out who the thief is! I can't wait to call Nora and tell her!"

"No! You *mustn't*!" Lucinda Payne's aristocratic, arrogant face suddenly cracked before their eyes into a starburst of lines and fissures, and with a rusty creak, like a faucet being turned after years of neglect, she burst into tears.

For a moment the five Hot Flash Club friends stood frozen with shock.

Then Faye gently suggested, "I think we should all sit down."

"I'll make tea," Polly added softly. She approached the stove slowly, as if afraid to startle the white-haired woman standing next to it. With careful moves, she bent, picked up the ice bucket and flashlight, and set them gently on the counter.

Shirley, who now felt hideously guilty for driving the older woman into what looked like the first crying jag of her entire life, crossed the kitchen floor and pulled a chair out from the table for her. She wasn't brave enough to touch the haughty older woman, even if Lucinda was in tears.

Lucinda sank into the chair. She covered her face with her hands, then pulled her hands away, looking mystified at the wetness on her fingertips.

Marilyn rushed to pull some tissues from the dispenser. She handed them to Lucinda.

Polly bustled around, setting the tea kettle on the burner and filling the Limoges teapot with hot water to warm the pot, the way she knew Lucinda would want it to be done. Alice opened the cookie jar and assembled an assortment of ginger snaps, almond macaroons, and lemon bars on a delicate, painted porcelain plate. She set the plate on the table, near Lucinda. Marilyn poured cream into the antique Limoges cream pitcher. Faye zipped into the dining room to fetch silver teaspoons and heavy cloth napkins which she brought back and placed around.

When Lucinda lifted her face from her soggy tissues, she looked even older than she had before. Her eyes were red-rimmed, her nose bright magenta, her wrinkled skin deathly pale. She looked haggard. She looked exhausted. She looked crushed.

"Here you are." Marilyn placed a thin china teacup on its matching saucer in front of Lucinda.

Polly poured tea into the pot. "Sugar? Cream?"

Lucinda shook her head abruptly. Then she sighed, an enormous, surrendering sigh, picked up the cup, and sipped her tea.

The five other women settled in their chairs and for a few moments devoted themselves to preparing their own tea.

"Well?" Alice coaxed, her voice gentle but firm.

"This is mortifying." Lucinda Payne's voice was so low they could scarcely hear.

"We're all friends here," Shirley assured her.

Lucinda tried to look disdainful, but could not quite pull it off. "It has never been fair, you see."

The Hot Flash Club women exchanged anticipatory glances.

"Nora has always had everything. Nora has always *won. Her*

grandfather got Amelia. Everyone *knew. Her* house is larger than ours. *Her* father always had more money than mine. And now"—she choked as emotion swathed her words—"now *her* two children are alive, and my two sons are dead. I'm alone. She is not."

Everyone sat in silence, contemplating this unexpected confession.

Shirley spoke up. "I understand, Mrs. Payne. All my friends here"— she gestured around the table—"have children. I don't. As much as I love them, I envy them."

"Oh, I don't *love* Nora!" Lucinda snapped, pique sending color back into her cheeks. The tea was reviving her. Her posture straightened, her features tightened.

"What I want to know," Alice said, "is how you got in here. I checked all the doors tonight before I went to bed. Do you have a key?"

"Of course not!" Lucinda shot Alice an impatient look.

But Alice had a few looks of her own to deploy. After a moment of Alice's most ferocious glare, Lucinda admitted, "I came through the tunnel."

The tunnel? What tunnel?" All five women exclaimed together.
Lucinda took another sip of tea. An element of sly pride stole
over her features. Obviously she enjoyed knowing something the
others didn't.

"Nora didn't tell us about any tunnel," Shirley prompted.

Lucinda smiled triumphantly. "That's because Nora doesn't
know."

Polly clasped her hands together like a child at prayer. "Oh, show us
the tunnel, please!" Her light green sleeveless cotton pajamas with the
frog on the front gave her the appearance of a chubby child, and as always, her sweetness showed in her face.

"Very well." Lucinda rose. "Follow me."

She didn't have to ask them twice. They nearly knocked one another
over getting in line as she opened the door to the cellar.

Obviously familiar with the area, Lucinda flicked on the cellar light
and began to descend the wooden steps. The other women had been in
the cellar only once. They'd never had reason to go, and it was not an
enticing environment. The walls were brick, dusty with age, and the
floor was dirt. Naked lightbulbs hung from the wooden ceiling, the
black electrical cords stapled here and there to the beams. In a corner
stood the square, modern furnace and an enormous water heater.
Shelves ranged along one wall, holding old canning jars with faded la-
bels, and rusty tools, and dozens of gallon cans of Benjamin Moore
paint.

As she led them through the dim, cavernous basement, Lucinda informed them, "When Ford and Pascal were boys, they dug a tunnel between the two houses. It was just the sort of nonsense they always got

up to. My father told me about the tunnel when he was dying. To this day, I've never told anyone." Her voice resonated with sadness. "I never had anyone to tell. My siblings are all dead, as are my sons."

They went through an open doorway into another dirt-floored room. Lucinda pointed to a door in the wall. "That leads to the old coal bin." Squeezing around a brick foundation for a fireplace, they arrived at a little compartment cluttered with old cardboard boxes. A low entrance, a dark upside-down U not quite five feet high, gaped in the brick wall.

"The door is here. When I leave, I simply pile these boxes up and back in. Like this." She demonstrated. The cardboard boxes hid the opening. For a moment, Lucinda was out of sight. Then she knocked aside the empty boxes as she reappeared. "All right. Follow me. You'll have to stoop."

At the entrance to the tunnel, the five Hot Flash women hesitated, gripped by a natural fear of dark, low, narrow, underground places. Lucinda had flicked on the flashlight and was shuffling ahead, nearly bent double, her back almost scraping the uneven bricks of the tunnel roof. The beam of the flashlight danced eerily in front of her, making her figure seem enormous, and dark.

"I'm scared," Shirley whispered. Somehow, she'd ended up at the front of the line.

Faye reached out and held Shirley's hand. "I won't let go," she promised.

Shirley folded up and duckwalked into the tunnel. Faye came behind, one hand holding Shirley's, the other feeling the uneven brick wall. Polly scuttled along after them, then came Alice, grumbling that she was surely going to be stuck in the tight passageway like a cork in a bottle. From behind, Marilyn assured Alice that if she got stuck, she'd push. Nervousness made Faye giggle at the thought, and soon all five women were snickering as they crept along through the dark, constricted dankness.

They popped out of the tunnel into a room floored with wood, with plastered, painted walls. Lucinda's clean, well-lit basement gleamed like morning.

"Civilization after a few moments of Cro-Magnon life!" Marilyn sighed gratefully.

They paused to catch their breath and stretch the kinks out of their backs. Then Lucinda led them through her basement rooms, which also held cartons of miscellany. Here, each box was carefully marked and stacked at right angles, according to size. In the last room, handsome white shelves held modern discards, seemingly waiting for repair: an electric shoe buffer, a wicker picnic basket with a broken handle, a record player and a stack of old 78s. The Hot Flash five scanned the shelves for any of Nora's items—the silver pheasant, a teacup—but saw nothing like that.

"Where's all Nora's stuff?" Alice demanded.

Lucinda paused, her head high, her posture rigid. "I'll return it."

Alice looked suspicious. "Or maybe you've sold it already."

The older woman whipped around to glare at Alice. "I would never sell heirlooms!"

"So you say," Alice countered.

Faye held her breath. She worried that Lucinda's lucidity was balanced on a thin line between sanity and madness. The older woman was clearly under great emotional strain. And yet Faye detected a kind of bright eagerness in Lucinda's eyes.

"Yes, yes. I'll show you." Lucinda headed for the stairs to the first floor.

The overhead lights, set in attractive glass fixtures, brightened their climb up the stairs and into Lucinda's kitchen. Here it was as Polly had remembered, organized and clean to the point of sterility. Without a word, Lucinda continued to walk through the long hallway to the front of her house. The rooms off the hall were in darkness, but everyone could tell by the ambient light from the street that the furniture in the rooms was modern, spare, and elegant. The rooms were uncluttered.

"Your home is beautiful," Faye told the older woman.

Lucinda flicked on the hall light. They were all suddenly exposed by the brightness, an odd little party in their nightgowns, pajamas, and slippers, their hair mussed, their tan lines showing beneath the thin straps of their nightgowns.

"If I show you this, it must be under the condition that you do not inform any authorities. No attorneys or police officials can be involved. I understand you'll want to tell Nora, but no one else. Agreed?"

"Agreed." Alice spoke for them all.

"Very well." Lucinda started up the stairs, her satin bedroom slippers whispering against the handsome needlepoint runner.

The second floor was as shipshape as the first, dust- and clutter-free. When they passed a door opening into a small bedroom, they looked in. The room, with its narrow bed covered in a white chenille spread and its spartan bureau and side table, could have belonged to a monk. Lucinda continued walking until she reached the bedroom at the back of the house. Here she paused, and for a moment hung her head, almost as if praying for courage. Then she turned on the bedroom light and gestured to them that they were admitted.

It was a large room, taking up the entire width of the back of the house. Windows ranged along the far wall, which, in the daytime, would display fabulous views of the harbor. Against the facing wall was a handsome four-poster double bed, the covers folded neatly back.

The rest of the room was a chaotic jumble of stuff. Two walls were lined with shelves. In front of them, tables crowded the bed. Every flat surface was crammed with items: candlesticks, vases, picture frames, clocks, figurines, paperweights, cloisonné boxes, silver salt and pepper shakers, pitchers, trivets, bowls, hatboxes, ladles, needlepoint pillows, perfume atomizers, hand-painted seashells, lightship baskets, porcelain soap dishes, papier-mâché wastepaper baskets, books, coasters, a single red shoe—it was an explosive abundance of *stuff*. So many tables groaned beneath the weight of so many items crowded in around the bed that there was only a narrow path to the bed.

Each of the Hot Flash women was quiet with her own thoughts, imagining Lucinda, ancient, brittle, and alone, lying like an Egyptian queen in her bed, surrounded by this profusion of possessions.

"Shades of Edgar Allan Poe," Marilyn murmured.

Lucinda cleared her throat. "*Some* of this is my family's, of course. I prefer to present a façade of simplicity to visitors to my home, and I've been strict in culling through all the items my family has accumulated over the years. But of course, a few things I was unable to part with. And then, a couple of years ago, I started collecting again."

"Collecting Nora's things," Alice clarified.

Lucinda nodded regally. After a few moments of silence, she said defensively, "Nora has so much, after all. A house full in Nantucket, and I know she owns a house up in Boston. It was only right that I even out the inequities between us."

Shirley widened her eyes at Polly and mouthed, "Cuckoo."

"Well, you know we're going to have to tell Nora about this," Alice said briskly.

"Or maybe not," Faye quickly intervened. "Perhaps if you agree to stop . . . 'collecting' . . . we could just forget about this."

Lucinda passed her eyes over the motley crew gathered in her bedroom. "Five women keeping one secret?" she scoffed.

"We can at least *think* about it," Faye insisted. "We don't have to decide anything right now. It's the middle of the night. We're all exhausted and not thinking clearly. We've all had a shock to our systems. Now is not the right time to make a decision."

As she spoke, the other four Hot Flash women *got* it: As Lucinda Payne stood before them, she was ashen pale, and trembling all over. Yes, they'd *all* had a shock, but Lucinda was older, and she was proud to the point of battiness. And she was all alone.

No one wanted Lucinda to have a heart attack tonight.

"Yes," Polly spoke up. "I certainly can't think straight. Let's all go back to bed. Lucinda, perhaps you can come over to tea tomorrow to discuss this."

Lucinda inclined her head regally.

"Good," Faye concluded with cheerful ease, as if they'd all just run into each other at the grocery store. "We'll just go back to bed now, and we'll see you tomorrow, Lucinda."

"Can you find your own way out?" Lucinda asked, as she allowed herself to rest one hand on a bedpost for support.

"Can we borrow your flashlight?" Alice inquired.

"Very well." Lucinda sounded as if she were making an enormous concession.

"Then we're good to go," Alice told her.

"Then turn out the lights and shut the doors behind you," Lucinda ordered.

"We will," Faye said. "Good night."

They each said good night, then filed out into the hall and down the stairs.

"Stephen King!" Shirley whispered.

But Faye shook her head and put a warning finger to her lips, shushing her. The five moved along in silence down the stairs, through the hall, into the kitchen, and down the stairs to the cellar.

When they reached the entrance to the tunnel, Shirley said, "Now may I please say this is all so creepy I want to barf?"

Polly whispered, "Actually, Lucinda reminds me a lot of my mother-in-law."

"That's right," Faye recalled. "Claudia *was* a domineering, brittle old bat."

"Let's never get that way," Shirley pleaded. "Let's never put possessions before people."

"Let's not worry about *ever*," Alice said practically. "Let's stop stalling and get through this horrible little tunnel and back to bed!"

"Agreed." Faye, who this time was first in line, doubled over and began to creep forward.

Next came Polly, then Alice, then Marilyn. Shirley was last. She held her lavender froufrou negligee between both hands to keep the hem free of dust, but as she crept along, the lace frill of her ruffled cap sleeve caught on the rough edge of loose brick angling slightly out of the wall.

"Wait!" she cried. "I'm caught!"

"Hurry up," Alice said. "I'm bent over like a croquet wicket."

Shirley reached up to ease the lace from the brick. Instead, with a scraping sound and a puff of dust, the brick came loose, falling to the floor, taking a section of Shirley's gown with it. "Oh, for heaven's sake," Shirley said. She picked up the brick and tried to wedge it back into the tunnel wall. "Hey!" she cried. "Faye, shine the flashlight over here."

Faye aimed the light at the space where the brick was.

"There's something in here," Shirley said. She forgot the hem of her negligee and the lace of her sleeve. She forgot she was cramped inside a narrow passageway. She gripped another brick and pulled. With a rasping noise, almost like a cough, the brick dislodged, exposing a small square chamber, and inside the chamber, a rusty metal box.

49

W hat's in it?" Polly asked breathlessly.

"I don't know." Shirley ran her fingers around the edges. "It's not locked, but it's been forced shut . . ."

"Bring it with you," Alice ordered. "I'm getting claustrophobic." She gave Faye a little poke.

Faye obligingly crept forward, the other four women following. When she reached Nora's basement, she said, "Now, let's see!"

But the hidden cubicle was so crammed with cardboard boxes there wasn't room for all five women to stand comfortably.

"Could we please go upstairs?" Polly begged. "This basement is so gloomy."

"Right." Faye hurried through the dank, shadowy rooms and up the stairs.

Nora's kitchen glowed, familiar and cozy. The table, set with all the accoutrements of tea, rose like an island of civility in a dusty world. Shirley put the metal box on the table. Alice slammed the cellar door shut, muttering that she wished it had a lock. The others gathered around the table. Faye sipped her tea to see if it had grown cold—it had. Polly nibbled on a ginger snap for sustenance. They all kept their eyes fastened on the metal box, as if expecting it to attempt escape. It was only about three inches deep, eight inches long, and eight inches wide. It was made from brass, which had darkened with age.

"Okay," Alice directed. "Now open it, Shirley."

"Drumroll, please," Shirley joked. She reached out, then hesitated. "Shouldn't we do this with Lucinda present?"

Polly groaned.

Marilyn said, "Shirley, Lucinda looked worn out. It wouldn't be a kindness to her to get her out of bed again . . ."

"And *I* won't be a kindness to you if you don't open it now," Alice growled impatiently.

"We'll tell Lucinda about it first thing in the morning," Faye said.

So Shirley lifted the small brass latch, which was not fastened by a lock. She pulled the lid up and back. It creaked on its rusty hinges.

Inside was a small, dark glass vial and a small bundle of letters tied with a ribbon.

Faye lifted the vial out and turned it in her hands. "Laudanum," she said. "I'll bet anything."

"What's laudanum?" Polly asked.

"It's a derivative of opium," Shirley told her. "It was used in childbirth, to ease pain."

"And it was used by the wives of sea captains to ease their boredom," Faye added.

"And the letters?" Alice prompted.

Shirley lifted the bundle out, untied the ribbon, which fell away in a stiff curl of red silk. She scanned the first page. "Oh, my." She breathed.

"What!" Alice growled.

Shirley handed the missive to Alice. She flipped through the rest, then said, "They're letters between Amelia, Nora's mother, and Ford, Lucinda's father. Just after their affair."

She picked up the second letter and read it. "Amelia's telling Ford that she's pregnant. She's sure it's Ford's child."

She handed the page to Alice, who handed the first letter to Polly. In this way, all seven letters were read and passed around the table.

"They agree to remain with their spouses, to protect their children. Amelia's had carnal relations with Pascal so he'll believe this child is his. Amelia is hiding these letters in the tunnel until the day when the feud between the two families is mended."

When they had all read the final letter, Shirley said, with wide eyes, "Do you know what this means?"

Faye nodded. "It means that Ford Payne was the father of Nora Pettigrew."

"Oh, my gosh." Polly clasped her hands to her face. "Isn't this amazing! That means Nora and Lucinda are half-sisters!"

"Good grief, Gertrude," Alice mumbled.

"How wonderful!" Shirley's eyes were shining. "This means Lucinda isn't really alone in the world."

"Get a grip," Alice told Shirley. "Lucinda and Nora hate one another. I don't think they'll run into one another's arms with cries of delight when we tell them."

"*If* we tell them," Faye amended.

"Right," Marilyn agreed. "We stumbled across this cache by accident. We could put it back in its hiding place and never say another word about it."

"No." Shirley crossed her arms and looked adamant. "We found the box. After seventy years, more or less, *we found the box*. You could say it pretty much jumped out at us. I mean, Lucinda's been using that tunnel for months now, and *her* sleeve never caught on it. Mine did. I think Fate *meant* for us to find the box, so we can help Lucinda and Nora deal with this information."

Alice buried her head in her hands. "Oh, Shirley."

Polly spoke up. "I agree with Shirley. I mean, I'm not so sure about Fate meaning for us to find it, but I do think we should tell Lucinda. After all, the motto of the Hot Flash Club is INTERFERE."

Faye said, "I agree with Shirley, too."

Marilyn said, *"Look."*

Alice groaned. "What now?"

Marilyn pointed to the window. "The sky's getting lighter. It's almost morning."

"Let's go to the beach and watch the sun rise!" Shirley cried.

"Yes, let's!" Marilyn agreed. She stood up, pushing her chair back. "Come on, hurry!"

"We can't go in our pajamas!" Alice protested.

"Why not?" Faye asked. "Who's going to see us?"

"Maybe no one, but it's crazy," Alice said.

Polly giggled. "Okay, then, let's do something crazy!"

"I agree!" Faye grabbed Alice's hand and pulled her out of her chair. "Come on! Let's do this!" She grabbed the keys hanging from the hook by the back door.

Shirley bundled the letters back into the metal box and shoved the box into a kitchen drawer. Just slightly dizzy and daffy from lack of sleep, the five women scurried out to the car and crowded in.

Faye drove. " 'Sconset?" she asked. "That's the furthest east."

"Right," Marilyn told her. "And hurry."

"I don't want to break the speed limit," Faye said. "We don't want to get arrested."

They all glanced at one another, surveying their various nighttime ensembles, and they laughed like schoolgirls playing hooky.

The material of Polly's green pajamas wasn't see-through, but it was obvious, even behind the giant frog on the front, that she wore no bra. She'd tied her white-streaked auburn hair into a pigtail on each side of her head so her hair wouldn't get mussed while she was sleeping, but by now most of the strands had escaped to corkscrew outward in the early morning humidity. Faye wore an expensive white linen nightgown with an embroidered and smocked yoke with white cotton rosettes. Her white hair, usually caught back in a chignon, hung loosely around her head, falling just past her shoulders. Marilyn was in a long T-shirt, her auburn hair limp in the humidity. Alice wore a knee-length, sleeveless slash of crimson silk with a mandarin collar, beautiful enough to wear to a party, if only she were wearing a bra. And Shirley wore her lavender peignoir, one cap sleeve missing a section of lace.

The town around them still slept as they passed through. Here and there a lamp glowed in a window, and the evenly spaced streetlights turned their path into a checkerboard of dark and light. They circled the rotary and headed out the long straight 'Sconset road, bordered by slumbering woodlands. Above them, the black sky slowly faded to gray. From overhead came the drone of the first plane, bearing the morning papers. A truck, its headlights two circles of white glare, came toward them, but they were the only vehicle going east.

"You can go faster," Alice urged Faye, who obliged by pressing her foot on the gas pedal, bringing them up to fifty-five miles per hour, ten miles above the speed limit, as fast as anyone could go on this island.

"I can't believe all that happened tonight," Shirley babbled. "My heart feels like it's been on a roller coaster. Hearing Marilyn scream! Finding that prim old Lucinda in our kitchen! And going through that scary tunnel. And seeing her bizarre bedroom, crammed with stuff—

how crazy was that? And then, finding that box, although I really do believe that box found me, I think it reached out and grabbed me, it *did,* it caught hold of my gown!" She gulped. "Then reading those letters, learning that Lucinda and Nora are half-sisters."

"I wonder whether all families have secrets like that," Marilyn mused.

"I doubt it," Alice said sensibly. "Mine sure doesn't."

"I don't know about that," Faye argued. "If you go back a generation, who knows what your mother and father hid from you. We all hide things, don't we? Perhaps not anything as significant as Amelia hiding the paternity of her child. But we hide dreams, or fears, or memories . . ."

"Turn here," Polly pointed.

Faye steered the Jeep down the narrow road, beneath the white footbridge, and parked at the small lot where the road ended at the beach. By now the sky was silver, and a line of violet glimmered on the horizon. The beach was a soft blur of sooty gray, like a smudged thumbprint, the ocean black.

They spilled out of the Jeep. No one else was around.

"Leave your slippers in the car," Alice advised them. "Or they'll get full of tiny grains of sand and you'll never get them all out."

They all hopped on one foot and then the other as they removed their slippers, which they tossed, willy-nilly, into the Jeep. The feel of gritty sand against their soles was intimate, engaging, a physical grounding in the moment. Barefoot, they hurried down to the shoreline.

Now a ribbon of gold glimmered beneath the violet streak, and they could see the white ruffle of foam surging up toward them, pulling the dark cover of ocean behind. The sky brightened into the iridescent gray of a pigeon's breast, illuminating the shoreline. They settled down on the sand at the water's edge, shoulder to shoulder, because near the water it was slightly cool, and there was a gentle breeze that teasingly lifted their hair away from their faces. They drew their knees up to their chests and wrapped their arms around them, nudging their chins into the V of their knees. They had front-row seats to the best view on earth, and here it came, the golden sun, majestic, radiant, moving in its own sweet time. The sky around it went pink, and the ocean beneath it blushed in response.

With splendid indolence, the sun ascended, unveiling the sky like Salome, in gauzy swathes of coral, then violet, then robin's egg blue, and the ocean beneath deepened to sapphire. The light was so strong it seemed a living presence, aware of them sitting there on the edge of the world, and pleased they'd come for the performance. They couldn't help but think how old the sun and the ocean were, and yet as fresh today as if it were all brand new. They couldn't help but think how small they were, and really, how relatively young.

I want to be with Ian, thought Marilyn to herself.

I want to paint a sunrise, thought Faye.

I want to be with Harry, thought Shirley.

I want to collect shells and make my own sailor's valentine, thought Polly.

"I want to eat!" said Alice, breaking into all their thoughts.

"Me, too!" Polly seconded.

"Plus," Marilyn added, "if I stay in this sun much longer, my nose will burn."

Rising, they brushed sand off their bare legs and nightgowns, then stalked through the sand back to the Jeep, arriving just as another car arrived at the parking lot. The young couple looked stunned at the sight of five women in their unusual state of undress, and their startled faces made the Hot Flash five laugh uncontrollably all the way back home.

50

'Bye!" Shirley called.

" 'Bye! Have fun!" Faye yelled back.

Shirley slung her backpack over her shoulder, skipped down the back steps, grabbed her bike, steered it to Orange Street, and hopped on. Huffing and puffing, she rode it to the top of the hill, then nipped into a side street, where Harry sat in his red truck, waiting for her, reading the *New York Times*. Reggie, his golden Lab, barked once in greeting, and hung her head out the window to be petted.

"Good morning!" Harry called, carefully folding his paper. He ambled out of the truck, gave Shirley a sardonic grin, and lifted her bike into the cab. Then they both got in the truck, the golden Lab sitting happily between them. It was Thursday morning, and Shirley hadn't seen Harry for over a week.

"I'm not sure I understand just why we have to go through this charade," Harry told Shirley. "It seems like an awful lot of fuss."

Shirley squirmed. Eventually, Harry would meet her friends, but when? One look at the two of them together, and the Hot Flash Club would know Shirley was gaga over this guy.

She waved her hands, trying to explain. "It's just that this week is supposed to be *our* week. The five of us all doing stuff together. Being with you is kind of like cheating. But Faye's going off painting by herself, and Marilyn's going off to some science project by herself, and Alice likes to sleep late, and Polly's working on a sailor's valentine and has the dining room table covered with shells and gets irritated if anyone so much as *breathes* in the room, so I don't feel guilty about spending some time on my own. Well," she amended, squirming, "kind of on my own."

Harry looked quizzical. "So what *do* you feel guilty about? Being with me?"

"No!" Shirley automatically replied. She slumped in her seat. "Well, maybe a little. I mean, they're doing stuff tied in with artistic pursuits, or intellectual activities."

"Sleeping late's an intellectual activity?" Harry joked.

She gently cuffed his shoulder. "Let me finish. Whatever they're doing, it doesn't involve a man. A man and sex. And what I'm doing . . ."

"Definitely involves both." Harry reached across the seat to put his hand on Shirley's thigh.

Shirley smiled.

Reggie, picking up on the romantic vibes, licked a slobbery kiss on Shirley's cheek.

Harry said, "I thought I'd show you Coskata today. You have time?"

"Sure," Shirley said. "We're going out to dinner and a play tonight, but I don't need to be back before about four."

Harry chuckled. "I feel like an adolescent. Like your mother's going to catch us and ground you and report me to my parents."

Shirley gently repositioned Reggie's enormous noble head so that she could see Harry's profile as he drove. "My friends are all really terrific," she assured him. "It's not really about you." She paused. "It's more that I haven't always made the best choices in the past."

Harry laughed. "Who has? But you know, you're going to have to introduce me to them sooner or later, because I'm hoping you'll spend a lot of time down here with me in the off season. If you think Nantucket's nice in the summer, you've really got to see it in the fall."

Shirley was so delighted by his words, she had to put her cheek against the cool metal of the door to cool down. "Well . . ." She put her feet up on the dashboard and snuggled against the seat. "Faye and Polly are thinking of renting a house this fall. . . ."

"That's not what I meant. I want you to stay with me. Keep your stuff in my cottage. I've got room for you. I'd clear out a few closets and drawers. I think the two of us would bumble around pretty happily together."

"Oh." Shirley's heart began to pound. "So I guess what we have isn't just a casual relationship."

Harry's blue eyes blazed. "I don't have 'casual' relationships." He laughed, easing off. "Hell, most of the time I don't even have relationships. I find I prefer the company of my dog to most people. But the truth is, I'm just happier when you're around, and I'm too old not to move as fast as I can."

Shirley rolled her thoughts around. "Would you come visit me in Boston?"

"Honestly? I don't think so. I hate leaving the island. I don't enjoy cities anymore."

"Oh."

"Well, I suppose I could come up once or twice," he conceded. "But I guess I'm hoping that in the future, well, it's not impossible that you might want to retire down here to Nantucket. It seems to me if you took that deal the Rainbow people are offering, you'd be financially set and you wouldn't have to work. I think you'd love life here on the island."

Shirley couldn't breathe. "Are you asking me to move in with you?"

"I suppose I am," Harry said. "Don't freak out. I'm not talking marriage, not yet, anyway. That's too weighted with laws and civil complications. I don't like corporations, and marriage seems to me like a kind of corporate principle. But you and I have such a good time together. I don't like it when you've gone back to Boston. I want you here as much as I can have you. And if I seem to be rushing you, well, I suppose it's because I'm aware that I'm getting old. I've been old and reclusive and contented for a long time. I *thought* I was contented. Now I see I've got the chance to be old and happy and sexy, and that feels a great deal better to me."

Shirley said softly, "I'm kind of overwhelmed."

Harry reached around the dog to take her hand. "Yeah, so am I. But at my age, I don't want to waste any time."

"I don't know what to say, Harry. I need to absorb all this." She was so happy she wanted to giggle and squeal. But one thought clearly pierced the bubbles of her glee. "I want you to meet my friends."

"I'd like to," Harry said. "Just tell me when and where."

Alice carried a mug of coffee up to drink while she showered and dressed. The Orange Street house was quiet. On the message board near the refrigerator, all the others had scribbled their day's plans: Faye was painting, Shirley was biking (and probably sneaking off to meet that guy, Harry), Polly looking for shells, and Marilyn was at the Maria Mitchell Museum. Tonight they were all going out together for dinner and then to a play.

Today Alice was going to go for a goddamned walk.

She didn't want to, but she knew it was the right thing to do. So she jumped in the shower, then pulled on a pair of batik cotton pedal pushers—or at least that was what she'd called them the first time they'd hit the fashion scene. Now she guessed they were Capri pants. She pulled on a poncho-shaped fringed orange top, added some heavy topaz and wooden beads, stepped into her comfy walking shoes, plopped a floppy sun hat on her head, and went out the door.

She checked her watch as she strode down Orange Street away from town. She'd walk for an hour, she decided. That ought to give her heart a suitable amount of aerobic activity. And she would observe the houses and gardens as she passed, and she would *appreciate* them. The other four Hot Flashers *got* Nantucket in a way Alice just couldn't. The whole thing about Quaker simplicity bored her silly. Lying on the beach wasn't half as comfortable as lying on a bed, plus she got sand in her suit and her teeth and her hair, and if she tried to read a book, either a breeze ripped at the pages or the sun's glare made her carve frown lines into her face.

But it was clear her Hot Flash friends would be spending a lot of time here in the future. Faye and Polly were discussing renting a house. Faye definitely planned to spend the winter here, painting landscapes. And Polly loved all that craft stuff—she wanted to take a course in lightship-basket-weaving. And Shirley—Shirley had gone lightheaded over this guy, Harry. Shirley would be coming down here a lot, for as long as this Harry kept her dangling on the line. When it came to men, Shirley had the acuity of a flounder. Alice hoped and prayed Shirley wouldn't get hurt *again*.

Alice ambled onto Fair Street. She sauntered along, studying the houses, picket fences, privet arbors, trellised roses. Away from the main part of town, the houses were modest, family-size but not ostentatious. The yards were nicely kept, but not professionally *landscaped*. Real families lived in these homes. She passed a woman snoozing in a striped hammock, her magazine resting on her chest. She passed a yard with a swing set, and a tree house with a rope ladder. Perhaps it was the chirps of the birds flitting from holly tree to birdbath, or the sight of a blue tricycle, or the little old man down on his knees weeding who paused to wave hello, but to her surprise, she was time-warped back to her Kansas childhood. She remembered hiding with her best friend behind mulberry bushes, making dolls of hollyhocks turned upside down, their petals like skirts, climbing on top of a neighbor's garage to spy on the world from an exciting new vantage point. Like a fresh breeze, the memory of freedom, childhood, laughter, swept through her. Perhaps this was what people loved about Nantucket, that it brought them back to a more innocent time.

Turning a corner, she found herself on York Street. At Five Corners stood the African-American Meeting House. She'd walked by it before, but hadn't thought there was much to see. It was such a modest little structure, gray-shingled, only one story high and one room large. She'd read in a guide book that it had been built in 1827 and served since then as a church, a school for African children, and a meeting house.

The door was open. On a whim, Alice wandered in.

A handsome black woman in her fifties sat at a small table, reading a book. She wore white cotton slacks and an oversized white cotton shirt just like one Alice had bought in Boston. She smiled. "Hello."

"Hello." Alice picked up a brochure and scanned it. "Huh. I didn't know this place was owned by the Museum of Afro-American History in Boston."

"Oh, yes. We purchased it in 1989. It was rededicated in 1992. We've worked to get it on the map as part of Nantucket's history." The woman held out her hand. "I'm Gloria Price. I live in Boston, but I come down here in August to help out. The Meeting House is open for tourists only in the summer. We'd like to do more to research and raise awareness of African-American history on the island, but of course that takes money, which means fund-raising."

"Uh-huh." Alice nodded and strolled around the little room.

Two rows of wooden pews lined either side of a narrow aisle to a small stage. The place was plain, but nicely restored. A framed portrait of a stunningly beautiful young black woman caught her eye.

Alice stopped to study it. The woman was seated in an ornate chair, its high, heraldic back suggesting a throne. She was magnificently dressed in a coat with fur on the cuffs and lapels, and her elegant head sported an enormous wide-brimmed hat adorned with ribbons and feathers. "Now that's what I call a *chapeau,*" Alice murmured appreciatively.

Gloria rose and came to stand next to Alice. "That's Mrs. Florence Higginbotham. She came here in 1911 to work for a summer family. In 1920, she bought this house and lived in it for the rest of her life. When she died, she willed the house to her son, but asked that the house's history be recognized. And gradually, although it's taken decades, that's what we're trying to do."

Alice looked at the portrait. She didn't know when she'd seen such an optimistic, charismatic face. Florence Higginbotham looked proud, but not angry. She wasn't jutting her chin out defiantly. Her expression was confident, and inviting. Why, she looked like she was about to laugh. She looked like someone Alice would dearly love to know.

Alice said, "She possesses a remarkable countenance."

Gloria said, "She was a remarkable woman."

Alice felt like she was under a spell. Like she was in some kind of mutual *communication* with Florence Higginbotham. Alice had never joined any organizations devoted to promoting Black heritage or African-American progress. She'd never had time. She'd always been too busy ensuring her own and her sons' safety, education, and future. But she was absolutely enchanted by Florence Higginbotham. And Alice was old enough to know she still had a lot to learn and she could learn from someone younger, even from someone who had lived in the past. In a flash, Alice saw how her own expertise at organizing, communicating, brainstorming, and managing could be helpful to this historical organization. It was as if Florence Higginbotham, with her splendid plumed hat, was holding a door open to a world Alice hadn't known existed, and Alice couldn't wait to enter.

She turned to Gloria Price. "I'm Alice Murray. I live in Boston, too. I think I might like to help with your fund-raising."

After a day of bright sun and intense heat, a delicate fog was drifting over the island, blurring the light and bringing a welcome coolness. The Hot Flash Club lounged companionably on the small back porch of Nora's Orange Street house. Marilyn and Alice each had one of the two wicker rockers, while Polly and Faye, with much giggling over the positioning of their plump backsides, shared the wicker loveseat with the blue-and-white striped cushion. Shirley, the most supple of them all, sat cross-legged on the pale gray wooden floor. From time to time, she leaned back against the white porch railing. She was the only one not enjoying one of the strawberry daiquiris Faye had just whipped up in the blender. Faye had made Shirley her own drink of fresh strawberries and ginger ale, adorned with lots of crushed ice and a bright slice of lime.

"Shirley . . ." Alice lolled among the rocker's cushions. Her voice was low and mellow. "Weren't you going to look for some yoga classes on the island?"

Shirley scooped a spoonful of crushed ice into her mouth. "Mmm. I was. But I got more interested in doing outdoor things."

"I doubt if I'll ever take yoga again," remarked Faye lazily. "I can't bend over to fasten my sandals without passing gas. Plus, my knees creak. In fact, any exertion makes me grunt like a sow."

"You're a regular Hot Flash Symphony," Alice teased.

"Someone should invent Hot Flash Yoga," Polly suggested. "To help specifically with hot flashes, forgetfulness, mood swings—"

"Irritability, weight gain, sagging," Faye added.

Marilyn giggled. "You know how yoga poses have names? Like Lotus Pose, or Warrior Pose, or Mountain?"

"Yeah!" Alice chuckled. "I see where you're going." She squeezed her knees together. "We could have the Hot Flash Leaky Bladder Thigh Press!"

Polly snickered, crossed her arms over her chest, and inclined her head. "And the Oh No I'm Growing Whiskers on My Boobs Bow."

Faye stood up. She tilted forward slightly, letting her jaw fall open and raising her hands, palms up. "The I Forgot What I Was Doing Affirmation of Paralysis."

Alice placed her hands on her belly. "The I Love Myself Even Though I Ate That Entire Bag of Chips Squat."

Marilyn made a face and stuck her hands out in front of her. "The You Don't Even Want to Be Messing With Me, I'm Constipated Crouch!"

Polly twisted her arms behind her. "And let us not forget the ever popular My Bra Is Biting Into My Back Blubber Twist."

Shirley laughed. "You guys are so silly."

"Hey," Alice said, dropping back into her rocking chair. "How is a bra like a friend?"

"How?" Marilyn asked.

"It's close to your heart and it never lets you down."

"I'll drink to that!" Shirley raised her glass.

All the others toasted, too. They sipped their drinks and relaxed into silence, savoring this moment of mutual harmony.

Finally, with a little sigh, Shirley said, "We really need to decide what to do about Amelia's letters and Lucinda Payne and Nora Salter."

Faye straightened on the loveseat. "I think one of us has to go back to Boston and tell Nora in person. This news is too overwhelming to be tossed off over the telephone."

"But this week was supposed to be just for us!" Alice objected.

"True," Faye agreed. "And if we all agree, we can always wait until next week to tell Nora. But it makes me uncomfortable to be in possession of these letters and this information and not act on it."

"Why can't we be flexible?" Marilyn suggested. "We've certainly changed plans before at a moment's notice. Let's take a day or two to go back to Boston, and then we'll add a day or two for us all to be together next week. Or the week after that. We've got the rest of the summer."

"You just want to go back to Boston to see Ian," Alice teased.

"No, actually, I don't," Marilyn assured her. "I don't want Ian to think I'm checking up on him. Shirley's the one who should go up to Boston. She's the one closest to Nora. I'd be glad to accompany her, but I'd be glad to stay here, too."

Polly wiped a bit of pink froth from her lip. "I'm slightly concerned about Lucinda. When I phoned her yesterday, she didn't even answer. Well, that wasn't too worrisome. We had been up all night. She was probably exhausted. I did get hold of her by phone today, but she wouldn't let me stop by. She claimed she was suffering from 'catarrh' and couldn't see anyone."

"What's catarrh?" Alice wondered.

"An old-fashioned word for a cold," Polly informed her. "Inflamed nostrils, mucus in the throat, that sort of thing."

"Ah," Shirley said. "Of course. All that crying probably opened up tear ducts that hadn't been used for years."

"Anyway," Polly continued, "sooner or later we've got to get together with Lucinda again."

Shirley said, "We can't tell Lucinda about the letters until we tell Nora. I just don't think that would be right."

"And of course Nora's got to decide what to do about Lucinda's thieving," Faye added. "I think if we presented Nora with all the facts, she might be more forgiving."

"And when we tell Lucinda," Polly suggested, "let's have Adele Singleton with us. What do you think? I mean, Lucinda is so alone. At least she's known Adele all her life. It will seem like someone is on her side."

"That's a really good idea, Polly," Faye said.

"Imagine." Shirley pulled her knees up to her chin and wrapped her arms around her legs. "Imagine being in your seventies and discovering you have a half-sister. Isn't life ever calm?"

"Well, *tonight's* calm," Marilyn pointed out. "Here we all are, all five of us, lounging around on a summer's evening, talking, planning, catching our breath, just like we said we would."

They all murmured agreement. Again, they sat in a companionable silence, soaking in the gentle air, enjoying the taste of their drinks and the feel of their light summer clothing against their tanned skin.

Shirley traced a swirl of paisley on her lavender and scarlet gypsy skirt and allowed herself to enjoy some secret thoughts of Harry. The board of directors of The Haven had called a special meeting in the middle of the month to discuss the Rainbow Group's offer, and just now, as she relaxed on this enchanting island, she was hoping they'd vote to sell.

Faye gazed out over the small garden with its new dawn roses and honeysuckle vines spilling over the fence. The green clouds of maple trees in the yard behind framed a bright glimpse of blue ocean. A fat, clunky necklace of heavy azure stones lay across the bodice of her loose white silk shift, and she absentmindedly rubbed the stones between her fingers as she reviewed the various advantages of the several rental houses she'd seen with a Realtor that week.

Marilyn lifted a Band-Aid to check on a cut she'd sustained on the sole of her foot after stepping on a shell while investigating the saltwater plants and invertebrate animals living at the tidal lines in the harbor. The cut was healing nicely. She pressed the Band-Aid back down. She wished, just a little, that her love life could be as simple as a clam's. She knew Ian loved her, but Fiona was so voluptuous, so *feminine*. While here Marilyn sat in tan shorts and a white T-shirt, and this was *stylish,* for her. She was trying not to obsess about Ian with Fiona, but she couldn't stop worrying.

Alice admired her turquoise bracelet against her skin. She'd worn it constantly since she bought it at the beginning of the summer. She just liked it for some reason, just like she just liked Florence Higginbotham. She thought she might go up with Shirley to Boston. Shirley could see Nora Salter, and Alice could stop in at the Museum of Afro-American History. She hadn't been there for a long time. Now that Jennifer's nephew Greg was helping at the bakery, Alan's depression had lifted. It felt good, not to worry about him and Jennifer. It made her feel lighter, more energetic. She was ready to take on a new project.

Polly thought the pink in her overlarge pink-and-white striped cotton shirt matched almost perfectly the pink of her strawberry daiquiri. She rocked idly in the white wicker rocking chair, humming lightly to herself. She felt more at ease than she had in ages. Partly that was because she no longer had to deal with Havenly Yours. Partly it was because of the rum in the daiquiri. She'd better enjoy this moment of peace, she told herself. She had her own secrets, her own complications. Today Aubrey Sperry had left a message on her cell phone. Next week was the annual company picnic at the Sperry Paper Company, and of course Carolyn Sperry and her husband Hank would attend, because Carolyn was the CEO. And of course Carolyn's baby would go along, adorable little Elizabeth, who was, after all, Polly's goddaughter. So Polly was invited to the company picnic, and it was so much fun, she'd been the last two years. All Aubrey had asked on his phone message was whether Polly might like for him to pick her up and drive her out to the company's grounds on the banks of the Rock River. That didn't constitute an actual *date*, did it? And was she honor-bound to mention this to Faye? Or even to garner Faye's reaction to this before she responded to Aubrey? And what was her own reaction to being alone in a car with Aubrey? Honestly, life really was so complicated!

"Polly." Faye's voice startled Polly, who jumped guiltily, spilling just a bit of her drink on her shirt. "I think you and I should be the ones to be with Lucinda when she learns the news. And Adele, of course, if she'll join us. Lucinda had us for tea, after all. She'll feel a little more comfortable with us, I think."

Polly's voice began in a squeak, but gradually modulated. "Great. Whenever. But, um, I have to be back in Boston at the end of next week for the Sperry company picnic."

"Right," Faye said. "Well, first thing, Shirley's got to tell Nora."

"I'll ride up with you, Shirley," Alice said. "I've got some things to do in Boston."

Go by yourself! Shirley wanted to yell. *I don't want to leave Harry!* But she answered mildly, "Okay. Let's go on Friday."

Marilyn sighed, a long, deep breath. "I suppose I should go up to Boston with you two. I can spend the day with Ruth. Maybe take her out to lunch or something. At least I can check to be sure her kitten's litter box is getting cleaned out."

Shirley poked Marilyn's flip-flop with the toe of her own lavender sandal. "Can't you just ask Ian?"

"Ask Ian what?" Ian asked, as he came walking around the corner of the house.

All five women screamed. Polly spilled more of her drink on her shirt. Alice, startled, rocked back so hard in the rocker she nearly went ass over teakettle. Faye put her hand to her surprised heart. Shirley clasped her hands to her face.

Marilyn just sat there, stunned.

Alice recovered first. "What are you doing here, Ian?"

Ian leaned against the wooden steps leading up to the porch. He still wore city clothes—khakis, a white shirt, a tartan tie—and he had a lightweight summer jacket hooked over his shoulder by one finger. With his thick glasses, his egg-shaped head, and his white, indoor, city complexion, he was not handsome, but he was very male, and to all five women, very dear.

He spoke to them all, but his eyes were on Marilyn. "I just missed Marilyn too much. I apologize. I know this is supposed to be your Hot Flash week, but I thought you might take pity on me and let me have an evening with my fiancée."

"But why didn't you phone?" Faye inquired gently.

"I tried, but Marilyn's not answering her cell. She must have it turned off."

Marilyn nodded in mute acknowledgment.

"You surprised Marilyn before, when you asked her to marry you last Christmas," Alice remembered.

"Yes," Ian agreed. "I seem to have to chase this woman to ground."

"This is so romantic!" Shirley blubbered, as tears welled in her eyes.

Marilyn was blushing so hard she sent herself into a hot flash. She lifted her hair off her neck. Still too flustered to speak, she fanned her face.

Faye rose. "Ian, I'll make you a drink. Strawberry daiquiri?"

"Do you have gin and tonic?"

"We do." Faye went through the screen door into the kitchen.

Polly suggested, "Marilyn, let's trade places."

Polly moved to Marilyn's chair, and Marilyn sat on the wicker sofa next to Ian. She gazed at him with amazement, as if he'd been newly minted. "I'm overwhelmed."

Since Marilyn was still trying to compose herself, Alice took on the conversational responsibilities. "How is Ruth? How's Fiona? How's Angus?"

"Ruth is well. In her words, she's as happy as a pig on a ship. And *Angus*! Angus is out on a date tonight."

Marilyn croaked, "Angus has a date?"

"Yes. Last week, when your computers went berserk at The Haven, Wendy had already phoned Julie Martin to ask her to come help, when

Alice phoned Angus, and they both showed up. Not only did they bring the computer back from outer space, they quite liked one another."

"Oh, my gosh." Shirley was thrilled. "That's so karmic!"

"And Fiona?" Alice asked dryly.

Ian rolled his eyes. "Fiona's driving me bats. I'm sorry for the woman, but to be honest, she's always irritated me a bit. She's so dependent. Not like you at all. I admire you ladies, the way you just get things done. I thought if I left her alone for twenty-four hours, she'd get lonesome for her friends back in Scotland and go back home. I can only leave the house overnight, you know, because I can't trust Fiona to deal with everything."

Faye came out, bearing a tall glass clinking with ice and gin and tonic. She handed it to Ian.

Alice stood up. "Well, you and Marilyn can have the house to yourselves for the evening, because the four of us have plans to eat out."

"We do?" Shirley looked surprised.

Alice shot Shirley a look.

"Oh! Right! We do!" She scrambled up off the floor.

Polly stood up, too. "I'll just get my purse and I'm ready."

Faye said, "Marilyn, there's some wonderful cheddar in the fridge, and a container of pasta salad, and lots of fruit. If you and Ian get hungry, I mean."

"Thanks." Marilyn was still dazed.

Polly scrutinized Faye's face as she spoke to the lovers. Faye seemed one hundred percent happy, not the slightest wistful.

As Alice grabbed Shirley's wrist and pulled her into the house, she saw how Shirley's face was soft with yearning, and so, because the salt air was so shimmering and romantic, and because she loved Shirley so much, she said, "You know what, Shirley? Maybe tomorrow we can all meet this Harry you're so crazy about."

Shirley's smile flashed like the summer sun.

As Faye pulled back the faded curtains in the front bedroom on the second floor of Adele Singleton's house, the calico material nearly disintegrated at her touch. Gently, she tucked the fabric behind a bookcase slanting next to the window, allowing sunlight to illuminate the room.

A double bed with an iron bedstead stood against one wall, covered with a patchwork quilt. Polly would go wild over the handwork, Faye thought, running her fingers over the soft cotton. An old rag rug lay next to the bed, but most of the floor was bare wood, wide boards, scraped and scarred by years of living.

There were no closets in the room. An ancient pine armoire served to store clothing. One door hung open. Faye pushed it shut, and slowly it swung back open, creaking, pulled by the slant of the floor.

On an old oak chest of drawers lay an embroidered cloth runner, and centered there was a glass vase containing a sheaf of hydrangeas, dried and withered by time into brittle brown papery petals. Faye touched the dusty vase. Who had last been in this room, brightening the day with this small bouquet of flowers? Next to the vase lay an embossed silver-backed brush, comb, and mirror set, and a silver picture frame containing a photo of Adele's three children. They were captured in their adolescence, two girls and a boy, laughing, sun-browned, hair as disheveled as haystacks. Adele had attended the funerals of her son and one of her daughters. Only one daughter remained, and she was older than Faye.

Trailing her hand over the walls, Faye toured the rest of the upstairs, two smaller bedrooms and one bathroom. In all of them, the plaster walls held cracks like frozen lightning, and the ceiling's plaster was fractured into loose jagged fragments like upside-down icebergs. Faye was surprised they hadn't fallen. The window frames were loose. The floorboards were splintered. The entire house tilted sideways, like an ocean liner slowly sinking.

She opened the door at the end of the hall. The attic, Adele had informed her, had no electricity, and so no light, and the moldy darkness did not entice Faye to climb the wooden stairs. She shut the door. She'd check out the attic later, when she had a flashlight . . . and a friend at her side.

Returning to the bedroom at the back of the house, she pulled back the dotted Swiss curtains and gazed around the room. The wallpaper of cabbage roses and giant ribbons and bows was pretty dreadful, but this room had two windows and faced north. Probably she could paint here. She'd met several painters on the island who had their studios in their homes and managed, even in the winter, with the use of good lighting, to have sufficient illumination for their work.

Yes, she could work here. She could envision it clearly. Her soul, her instincts, urged her forward. But her mind urged caution.

Adele Singleton had offered to sell Faye the house. Adele's one remaining child lived in Arizona. Adele's five living grandchildren lived all over the country. None of them had any sentimental tie to the island. All of them needed money. They wanted Adele to sell her house and let her estate split the proceeds. Adele wanted to help her children, and she admitted, sadly, she was finally getting too old, too weak, and too absent-minded to live alone. She had friends at the retirement home on the island, where trained, strong, young people could help her get into and out of bed, her chair, her clothes.

Adele had resisted selling in the past, she admitted to Faye, in large part because she didn't like the newcomers to the island, who knocked the venerable old homes to the ground and erected modern fakes in their place. But she'd gotten to know Faye, and to appreciate her artistic sensibility. Faye might restore the old house, but she wouldn't rip out its soul.

This was true, Faye knew. It would be a labor of love to restore this old place, and it would *take* labor and love, and lots of money to do it right. She couldn't buy this house unless she sold her house near Boston, and was she sure she could survive a winter on this island without all the cultural delights of the city? Of course Alice, Marilyn, Shirley, and Polly all assured her she could have use of their guest rooms whenever she wanted. Then they would come stay with Faye in the summer! Also, Shirley confessed, blushing and giggling like a schoolgirl, she intended to spend lots of time on the island during the off season. She would stay with Harry, but she'd have lots of time to meet Faye for lunch or a movie or a play. And perhaps—Shirley had rambled on exuberantly, optimistic as always—perhaps Harry even had a friend for Faye and they could all double date!

She didn't need a man, Faye had assured Shirley. At the moment, she wasn't even interested in men. She wanted to paint, and the thought of restoring this old house herself made her hands itch! She wanted to rip off the wallpaper, hire someone to sand the floors, and design a clever little kitchen that would have modern appliances but retain an old-fashioned ambience.

Was she unstable? she wondered. Since Jack died four years ago, Faye had moved twice. First, she'd sold the posh townhouse where she'd lived with Jack and their daughter for so many years, given some of the proceeds to her daughter and her husband for their own home, and moved into one of the condos at The Haven. That had been fun, almost like being back at college. But she'd missed having her own place, especially her own garden, so she'd bought a little Cape Cod located halfway between The Haven and Boston. She'd enjoyed the house, but it never had *claimed* her the way this house did.

But would it be reckless, to buy this house when she hadn't even lived on the island for a year? What about the doctors, and health care, Marilyn had asked. What about when Faye grew older? It was a valid question, and related to the question Polly had asked—if Faye moved to this old-fashioned island, would she develop an increasing estrangement from the real world? Already Faye was so separate from the culture of youth. She didn't play video games, couldn't use a skateboard or an iPod. She used a computer but hadn't ventured much beyond e-mail. Would moving to Nantucket be hiding in the past instead of welcoming the future?

Faye lifted a piece of peeling wallpaper. Beneath it lay another layer of wallpaper, an ivory background covered with blueberries. She could envision living in this house, restoring it, painting landscapes in good weather, painting the woodwork of the parlor when it rained outside. She could imagine opening up the old fireplace, selecting one of her art books, and curling up to read. She could imagine walking into town every day to post her mail, stop at the library, buy groceries, perhaps meet Shirley for coffee or lunch. She could imagine fetching Adele from the retirement home and driving her out to appreciate the crash of waves on a stormy day. She could envision painting. She knew the landscapes she'd done over the summer were her best work yet. A gallery owner on the island wanted to give her a private show here next summer. She felt she was just starting out.

And if it was reckless to move here, then why shouldn't she be reckless? She was old enough to be reckless!

And—for a good long time more—she was young enough.

On the eighth of August, Shirley traveled to Boston to Nora's house. There, over the reassuring social ceremony of Earl Grey tea and scones, Shirley presented Nora with the news of their discoveries. On Nantucket, Faye and Polly invited Lucinda to tea that same afternoon, where, as synchronized as spies, they waited for Shirley's phone call. At her signal, they told Lucinda about the letters. Then, using cell phones, Shirley, in Boston, and Faye, on Nantucket, began the difficult process of arbitration.

Both Nora and Lucinda reacted with disbelief and horror. In Boston and in Nantucket, the younger women rushed to strengthen the older women's tea with stiff shots of brandy.

As the first shock faded, both Nora and Lucinda went into tailspins of panic about the possible legal and financial consequences of this information. Lucinda worried that Nora, now that she knew her father was Ford Payne, would sue for some portion of Lucinda's estate. Nora worried that if her one living sibling and all the cousins knew that Nora and her children were not Pettigrews, her children would lose their share of the Pettigrew inheritance.

In addition, Nora had to deal with the fact that it was Lucinda who had been pilfering her heirlooms. And Lucinda had to suffer the embarrassment of Nora's knowledge of her strange thefts.

Shirley did her best to soothe Nora, while on Nantucket, Faye and Polly did their best to reassure Lucinda. Finally, Nora asked for some time to think things over. Both Nora and Lucinda agreed to a détente during which no one would speak of these matters to anyone else.

For two weeks, the women of the Hot Flash Club at last basked in a temporary sense of summery peace. Shirley hurried back to the island to spend the hot August days with Harry. Faye painted. Alice spent time in Boston with Gideon, occasionally visiting her granddaughter. When she came to Nantucket, she kept busy helping plan a fund drive for the Meeting House. Polly traveled to Boston for various social outings with Carolyn Sperry, which included, naturally, Carolyn's daughter, Polly's goddaughter, Elizabeth, as well as, *naturally,* Carolyn's father Aubrey. Marilyn and Ian split their time between their chaotic Cambridge home and blissfully idle island days, when they finally were able to plan their wedding.

Toward the end of August, Nora Salter phoned her Nantucket house. Shirley didn't answer—she was pretty much living with Harry—but Faye was there, and the two women knew each other because they both served on the board of The Haven. After a brief consultation, Faye phoned Shirley, who flew back to Boston, and once again, using their cell phones, Nora, with Shirley as arbiter, and Lucinda, with Faye and Polly, struggled toward a rocky rapprochement.

Nora assured Lucinda she would place no claim on the Payne estate or make it public that Lucinda had been stealing Nora's possessions, as long as Lucinda did not make public the newfound fact of Nora's heritage. Lucinda agreed. Their verbal contract was based less on mutual trust than on mutual blackmail, but it was a start.

Faye and Shirley were instructed by both women to make copies of the letters between Amelia and Ford so that Lucinda and Nora each could retain them in safe deposit boxes in their separate banks. The pages of the original letters were divided equally between them.

And then, Nora announced, she wanted to come to Nantucket.

She didn't want to inconvenience any of Shirley's friends, who had been promised the house for the summer season. But her hip was healing nicely, and the truth was, curiosity about the tunnel between the houses was rather consuming her. Faye assured her she was welcome in her own home, and made plans to pick Nora up at the airport.

On the last Saturday in August, sunlight poured down, turning the humid air of the island into a giant steam bath. It was relatively cool in the basement of Nora Salter's house, for which Shirley and Faye were grateful. Their hearts were already tripping as they assisted Nora Salter down the stairs and across the dirt floor to the tunnel. Even though they knew that Polly and Adele were with Lucinda, awaiting their arrival, they still dreaded the forthcoming confrontation. Both women were formal and proud—and in their seventies, the perfect age for a heart attack.

"My, my." Nora leaned heavily on her ivory-handled cane as she peered into the entrance to the tunnel. "How inordinately peculiar. This was here all my life, and I never knew it. Would you shine the flashlight, Shirley, so I can see to enter?"

Shirley hesitated. "Are you sure you want to go through it? You have to sort of scrunch up and bend over—"

Nora chuckled dryly. "Since my hip operation, I've become quiet adept at stooping."

Shirley shone the light into the tunnel. Nora peered around, investigating, then moved forward, slowly, resting her more vulnerable side on her cane with each step. Shirley followed, with Faye behind. They paused to show Nora the loose brick and the small space where the metal box holding the letters had been hidden. The tunnel was only eight feet long, but it was small enough to make them all claustrophobic, so they quickly moved on, out into the light and modern ambience of Lucinda's basement.

Nora looked around. "I'd heard that Lucinda had turned her basement into a family room. This is nicer than I expected. Although the windows provide very little light." Eagerly, she moved toward the stairs to the first floor. "I've never been inside the house in all my life," she whispered to Shirley.

In spite of Nora's enthusiasm, the climb up the stairs took time because of her hip, and Shirley and Faye kept alert, ready to catch the older woman should she fall. From their vantage point one and two steps down, Nora's girdled, silk-trousered bottom loomed like a boulder.

"I think this is what's called 'bringing up the rear,'" Faye muttered to Shirley with a grin.

"What's that?" Nora asked.

Shirley quickly improvised. "The basement's so cool it makes you feel like spring is here!"

Polly was at the top of the stairs, holding the basement door open.

"Greetings, travelers!" she called as the three women arrived in the kitchen. "If you'll follow me, we'll take tea in the front parlor."

"Well!" Nora stared around her admiringly. "Lucinda has done a very nice job modernizing the place. Very nice."

Slowly they made their way down the hall and into the front parlor. Lucinda was enthroned in a wing chair. Clad in ivory silk, she looked regal, but her hands clutched the arms of the chair, belying her facade of calm. Seated at one end of the sofa, Adele, with her white curls and bright eyes, looked like a very old child at the opening curtain of a play.

Nora's green eyes met Lucinda's green eyes across the expanse of the room. Nora was a bit plumper than Lucinda, and she kept her hair colored brown and cut short and styled loose and modern. Both women wore trousers and overshirts, but Lucinda's look was classic, while Nora's was more current. Both women's cheeks were flushed.

"Sit down!" Polly invited, nearly squeaking with nerves. "Please!" she added. "I'll pour tea."

For a few moments, everyone was diverted by the business of getting Nora settled and tea poured and served. Then the room was silent. Because it was Lucinda's house, Shirley assumed Lucinda would speak first, but Lucinda was so rigid she was nearly trembling. Polly glanced back and forth between Nora and Lucinda, using every ounce of willpower to stop herself from filling the silence with babbling. Faye and Adele exchanged glances, smiling at each other. Nora had the upper hand here. Lucinda had been sneaking into Nora's house, stealing Nora's possessions. Nora had the moral right to castigate Lucinda, or to sneer.

Nora sipped her tea, then looked at Lucinda. "I've occasionally wondered if we weren't related. Our earlobes, you see."

Lucinda touched her ear. Squinting, she studied Nora's earlobe. "Yours are overlong, as well!"

Nora nodded. "I've never seen anyone else with such long earlobes. Well, my daughter has them. I seldom wear earrings, because I feel they call attention to the abnormal length. As a child, I was very self-conscious about them."

"As was I." Lucinda shook her head, remembering. "I felt rather like a Ubangi. I never noticed that yours were overlong."

"We seldom saw one another," Nora reminded her.

"True." Lucinda sipped her tea.

"But your *subconscious* must have known!" Shirley eyes shone with excitement at this touchstone. She turned to Lucinda. "I mean, you took so many *earrings*. Maybe your mind was trying to give you a message."

"I never took any earrings," Lucinda asserted.

Shirley and Faye exchanged worried looks. Was Lucinda going to sit here in front of them and deny her thieving?

"I admit I took many things from Nora's house. But I never took any earrings. Go check if you wish."

"But we all lost earrings," Shirley insisted.

Adele spoke up. "It was probably a ghost. Perhaps Amelia's ghost, or Ford's, trying to get you girls to notice and start communicating."

Faye, amused, smiled down into her teacup at such nonsense. Polly looked skeptical.

But Shirley caught the look that flashed between Nora and Lucinda.

"I've always thought we had a ghost." Nora's eyes misted slightly. "I've always thought it was a woman, and I never felt endangered by her presence. Perhaps it was my mother." She smiled. "I'd like to believe it was my mother."

Shirley scooted forward on her chair. "They say young children are more sensitive to extraordinary phenomena, but they lose it as they become educated in the ways of this world. Perhaps people, as they grow older, begin to regain this ability."

"What an interesting idea!" Adele looked thoughtful.

But Nora and Lucinda both bridled.

"We're hardly that much older than you!" Lucinda reminded Shirley coolly.

Nora nodded sharply, agreeing with Lucinda.

"That's true, of course." Shirley, appropriately chastised, settled back in her chair.

Lucinda, emboldened by this much rapport between herself and Nora, cleared her throat, straightened her already ramrod-straight shoulders, and lifted her chin high. "I'm in the process of packing several boxes with your little, um, bibelots. Since these women are so much younger and stronger, they'll be able to carry them back to your house for you."

Nora responded mildly. "I would appreciate that." Looking around Lucinda's parlor, she commented, "This room looks very tasteful without embellishments. The Quakers would have approved. I often think I have too many items scattered around."

Adele spoke up. "My children have made oodles of money, selling a lot of the family stuff on eBay."

Nora, who was an investor in The Haven and an active member of several important charities, was savvy. "Not a bad idea."

Lucinda looked puzzled. "What is eBay?"

Faye opened her mouth to explain, but was halted by Adele gently placing her hand on Faye's. Faye looked questioningly at Adele, who nudged her to observe the two adversaries.

Nora inclined toward Lucinda. "EBay is a sort of computer marketplace. You *do* have a computer?"

Lucinda sniffed. "I do not."

"But you should have one!" Nora exclaimed. "They're wonderful for keeping in touch with friends. And it opens up a whole new world."

"I have no interest in computers," Lucinda said with a touch of defiance.

"That's because you've never used one," Nora retorted. "Look, come over sometime and I'll let you try mine out. You'll be amazed."

"*I* use one," Shirley put in. "And I'm hardly part of the college set."

"I don't use one." Adele let an elderly quaver enter her voice. "I'm really too old to learn the things." Stifling a grin, she allowed herself to meet Shirley's eyes. Vain Lucinda would want to distinguish herself from Adele.

Lucinda looked annoyed. She knew she'd been boxed in. "Very well. I'll give it a try. Would you like to set a time?"

Nora took a small black leather notebook from her purse and checked it. "What about tomorrow? Around eleven in the morning? I always feel fresh in the mornings."

"I have to check my calendar," Lucinda told her.

"Would you like me to get it for you?" Polly offered.

"I'm hardly lame," Lucinda responded. Rising, she crossed to the handsome desk on the other side of the room and opened a leather diary lying there. "Tomorrow morning at eleven will be fine."

"Good." Nora set her teacup on the table.

Adele stirred her plump limbs. "Girls, I'm sorry to break up the tea party, but I believe I need to go home."

"That's fine," Nora said. "I'm ready, too."

Polly and Faye helped Adele up and stood back like maids-in-waiting as Adele and Nora slowly perambulated to the front door. Shirley opened the front door and the covey of women, politely thanking Lucinda for the tea, bustled out into the hot August day.

Just as they were almost out the door, Nora turned back. She looked at Lucinda, archrival, thief, and half-sister. "Oh, and Lucinda." Her voice was cool, but tinged with the beginnings of laughter. "When you come tomorrow, you won't need to use the tunnel. This time you can come in the front door."

Lucinda looked piqued, but replied, "Yes, of course," before firmly closing her own front door.

Marilyn and Ian decided to be married on Nantucket, because it was such a romantic location, comparable in its way to the Loch Ness area in Scotland where they had first met and walked and talked together.

Shirley, genuinely excited, offered to purchase a giant air-filled dinosaur replica, tie it to the bow of Harry's boat, and steer the boat back and forth across the water near the beach where Marilyn and Ian would be married. It was a measure of Harry's commitment to Shirley that he actually agreed to take part in this unusual scenario. Marilyn assured Shirley she appreciated the thought, but insisted she'd rather have Shirley right there, with the others, during the ceremony.

One day, Marilyn took Ian on a picnic on the moors, and they decided that Altar Rock was the perfect spot for their nuptials. As paleobiologists, they felt a connection to this relatively small landscape with its enormous geologic complexity. The low-growing heath plants reminded them both of Scotland. Also, the moors were more private, seldom seen by tourists, and the summit at Altar Rock, with its panorama of rolling green earth and shining blue water, gave them the sense of being on top of the world.

They invited only close family members. Marilyn's only child, Teddy, and his wife Lila, and their adorable little daughter, Irene, almost three, came. Teddy, who had all the money in the world, assured his mother they would stay in one of Nantucket's wonderful inns, but Marilyn thought it would be more fun if they stayed in the Orange Street house, and so Shirley, who now spent most of her time and had most of her things out at Harry's, gladly moved the remainder of her stuff up to one of the tiny, dusty bedrooms in the attic and gave Teddy, Lila, and their little daughter her room with its spectacular view.

Ruth, at eighty-seven, could manage the trip to Nantucket, but needed someone to accompany her, so she traveled with her grandson Teddy and his family to the Orange Street house, where she was given the other twin bed in Polly's room. Ruth was content to leave her kitten Marie at home for a neighbor to look after.

On Ian's side, there was Angus, who surprised them all by asking if he could bring his girlfriend Julie down with him. Since Julie was one of the major investors in The Haven, and had once been one of Shirley's massage clients, all the women knew her, and were thrilled at this little romance that would never have happened if Shirley's computers hadn't gone wild. Of course, they told Angus, bring Julie, and when he begged to bring his bulldog Darwin, they agreed to that, too. Angus, Julie, and the bulldog shared another attic bedroom. Angus reminded his father he had once had bagpipe lessons, and asked if he might provide the music for the wedding. Nervously, Ian and Marilyn agreed.

Fiona was also invited to the wedding. Marilyn had secretly confided to the Hot Flash Club that she wasn't thrilled about this, but Marilyn had so many more people on her side—four family members, and four Hot Flash friends. It seemed only fair to invite Fiona. Fortunately, Fiona was eager to return to her own home. And, she confessed to Ian and Marilyn, she was afraid she'd weep all through their wedding ceremony. She offered to remain in Boston, taking care of Marie, until after the ceremony, but Marilyn assured her a neighbor would do that. So Fiona flew back to Scotland a few days before the wedding. Marilyn secretly considered Fiona's absence a present.

Because Faye had no gentleman friend, she moved out of the other big bedroom, with its amazing view, into Alice's small bedroom at the front of the house, which allowed Gideon and Alice to have the larger room. Gideon and Ian had become friends over the past year, so Gideon would stand with Angus on the groom's side.

After some discussion about whether or not Harry should attend the wedding, because he didn't know Ian, it was decided that he should come, because it would make Shirley happy, and it would add another man to the mix.

That made twelve people and one bulldog as guests at the wedding. Bette Spriggs, a local justice of the peace, was asked to perform the ceremony. Because there would be eight guests, the Hot Flash Club decided it would work just fine if Marilyn had four attendants. They decided to use the title "maids of honor" because Alice refused to be a "matron of honor" and Shirley wondered if you could even *be* a matron of honor if you weren't married and didn't have children. The five women went to Boston for one madcap day of shopping for the perfect dresses.

And finally, the day arrived.

The ceremony was set for eleven in the morning. The day was warm and humid, blue-skied, but drifting with high clouds and occasional sea mists.

Gideon rented an SUV in which he drove Ian, Ruth, Angus, Julie, and the dog Darwin, and Teddy, Lila, and little Irene to the moors. Harry met them there in his red truck, and showed them where to park, at the base of the hill in a spot where the sand wasn't so soft it would strand the vehicles. Gideon and Harry lugged a cooler of iced champagne and a carefully packed box of crystal flutes to the top of Altar Rock Hill and tucked it behind a pine tree. Angus paced the dirt roads below the hill, practicing on his bagpipes and frightening the wildlife.

Ian waited to greet the justice of the peace, who looked official and formal in a black suit with a white shirt. Ian wore a white dress shirt and a kilt in the black, navy blue, and green tartan of the Foster clan. They climbed the winding, narrow dirt road to the top of the hill and Bette took her place, with her back to the sweeping view. Harry and Gideon, both wearing white flannel trousers and Hawaiian print shirts, stood on the left. On the right stood Julie Martin, transformed from her computer geekiness by her simple blue dress into a pretty young woman. Julie kept a tight hold on Darwin's leash as the dog twined in circles around her legs, trying to reach the celebratory bows tied onto his collar. Ruth, fabulous in an azure mother-of-the-bride organza frock with a matching hat, was supported by her grandson Teddy, also in white flannels and a wild summer shirt. His wife Lila wore a blue sundress, and Irene wore a yellow organza dress and a matching yellow bow in her red curls. Together mother and daughter scattered a carpet of rose petals up the road to the summit, then took their place with Teddy, Ruth, Julie, and Darwin.

Just before eleven, Faye's rented red Jeep came bouncing along the dusty road, cutting through the heather. It stopped by the other cars, and the women in their brilliant sundresses all spilled out like candies from a box. Angus met them there, and they lined up in the order that had been decided the night before when they drank champagne and drew numbers from a hat, because otherwise they couldn't decide who should go before whom.

Angus, in a kilt and white shirt like his father, headed the procession, skirling out "Here Comes the Bride" on his bagpipes. To everyone's relief, he played well, and the haunting, measured music gave a sense of solemnity to the open-air occasion.

Alice, in a sea-foam green sundress, came next. Then, Shirley, in lavender. Faye, in royal blue. Polly, in turquoise.

And Marilyn, in a simple ivory silk sundress. She held a bouquet of yellow roses in her hands, and a tiara of yellow and white roses lay in her upswept hair.

A breeze shivered their skirts as they climbed the hill. Because the road was unpaved, they all wore sandals. The poignant sound of the bagpipes and the sheer beauty of the moment had them all nearly dissolved in tears, but this was Marilyn's day, and they each vowed not to blubber, at least until the ceremony was over.

They reached the top of the hill where Ian and the others stood waiting. The guests began to smile, but the dog reacted to the sound of the bagpipes by breaking into howls, which terrified Marilyn's granddaughter, who began to howl, too. For a few moments, everyone bustled around, giving Darwin biscuits and soothing little Irene.

Then Marilyn and Ian stood side by side in front of the justice of the peace and the age-old words were spoken. At this, Shirley, Polly, Faye, and even Alice began to cry—quietly, joyfully, with radiant faces. Indeed, *radiant* faces, they agreed later, because their emotions sent them into what was probably the first ever combined Hot Flash Club hot flash.

Ian kissed his bride, and the newlywed couple turned to greet their friends and family. Ruth reached into her purse and brought out a Baggie full of bread crumbs, which she flung at the couple, explaining, "I considered rice, but uncooked rice might give the birds and animals indigestion and cooked rice would clump, so I thought this would work."

The bulldog thought the bread crumbs were for him—after all, they were thrown on the ground, except for the ones which got caught in Marilyn's hair. Darwin shuffled around their feet like a canine vacuum cleaner, snuffling as he licked and munched, and Teddy steadied his grandmother every time Darwin's big head knocked her fragile legs.

Gideon and Harry brought out the champagne, popped the corks and handed champagne to everyone, and a flute of sparkling water to Shirley. They raised their glasses in a toast to Marilyn and Ian. Teddy took out his digital camera and shot photos of the group as they stood on top of the hill with the island and the sea spreading out around them.

Then they all piled into their various vehicles and sped back into town for a wedding luncheon at Fifty-Six Union Street. Their party had been allocated a separate room at the restaurant, off to the side and toward the back. Earlier that day, Faye, Polly, and Shirley had decorated the room with bowls spilling with lilies, roses, and ranunculus, while Alice had picked up the three-tiered wedding cake and brought it to the restaurant kitchen.

Now the group floated in, as colorful and celebratory as a bundle of balloons, and the other diners smiled to see them pass through. In the side room, Marilyn and Ian took their places at the head table, with Ruth next to Ian and Angus next to Marilyn and Julie, shy and blushing, next to Angus. Darwin had to wait in the car, but he'd been presented with a festive pig ear to celebrate the day.

The others settled in at tables dressed in snowy white linen. A waitress brought a child's seat for Irene, and a waiter popped a cork on more champagne. The party feasted on fresh scallops, mussels, steamers and oysters, lobster and fresh greens, with lots of fresh hot rolls and butter and many glasses of champagne.

Alice chatted with Harry, who knew all about the African-American Meeting House. Ian listened to Ruth describe her recent adventures with Ernest, while Marilyn gently coaxed conversation from Angus and Julie.

Faye and Polly allowed themselves to be charmed by three-year-old Irene, and Shirley listened, rapt, to Bette Spriggs talking about Harry, whom she'd known for a long time.

Gradually, Shirley realized that across the table, Alice was wriggling her eyebrows at her.

"*What?*" she mouthed at Alice.

"*Bathroom,*" Alice mouthed back.

The two women excused themselves from the table and went off to find the restrooms. There were two, side by side, both unisex. They slipped into one and shut the door shut behind them.

"This dress is too tight in the waist!" Alice hissed frantically. "It's slicing into my skin! Help me rip the seams."

"We can't rip this beautiful dress!" Shirley protested.

"Fine. Then I'll gag and die," Alice snapped, tugging at the waist.

"Okay, okay, I'll do it. Turn around." Shirley bent close to inspect the material. "Oh, dear, I'm not sure . . ."

"Just hurry."

A knock came at the door. Alice opened it to see Faye and Polly peering in. "What's going on?" they asked.

"Oh, good!" Shirley cried. "You both know how to sew! Come in and help me rip apart Alice's dress."

The two women squeezed into the little room.

"I've got the same problem," Faye assured Alice. "These dresses were a triumph of vanity over comfort."

"Vanity over breathing in my case," Alice panted.

Polly slipped her glasses out of her purse and studied the dress. "Look, there are two darts in the back. Let's open them up."

Shirley unzipped Alice's dress and eased it off one shoulder. Polly inspected the dart. "I need scissors."

Another knock came at the door. They opened it a crack. Marilyn stood there, looking left-out.

"What are you all doing?"

Faye chuckled. "Trying to give Alice some space in her dress. We need to open a couple of darts. Come on in."

"I know!" Polly unfastened the corsage on her shoulder. "I can use this pin." She set her corsage in the sink and wiggled the long pin out. "Now hold still, Alice."

"Wait a minute," Faye ordered. "Alice, slip off the other shoulder, and I'll work on this side."

Alice complied.

"Shirley," Polly suggested, "could you hold the fabric taut—that's right."

Alice stood squeezed into the corner of the room with her back to them while Shirley held the fabric and Polly picked apart the stitching on the left side and Marilyn held the fabric while Faye picked apart the right side.

"This is *so* unglamorous!" Alice grumbled. "How can I grow out of my clothes while I'm wearing them?"

"Speaking of which," Faye said, "did you get a good look at Lila today, Marilyn? I think she might be pregnant again."

"Oh, I hope so," Marilyn exclaimed. "I always regretted that Teddy was an only child. I hope Irene has a brother or sister."

"Lila does have sort of a glow about her," Shirley said. "And now that I think about it, her belly is bulging."

"I've got a glow and my belly's bulging," Alice joked.

"Maybe that's Mother Nature's way of reminding us we've still got potential," Shirley mused.

Alice snorted. "Potential to look like I swallowed a beach ball!"

Polly giggled. "That reminds me. What's the difference between a girlfriend and a wife?"

"What?" the other four chorused.

"Forty-five pounds."

"Oww!" Alice and Faye groaned.

"What's the difference between a boyfriend and a husband?" Polly asked.

"What?" the other four chorused.

"Forty-five minutes!" Polly crowed.

"Ha!" the other four laughed.

Faye patted Alice's shoulder. "There. I've opened that dart. See if that helps."

Alice slipped her arms back into the dress. Polly zipped the zipper. Alice sighed with relief. "Does it look okay?"

"You can't tell a thing," Faye promised. She turned to Marilyn. "Help me pin my corsage back on?"

"I'll fix yours," Shirley told Polly.

Shirley, buoyed up by the presence of all her friends, was brave enough to ask, "Alice, how do you like Harry?"

Alice was smoothing the dress over her front. "He seems like a good guy."

"He's really good-looking," Polly added.

"Hey!" Faye said. "I just remembered! Marilyn, you forgot to throw your bouquet!"

"Oh, right. I'll do it when we leave the restaurant." She looked around at her friends. "Who wants to catch it?"

"Not I," Alice said. "I'm quite happy in my present state."

"Not I," said Faye.

"Not I," said Polly. Then she turned bright red. "Not yet, at least."

"Why, Polly!" Alice pounced. "You've got a new man in your life!"

Everyone looked at Polly. "Oh, don't be silly," Polly protested, turning even more crimson. "This is only a hot sash."

"Ha!" Alice laughed triumphantly. "You said 'hot sash'! Why are you so muddled?"

All the women stared at Polly. In self-defense, she quickly deflected their attention by pointing to Shirley. "*She* should catch the bouquet!"

"I wouldn't mind," Shirley said with a great big smile.

"Shirley," Alice noticed, "you've got lipstick on your teeth."

"I do?" Shirley bent toward the mirror.

The other four women did the same, inspecting their teeth, rerouging their lips, smoothing their hair, powdering their noses.

"I know you just employed a deflective tactic," Alice said, meeting Polly's eyes in the mirror. "Trust me, we're going to find out who this mystery man is. But first, we've got to plan how to get the bouquet to Shirley."

Faye said, "When we get out to the parking lot, Shirley should stand on the side, so it doesn't look too staged. Marilyn, how's your aim?"

"Pretty good," Marilyn said.

Someone knocked on the door. They opened it to see Gideon standing there.

"What in heaven's name are all of you doing in here?" he demanded.

"It's a Hot Flash Club Emergency Summit Meeting. We'll be out in a minute," Alice assured Gideon. "We have a few more things to settle to our satisfaction." She shut the door and, with a conspiratorial smile, turned back to her friends.

ABOUT THE AUTHOR

NANCY THAYER is the author of many previous novels, including the Hot Flash series. Her work has been translated into nearly a dozen languages. Her first novel, *Stepping,* was made into a thirteen-part series for BBC Radio, and her ghost novel *Spirit Lost* has been optioned and produced as a movie by United Image Entertainment. In 1981 she was a Fellow at the Bread Loaf Writers' Conference. She has lived on Nantucket Island year-round for twenty years with her husband, Charley Walters.

Visit the author's website at www.nancythayer.com.

ABOUT THE TYPE

This book was set in Sabon, a typeface designed by the well-known German typographer Jan Tschichold (1902–74). Sabon's design is based upon the original letter forms of Claude Garamond and was created specifically to be used for three sources: foundry type for hand composition, Linotype, and Monotype. Tschichold named his typeface for the famous Frankfurt typefounder Jacques Sabon, who died in 1580.